JO BEVERLEY's
LOVE
STORIES
ARE

"Romance at its best."
—*Publishers Weekly*

"Delightfully wicked."
—*Library Journal*

"Expertly laced with danger and skillfully
sweetened with sensuality."—*Booklist*

"Wickedly delicious."—Teresa Medeiros

"Wonderful."—*Midwest Book Review*

Praise for the Novels
of Jo Beverley

Lady Beware

"A remarkable achievement. . . . It is the unusual combination of familial comfort and risqué pleasure that makes this book a winner. . . . No doubt about it, *Lady Beware* is yet another jewel in Beverley's heavily decorated crown." —*The Romance Reader*

"Enchanting . . . a delightful blend of wit (with banter between Thea and Darien), intrigue (as evil lurks throughout), and emotional victories (as love prevails in the end). . . . Watching Thea and Darien spar is entertaining, and watching them succumb to the simmering love and passion is satisfying." —*The State* (Columbia, SC)

To Rescue a Rogue

"Beverley brings the Regency period to life in this highly romantic story [with] vividly portrayed characters. [Readers] will be engrossed by this emotionally packed story of great love, tremendous courage, and the return of those attractive and dangerous men known as the Rogues. Her Company of Rogues series is well crafted, delicious, and wickedly captivating." —Joan Hammond

"With her usual beautifully nuanced characters and lyrical writing, RITA Award winner Beverley brings her popular Company of Rogues Regency historical series to a triumphant conclusion. . . . A quietly powerful romance." —*Booklist*

"Lighthearted and serious, sexy and sweet, this exquisitely rendered story is a perfect finale to this classic series." —*Library Journal*

continued . . .

A Lady's Secret

Jo Beverley

A SIGNET BOOK

SIGNET
Published by New American Library, a division of
Penguin Group (USA) Inc., 375 Hudson Street,
New York, New York 10014, USA
Penguin Group (Canada), 90 Eglinton Avenue East, Suite 700, Toronto,
Ontario M4P 2Y3, Canada (a division of Pearson Penguin Canada Inc.)
Penguin Books Ltd., 80 Strand, London WC2R 0RL, England
Penguin Ireland, 25 St. Stephen's Green, Dublin 2,
Ireland (a division of Penguin Books Ltd.)
Penguin Group (Australia), 250 Camberwell Road, Camberwell, Victoria 3124,
Australia (a division of Pearson Australia Group Pty. Ltd.)
Penguin Books India Pvt. Ltd., 11 Community Centre, Panchsheel Park,
New Delhi - 110 017, India
Penguin Group (NZ), 67 Apollo Drive, Rosedale, North Shore 0632,
New Zealand (a division of Pearson New Zealand Ltd.)
Penguin Books (South Africa) (Pty.) Ltd., 24 Sturdee Avenue,
Rosebank, Johannesburg 2196, South Africa

Penguin Books Ltd., Registered Offices:
80 Strand, London WC2R 0RL, England

First published by Signet, an imprint of New American Library,
a division of Penguin Group (USA) Inc.

First Printing, April 2008
10 9 8 7 6 5 4 3 2 1

ACKNOWLEDGMENTS

I dealt with a number of new things in writing this book, and as usual, the Internet proved to be a wonderful resource to add to my walls of books.

Thanks to Google for putting the texts of rare old books online with Google Book Search. You can read more about what I used in the author's note at the back.

The Internet provides connections to people, too, and I especially thank Maria Rosa Contardi for patiently helping me with Italian names and language. Ada Ferrari also helped.

I have no idea where Coquette came from, but Sharon Krikorian and Dorothy McFalls helped me to understand papillon dogs, and Marie Sultana Robinson gave me some useful details about both northern France and Italy.

I do know Kent, but it's been a while since I've been there and I don't think I've ever been to Folkestone. Jo Kirkham's assistance was invaluable, especially the old maps she found for me. My nephew Will and his wife, Jo, who live in Canterbury, helped fill in some spots.

Finally, thanks as always to my agent, Meg Ruley, and everyone at the Rotrosen Agency; to my editor, Claire Zion, and Penguin/NAL, who make this book in your hands possible; and to you, the reader, who make it all worthwhile.

Chapter 1

July 1764
The Tête de Boeuf Inn
Abbeville, France

It isn't often a man hears a cursing nun.

Robin Fitzvitry, Earl of Huntersdown, was finishing his meal at a table by the window and thus had an excellent view of the woman out in the coach yard. There could be no doubt. She was muttering curses, and she was a nun.

She was standing beneath the outside gallery that gave access to the bedrooms upstairs, so her gray clothing blended with the shadows, but her clothing was a nun's habit or he was a mother superior. Her plain gown was belted with rope, and a dark head cloth hung down her back. There was even a long wooden rosary hanging from the belt, and perhaps sandals on her feet. She had her back turned, but he thought she might be young.

"Maledizione!" she exploded. Italian?

The frivolity of fur known as Coquette finally proved useful. The papillon wriggled to put her front paws on the windowsill, to see what had made that noise. Her plumy tail swept Robin's chin, giving him an excuse to lean to the right.

Yes, certainly a nun. What, Robin wondered with growing delight, was an Italian nun doing in northern France, beseeching the devil, no less?

"So, sir, do we go on?"

Robin turned back to Powick, his middle-aged English manservant, who was sitting across their dining table beside Fontaine, his young French valet. Powick was square and weathered; Fontaine was slender and pale. They were as dissimilar in nature as in appearance, but each suited Robin in his own way.

Go on? Ah yes, they'd been discussing whether to take rooms here for the night or push on toward Boulogne and England.

"I'm not sure," Robin said.

" 'Tis not much past three, sir," Powick argued. "Plenty of traveling light this time of year."

"But a storm, she would turn the roads to *pottage*!" Fontaine exclaimed. "We could be stuck in the middle of nowhere."

He was probably correct, but he also wanted to linger in France as long as possible. With high pay and many privileges, Robin had tempted the valet to leave the service of a prince, but even after three years, Fontaine shuddered at each return to England. Powick, who'd served Robin for twenty years, grumbled all the time they were in France.

"Think on that lot as just arrived," Powick said, playing a very strong card.

An overloaded Berlin carriage had recently swayed into the innyard and disgorged howling children harried by a screeching mother. The party had pounded up the outside stairs, and now some possessions were being unloaded. They were staying for the night, and above, the children still howled and the mother still screeched.

In English. An English party might want to strike up an acquaintance with him. Robin was a gregarious fellow, but he chose his company. A crash and shriek of rage should have settled it, but he glanced outside again. His mother often predicted that curiosity would be the death of him, but what would you? It was his nature.

"You agree, don't you?" Robin said to Coquette, who twitched her enormous ears and wagged her plumy tail.

"Agree we should leave?" asked Powick.

"Agree we should stay?" asked Fontaine.

"Agree we should investigate outside," Robin said, picking up the dog and rising. "I'll get a better look at the weather, and ask advice of the local people."

With that, he strolled outside, tucking Coquette into his large coat pocket, which she seemed to enjoy. It was as well he liked to dress casually for travel, for the current fashion was for close-fitting coats with no useful pockets at all.

He approached the now silent figure, considering what language to use. His Italian was only passable, but his French was perfect, and they were in France.

"May I aid you, Sister?" he asked in that language.

She turned sharply, and his breath caught.

He was looking at a stunning face. It was oval, but the tight white cap she wore beneath the gray veil was made with a widow's peak that came down almost to her brow. The narrow frill continued all the way to the tie beneath her chin, forming a heart shape that seemed designed to emphasize large, dark eyes and full, soft lips that needed no emphasis at all. What demented bishop had thought up that cap? For a certainty, no mother superior would have done so.

Her complexion was pale, which he supposed common enough in the cloister, but it glowed with health, as perfect as the creamy rose petal tumbling over a nearby wall. Her nose was straight, with tiny dimples just above the nostrils, and those lips . . .

Robin inhaled. Such lips were made for kisses, not confessionals. And she was young. She could not be much more than twenty.

She disciplined those lips into a firm line. "Thank you, monsieur, but I need no help," she said, and turned away.

Good French, but not that of a native speaker, and people generally swore in their native tongue. Italian, for sure. What the devil was an Italian nun doing in Northern France, alone?

He moved into her line of sight, plying his most disarming smile. "Sister, I have no ill intentions, but I can hardly ignore a lady in distress, especially a bride of Christ."

She made as if to turn away again, but then stilled and studied him in a remarkably direct way. Robin hid a smile. Put that with the cursing, and what he had here was not a true nun, but an adventuress in disguise.

And to think he'd been bored.

"Permit me to introduce myself, Sister," he said, bowing. "Mr. Bonchurch, English gentleman, very much at your service." He felt a little uncomfortable at such a direct lie, but he always used a false name when traveling in France. His true name and title caused fuss, and sometimes people would even alert the local dignitaries and he'd be plagued with visits and invitations. And this, after all, was a mere amusement en route.

The nun continued to study him, as if making calculations. Before she decided whether to give her name, hard footsteps rattled the wooden gallery above and that strident voice yelled, "Sister Immaculata! Sister Immaculata! Where the deuce are you?"

"Sister Immaculata, I assume," Robin said with a smile.

She looked up balefully. "How many stray nuns can there be here?"

"And you arrived in the Berlin—"

"Sister Immaculata!"

She muttered something, but said, "I must go."

He moved to block her. "You are the children's nurse? My condolences."

"I am *not*." She punctuated it with a sharp hand gesture that was emphatically Italian. "But the nurse, she contracted an ague in Amiens, and milady's maid abandoned her in Dijon. Now there is only me."

"Sister! Sister! Come here immediately!"

"No wonder you were swearing at fate." Robin gestured toward a nearby arch. "If we were to go through there, we would be out of sight and could discuss your liberation from durance vile."

"There is nothing to discuss."

Again she moved to leave.

Again he blocked the way. "It will not hurt to talk."

She frowned at him, but thoughtfully rather than angrily. At another yell, she threw up her eloquent hands and hurried through the arch. Robin followed, admiring her brisk, light movements. She was so deliciously vigorous, perhaps more strikingly so for being veiled in shapeless gray.

Her gray veil brushed a fading rose, scattering petals but collecting one. When he plucked it off she whirled to challenge him, hand raised to point or hit. He exhibited the evidence. She simmered down, but he began to heat. There'd been a frisson of awareness at his lightest touch, and now pink touched her cheeks. This was no nun.

He crushed the petal and invited her to enjoy the perfume, but Coquette, the jealous minx, yipped.

Sister Immaculata flinched, then stared. "What is *that*?"

"A Coquette," he said. It was the dog's name, but in French it meant "a little nothing." "Ignore it."

Instead she put out a hand to stroke the tiny head. Robin was familiar with the effect. After all, he'd acquired Coquette to seduce a lady in Versailles, where the breed was all the rage. He took the dog out, willing to use any tool.

"So pretty!"

"Allow me to give her to you as a gift."

She drew back, frowning. "How heartless you are."

"It is my mission in life to fulfill all ladies' desires." He smiled into her eyes. "Come into the inn, Sister Immaculata, and tell me yours."

She hissed in a breath. Had he gone too far, too fast? But another screech from her employer made her turn and hurry through the arch. It took them to a small garden from which another door opened into the inn's entrance hall.

"Too public," he said, touching her arm to steer her into what looked like an empty parlor. She moved sharply ahead to outpace his touch. He followed, but didn't close the door. Yet. There was an old story about a princess and a pea. He generally found that such sensitivity to his touch indicated a woman was primed for pleasure.

"Now, Sister," he said gently, "your desires?"

"Stop saying such things. You show no respect for my habit."

"It's such a dismal garment. But," he added, raising his free hand to signal peace, "I merely meant your wishes about your situation. The lady's maid left. The nursemaid left. You are the screeching lady's only servant. . . ."

As he'd predicted, hard-heeled footsteps beat a tattoo down the steps to the innyard, and the demands started up again there.

"Her name?" he asked.

"Lady Sodworth." The English words spoken with a fluid Italian accent sounded like another curse.

Robin didn't recognize the title Sodworth, and the haut vollée of Britain was his world. Another imposter? Could this be some strange plot?

"What exactly is your position with the lady?" he asked, studying her.

"Companion. But now she expects me to do everything."

"And you've endured the lady all the way from . . . ?"

"Milan."

"Why?"

The simple question seemed to challenge her.

"I had reason to travel to England and needed female companionship."

Through the open window, he could hear the lady haranguing an ostler in atrocious French.

"The price seems high."

"She is under great strain."

"Which I suspect is entirely of her own creation. The voice alone would drive off angels."

Another flip of fine-fingered hands. "I have no choice. I must go and pacify her." She headed for the door.

"Your destination is England?"

"Yes."

"Then may I take you there?"

She turned to face him. "Of course not."

"Why not?"

"You're a man."

"A very safe one."

She gave a snort of disbelief. But she didn't continue on her way.

"Truly, Sister Immaculata, a man like me can't afford to add cuckolding God to his sins. But perhaps rescuing one of his brides would wipe away some years in purgatory?"

"You think me an idiot, sir? You are not a man any woman should trust."

"On the contrary, it's the hungry beast that is dangerous. You behold me, Sister, satiated by the ladies of Versailles."

The pink that flooded her cheeks made him dizzy, but her eyes remained steady. "Are you staying here tonight?"

He knew the necessary answer. "No."

Lady Sodworth was inside the inn now, her demanding voice cutting the air like a saw. Upstairs, something shattered, perhaps even a window.

The errant nun moved to hide behind the door. "Do you travel swiftly?" she whispered.

"As swiftly as roads and horses permit."

"Do you give me your word, sir, at peril of your immortal soul, that you will deliver me safe to London?"

"Safe" was a slippery term. Robin defined it to suit himself and said, "I do." Then he grinned. "How very matrimonial, to be sure."

Her expression turned wry. "You are beautiful and wicked, Mr. Bonchurch, and used to women falling into your hands like ripe fruit, but I assure you it won't happen with me. I want no complaints when we arrive in London with your lust unsatisfied."

"Not a one," he promised, drowning in delight. "But you do realize that constitutes a challenge?"

"One I'm bound to win. As you said, you can't afford to cuckold God. You have a carriage?"

"A chaise. I need only order horses put to."

"Excellent. But even better if I get into your chaise now, don't you think?"

"You're a conspirator after my own heart, Sister, and you're right. Your Lady Sodworth's next step will be to have the whole inn searched."

As if to confirm his thought, the harassed innkeeper popped his head into the room. Robin pulled out a gold coin; the man saw it, nodded, and hurried on. Robin opened the casement window and looked out at a lane alongside the inn. "All's clear." He moved a chair beneath it.

She hesitated, but then hurried over and climbed nimbly out, showing him sandals and bare ankles. He replaced the chair and followed, grinning. "This way," he said, gesturing toward the back of the inn.

They entered the yard close to Robin's post chaise, which sat axle down, awaiting a new team of horses. He hurried his adventuress to it and handed her inside. Another touch, another frisson. Her position was awkward in the slanted coach, but she managed.

"I'll order the horses."

But she suddenly clasped her hands and raised them to her lips. "No, I can't. I need my possessions, my traveling trunk."

"I will buy you anything you need."

"I will not be so indebted to you."

He shrugged. "Where is your trunk?"

"It was in the boot of the coach, but it might have been carried inside."

Robin turned to study the Berlin. Baggage was piled on top of the big, four-wheeled coach, but that was not being disturbed. The boot was open and already half empty. As he watched, a man came out of the inn, grabbed two bundles, and carried them inside. Bedding? Robin could have told Lady Sodworth that the sheets at the Tête de Boeuf were clean and aired, but from the sounds of her, she wouldn't listen.

"What does your trunk look like?" he asked.

"Plain wood with black straps. A brass plate with a cross."

"I'll see to it. Stay out of sight."

He lowered the blind on the inside of the chaise window and began to close the door, but realized he still had Coquette. He put her on his nun's knee. "Discuss desire," he said, and shut the door. He scanned the area but saw no danger, so he strolled over to the Berlin. There inside was the sister's small trunk.

Two men came out and unloaded a fancier, leather-covered trunk, carrying it between them. Robin decided he needed his men, anyway, and went into the inn to beckon them. When they came over, he explained the situation and gave them their orders.

Fontaine—sighing because they were leaving—lurked to distract any porters, while Powick, sighing at Robin's new game, pulled out the small chest, hoisted it on his shoulder, and carried it over to the chaise.

A nun or not a nun, that was the question. That was a very plain, nunlike box, but even if Sister Immaculata was genuine, she was still up to something odd. In two days' travel he should be able to uncover all her secrets.

Powick was making room in the boot for the box. Robin turned to tell Fontaine all was clear.

"You there!"

He turned to face a furious woman. It had to be Lady Sodworth, but she didn't match her harsh voice, being petite, beribboned, and even pretty in a bad-tempered way.

"Have you seen a nun here?" she demanded in her bad French, not seeming to recognize that he was a gentleman, never mind an Englishman.

Robin looked around in puzzlement. "Here, madame?"

"Anywhere here, you fool!"

He gave a mischievously Gallic shrug. "If you need a nun, madame, you should perhaps go to a convent?"

"Dolt!" she spat in English, and rushed off in her chaotic search. Another Coquette, and with a worse temperament. Robin wondered at any man marrying her, despite her looks. He searched his memory again for a Lord Sodworth, but felt certain there was none. So, a knight or baronet, and probably of recent creation. Excellent. That made it unlikely he'd meet Lady Sodworth again.

He collected Fontaine and headed for his chaise, where ostlers were putting horses to under Powick's scrutiny. He'd been a groom in his youth, and knew the trade.

Powick had put Robin on his first pony and then become his tutor in riding, hunting, fishing, and other country lore. Eventually he'd become a kind of manservant-companion of endless usefulness. Having steered Robin into adulthood, however, he still thought he held the reins. Even Robin becoming earl a year ago hadn't convinced the man that he was able to manage his own affairs.

"The nun's coming with us, sir?" he asked in a forbidding tone.

"A damsel in distress. What would you?"

"I, sir, would return her to her mistress."

"As would I," said Fontaine. "The chaise, it will not fit three."

"Therefore," Robin said, "you will ride."

The valet normally traveled in the coach. "Impossible. It might rain."

"Think of it as a favor you are doing me in thanks for all the times I've ridden and you've had the chaise to yourself."

"Not in the rain, sir," Fontaine protested.

"Sir—" Powick protested for other reasons.

"I'm all innocence," Robin insisted. "The holy lady needs to reach England, and do you really want me to abandon her to that harpy?"

"We could be days on the road if the weather turns. Days and nights."

"And she will have a room to herself, I promise."

"The weather. . . ." Fontaine tried again.

Robin held on to his patience. "We need only go as far as the next stage. What is it—Montreuil?"

"Nouvion," Powick said.

Robin shrugged. "As long as we're away from all things Sodworthy. Let's be off."

In the end his word was law, so soon Fontaine and Powick were mounted. A postilion took his seat on the leader of the chaise horses, and Robin took delivery of the basket of food and wine he'd ordered earlier. He opened the door, winked at the shadowy nun, and placed the basket on the carriage floor. Coquette leaped out to relieve herself.

Once the dog was ready, Robin glanced around, saw no problems, and put the dog in the chaise. Coquette leaped right onto Sister Immaculata's lap.

"If you think to make me jealous," Robin said to the dog as he sat beside the nun on the one seat, "prettier ladies than you have failed."

The nun stroked, and the damned dog seemed to smirk. The chaise rolled out onto the Boulogne Road, leaving the screeching and howling behind.

"Welcome to tranquillity," Robin said.

"Can you promise that?"

"If it's what you truly desire." Her reaction to the word "desire" seemed to be a weary sigh. Very well; she wasn't ready for the game.

"I must confess," he said, "that I've suffered tranquillity for days. I was hoping you would remedy that. But not in any naughty way, Sister. See, I've even provided female companionship."

She glanced down. "She's a bitch?"

"With a name like Coquette, she'd better be."

"Why don't you like her?"

He shrugged. "I can tolerate tiny, frivolous women, but not tiny, frivolous dogs."

"Then why own her, poor thing?"

"With a collar of gold and pearls, there's nothing poor about her."

She looked down at the collar. "It's *real*? Why?"

"You tell me your stories and I'll tell you mine."

She gave him a scathing look and turned away, as if fascinated by the outskirts of Abbeville. So she did have secrets, and some must relate to why she'd accepted his invitation. There was time. To increase her comfort, he angled into his own corner and stretched his legs, widening the space between them on the seat.

"You can still change your mind, Sister. We can return you to Lady Sodworth."

She clearly thought about it before saying, "No, thank you."

"Then perhaps you would like to return to your convent."

She turned, frowning. "You would take me to *Milan*?"

"I'm a wealthy man. It would not discomfort me."

"You're a madman!"

"What a shame you've cast your lot with me, then."

Her reaction seemed to be irritation rather than fear. "You don't appear rich."

"I'm modest, and don't flaunt it."

"If you truly are rich, you could arrange for me to travel to London in a more respectable way."

"But how would that benefit me?"

"How does this benefit you?"

"It amuses me."

Perhaps she tightened her hand, for Coquette jumped down with an affronted twitch. The dog considered Robin, but then circled and settled onto her pink velvet pad.

"I'm your amusement?" Sister Immaculata demanded.

"Of course. Would you really wish me to pay strangers to escort you to England?"

"*You* are a stranger."

It startled a laugh out of Robin. "So I am. But I've taken charge of you, you see, so now my honor requires that I personally see you safe."

That created an intriguing, wary silence.

"So where, Sister Immaculata, does your safety dwell?"

"In England."

"Any specific place?"

"None that need concern you, sir."

"I am to deliver you to Dover and abandon you? I think not. Do you even speak English?"

She smiled and answered in that language. "Perfectly."

As best he could tell from one word, that was the truth. Yet more dazzling twists to his puzzle.

He asked his next question in English. "Where do you plan to go in England?"

"London. At least to begin with."

Ah, now he heard the accent, but perhaps only one of extra precision, which gave it an almost liquid charm.

"And after?"

"Again, sir, that need not concern you."

He didn't argue at this point, but she'd not shake him off so easily. He'd acquired a mysterious adventuress, who had not, he suspected, joined him merely out of temper. He perceived urgency and some fear. Of what? He really should be more worried about that, but he was entranced.

He had mysteries to solve, wits to challenge, and a companion so beautiful that simply looking at her enriched his day. Her every action and reaction thus far promised more. She had courage, spirit, and a spicy temper. Given a few days on the road, he'd explore all her secrets, including those only discovered in a passionate bed.

Chapter 2

Petra d'Averio knew she'd leapt out of a pan into another boiling pot.

Lady Sodworth and her impossible brats had been almost unbearable, but she was accustomed to penance. The real problem was that Lady Sodworth traveled like a snail. Now that Petra had glimpsed Varzi—thought she'd glimpsed Varzi—the pace was unendurable.

Once she'd won free of Milan, and then of Italy, she'd prayed that even Ludovico wouldn't pursue her across Europe. But Varzi was Ludo's hunting dog, and surely the man she'd seen in the streets of Abbeville had been he.

She'd been trying to persuade herself that she was wrong. The man she'd thought was Varzi had been in the street as Lady Sodworth's carriage had approached the inn, and how could the hunter be ahead? She knew he could, however. If he'd learned that she was with Lady Sodworth, then he knew her route and destination. It would be in keeping for him to ride ahead and station himself in her sight to warn her of defeat. Such a rotund, swarthy, ordinary-looking man to shoot terror through her, but everyone knew that Varzi never gave up a pursuit and would do anything to make the capture.

She wished she could see his face when he realized she was no longer in Lady Sodworth's party. *But at what price, Petra? Why this man? He's danger on long, elegant legs.* He'd been her only chance, however, and she'd seen only a wastrel rake with a ridiculous dog. A man she could manage.

Now she wasn't so sure.

His dog rose and demanded attention again, so he picked her up. Stroking the fluffy white thing, he should look weak, but though he was relaxed as a cat she sensed danger and almost felt the carriage was too small, too short of air.

Don't be idiotic. Just because the man assumed that a smile and soothing words would get her into his bed didn't constitute danger. She, above all, could resist seduction.

He was simply her means to an end, to safe arrival in England, so she assessed him with that in mind.

He'd claimed to be wealthy, but he didn't look it. His brown frock coat was loosely cut, as were his buckskin breeches. He wore well-used riding boots, a beige waistcoat that hung unfastened over an unruffled shirt that lay open at the neck. No form of neckcloth. Even his light brown hair hung loose around his shoulders, like a countryman's.

Yet his poor excuse for a dog wore a collar of gold and pearls—or so he said. She'd inspect it later, for she knew gold and pearls. She'd once possessed some and would still, except for her brother, Cesare, God send him what he deserved.

This Bonchurch was handsome, she'd grant him that. No wonder he expected her to fall into his arms.

Women probably did that all the time. He had almost magical eyes—blue, but not a common blue. A sapphire blue that only an unfair God would give to a man, especially with long lashes as trimming.

His fine profile could almost be beautiful, but no one would call him feminine. His cheeks were lean, his jaw square. Even though he couldn't be much older than she, he had the self-assured arrogance of his sex and an almost palpable aura of the erotic. He was sinfulness incarnate, and spoiled—the type used to getting what he wanted.

And he wanted her.

He hadn't even tried to hide it.

To her annoyance, that game had stirred a coil of pleasure. What young woman doesn't want to be desired by a devastating man? And it had been so long. . . .

She pulled her mind back from that pit. He didn't admire her. He didn't even know her, and he could hardly be overwhelmed by her charms in her nun's garb. He wanted a nun as a hunter might want a trophy to hang on the wall, and in this hunting game the advantage would go to whoever broke this silence. Which language? She was more comfortable in English than French.

"Wise of you to travel simply, Mr. Bonchurch. Lady Sodworth flaunted her wealth and title."

He turned to her. "And was doubtless fleeced left, right, and center. She travels without some man to arrange details for her?"

"She has outriders, but no one with authority since somewhere in La Vanoise. She dismissed the man her husband appointed, for calling her, more or less, a twit."

"A man of discernment. Where is the husband?"

"He found some pressing reason to travel home by a different route."

"Sister Immaculata, you're a cynic."

"Mr. Bonchurch, three weeks with Lady Sodworth would turn St. Francis of Assisi into a cynic."

He laughed. "I'm surprised you lasted so long."

"So am I, but to begin with Lady Sodworth had a lady's maid, and the children had a nursemaid."

"The latter, I remember, fell ill in Amiens."

"And the former abandoned us. We encountered another party interested in her services, and off she went, wise woman. Anna had no means of escape until she developed a fever. I wonder if it's possible to fall ill on purpose."

"Quite probably. What happened to her?"

"She was left in a convent."

"That sounds like a tranquil alternative."

"But Lady Sodworth gave only the most miserly donation for her care, and how is she to get home? She's only sixteen, and has never been out of Italy before. I don't know what will become of her."

Petra had added a few of her own coins, but she knew it wasn't enough. She would send more if she was ever in a position to.

"Give me the name of the convent and I'll provide for her."

"Why?" she said, sharp with suspicion.

"So you'll pay the debt with your body." When she shrank away, he waved a hand, a smile tugging at his lips. "Forgive me. I have an impish sense of humor. Why should I not provide for her? The price is likely less than I'd pay for buttons."

She eyed his horn buttons.

"I mean my better ones."

"I don't think you're rich at all."

"I don't think you're a nun."

At that challenge, Petra took her well-worn prayer book out of the leather pouch she wore on her rope belt and turned her eyes to the Latin. *Take that, you wicked rake, and chew on it.*

She tried to concentrate on prayer, but was aware of him to an infuriating degree. On the edge of her vision, he still stroked his dog, and she began to imagine those long fingers stroking her.

"If I removed your headdress, would I find long hair?"

Petra didn't look up. "No."

"Is that the truth?"

"What difference if I answer yes or no?"

"A point. Let's make this more interesting. Promise to always speak the truth."

She frowned at him. "Why?"

"For amusement."

"I don't need amusement."

"I do, and we have two, perhaps three, days' travel ahead. I'm providing free transportation and protection, Sister. You might give a little in return."

He had a point, and Petra knew she needed to learn more about him. "If I promise truth, you must do the same."

"I have nothing to hide."

"You think I do?"

"Sister Immaculata, you are a box of secrets, and I intend to discover every one. Let's establish the rules."

"Let's not."

He ignored her. "We may ask anything of each

other. We need not answer, but if we do, we will tell the truth."

"Why on earth should I indulge you in this?"

"As I said, in payment."

"If you wanted payment you should have said so before I joined you." She returned firmly to her prayer book.

"Seek guidance from heaven, Sister," the taunting voice said. "I'm sure God will see that I have right on my side."

Petra had to fight not to return to the fray. She won, but only just. She knew her own weaknesses. Force would not break her, but gentle seduction, especially seasoned with humor and whimsical delights, might melt her before she recognized her danger.

She tried again to concentrate on prayer, for she surely needed it, but the presence of the man beside her, his body occasionally brushing hers with the swaying of the coach, made it impossible. She began to sweat, and not just because of the oppressive weather. She tried to avoid all sight of him, but his long legs were always in front of her, his body in the corner of her eye.

Two, maybe three days. . . .

She gave up, closed the book, and put it away, shifting slightly to face him. "There are some matters to be discussed," she admitted. "Where will you take me in England?"

"Our agreement, Sister? Truth for truth?"

She sighed, but said, "If you insist on such folly, I agree. Well?"

"I'll take you wherever you want to go."

"Scotland," she said promptly.

His eyes twinkled. "Is not in England."

Irritating man. "I know that. I was countering non-sense with nonsense. I won't be obliged to you, sir, so I will not take you out of your way."

"I will ask no payment that you are unwilling to make, Sister, but let's say London."

"That will suit me perfectly. Thank you."

"London is your destination?"

"It will suit me," she repeated.

"Where in London?"

"That need not concern you, sir." Before he could protest, she asked, "Where in London do you go?"

"I'll merely pass through. It's moribund in summer."

"But it's the greatest city in the world."

"Which everyone flees in the warm weather. London's a crowded, dirty place at the best of time, Sister. In summer it's all stink and disease; thus anyone who can flees to countryside or seashore. Are you sure you want to go there?"

She was wondering, but had to say, "Yes. You go north, then?"

"To Huntingdonshire, but I'll linger long enough to see you settled. Where?" he asked again.

She supposed he couldn't simply leave her on a London street. "You may take me to a convent there."

"Sister Immaculata, there are no convents."

"We promised truth."

"I speak the truth. We're a Protestant country."

"But you have Catholics. I know you do. And they are no longer persecuted."

"Not tortured and executed, certainly, but there are restrictions on them. For all I know there are still laws forbidding religious houses, but for sure, any Catholic lady who wishes to become a nun travels to the continent. Which makes me think—do you have any other clothing?"

"A spare habit. Some changes of linen. A cloak."

"Then we must purchase something. There may be a law against wearing a nun's habit in England, but of a certainty wearing one will make you conspicuous and even put you in danger of unpleasantness."

Petra's head was spinning. "Unpleasantness?"

"Catholics are not loved and sometimes mistreated."

"That is barbarous!"

"Is it? Less than twenty years ago a Catholic claimant to the throne, supported by the Catholic King of France, invaded and tried to seize the crown. Memories of the Armada live on, when the Most Catholic King of Spain attempted to seize our country and return it to the rule of Rome."

Petra looked down in dismay at her gray habit. What she'd seen as protection might now be her peril? Her courage was shrinking by the moment. Religious persecution was notoriously cruel, and she was not the stuff of martyrs.

"Lady Sodworth said nothing of this."

"Perhaps she simply didn't think of it."

"She never thinks of anything but her appearance. But we had an agreement, she and I. I would assist her with the journey if she transported me to England and advised me there."

"And you trusted her?"

His skepticism stung, but she could hardly respond with the truth, that she'd been desperate.

"Her title . . . but when I asked her about aristocratic ways, she was evasive. I think she is not a lady at all."

"In some senses you might be right. What's her husband's name?"

Petra thought about it. "She only ever refers to 'my husband' or 'dear Samuel.' I see now it is all a lie."

"Perhaps not. He could be Sir Samuel Sodworth and she would be Lady Sodworth."

"A mere knight?"

He seemed amused. "Most would hardly think it mere. He could be a baron or higher, but I don't recognize the title."

"And you would?"

She knew the answer before he said, "Yes."

Could he provide the knowledge she needed? "You are nobly born, sir?"

"Right back to the Conquest."

"Then why are you a plain mister and she is Lady Sodworth?"

He settled more comfortably, apparently willing to inform.

"In many countries, the children of nobles are all titled, and that can continue through the generations, but that's not the way in England. For example, the younger sons and daughters of a duke have the courtesy title of lord or lady, but that's not inherited, so their children are plain misters and misses."

"That is your situation?"

He laughed. "The grandson of a duke? No."

"But wealthy and nobly born?"

"Yes. The point is that plain misses and misters can be rich and important in England, and ladies can be upstarts. Many a foreigner comes to grief by not knowing that."

Petra nodded. "Thank you."

"What else do you want to know?"

Alas, she couldn't ask about the person she'd traveled so far to find. She'd not let a stranger close to that.

"Tell me about the royal court," she said. "It is the Court of Saint James, I know, centered on Saint James's Palace in London."

"True"

"That is where the king lives."

"Not true."

"No?"

"The palace is a rambling old warren which the king only uses for official functions. He lives at the Queen's House—that's its name—in a more rural setting."

"And the court? His courtiers?"

"Live in their London houses when necessary and their country ones when they can, as now. In summer even the king moves farther into the country, to Richmond Lodge."

"How far is that from London?"

"About ten miles."

Not too far. She could walk that distance if a carriage would be too expensive.

"You seek someone who will be at court?" he asked.

Trapped, Petra said, "Perhaps."

"Who?"

"I can't tell you that."

"You could trust me."

"I've known you less than an hour, sir."

"Even so."

"Exactly so," she said.

"Stubbornness is not a virtue."

"Nor is persistence."

"Isn't it? Sister Immaculata—if that is your real name—I predict that you'll encounter difficulties in England. You will need me."

She met his eyes firmly. "And I know that I will not."

Her declaration was hollow and he must have known it, but she could not allow him to take over her life. She understood his price for that.

He shrugged with irritating confidence. "So you seek a gentleman of the court. If you won't supply a name, I will. A title?" When she didn't respond, he said, "Why not? Lord, as it covers everyone except dukes. I assume he's not a duke?"

"You are irritatingly flippant, sir."

"If you won't amuse, I must. Let's see. Lord Mystery, Lord Conundrum, Lord Puzzle, Lord Riddle . . . Riddle!" he declared. "You seek Lord Riddlesome."

"As you wish." Petra smiled despite herself. By chance he had the first letter right.

"But unless Riddlesome is part of the king's household, Sister dear, he won't be at Richmond Lodge. He'll be enjoying bucolic pleasures at his country estate—Riddlesome Hall. So where is that?"

She remained silent.

"North of London?"

That tricked a "No" out of her and she tightened her lips.

"You are a very irritating woman," he said. His silly little dog suddenly whined and came to her feet. He scooped her up. "She irritates you, too?" He smiled at Petra. "She says yes."

"She'd say yes to anything you said," she snapped, then realized she'd been tricked into his nonsense. "Just because you can win over a dog so easily doesn't mean you will win me."

"No?" Long fingers playing in fur again, stroking the dog to besotted contentment.

She forced her gaze up to his face. "Not even with your beautiful blue eyes."

He smiled. "Are they beautiful?"

Why, oh, why, had she said that? Grateful that growing darkness stole their power, she said, "You know they are, sir, and you enjoy using them to devastating effect."

"Are you devastated?"

"Not at all."

"Of course, you're not lying in my lap, being stroked. We were talking of Coquette, weren't we?"

Heat flared in her cheeks. "It's wicked to say such things to a nun!"

"It's wicked for a nun to respond."

"I didn't!"

He silently accused her of lying, and he was right. But then he said, "I apologize. Unfair to play such games when you have no escape. I'll try to be good. So what is your native tongue?"

Petra felt tossed breathlessly from near drowning onto dry land.

"Italian."

"Then your linguistic abilities are impressive. Your French is good and your English almost perfect."

"Only almost?"

"Alas, a slight accent, but lovely."

She smiled, but then realized she was being stroked in another way.

"How did you learn so well?" he asked.

Petra searched the question for traps, but found none. "I had an English nurse, then later an English governess. How do you speak such good French?"

"I had a French nurse and governess, but my

mother is French and spoke French to her children. Your mother was English?"

"No."

"Your father?

Petra hesitated, then said, "Yes."

"He spoke English to you?"

"No."

"Alas, he died when you were young?"

Petra knew then that she shouldn't have gone in this direction. "He left."

"I see. Your mother?"

"Died recently."

"My condolences." He seemed to mean it. "Is that why you became a nun?"

"I've been in the convent for some years now."

He hadn't expected that and didn't welcome it. She saw no hint of peevishness, however. By Saint Peter, she was beginning to like him, and that was truly dangerous.

"How old are you?" he asked, but then rain rattled sharply against her window. She turned, and he exclaimed, "Plague take it!"

Lost in their competitive conversation, they'd missed the change in the weather. Dark, heavy clouds roiled toward them, and sudden lightning flared. Too soon afterward, a crackling roll of thunder shook the air. The carriage jerked as the horses reacted and then sped up.

The little dog yelped and burrowed beneath Mr. Bonchurch's coat. Petra wished she could do the same. She hated lightning, and the storm was on her side of the carriage. Another spear of lightning lit the inside of the coach with unnatural white light, making her flinch away from the window up against him. Instead of protecting her, he thrust the trembling dog into her hands, then let down his window to call out to his rider racing along on that side. "Is there any shelter nearby, Powick?"

"Not in sight, sir!" the man yelled back, hunched against the slashing rain, his horse wild-eyed.

Petra covered the quivering bundle of bones and fur in the skirt of her habit, murmuring reassurances she wished she could believe.

"Any idea how far we've traveled?" Bonchurch was asking.

"Perhaps five miles, sir."

He closed the window and swept wet hair off his face—but spared a moment to glance down and smile. Petra realized her bare legs were exposed up to the knee.

"Well?" she asked sharply.

"Exceedingly well." But then he returned to business. "Too far to go back. Too far from the next town." He dug a slim book out of his coat pocket and opened it to consult a road map and guide.

He was a reprehensible rake, but there was nothing indolent or idle about him now. Given the situation, Petra was glad of it. But dog or not, she'd been right to think him dangerous. He wouldn't be easy to handle or easy to get rid of.

Wanting to cover her legs again, she pulled her Saint Veronica cloth off her belt and bundled the dog in that, holding it close to murmur, "Out of the pan but into the fire, Coquette. Both you and me. But I won't let you burn."

Chapter 3

Robin was cursing himself upside and down. He'd known there was danger of a storm, but he'd slid into games and lost track of the situation. Even Coquette had tried to warn him. Now they were exposed in open countryside with the thunderstorm almost on top of them. If the chaise was struck, it could go up in flames.

Then the full force of the rain hit like a drenching sheet, blinding the view through the windows, drumming on the carriage roof. In minutes the road would be mud; not long after, a quagmire. They could be literally stuck. If they survived the storm, they could still be locked in place overnight.

He stabbed his fingers at the map. "Nouvion's the next stage," he shouted over the noise. "We'll try for that, but watch out of your window for any kind of shelter."

She looked as terrified as poor Coquette. At least the dog was swaddled, but nothing could protect it from the noise.

He let down the window again to shout his orders, commanding all speed. The chaise lurched ahead, but then slid violently sideways. Sister Immaculata bounced

into him. Robin caught her. Even though he instantly
released her, a jolt that could be lightning of a different sort shot through him. He thought he saw a similar
response in her. The coach straightened and hurtled
on.

"That could have crushed Coquette," she yelled.

He opened the food hamper on the floor and tugged
out a wicker-wrapped wine jug. Then he grabbed the
bundle of dog and tucked it into the spot, making
sure Coquette could breathe. He closed the hamper,
considered the jug, uncorked it, and took a long swallow. Then he offered it to his nun. His nun with
shapely legs and deliciously trim ankles.

She shook her head, clutching the strap on her door
but still being tossed around, her eyes white edged
with terror.

He put down the wine jug. "Come here."

She shook her head, so he grabbed her and pulled.
"I can brace my legs to keep in place. Yours are too
short. Let go."

She surrendered. He held her close with one arm.
She clutched his coat for purchase. The chaise hurtled
wildly now, with an orchestral accompaniment of
cracks, rolls, and rumbles. A dazzling flash was followed by an explosion that felt right on top of them.
The coach lurched wildly toward his side, and Sister
Immaculata rolled completely on top of him. He
cinched her close.

He was ensuring her safety, but he'd have to be
dead not to notice full breasts pressed against him
with no hint of stays to spoil the fun. A firm bottom
was almost under his hand, with no hoops or quilted
petticoats to muffle it.

He couldn't resist sliding his hand farther south. If

heaven's wrath incinerated him now, at least he'd be doing something to justify it. If only she were another sort of wench. Her sheath was mere inches from his blade, and a love joust in a storm could be magnificent.

At his touch she stiffened, bracing her hands to push away. He tightened his hold, lowering his lips close to her ear. "Apologies to your heavenly bridegroom, Sister, but I think he'd prefer me to keep you safe."

She squirmed, and a lurch in the other direction slid her astride him. She cried, "Stop it!"

"I have many talents," he laughed, "but controlling the weather isn't one of them."

"You know what I mean—"

Another blinding light and roar ended her protests. She sealed herself to him with hands and legs, head tucked down as if to make a smaller target. Robin grinned, reveling in the wild power of the storm and the lightning energy between their bouncing bodies.

Just how close was he to her secret delights? Did nuns go naked underneath? Or did chastity demand confinement? He'd read that some monks wore tight drawers day and night to guard against self-pleasure. Sometimes they were of leather or even sheepskin. He'd need plate metal to guard against the pleasure of his nun bouncing around his hard cock.

He laughed again. He couldn't help it.

She looked up at him, wild-eyed, headwear askew. "You're mad!"

He kissed her. How could he not?

Her parted lips pressed shut, but not immediately. She pushed away again, but not desperately.

She was half-willing. He coaxed her lips open, explored her mouth, and began to inch up her skirts. She began to kiss him back. . . .

But then she wrenched her mouth away, stiffening, preparing to thrust away entirely.

"My apologies, Sister," he murmured. "The storm . . ."

She stared at him, eyes dark and huge, and then licked those lips.

Oh, don't.

"You're afraid, too?" she asked.

"Very."

"It's silly, I know. . . ."

"Are you calling me silly?"

"No, but I don't like storms."

"I do. They excite me. But I'll be good."

He kissed her temple, hoping it felt soothing. It didn't soothe him. Nothing could soothe him as long as they were locked together like this, but he'd fight armies not to separate.

"It's not foolish to fear danger," he said. "My own heart is galloping. See, feel."

He pressed her left hand to his chest. With his waistcoat undone, only his shirt lay between his skin and the heat of her palm. She remained like that, numbly trusting—until she became aware of their position and pushed fiercely away.

But then the coach rocked violently to the left, perhaps even sliding toward a ditch. Robin braced for complete disaster, preparing to shield her as best he could, but then it corrected and hurtled on. He hoped the postilion still had command of the horses, but if not there was nothing he could do now other than ride the wild motion and keep his charges from injury.

Sister Immaculata had stopped trying to escape, but she was trying to close her legs without losing safety, wriggling in the process. When she accepted defeat she was still straddling him, but he was in danger of firing off. And oh, Jupiter, her scent—earthy, not perfumed, but intoxicating.

One day he would have a perfume designed for her. Nothing heavy or cloying, but not sweet, either. Something fresh, even astringent, to be used lightly, very lightly. Perfumed water for her silken underclothes, perfumed lotion for her skin, perfumed oil for her bath. Which he would share with her . . .

He needed her breasts in his hands, her nipple in his mouth. He needed to be pounding into her with each jolt of the coach, needed another kind of lightning storm.

Maledizione, as she had so aptly said.

"Is it over?" she whispered, as if the god of storms might hear.

Robin realized the lightning and thunder had definitely moved on, though the rain still pounded and the carriage still rocked. One storm was diminishing, but the other still raged, and she looked so very ripe for love.

Over? My sacred jewel, it has only just begun.

Then the coach stopped.

Her eyes widened. "What now?" But then she realized her position and pushed away from him just as he let her go. She flew back across the coach to thump into her corner. Her "No!" clashed with his "Are you all right?"

They stared at each other, both breathing hard.

Robin turned away, glad of the excuse to lower the window and find out their situation. Deep in the mire, he thought, and he was not thinking of the road.

"Are we stuck?" he called.

"Not yet, sir," said Powick, "but soon. There's

something ahead. A light probably coming through shutters."

"Thank God. Tell the postilion to go forward carefully, and you ride ahead to ask for shelter."

As the coach moved forward, Robin peered down, ignoring the rain on his head.

"How bad is it?" Sister Immaculata asked.

He pulled his head in, raised the glass, and turned to her, pulling out a handkerchief to soak up some of the wet in his hair. She offered him her own—a square as plain and white as his, but smaller.

He thanked her and used it. "There's six inches of mud, and the rain's showing no sign of ending soon. Pray, Sister, that this place will offer shelter."

She grasped her rosary. "Of course, but how long will we have to stay?"

"Until the road firms up again. We're in no hurry. At least," he said, considering her, "I'm not."

Her pale face was now tight. Had her only problem been the screeching Sodworth? He suddenly wondered if she were a thief. He'd taken her word that the trunk belonged to her. It was a very nunlike piece of luggage, to be sure, but perhaps he'd been too trusting.

A faint whine startled him. He'd forgotten Coquette. He opened the hamper and grimaced. "She's stained your cloth in her fright. Is that sacrilege?"

"No."

He extracted the still-frightened dog, leaving the soiled cloth behind. "What is it?"

"A reminder of the cloth Saint Veronica used to wipe the face of Christ. The Sisters of Saint Veronica care for the poor and injured in the streets."

Comforting the dog, he turned that over in his mind. A strange detail to invent. And if true, an extraordinary calling—and one that made her journey to England even more puzzling.

Robin suddenly wanted to smash something. She was a nun, after all, and even to him a true nun was untouchable, no matter how beautiful, how enticing her body, how hotly she kissed.

"Your food's ruined, too," she said.

"Ours. A shame, that, for heaven knows what we'll eat tonight."

Where the hell were they and what was this place? It shouldn't be so dark this early, but the storm had brought its own night and rain still blurred the windows. All he could make out was a long, low building on Sister Immaculata's side of the coach. He leaned across to lower the window.

She flinched back. "Sir!"

He probably had brushed against her breasts, but no more firmly than a butterfly's wings. "I need to open the window to see better."

She shoved him away. "I'll do it."

She struggled with the catch, but he judged it wiser not to assist. When she loosed it, the window rattled down too fast. Just possibly one of those Italian curses escaped her.

He'd forgotten those promising curses.

A nun or not a nun, that was the question.

Then again, not all nuns were virtuous.

A saint or a sinner? Could a person be both?

"It's a long, low building," she said, "but it doesn't look promising."

He leaned to see, careful not to touch her. "It's here or nowhere, and it promises dryness, warmth, and a bed for the night."

"Beds," she corrected, raising the window again with a fierce push.

Robin settled back onto his side. "I meant nothing else, Sister."

She glared. "You *kissed* me."

"You kissed me back."

"It was the storm. I was frightened."

"I was born during one, they say, and they drive me mad." He smiled at her bafflement. "Your headdress is awry. Would you like me to straighten it?"

She blushed and gave it a sharp twist, but a dark tendril still showed, and her blush turned beauty into magic. Robin could hardly breathe. He hid his expression by considering the damage to the contents of the hamper.

"You must never do such a thing again," she said.

"Put Coquette in a safe container?"

"Kiss me!"

"Or?"

"I thought you feared God."

"Sister Immaculata, He already has so many counts against me that a mere kiss, even with a nun, will hardly weigh an ounce."

"Then why aren't you raping me?"

Robin simply stared. "I don't rape," he said coldly, "and I promised you safety. The one sin I have never committed is to break my given word."

She flinched back. "I'm sorry, but cease such folly. I will never succumb."

"The future is a mystery."

"No. It is ours to shape."

When she turned to look outside, Robin absorbed that statement with admiration and doubt. Mysterious as the future was, he predicted trouble for Sister Immaculata. She was alone and vulnerable in a dangerous world.

He saw Powick arrive at the building. The people there would have to give them some sort of shelter. Which could present some problems.

"Sister."

She turned back to him, prepared for another fight.

"We may need a story."

"Why?"

"Our hosts may wonder why a nun is traveling without female escort. Especially with a man such as I."

"You are every inch a rake," she agreed.

"Then why come with me?"

"Lady Sodworth." But her eyes slid away.

"Then I hope you've learned your lesson. She's doubtless enjoying a cozy supper before settling into a warm, dry bed, and we're faced with, at best, straw and soup. Come to think of it, I could be in the same comfort. I'd have stayed safe at Abbeville if not for you."

Her eyes widened. "Are you suggesting this is all *my* fault?"

Robin addressed the rapidly recovering dog. "She's an unreasonable, argumentative woman, is she not?"

"I am not!" she protested.

"Facts are facts." Before she could complain about that, the carriage jerked to a stop. "Open the window and tell me what you can see."

Muttering her opinion of him, she did so, letting in cold, wet air. "We're by a lane leading to the back of the house. Your man is talking to someone at the front door. The ground's covered with water."

Robin leaned across her to call, "Fontaine!"

"Yes, sir," said his valet, the very picture of dripping misery.

"Are the wheels sinking now we've stopped?"

"No more than they were, sir. I am *very* wet."

"So you are." Robin closed the window and sat back.

"Your master," Sister Immaculata said to the dog in his lap, "is cruel and heartless."

"Is it not entirely her fault, Coquette, that my poor valet is exposed to the storm?"

Coquette yipped in agreement.

"Sycophant," she accused.

"Termagant," he retorted. "And I don't mean the dog."

"Of course not. She never disagrees with you."

"She doesn't always obey. Damn this never-ending rain. Our story," he said. "Here we are, traveling despite bad weather, a nun and three men. Suspicious. They might think we're eloping. One winces at the possible punishments for ravishing a nun."

"Like Abelard," she said, a glint in her eye.

"You want to see me unmanned, Sister?"

"Not yet," she said.

"Terrifying woman. I see Powick returning. Pray for good news."

She turned to look out. "Even if these people wonder, they won't do anything."

"Better not to raise alarm. We'll be brother and sister."

"But we don't look at all alike."

"Half brother and sister, then. Your mother was Italian. Your father, also my father, was English. See my devotion to truth?"

"After a fashion," Petra said dryly. "Why, then, are we in a desperate hurry?"

Yes, why? Robin thought at her turned head.

"I could be more inventive, but let's say we're racing to your dear mother's deathbed. We're a staunch Catholic family. You discovered a vocation to the holy life and entered a convent—I like the way this ties together—entered a convent in your mother's hometown of Milan."

She frowned as if on principle, but said, "I suppose that makes sense."

"It is pure brilliance."

"It is not a matter for pride to be a brilliant liar."

"Consider it theatrical invention, then. I shall write a play about our adventures and call it . . . *The Rake and the Nun*."

Perhaps she growled, but Powick was approaching the coach, hunched against the rain.

"We are both Bonchurch?" she asked quickly.

"We share the same father, so yes. Your mother's name?"

"Amalia." It came out so automatically that it was probably the truth. "And your name? Hurry. Immaculata is not convincing for an English lady."

"Not even with an Italian mother?"

"The English father would object."

She hesitated, so when she said, "Maria," he asked, "Truth?"

"Are we still playing that silly game?"

"Yes."

"My name is still Maria." But the tilt of her chin suggested a half-truth at best.

He let it pass and turned to let down his window to hear Powick's report.

"They'll give us shelter, sir, but there's only women there right now, so they won't let us in the house."

"Women? I should have gone to talk to them."

"More than likely, sir," Powick said, dripping. "The best I could obtain was a barn of sorts out the back."

"Beggars can't be choosers. Can the coach get back there, or do we walk?"

"There's a cart track, but it's rough."

"We'd better try it. But first, what did you tell them?"

"Just that we're English. sir. Couldn't help that, me with my mangled French."

"Damnation, I really should have gone myself. Listen, Sister Immaculata is my half sister, Maria. My mother died and my father remarried an Italian woman." He saw rather than heard Powick's sigh. "We've no choice. They're going to wonder about a nun with four men. Tell Fontaine."

"Very well, but you'd better hope they don't want to gossip, or they'll get a dog's dinner of details."

"Impudent rascal," Robin said, shutting the window.

"But right."

"He generally is. I apologize for our lodgings, Sister."

"I suspect I'm more accustomed to Spartan living than you, sir."

"Then I look forward to your assistance in the night."

As she sighed and turned away, his conscience tweaked a little. But only a little. The coming night could be very, very interesting.

But then the coach lurched down at least a foot. "Plague take it! Pray fervently, Sister, for the axle."

"If God heard my prayers," she said bleakly, "I wouldn't be here at all."

Chapter 4

Petra regretted those revealing words as soon as they escaped, but how could God let things get to this dire state?

When she'd joined Mr. Bonchurch, she'd expected an ordinary man and thus someone who would be easy to handle. He was anything but. She'd also expected to race ahead of Varzi, but here she was, stuck for the night in the middle of nowhere. Tomorrow, Varzi would catch up with ease—especially if the coach broke. It was groaning and squealing as it navigated the rough track.

At every turn—every turn!—God's hand seemed raised against her. Was her flight so wicked? Did He want her to be Ludovico's whore?

"Powick's right," he said. "We should settle a few more details. How old are you?"

She could see no reason to lie. "Twenty-one. How old are you?"

"Twenty-five."

She frowned. "Truth?"

"You think me older or younger?"

"Older."

"A year as head of a family can turn a man gray."

"Your father died? I'm sorry," Petra said, thinking of the pain of her mother's recent death.

"So am I," he said, but then the coach bounced down jarringly, and he winced. "Only think, we have to get out again tomorrow."

"Perhaps we should have gone on," Petra said.

"We'd have been stuck within a league."

He was looking at her in a way that made her twitch. "What?" Disconcertingly, it again came out in Italian. *"Che?"*

"Maria is your second name, isn't it?"

The coach seemed to have achieved level ground and was turning around the back of a walled yard. Rain still drummed on the roof, however, and the dim light made everything grim.

"How did you guess?" she asked.

"It's not right for you. So?"

Again, the truth didn't seem worth a struggle. "Maria is my second name. My first is Petra. Petronilla, in fact. No more convincing than Immaculata for an Englishwoman."

"Stranger ones have been known. Is there a Saint Petronilla?"

"A holy virgin martyr of the early church, possibly a daughter of Saint Peter himself."

"A bride of Christ with a saintly lineage. How can anything possibly go amiss? Except," he added, "that God does not listen to your prayers."

Petra looked away. "A foolish statement because of the interminable rain."

The coach swayed to a stop then, at a tilt that meant Petra had to use every bone and muscle not to slide on top of him. Every scrap of willpower, as well, because part of her wanted to. Part of her wanted to surrender to strong arms and kisses, to allow someone else to make all the decisions. To have someone take care of her. This man wasn't interested in protecting her, however, except in the sense of making her his mistress. And now she had a perilous night to survive.

"May I know your family name?" he asked.

Again, Petra hesitated. He was wearing away at her, but it couldn't matter. He wouldn't suddenly realize that she was il conte di Baldino's shamed sister, or turn her over to Varzi. If Varzi caught her, all her secrets would be exploded.

She turned back. "Averio."

"Petronilla Maria d'Averio?" He said it as if he was relishing it, and for some reason she liked hearing it roll off his tongue.

But she corrected him. "Petra d'Averio. The Maria I do not use, and the Petronilla was only to give me a saint's name. My father insisted. Petra was my mother's mother's name. It's common in German lands, but not in Italy. And your first name, sir?"

"Robin."

She couldn't help but smile. "The small bird with the red breast?"

"Cheerful and friendly." She must have made a sound, because he said, "Have I not stood your friend? And I am willing to be more so."

"You're tiresome."

"I'm wounded, Sparrow."

"I know that allusion. *'Who did kill Cock Robin? I, said the Sparrow, with my bow and arrow. . . .'* I mean you no harm, sir, whereas you are wearing at me like water on stone."

"Devilish slow, water on stone," he said, good humor undented.

More like sun on ice, which was often not slow at all.

"You must stop this. You must treat me like a sister, because anything else and even French peasants will recognize the truth."

He sobered at that. "Alas, you're right. Brother and sister it is, then—at least for this night."

Thank heavens. On those terms, she might survive. The carriage made a sharp left turn into the walled farmyard and then the gates were closed with a thump. The noise made her jump with fear. Nonsense. The wall and gates were for safety, and with her tucked in here, Varzi could pass by and never guess she might be near.

Two women ran past her window, splashing through mud, eager to be back in the house. A house of women. Nothing to fear. And it was kind of them to come out in the wet to let them in. They ran in past a sturdy, middle-aged woman who was standing in the open farmhouse door, pointing and yelling instructions. The coach moved slowly forward, and then sudden quiet told Petra they'd reached shelter.

"Thank you, God," she said.

"Amen, though after so long, quiet feels almost eerie. Here, take Coquette and don't let her follow me. The last thing we need is her covered in mud."

He passed over the dog, opened his door, and climbed down. After inspecting their shelter, he turned to offer a hand. "It's merely an overhang, but the ground's dry."

Dog tucked in her arm, Petra left the coach.

The farmhouse door was shut again, so this was their haven for the night. As he'd said, the "barn" was merely a rough roof supported by three wooden poles in front and two sides of the wall in the back. Rain poured off the edge of the roof into a pungent, muddy lake between them and the farmhouse.

"Not the accommodation I hoped to offer you tonight," he said.

"Then probably safer for me."

The dog was wriggling so she passed her over, but he put her down. "She's fastidious, so I doubt she'll go out into that sort of mud." Coquette shook herself and began to roam.

Petra shook, too, but because of damp night air. "I need my cloak. And so do you."

"You're worried about my health," he declared. "How delightful."

She smiled sweetly. "Simply playing the part of loving sister."

"Loving! We make progress, indeed we do."

"Only toward survival," she said, marching to the coach to find her luggage. He reached past her to open the boot for her, brushing against her arm. Petra ignored the play and unlocked her trunk to take out her gray woolen cloak. She allowed him a clear look at the innocent contents before closing it again.

He didn't seem disturbed, and took the cloak to put it around her shoulders. That was nothing to make her shiver, but it had been so long since any man had performed such a simple courtesy.

Ludo.

A winter garden, glittering with frost.

A fur-lined, velvet cloak.

A searing kiss . . .

"What is it?" he asked.

"Just cold," she said, stepping away, fastening the clasp at her throat. That memory had been an excellent reminder of what happened when a woman allowed a man to play such games. "Can we make a fire, do you think? There's a woodpile over there."

"We'd better ask. We don't want to be accused of theft."

He took out a dark, heavy cloak and swung it on, instantly becoming more ominous, especially when he raised the hood. She recognized a riding cloak of supple leather, which would shrug off rain, but the forbidding effect persisted even when he smiled at her and said, "Perhaps these ladies will not be so immune to my beautiful eyes."

She couldn't stay out here all night with him. She couldn't.

"Perhaps they could win me a bed inside," she said. "After all, I'm a harmless female."

"To other women, perhaps."

He set off, but yipping halted him. Coquette was frantic at being abandoned. With a sigh he picked her up and put her in his pocket. Then he strode out into the rain in a lordly manner. But his booted feet sank into slippery mud, so instead of a masterful march, the hooded, dark warrior slogged his way across the yard.

Petra smothered a giggle, but she prayed the women would agree with a request to let her sleep inside.

He arrived at the door and knocked. The door opened a crack, then a little wider. He talked to the woman, and then set off back to the barn. Once he was under shelter, he pushed off his hood and stood dripping. "Triumph for *mes beaux yeux*. For a price they'll provide some food and drink, some spare coverlets, and the use of their woodpile."

"And me?" Petra asked.

"So anxious to flee me. It seems a rough place, but if you want to sleep in there you have Madame Goulart's agreement."

Petra hurried to her trunk to take out her bag containing necessities and a spare shift for tomorrow. She turned eagerly toward the house, but then realized a problem. She was wearing sandals. She'd have to cross in bare feet. She bent to unfasten them, but her tormenting escort said, "May I have the honor of carrying you?"

He was straight-faced, but she heard laughter in his voice.

Petra was torn, but being in his arms won over wading through farmyard mud.

"Thank you," she said, and tried not to stiffen as he lifted her into his arms.

Ludovico carrying her, sweeping her into his arms simply to show off his strength. She protesting but loving it—loving the intimacy, the closeness, feeling fragile in his strong arms. . . .

"Pull my cloak over yours as much as you can. It's waterproof."

She started out of memories of folly and did her best, though the wet leather had a slimy texture and wasn't easy to manage.

He stepped out into the rain. "My sincere apologies for any shortcomings."

"As a porter, sir, you excel."

"Reserve your applause until I get you to the door without dropping you. This mud is slime."

As if on cue his foot slid sideways. Instinctively Petra clutched tighter, then instantly realized her mistake and let go, trying to lean the other way to correct the tilt. That almost tipped them over, and a stupid screech escaped her as she braced to slam down into foul mud.

He staggered two steps in one direction, then another back and stilled, precariously balanced. They looked at one another, and perhaps he, like she, was holding his breath.

But his eyes were bright and then he grinned. "We must dance again sometime," he said, and moved forward with extreme caution.

Inside Petra, folly sighed, *Oh yes*.

He was struggling with the mud, but not with her weight. Of course, carrying ladies would be a required talent for a rake. Doubtless they trained in it. And in kissing. Kissing ladies. Fondling ladies—loose ladies draped in silk. Ladies with rouged cheeks and reddened lips, drenched in perfume of musk and roses . . .

But the coarse wool of her habit must rasp against his hands, and her smells were all her own and there were too many of them. At least he wasn't fresh himself beneath the damp wool and tangy leather. Surprisingly, the medley of smells was not unpleasant, and could even be sweeter than memory of Ludo's expensive perfumes. . . .

What if her venture turned out even better than she dreamed? Might she one day attend a ball in England, and there meet Robin Bonchurch, gentleman, both of them smelling sweetly in silken finery? Dancing, stepping lightly to lovely music, eyes locked, teasing, flirting. He flirted as easily as he breathed.

He wasn't breathing easily now, as he staggered the final steps, but he grinned triumphantly as he set her down beneath the small porch.

Fresh from her dreams, she gave him a full smile. "Thank you, my hero!"

He stared, and it was as if new lightning sizzled through the air.

A grunt made Petra aware that the door had opened again and the farmer's wife was staring at them. Petra quickly turned the smile on the woman. "God bless you for your charity, madame."

The woman wasn't charmed. "Come in, then." Her accent was so heavy Petra had difficulty understanding, and she was dirty and missing a number of teeth.

Petra was suddenly reluctant. "I'm sorry you'll have to sleep in the barn, Robin. Perhaps—"

"Don't worry about me."

"You'll be so uncomfortable." Petra turned to the woman. "Could my brother—"

"No men." The woman grabbed Petra's arm and hauled her inside, slamming the door in Robin Bonchurch's face.

Chapter 5

Petra almost wrenched it open and ran back out again, but she was being ridiculous. So these people were poor and from the smells, unclean, but they offered what they had. She gathered her manners and thanked her hostess again.

The woman grunted and waved her to a seat.

A table took up half the room, with a crude chair at head and foot and a bench down either side, but some wooden chests against the walls could also be seats. Petra walked to one of those, not liking the way the floor squished. It was covered with rushes, but clearly they lay over earth and the rain was seeping up.

These poor people. At least they had a fire, burning in a hearth that made up most of a side wall. On either side shabby curtains hung over arches that must lead into the other half of the house. They had food, too, for a cooking pot hung over the fire, attended by an ancient, humped-backed woman. The old woman was staring at Petra—if she could see out of eyes so pouched. Her yellowish skin lay thinly over bones, giving her an almost skeletal appearance. Petra found a smile and wished her a good evening.

The woman grunted, swigged something from a flagon, and returned to her pot.

Petra sat, trying to gather her cloak around her, both for warmth and to stop it trailing on the dirty floor. The few windows were high and shuttered and she doubted they had any glass in them, for drafts wavered the solitary candle on the table. From the smell, it was tallow, but there were other smells, and some, she feared, came from the cooking pot.

Madame Goulart went through the left-hand arch and Petra heard muffled voices. For a moment she was suspicious, but she remembered the two women who'd opened the gates. They'd be changing their wet clothing. They'd gone out in the rain to let in distressed travelers, even though fearful because their men were away.

These people were very Good Samaritans, and she must remember that.

Madame Goulart returned bearing a large earthenware jug and a leather pouch. She gave the pouch to the old woman and put the jug on the table. She took down a wooden beaker from a shelf and poured into it, then brought it to Petra.

Petra thanked her but had to ask "What is it?" Travel had taught her that local food and drink could be peculiar.

"Poiré."

Ah, the pear cider of northern France. Petra longed for good wine or coffee, but this was wholesome. "Thank you. Most refreshing. I am Sister Immaculata."

"Where you from, then?" the woman asked, studying Petra with eyes almost as pouched as the crone's. She was fleshy rather than skeletal, but her skin, too, was sallow.

"Milan," Petra said.

"That is in England?"

Petra realized she should have given an English place, and was tempted to agree, but it was too strange a lie. "No, madame. It is in Italy."

Madame Goulart reared back. "Your brother claimed to be English!"

"Oh, we are, madame, but we have no convents in England, you see, so I had to travel to Italy to join one."

The woman still frowned, and Petra was glad to see no crucifix here or other sign of devotion. "My brother and I shouldn't have pressed on, but I weep to think my poor mother might die before I see her one last time."

Madame Goulart still frowned, but then the other two women entered.

They were about Petra's age, and unlike their elders seemed healthy and cheerful. One wore a green skirt, the other a yellowish-brown one. Both wore dark red country bodices, laced in front, over plain shifts, and wooden clogs on their feet. All the women wore clogs, and given the state of the floor, Petra wished she did, too.

The one in the green skirt stared at Petra and said, "Oh, but you *are* beautiful."

It made Petra blush, but she could think of nothing to say other than, "Thank you."

Brown Skirt poked a pointed elbow into her sister to remind her of her manners, and they both sat on a bench. But they kept flickering glances at Petra, as if she fascinated them. Of course, with most nuns living in cloister, they might never have seen one before.

They were old enough to be married, but wore no

rings. Petra wasn't entirely surprised. Green Skirt seemed a bit slow, and had large eyes that should have been appealing, but which put Petra disconcertingly in mind of a cow. Brown Skirt's eyes were small and too close together, and when she smiled, she showed small, sharp, crooked rat's teeth.

Petra, you've never studied a rat's teeth. Be charitable!

Promising to do penance, Petra smiled at both and said, "Good evening."

Cow Eyes smiled back, but anxiously. The other showed those teeth. Perhaps neither was normal. This seemed a very unfortunate family.

"Solette and Jizzy," Madame Goulart introduced. The slow one seemed to be Jizzy and the sly one Solette. "And my mother attends the pot."

Petra had seen the woman add things to the pot—some herbs from the pouch and more vegetables. Trying to make their poor meal stretch to five more mouths. Petra wished they had some food to offer.

"That is a dog your brother has?" Madame Goulart asked.

Petra was still having trouble with the dialect. "Yes, an absurd thing, is she not?"

"Pretty collar. Your brother, he is a rich lord?"

Were they planning to demand an outrageous amount for a night's shelter?

"We're simple people, really, but we will pay generously for your hospitality."

"Good, good. Come, Sister. I'll show you where you'll sleep."

Petra followed her through the right-hand curtain, praying for better than she expected. She found herself in a room containing just one bed. The bed was low and large, and she saw no doors or stairs that could lead to other rooms. She was going to have to share one bed with the whole family? But Madame Goulart walked toward the back wall, which was entirely covered by dark red curtains. Petra hurried after. Thank God.

The woman parted the curtains in the middle to reveal something quite like a nun's cell, with other curtains making side walls. The end of the room held curtained sleeping alcoves—perhaps five of them? Peculiar, but Petra could have cried hallelujah with relief.

She hurried forward but halted, hit by yet more smells. The prevailing damp and rot was joined by unwashed sheets, old spilled wine, perhaps even urine, and something else. A rank, musty odor that turned her stomach.

"Oh. I . . ."

"What?"

Inspiration flew to Petra like an angel. "I cannot sleep in a room without an open window. I'm sorry. It is the rule of my order. I must be ready for God to take me at any moment."

"God needs a window?" the woman asked with surprising perception.

Petra spread her hands. "It is the rule. I will return to my brother. . . ." *Please.*

But Madame Goulart said, "That wouldn't be right, Sister," and stumped off to the right.

The woman dragged back the curtain at the end of the row to reveal an identical sleeping space. It was as filthy, but had a shuttered window. Petra opened the shutters and inhaled damp evening air. "Thank you, madame. God bless your holy kindness."

The woman grunted, but seemed to expect Petra to

return to the kitchen. Petra needed a moment to pull herself together. "I have a few prayers I must say, if you don't mind."

Mère Goulart shrugged. "I'll send for you when the meal's ready."

She left, dragging the curtain closed behind her, but at least left the candle. Petra pulled back the coverlet but saw, as feared, a stained sheet. She hastily covered it again. She'd sleep on top of the coverlet, wrapped in her cloak. It would be chilly, but she could offer up all her sufferings as penance for her many sins.

Especially that of responding to Robin Bonchurch's kiss.

Not only was it foolish, it was wrong. She might not truly be a nun, but she'd worn the habit for three years and had always believed that as long as she did so, she should follow the rule of the Community of Saint Veronica—the rule of poverty, chastity, and obedience. Yes, she'd made the right choice to avoid night out there with that man and temptation.

She went to the window and inhaled fresh air—then laughed to herself. In other circumstances, the smell of a farmyard would not have been so welcome.

Her spurious brother, Robin, was right. She should have stayed with Lady Sodworth. Even though she'd have had to take care of the little monsters, she'd be warm and fed. As for Varzi, she must have imagined him. The world wasn't short of round men of medium height who dressed plainly, but she'd leapt to a conclusion, acted impetuously, and was being suitably punished. She had a cold, damp, dirty night ahead of her.

The view outside was equally forbidding. The walls of the old house were feet thick and the window chest high, restricting her view to the rectangle in front of her. All she could see was mud, sheds, and the high wall with cloudy twilight beyond. Were the men still out there? Ridiculous to think they weren't, but she had to check.

She hooked her arms over the sill, jumped, and pulled herself up to balance there. Laughter almost tipped her over. If her hostess returned, how could she explain this? Obligatory convent exercises? Laughter died because it hurt her ribs, but she had the reassuring glimpse she sought.

Reassuring but painful.

Four shapes sat around a cheery fire. When they laughed, she longed to be with them. She freed one arm to wave, but no one saw her so she slid back down to her feet and brushed flaked stone off her habit, stupidly close to tears.

"You looked like a medieval princess in a tower pleading for rescue."

She spun around, and there he was, arms on the sill, looking in, dimples in his cheeks. Coquette sat on the sill at his elbow, ears twitching. Petra could almost imagine the dog was wrinkling her nose at the smell.

"What are you doing here?" Petra asked, keeping her voice low. She didn't want to be heard in the kitchen.

"Coquette saw you wave and insisted. I think she misses female company."

Petra stroked the pretty dog. "I doubt it. It's you she loves."

"Then she's a fool. If there was any meat on her I'd sell her for soup."

Petra shook her head at him, but she was smiling just for the pleasure of his company. "You take good care of her."

"I'm a dutiful fellow burdened by desirous females. So, what do you desire, princess? Rescue?"

She remembered why she'd needed to be away from him for this night. "No, of course not."

He peered past her. "Not the most inviting chamber."

"They're poor."

"The poor can be clean."

"So can the rich, and they're often not."

"True enough. Are you all right?" he asked seriously.

Petra eased back the curtain to be sure no one was in the room beyond.

When she turned back, his eyes were watchful. "Why the caution?"

"I don't want to hurt their feelings."

"But?"

"They're a strange lot."

"Strange? In what way?"

"I don't want to be unkind, but one of the daughters might be simple and the other . . . I don't know." She touched her head.

"Probably too many cousins marrying."

"Probably. Though, in fact, they're not much alike."

"There's just the three women?"

"No, there's a grandmother. She's horribly hunched, poor thing, and drinks, perhaps to kill the pain. They're an unfortunate family."

He was leaning his arms on one side of the sill, she on the other so their faces were only a foot away. The tallow light was dim, but if anything it cast drama onto the elegant lines of his face and lips. Lips she remembered against hers.

"Something's the matter," he said.

You. But Petra only said, "Tiredness, probably, but I don't expect to sleep well."

He rested his hand on hers. "I'll do better for you tomorrow. State your wish, princess."

Petra knew she should pull away from that warm touch, but she needed human contact right now. "A palace," she said lightly, but then shook her head. "A clean, well-aired bed will do, in a clean room—a room entirely to myself."

"Not quite what I had in mind," he said, but the light humor in it stole offense. "We'll stop early tomorrow to be sure of it. Perhaps in Montreuil. The luxury of the Court de France should compensate for this."

"The French court?" she asked, puzzled.

"It's a hostelry. A very grand one."

"I don't require grand. I'd rather we made haste to England."

"Why? Why the hurry?"

Petra shook her head. "Don't pry at me now. I don't have the wit to amuse."

His hand tightened slightly in comfort. "Very well. But later, after you've had a good night's sleep in a clean, well-aired bed entirely to yourself . . ."

"Even then you won't get my secrets, sir. Not even with torture."

"It wasn't torture I had in mind. . . ."

She moved her hand away, but he captured it and raised it to his warm lips. "Trust me, Petronilla *mia.* Whatever your urgent purpose in England, you will need me."

Her breath felt thin, but she tugged. "Your price will always be too high."

He released her. "See, I set you free. I will never

force you to anything. But reality will. I predict failure
if you escape from me."

If the two-feet-thick wall hadn't been between them
she might have hit him.

"How can I be free if I must escape?"

His eyes met hers. "Alas, you're right. I'll try to
respect your wishes." He drew back, taking his dog.
"Good night, sweet lady of the secrets."

Petra watched him disappear into the darkness,
fighting an urge to climb out after him, but also wishing she could flee him now.

She had pursued her plan thus far and made it almost to England. She only needed Robin Bonchurch
to get her there, and then she would escape him. She
had a dagger in her pouch and twenty guineas hidden
in the end boards of her prayer book. Once in England, she would find her father, and then all would
be well.

She hoped and prayed.

Chapter 6

The curtain rattled back without warning, and there was Solette, eyeing Petra suspiciously. Petra gave thanks that she had instinctively gripped her rosary and would look as if she prayed. She followed the young woman back to the kitchen, carrying her guttering, smoking candle. She placed the candle with another on the table, and with the fire, the room seemed positively merry after the dank cell. For greater cheer, a hunk of yellow cheese now sat beside the coarse bread.

Madame Goulart sat in a chair at the end facing the fire and waved Petra to a seat on the bench to her left. Jizzy sat on the other bench, still looking anxious. Petra smiled at her, but it didn't seem to help.

The old woman ladled soup into bowls that Solette carried to the table, serving her mother first and then Petra. Petra thanked her, but she'd forgotten the smell of this brew. Perhaps a meat bone had been used when past its best. Perhaps the cook had tried to mask decay with extra herbs. Perhaps the old woman had lost her sense of smell. There was certainly a lot of sage, a herb best used in moderation in Petra's opinion, but no one else showed any sign of minding.

Once the soup was served, Solette helped her grand-mother to hobble painfully to the empty chair opposite Madame Goulart, then sat beside her sister. When Monsieur Goulart was home the chair at the head of the table would surely belong to him. . . .

"Perhaps you'd offer grace, Sister."

Madame Goulart's words pulled Petra away from the half-formed thought. Petra said a brief prayer of thanks for the food and also asked God for blessings on this household, for they surely needed them. Everyone picked up a wooden spoon and began to eat.

Petra filled her spoon and took a mouthful—then had to force herself to swallow it. It must have a bushful of sage in it, and there was definitely an unpleasant taste beneath. She stirred it as the others ate with relish. Truly, local tastes were different.

"Eat, eat!" the old woman croaked, showing a few long, blackened teeth.

Petra looked back at the stew, bracing herself to force it down as penance, but then a whole clove of garlic bobbed up. She remembered an unfortunate sister in the convent. "Oh! Is there garlic in this?"

"Of course there's garlic," the crone said. "What's soup without garlic?"

"Yes, yes, but you see, I can't eat garlic. It makes me terribly ill."

"Garlic?" queried Madame Goulart. "How can anyone be made ill by garlic? It's good food, Sister. Eat."

That shot out like a command, but Petra put down her spoon, the focus now of unfriendly eyes. She felt bad, but she couldn't eat the stuff. "Truly," she assured them, recalling Sister Beata's sufferings. "It gives me terrible cramps and foul gases. You wouldn't want me in the house if I ate this."

After a tense moment, Madame Goulart waved toward the bread and cheese. "Make up with that, Sister."

Petra thanked her with true sincerity and sliced into the loaf, then cut a wedge of cheese. The bread was coarse and chewy, the cheese pungent, but she had to struggle not to gobble it. When the pear cider came around, she drank deeply and praised that, too.

Perhaps the mood eased, but apart from her thanks, everyone ate in silence. It was clearly their normal way, and in the convent meals had been silent, but Petra found herself longing to speak. She wasn't sure how long the family might sit here in silence, but once she'd eaten her fill, she used the soup as escape.

"Please excuse me. Even so little garlic has stirred my insides. I will retire to my room."

Madame Goulart's face was stony, but she said, "The privy's in the yard, but the mud's bad. Jizzy, give the holy sister a bowl."

Jizzy took a mixing bowl off a shelf and thrust it into Petra's hands. Petra thanked her, said, "Good night, and blessings upon you all," and escaped.

Probably they were as pleased to see her go as she was to leave.

Once through the curtain, Petra realized that she had no light, but she didn't want to return. The clouds must have cleared a little, for some moonlight enabled her to make her way past the bed to her dirty cubicle. Who slept where? Monsieur and Madame Goulart in the big bed, the grandmother and girls in the cells? Perhaps there were sons.

She put the bowl down on the floor and sighed, going again to the window. The moon lightened the scene a little, but the night air was damp. She wouldn't look toward the warmth again. The rake would only take it as encouragement.

How long must her strength last? Perhaps only one day. She had studied maps, and though Lady Sodworth would have taken two days from Abbeville to Boulogne, it was possible in one day if they left early and traveled long. The packet ship to England would leave in the evening. She could be in England on the day after tomorrow, if God would for once be kind. Then she had only to find her father.

If only that were so easy.

She knew the location of his various houses, but not where he was right now. He was an important person at court, so she'd assumed he'd be where the court was, but now it seemed that might not be so. She would check his London house first, and then the one in Hampshire.

If she found him, there was always the risk that her father would deny her. Her mother had been adamant that he wouldn't, but with time Petra's faith in her mother's certainties had faded. Her mother had been ill and desperate and thinking of a man she'd known more than twenty years ago. The only proof Petra had to offer him was a letter from her mother and a picture—a picture of an eye.

Her mother had explained that such images had been the height of romance back then, especially in the whirling mysteries of a Venetian masquerade. Artists had sat in the streets ready to execute such miniatures on the spot, sometimes even without the sitter unmasking. To her mother it had been impossible that the then Lord Grafton would have forgotten her, but Petra had wondered all along. A young English lord traveling through Italy and Greece, supposedly for his education.

How many liaisons had there been? How many were remembered weeks later, never mind decades?

And even if he remembered, even if he believed the story, why should he embrace a bastard daughter who turned up out of nowhere? Petra sighed. She'd doubted all along, but this had been her only hope. Her brother was now the head of the family and he had turned against her. Her other brother and sisters feared his displeasure, and once Cesare had revealed her paternity they'd used that as excuse to ignore her mother's pleas. Her mother's family, far off in Austria, had fallen from favor and didn't have the resources to intervene.

As for aristocratic Milan, she'd been foolish with Ludo and not discreet enough, so when Cesare had let word spread that she was not his father's true daughter, most had shrugged and said that being the acknowledged mistress of il conte di Purieri wasn't so bad a fate for one such as she. No one wanted to offend the Morcini, Ludo's family, least of all Cesare. He might be il conte di Baldino now, but he needed the alliance with the Morcini to pursue his ambitions.

Politics, politics. She'd raged to her mother that politics and the ambitions of men could cripple her life, but her mother had been able to do nothing but shrug. She herself had been married to a foreigner she didn't love for political advantage.

Politics. They had politics in England, too, and her father was deeply involved in such things. If he accepted her, would he see just a new pawn in his games? Could Ludo bring pressure to bear in England? Austria ruled Milan, and Austria had been Britain's enemy in the recent war, so she hoped not. But could she be seen as an enemy?

Even aware of all these problems, she'd been sure that if her plan failed, she could find a place in a convent and take full vows. Anything was better than being Ludovico's whore.

Now it seemed that wasn't possible, and she might have Varzi in pursuit. Which meant, she suddenly realized, that she was putting Robin and his men in danger.

That nursery rhyme came back to her.

Who did kill Cock Robin?
I, said the sparrow,
With my bow and arrow.
I did kill Cock Robin.

She shivered from mental and physical exhaustion, feeling she'd sleep as soon as she lay down anywhere but here. Here, she was reluctant to lie on a dirty bed, but also strangely reluctant to surrender to oblivion.

What, did she think her hosts were going to creep in and murder her? She was no threat to them.

She unpinned her veil from her cap, setting the pins in the gray cloth for storage, and then looked around for a place to put it. Not liking the look of any surface, she tucked it over her belt, remembering the Saint Veronica cloth. Perhaps tomorrow night she'd be able to wash that.

She'd like to take off the belt and pouch, but again there was nowhere to put it. She realized she'd put her bag containing soap and toothbrush down in the kitchen, along with her clean shift. She wasn't going back out there for them, and what was the point? She hadn't been offered washing water.

She pulled her cloak completely around herself and lay on the bed, keeping her sandals on. Then she said a prayer against fleas and composed herself for sleep.

Her mind jangled. What was it that had struck her as odd about the table?

Stop it, Petra. The atmosphere here is strange because the poor women are terrified without their men.

She sat bolt upright. Their men! This evening, with five people at the table, only one space had remained. Was there only one man in the family—Monsieur Goulart? No, there could be two, with a son to take her place on the bench.

Whatever the truth of that, the man of the house would sit at the head of the table, so when he was home, where did the old woman sit? Petra doubted she could climb onto one of the benches. Hard to imagine Madame Goulart lowering herself to sit on one.

The truth was, there were no men. They were women alone, poor things, which explained their poverty and fear. All was explained, and perhaps Robin could be especially generous to them tomorrow.

Petra was awakened by muttering voices. Was it morning already? No, it was dark.

Two or more people were talking in the kitchen, so she'd probably dozed off for only minutes. She huddled into her cloak and concentrated on sleep, but the voices warred with exhaustion. She rolled onto her back, wishing she could go out there and tell them to shut up.

Was it the young women sharing secrets, or Madame Goulart complaining to her mother about the visiting nun who wouldn't eat garlic and insisted on keeping the window unshuttered? Petra pulled her hood over her ears to block the sound, but her mind wouldn't calm. It insisted there was something wrong about those voices, something suspicious.

Grumbling to herself, she rose and went to the curtain. She eased it back an inch and the voices became a little louder, but she still couldn't understand a word. The room beyond was dark, but a bit of light leaked around the edges of the curtain. The big bed looked empty. They were all still up?

They have a right to sit by their fire talking, she told herself. *Go back to sleep.* But she couldn't. Ready with the excuse of wanting her things, she slipped across the bedroom and up to the left-hand curtain.

"One of you make sure they're . . ." Petra couldn't understand the last word, but it had been the old woman's raspy voice.

"Course they are." That might be Solette. "There was enough"—another unknown word—"to make them sleep for a week."

Petra's breath caught. "Them" could only be the men. They'd given them something to make them sleep?

She wasn't drugged—but she'd eaten only a mouthful of that strange soup. Everyone at the table had eaten from the same pot—but the old woman had ladled it into bowls and Solette had delivered them. Could there have been something extra in the one delivered to her?

Something from that pouch?

But why? It could be because they were afraid and wanted the men to sleep deeply in the night, but that didn't explain their current conversation. Madame Goulart was talking now, in such a rapid, low voice and heavy accent Petra couldn't understand a word, but it sounded unpleasant.

Think, Petra, *think*!

She remembered the persistent questions about

Robin's wealth. He'd said that the French thought all Englishmen were made of gold. The woman had mentioned Coquette's collar. Had these impoverished women decided a treasure had fallen into their hands and planned to steal from the sleeping men? They'd have to be mad. Tomorrow the theft would be discovered, and as soon as they reached the next town . . .

Her imagination skidded to a halt.

Unless they weren't to be allowed to reach the next town.

Saint Peter aid us! It seemed unbelievable, but Petra had heard of travelers disappearing without a trace. She retreated shakily to her cell, struggling to think over a racing heart. If the sleeping draft had been in the soup, the women knew she hadn't eaten much. They'd know she'd cry the alarm if anything happened to the rest of her party.

But they wouldn't need to drug her to kill her—three strong women against one, with the old woman to help if necessary. Petra fingered the shape of the dagger in her pouch, but doubted it could hold them all off. With a shudder, she remembered the big knife on the table that had cut so easily through chewy bread and hard cheese.

Saint Peter aid them all.

Then yelling made her almost leap out of her skin, but it was only Madame Goulart yelling at Solette, and Solette screaming back. Then a door slammed. Solette had finally done as she was told, but clearly none of them expected the men to be awake.

Or alive?

Chapter 7

Petra thrust her fist into her mouth, shaking now. But surely these peasants wouldn't have strong poison on hand, a poison that could overwhelm without chance of struggle or screams of pain?

A sleeping draft was a different matter. Gall, poppy seed, henbane, even hemlock in small amounts, would put anyone into a deep sleep for hours, and the men might have thought sleepiness natural after the hard journey.

Petra heard a noise and quickly lay back on her bed. She was only just in place when the curtain rustled and candlelight shone through her closed lids for what felt like an excruciating eon.

Then it went. After a moment, Petra risked opening her lids the merest crack. She was alone. She slipped to the curtain and saw the solid back of Madame Goulart returning to the kitchen. Petra just stood there, all doubt gone. The woman had come to see if she'd been awakened by the noise, but why hadn't she killed Petra then and there?

Perhaps she was waiting to see if the rest of the plan worked. If one of the men woke, the women could probably think up an excuse. Nothing could excuse a corpse. Petra was sure now that the women were intent on evil, and she might be the only one able to stop it. She had to get out and wake the men.

If they couldn't be woken?

She'd have to deal with the women alone.

If only she had a better weapon. Robin must travel with pistols. She didn't know much about guns, but if one were primed and loaded, she knew how to cock it and fire.

Wouldn't he also have a sword? Thanks to Ludo, damn his black soul, she could use a sword. Not brilliantly, but well enough—

The distant door squeaked open again, banged shut again. Petra risked creeping out to the curtain.

"All snoring," Solette reported sulkily.

Not dead, not dead. Thank you, God!

Madame Goulart asked something.

"Three near the horses. Milord must be in the carriage."

"Too good to sleep on the ground," the old woman sneered at a deaf woman's volume. "A rich milord for sure."

"And we'll have that pretty dog collar, and his other treasures," Madame Goulart said. "Get ready, girls."

Whatever Petra did, it had to be now, and the only way out was through her window. She slid back into her cell and heaved herself up onto the windowsill again, praying that she not be heard. Her blood was pounding so fiercely in her ears, she was all but deaf to other sounds.

Balanced, shaking, and sucking in breaths, she realized that getting out wouldn't be as easy as she'd imagined. She could fit through the opening, but it was too small for her to turn. The only way was to keep going as she was, headfirst.

Into the mud.

Silently.

Praying fervently, she tipped forward and attempted to slither down the outside wall. Not being a snake, she got only so far, then tumbled to the ground. This close to the house, the ground was damp rather than muddy, but that meant it didn't break her fall well. She'd be bruised tomorrow.

If she lived.

She pushed to her feet, looking for Robin's fire. It must have died, but there was one faint light—a candle in one coach lamp, she thought. She tried to sprint across the dark yard, but within feet, her sandals sank in mud. The best she could do was slip and slog as Robin had done when carrying her.

Sweet, wicked Cock Robin. He was doubtless destined to rake coals in hell, but please God, not yet.

At least the darkness hid her. The kitchen shutters must still be closed, and the moon was mostly behind clouds. She remembered she'd taken off her veil and pulled her hood over her white cap, then labored forward, focused on the coach lamp like a ship on a harbor light, ears stretched for sounds from the house.

Finally, her feet found firmer ground. She was under the overhang and took a moment to catch her breath. No movement from the house. She shuffled toward the lamp, trying not to trip over anything.

Then behind her, the farmhouse door opened.

Petra froze, praying she was beyond the range of any light. She turned slowly to look behind.

Madame Goulart stood in the doorway. She made no move forward, but the women were coming, coming, and Petra hadn't woken anyone or found a weapon. Trusting to her gray cloak, she edged toward the coach, watching the woman.

Her back hit a wheel, almost making her gasp.

She looked left and right, able to make out some details in the darkness. They'd propped the coach pole on the side of the horse's stall so it was level. Because Robin was sleeping in it, she remembered. She couldn't see any of the other men, so she'd try him first.

With her back to the wheel, the door was to her right, but high. Still watching the silent woman, she stretched for the handle. Got it. Did the door creak when opened? Nothing must steal her element of surprise.

Someone in the house spoke, and Madame Goulart went back inside. She left the door open, but was no longer watching and listening.

Petra turned and eased the handle down. It made only the dullest click. She pulled the door open. No noise. *Thank you, God!* The floor of the coach was at the level of her waist, but Petra didn't want to risk noise by climbing the steps.

"Are you awake?" she breathed.

No answer. Her voice was too quiet to wake someone in a normal sleep, never mind a drugged one. She needed to poke or shake. She climbed up one step. The coach dipped a bit and let out a squeak. She froze, but a glance behind showed no one.

Her cloak was getting in the way, so she unfastened the clasp and let it drop, trying to visualize the interior of the chaise. The seat was to her right, but it was far too short for Robin to lie along it, so he'd be slouched in one corner or another, his long legs crossing the space in front of her. Had he taken off his boots? She couldn't wake him with a poke through boots.

Where was Coquette? She must be drugged, too, or she'd be yapping welcome or alarm.

Petra was reaching out carefully when she heard low voices behind her. She thrust her hand out—and hissed when she jarred her fingers on something hard only inches away. What? Quick hands found a solid barrier. He'd barricaded himself in already?

Muttering under her breath, she climbed higher and tried to reach over—but it was a solid surface. A box? Covered with some thick cloth? An improvised bed! The clever man, but he'd be a clever corpse if she didn't wake him. She scrabbled over the surface, seeking a man's body, trying to see through her fingers.

Cold metal.

A cylinder.

A pistol! She curled her hand around the butt and lifted it against her breasts, thanking the universe. Armed, she turned to face danger.

There they were, Madame Goulart and her daughters, coming, but making slow progress in the mud. Perhaps they were also cautious, even afraid, and so they should be. Of damnation, if nothing else.

Madame Goulart carried a lantern. No light reached the coach yet, but it soon would. Petra arranged herself right hand outward, ready to raise the pistol. With her left hand, she groped for any bit of Robin Bonchurch she could hurt.

Ah, warmth. Still watching the women, she poked, but he was at the limit of her reach. She weighed options, turned, put down the pistol, and stretched out both hands. A hard bit—hip?

Oh!

Well, men were supposed to be sensitive there, so

she gripped the shape beneath his breeches. His breath caught, but he stayed dead to the world.

Don't think dead.

"Wake up!" Petra whispered, getting a knee on the top of the box and pounding what she hoped was his chest.

She was grabbed and dragged in and under him. "Desperate, are you, my lovely?" he asked, laughing.

"It's me!" she hissed. "Sister—"

He kissed her.

Petra froze, but only for a moment. Then she fought. He was all over her, however, his mouth silencing her, his strength conquering her—while irrational bits of her were trying to forget their danger and succumb.

She felt skin and raked her nails.

He jerked back, hissing.

"Idiot man!" she spat. "The women. They're coming to kill you."

"What?"

Petra heaved him away. The women had to have heard. They might even be able to see the coach rock. She grabbed the pistol and scrambled out of the coach to swing the gun two handed toward the three. She cocked it, the click startlingly loud.

The women stopped, but only yards away. Jizzy seemed to carry some sort of club, and Solette had that sharp kitchen knife.

"Well, well," said Madame Goulart, face positively evil in lamplight. "Perhaps she's not worth as much as I thought."

Petra frowned at her. "Me? I'm a nun."

"Who holds a gun like that? And sneaks out to join her brother in his coach?"

Petra almost argued, but could she pretend to be unaware of the danger?

"What are *you* doing out here?" she demanded.

"We heard intruders," the woman said. "Someone stealing the chickens, perhaps."

"We're not stealing your chickens, so all's well."

"All's well, except for your wicked sin, Sister. Shameful, that is."

"With your brother, too!" exclaimed Solette. "That'll send you right to hell, that will."

They were conversing as if no one held weapons, but Petra was willing to play that game if it would send them back to the house.

"Not a virgin, though, Mère," Solette said. "Pity."

"I can stitch her."

"And she does the nun thing well."

Petra suddenly understood. They were talking about making her a whore! A whore slave, sold off as a virgin nun. They were all whores. This was some low kind of brothel. Those sleeping cells. Perhaps there were sometimes more women here.

She clutched the pistol more tightly. "Return to the house. We'll leave in the morning and say nothing about this."

The evil mother laughed. "You could kill one of us, maybe, but then you're ours."

"I'm an excellent shot," Petra lied, "so one of you will certainly die." She moved the gun to point at each in turn. "Which shall it be?"

The two younger women shifted uneasily, but Mère Goulart said, "Kill one of us, and I'll cut out your tongue. A mute whore can have special value in some quarters."

Petra shuddered, but steadied the heavy pistol on her. "Then I'll kill you."

"Then Solly'll do it. Won't you, girl?"

Solette giggled. "With pleasure."

"Spread out, girls," Mère Goulart ordered. "Make it a harder shot."

The two girls obeyed, but they both looked nervous.

"Uno, due, tre. Uno, due, tre . . ." Petra counted as she moved the pistol to track the growing arc, but her hands were shaking now, both with the weight of the gun and fear. She didn't doubt their horrible threat, and it seemed that Robin had sunk back into a drugged sleep. Perhaps he'd never truly woken up. She'd end up a mute slave in a brothel, and the men would all die.

And she was counting in Italian.

"Un, deux, trois," she muttered. *"Un, deux, trois."*

Saint Peter, Saint Veronica, all the angels and saints, come to my aid!

She realized silence was useless now. "Robin!" she screamed. "Someone. Help!"

They all waited. Petra realized the women couldn't be sure Robin was drugged. When nothing happened, however, Mère Goulart said, "No one's coming to help you. Put the pistol down, and you can keep your tongue."

"Put your weapons down and you can all keep yours," said a cold voice from behind them.

Mère Goulart whirled, her lantern swinging wild light over her two alarmed daughters, and over wonderful Cock Robin, ghostly in white shirt and pale breeches and stockings, pistol steady in his right hand, sword in his left.

Jizzy and Solette dropped their weapons. but Mère Goulart whined, "Sir, sir, you mistake everything. We meant no harm! The chickens—"

"Shut up. Are you hurt, Sister?"

Petra's heart was knocking in her chest and she felt dizzy, but she managed "No."

He considered the women. "You," he said to Jizzy, "take off your skirt and cut it into strips."

"What?" Jizzy's startled query quavered with fear.

"Cut your overskirt into strips and tie up the other two, starting with madame. Get on with it."

At his tone, Jizzy squeaked in panic and fumbled with the ties of her skirt. It tumbled down, revealing her dingy, knee-length shift. Then she fell to her knees and crawled to the knife to hack into the cloth.

Robin Bonchurch watched all three, apparently relaxed, but in command of both sword and pistol. Petra felt as if she'd whirled from unimaginable horror into some sort of dream featuring a pale angel with rippling, burnished hair. . . .

She remembered other dangers and studied the farmhouse.

The door was shut and there was no sign of life other than a little light around closed shutters. The crippled woman wouldn't be able to attack them, but she'd be watching through one of the chinks and know the plan had failed. Would she try something?

"Put down the lantern."

At Robin's command, Petra twitched back and watched Mère Goulart obey, dark with sullen malevolence. He told the woman to hold out her wrists while Jizzy bound them. Jizzy quaked but she obeyed, clearly fearing Robin more than her mother. No, not mother. She and Solette were probably no relation at all.

Petra realized she should try to get help. None of
the other men had stirred to her screams, so they must
be drugged deeply, but she sidestepped toward the
bundles near the horses, keeping an eye on the women
and the house.

Her feet found something. She looked down. Powick. He'd be the most useful anyway. She kicked him.
The only result was a grunt, so she put her foot on his
chest and pressed down. He coughed but didn't wake.

"Any luck?" Robin called.

"They're drugged deep." She spoke in English so the
women wouldn't understand. "How is it you aren't?"

"I ate little of the stew," he replied in the same
tongue. "I assume that was it."

"Has to be. I only ate a mouthful."

"Why?"

"Too much sage."

"Too much everything, but unfortunately the others
found it edible. Sit back against that pole," he told
Mère Goulart in French. When she obeyed, he ordered Jizzy to tie her to it. The woman spat a curse,
but there was still no action from the house.

Petra moved to another bundle. The valet. A kick
to the body gained no response at all. He might as
well be dead, and being slightly built, the drug's effect
would have been stronger. He might indeed be dead.
She went to one knee and felt for a pulse. Slow and
steady, thank God, but he wouldn't wake soon. She
had the same result with the postilion, another small
man. She and Robin were alone for now, but at least
Madame Goulart was immobilized. She was the
leader.

Robin had set Jizzy to tying up Solette, who hissed
like a feral cat. Petra remembered the relish with

which the rat-toothed young woman and the brothel owner had discussed turning her into a whore. They were vile, and tomorrow they'd be in the hands of the law, but only if she and her party could survive the night.

"Maria."

It took Petra a moment to realize Robin was calling her.

"Come and tie up Jizzy."

Petra did, but hated the fact that the scared young woman was crying, lips quivering, nose running. She hardened her heart, put down the pistol well out of the woman's reach, and approached warily. There was no fight in Jizzy, however. She held out her plump wrists, begging not to be hurt. Petra cursed herself for not noticing plump wrists before. These "poor peasants" were well fed.

As Jizzy sat miserably with the other two, Mère Goulart caught Petra's eye and said, "Tongue and eyes, Sister. You're for it."

Despite everything, Petra backed away, stumbling over the gun. She grabbed and pointed it. "Another word and I'll kill you!"

The woman went silent, but her eyes were evil and cunning.

In English again, Petra said, "If there's any way to escape, she'll find it. And the old woman's still in the house. I don't think your men can be awakened—"

"We need only to keep alert."

"This is all because of Coquette's ridiculous collar. They think it's real. That you're a rich English milord."

"It is real," he said, "but if you remember the conversation, this is mostly because of your ridiculous beauty. Also real."

"I'm not worth four lives."

"You obviously don't know a beautiful virgin's worth in some quarters. A nun, as well. A premium for that."

The women were bound, but Petra felt the threat winding around her.

"Don't worry," he said. "It won't happen."

"We'll have to watch them all night. The house, as well. . . ."

"Take some deep breaths, my dear. I'll keep you safe."

He still seemed a gossamer warrior, but some deep breaths helped, and his calm comforted her. "I've kept all-night vigils in the convent," she said, satisfied with her steady voice. "I can do this."

"And I've enjoyed long nights in less holy pursuits," he said. "See? We're well equipped."

"But before vigils I enjoyed decent sleep the night before," she said. And she hadn't been afraid. Now she was shivering with shock and exhaustion, but must watch, watch, watch all night, or they would die.

Chapter 8

Robin saw how exhausted Sister Immaculata looked and knew he wasn't completely alert himself, even though all-night revels truly were common to him. He'd eaten two mouthfuls of the soup before giving up. Perhaps that had been enough to have some effect.

He worried about his men and suddenly about Coquette. If she was her normal self she'd be out here making a fuss. He'd fed her some chicken from the hamper, but she'd licked from his discarded bowl. She'd disdained it after one taste, wise dog, but perhaps she'd eaten enough.

Plague take these foul hags and plague take him. The dog was a pest and a burden, but he should have protected her better. He should have protected everyone. Instead a nun had been their savior, but now she looked at her limit.

They were standing side by side, and he'd like to take her in his arms, but as she said, they had to watch, watch, watch. He'd like to check Jizzy's knots, but it was too risky to get close to cunning Solette and the madame, and he didn't think Jizzy had the wit and courage to deliberately make the bonds loose.

The gun hung heavily at the end of Petra's arm.

"Why not put that down between us?" he said in English. "Then either of us can grab it as needed."

After a moment she did so, but said, "Give me the sword, or you'll not have a hand free."

Stubborn woman, but he passed his rapier. She took a practiced hold on the hilt and tested its weight and balance even as she resumed her watch on the bound women and the silent house.

He shook his head. "Care to explain familiarity with weapons, Sister?"

Eyes ahead, she said, "I wasn't always in the convent."

"Pistol and sword work are a routine part of a girl's education in Italy?"

"No, but not forbidden."

"Close enough, I'll be bound. Need I remind you we're in danger here? Your secrets could kill us."

She turned to stare. "This has nothing to do with me!"

"Doesn't it?"

Until he asked the question, he'd not seriously thought this mess could be her doing. "Sometimes people lurk at inns to steer passengers toward doom."

"You're mad! I arrived in Abbeville with Lady Sodworth. You heard her calling for me. How many stray nuns could there be at the Tête de Boeuf?"

Robin shook his head. "Only one. I apologize."

"So I should think. As if I'd have anything to do with *them*."

As she turned her attention back to the women, he couldn't help but smile at her outrage. She was right. Whoever she was, Petra d'Averio came from a different sphere than Mère Goulart and her nest of whores. Even now, muddy and exhausted, she was all fine lines and high spirit, back straight, shoulders square, chin angled proudly. She'd taken off her veil, and the tight white cap showed a fine line of skull and neck. Some dark wisps of hair escaped at her nape.

He wanted to brush his fingers through those wisps and feel her shiver of response. To run a finger down the fine bones of her spine. They'd been previously hidden by her veil, but now . . .

As if aware, she shot a frowning look at him.

He shook himself. "We need help. Try again to wake Powick."

She put down the sword and went to shake his groom. Powick stopped snoring.

"That's hopeful. Get a bit rougher with him. He won't break."

She slapped Powick's cheek, and the man swore at her. She didn't hesitate. She gave him a full blow that made Robin wince in sympathy.

"Wake up! Wake up!" she yelled. "Danger!"

"Huh?" Powick blinked and half rose, but then tried to sink back into sleep again.

The indomitable woman grabbed his shirt and bounced the big man up and down until he began to fight her off. When he almost caught her a blow on the cheek, Robin moved to help, but she scrambled out of reach, muttering, "Stupid men."

Robin assumed that included him.

Powick was sitting up now, looking furiously for someone to fight. Then he froze, staring at the scene. "What the . . . ?"

"A trifle of trouble," said Robin. "Sister, bring the wine jug from the coach. And check on Coquette."

"Yes, sir," she said, clearly resenting the order.

"Of your kindness, please," he amended, smiling despite everything.

She might have laughed as she went to the chaise, but Robin noticed the heaviness of her steps. She even wavered once, before wrenching herself straight again. He wanted to tell her to climb onto the makeshift bed and go to sleep, but he knew she wouldn't until Powick was able to stand guard with him.

He *knew* her. Astonishing after less than a day, but he knew Petra d'Averio. Not her secrets, but her nature—strong, brave, quick-witted, and stubborn. Tested by fire and proved true, and he meant a fire much fiercer than this.

As she poked around in the chaise, her prettily rounded bottom sticking out, he couldn't help but smile. Was she, too, remembering her earlier groping exploration? He marveled at his self-control then, and shifted now. Ah, the madness of a man's body that could stir in a situation like this.

"Coquette?" he called.

"Sleeping, but I think she's all right."

She worked her way out of the chaise, wine jug in hand. When she was back on the ground, she paused to take a good swig before carrying it to Powick. The groom had his head in his hands, but he looked up when she spoke, grabbed the jug, and drank deep. Wiping his mouth with the back of his hand, he looked over at Robin again.

"What trouble have you fallen into now, lad?"

"I'm demoted to lad, am I? This is hardly my fault. This pretty lot tried to kill us."

"What?"

"All of us. Except my lady sister. She was intended for a brothel, though a far more expensive one than this."

Powick swore, then begged Petra's pardon and took another long swallow of wine.

Robin gave him a more detailed account of events, and Powick shook his head. "Always into trouble of some sort," he muttered. "So, what do we do now?"

"Keep watch until we can leave, but it doesn't require all of us at once." Petra had weakened enough to lean on one of the posts. "You take the first sleeping shift," he told her.

She instantly straightened. "I can manage."

"I'm sure, but one of us needs to sleep now so as to be able to stand watch later, and I need to make plans with Powick." When she still hesitated, he said, "I'll wake you later. I promise."

He didn't specify when.

She made no further argument. He suspected it was an effort to walk to the carriage in a straight line, and the three steps up seemed to be a challenge. Her gray-covered bottom disappeared into the dark. He saw no more but was sure she was asleep as soon as she lay down.

"Reminds me a lot of your lady mother, sir," Powick said.

Robin turned to him in surprise. "What?"

"Doesn't stand for any nonsense when something needs to be done."

As best Robin knew, the Countess of Huntersdown had never handled sword or pistol in her life, and he couldn't imagine her climbing out of a window, but he saw Powick's point. He captured the wine jug and drank. "I've no idea what she's up to."

"Not a real nun?"

"She swears she is, but I think she has a nimble way with the truth. Even her names. Petra d'Averio and Sister Immaculata and Maria Bonchurch . . ."

"Maria Bonchurch, sir? But—"

"It's complicated."

"Now, there's a new start." Powick pushed himself to his feet, shaking himself like a big dog. "You need some sleep, too, lad."

"You're not alert enough yet."

"I can manage this lot."

"There's an old woman in the house."

"Nimble?"

"Crippled."

"Reckon I can handle her, too, then, and I'll see if I can wake the others."

When Robin found he was too tired to argue, he knew Powick was right, but a dirty quilt on the damp ground didn't appeal.

"I'm cold." The whine from one of the women startled him out of a half sleep.

The young whore with the big, stupid eyes was looking at him piteously. Her misery and fear stirred Robin's protective instincts, but he steeled himself against it. "You won't die of it."

Powick picked up his discarded quilt and tossed it to her. She fiddled it into place with her bound hands, but the other young one tried to snatch it and they ended up in a tug-of-war.

"Share it," Madame Goulart growled, and Robin gave her credit for that. He met her flat eyes, knowing she would be a formidable opponent, given any chance at all.

As if she could read his mind, she said, "Set us free when you leave and we'll say no more about this. Give us that dog collar, too. Anything else, and we'll say you attacked us. Forced your way in. Stole our food and drink. . . ."

Powick growled at her to shut up. He spoke English, but she got the message and fell silent. She had a point, though. Who would the local authorities believe? True, these were whores, but they were local whores, probably used by local men. It was always easier to blame outsiders, especially the old enemy, the English. Their accusations wouldn't stick, of course, but it could be damned messy for a while.

What was best, what was right . . . ?

When he couldn't follow through on that thought, Robin knew he was worse than useless at the moment. It was as if sleep, once thought about, became an invincible force. He headed for the chaise, discovering he wasn't too tired to smile.

"Sir," Powick said disapprovingly.

"I'm too exhausted for a willing woman, and I assure you, our nun is not at all willing. I have the scratches to prove it. She's not even awake. I do prefer my lovers awake. . . ." He had sense enough to stop babbling and simply climb into the coach. Realizing he was in stocking feet, he peeled the muddy things off and dropped them outside. His boots were out there, too, somewhere, where he'd left them when he'd first settled to sleep. . . .

His mind was wandering again.

The dim lights outside hardly reached inside, but Mère Goulart's lantern meant that Robin could make out Petra curled on her side facing him, covered by the silk tapestry he'd dug out hours ago to serve as cover. Hours that felt like days.

She was in the middle of the space. He sat on the edge of the makeshift bed, pulled the door closed, and then slid under the tapestry, staying as far from Petra as he could. He wouldn't take advantage of a sleeping nun, especially one who'd saved his life.

He couldn't help but touch her warm body.

She stirred and rolled, but only onto her back.

How could he be aroused and exhausted at the same time? He couldn't not look, not sense each breath, not detect her warm scent. Sweat intensified an essence that would remain after the longest bath and hum beneath the most expensive perfume.

That snug cap. It must be uncomfortable, tied so firmly beneath her chin.

Ladies often wear nightcaps tied exactly like that, his conscience protested.

But not such tightly made ones, down on the brow, close over the ears.

He was skilled at arguing with his conscience. And winning. He found the string tie and tugged. As he'd hoped, the bow slid undone with only slight resistance. In moments, he had it loose, and even the brush of his fingers against the skin beneath her chin didn't make her stir. Though it certainly stirred him.

He hesitated. He didn't need more scratches.

Not tonight, at least.

He couldn't resist. Breath held, he slid his hand beneath her head, enjoying the feel of her neat skull cradled there. She stirred and mumbled something with those soft, pink, kissable lips, but then settled again. He raised her head just enough to slip off the cap. As he slowly slid his fingers free, enjoying every second, she gasped.

He froze, but she simply turned away from him and settled again, muttering angrily. It sounded fearful as well as angry.

Who pursues you, Petronilla Maria d'Averio?

He lay down, eyes closing, sleep creeping over him.

Fear not. I won't let anyone harm you. But I'll have your secrets, all of them, before we part.

Chapter 9

Petra was awoken by a cock's crow.

Where was she?

What was this hard uncomfortable bed . . . ?

She shot upright.

Who was she sleeping with?

She was in Cock Robin's chaise. With Cock Robin. The wretched, wretched rake! She quickly felt her clothes, but everything seemed to be in order—except for her cap.

Her alarmed hands ran over her exposed hair.

How dare he!

She was tempted to scratch him again, but then she made herself calm. In fact, this was good. He'd discovered what she'd promised—short hair—so now he should believe her story. And it did seem that he considered a nun inviolable.

Where was her cap?

She felt around the bed and found it disconcertingly clenched in his right hand. She stared at that, disabled by a tangle of emotions. She tugged at it, and after a moment he let it go. She put it on, tucking away hair, tucking away perilous reactions at the same time. He was a rake, but he was also mischievous. He'd probably taken off her cap simply in hope of an angry reaction when there were more important things to think about.

She looked across him, out at the Goulart farmyard. How ordinary it looked in daylight. There really were chickens pecking in the mud, and a cock lording it over them. This wasn't a farm, however; it was a brothel, and the whores had tried to murder them.

She looked back down at Robin, thinking how close it had been. If he'd eaten the soup, if she'd faced the women alone . . .

He was sleeping on his back, one arm curled over his head, a tapestry covering him from the waist down. Above he wore only his loose shirt. The top two buttons of his placket were open, exposing his neck and a bit of chest. The morning light was still misty, but in a way that made him even more beautiful, more classical. A sleeping Adonis.

She eyed that inch of chest. Four buttons were still fastened. Tit for tat. Smiling, she stealthily undid one, then the next. He didn't stir, so soon all six were open and she could widen the cloth to expose more smoothly muscled chest. He was a lot stronger than he looked. When she saw inflamed scratches, however, she winced and her finger hovered, wanting to soothe.

They were justly deserved—the stupid, lust-crazed rake—but she sighed to have damaged perfection.

He was a lust-crazed rake, however. She remembered how he'd reacted to her trying to wake him. But then, he probably had women crawling into his bed all the time, pursuing him for his beauty and charm. Was it his fault if he obliged? What young man could resist such temptation?

Petra drew back her hand sharply. The point of

temptation was that it was hard to resist, but good people did, and she absolutely must. In fact, she must leave this sinful nest.

Where were her sandals? She remembered crawling into the coach, but nothing after that. She went on her stomach to peer over the end of the makeshift bed and came eye to eye with a peevish-looking dog. Did dogs get headaches?

"Yip?" Coquette said, rather pitifully.

Petra gathered up the dog, struck again by how small and fragile she was beneath her luxuriant coat. "There, there, little one, it's all right now. The bad people are tied up and we'll soon be away from here. Your master did quite well. Once I'd woken him up and fought him off, that is. He's a wicked wretch, isn't he?"

Coquette remained discreetly silent, but she wriggled free to first sniff at Robin, then go to the door. Of course, she needed to go out.

Petra saw her sandals on the floor and how muddy they were. She picked them up, intending to carry them outside. However, Robin was blocking her way to the door she'd used to enter, and the other door was so close to the wall that it would be a tight squeeze.

She reached over and opened the door for Coquette, wondering if the tiny dog could manage the steps. She did. Petra frowned at the man in her way, but couldn't help noticing the fine line of his jaw and the promise of his parted lips. If she were his wife, waking beside him, she could lean down . . .

She twitched herself straight.

Veil. Where was her veil? She'd felt nothing like this since putting on a nun's habit, and the last time she had felt like this, it had led to disaster.

She found the veil over her belt, horribly creased. She flapped it out, folded it, and pinned it on, feeling to be sure it was straight.

"There's a stray tendril on your forehead."

Petra froze, then glared down at his smiling, lazy eyes.

"You! How dare you take off my cap? It's sacrilege."

"It is no kind of sacrilege to reveal such beauty, Petra."

"And to sleep with me. You *slept* with me."

"It's the only bed around."

Petra opened and shut her mouth a few times. "It's scandalous."

"We spent hours together in this carriage yesterday," he pointed out.

"It was a seat then. It's a bed now."

"It's merely a carriage somewhat overstocked with boxes and packages."

"It's a bed. We shared a bed. What if anyone should hear about this?"

"Who, Petronilla *mia*?"

"Anyone. Your men will talk—"

"They won't talk about anything I don't want them to talk about." The calm certainty of that silenced her, but only for a moment.

"What about the whores, then?"

"Don't be foolish."

She made a fist and raised it, but instantly he gripped her wrist.

"No more claws."

She tried to twist free. "I made a fist, if you'll notice. Let me go."

"Stop struggling."

"Let me go!"

"Why?" he asked, grinning in a way that drove her

insane in all the wrong ways. And he saw it, knew it. She swung her other fist. He caught it, curling up effortlessly, smiling, focused on her lips—

Someone knocked on the outside of the chaise, freezing them in place.

"Monsieur? Pardon me, I beg of you, monsieur, but what are you doing to the blessed sister?"

It was the postilion, and at some point the cunning rake had closed the door. There could be no doubt about what he'd intended, and now they were caught.

Robin cocked a brow at her, not relaxing his grip an inch.

Petra mouthed curses at him, but called, "I'm safe, sir. We're preparing to leave the chaise and the space is somewhat limited."

"You shouldn't be in there with a man, Sister," the postilion persisted.

"I'm with my brother, sir. For protection during this dangerous night. Thank you for your concern."

"Yes, thank you," Robin said, eyes shining. Clearly he found the whole exchange hilarious. "Go and check the road, my man. If it's firm enough, we'll leave soon."

Silence probably meant the man obeyed.

"He should be helping to watch the women," she hissed.

"Powick is up to the task, and Fontaine should be awake by now."

"You . . ." But the wretched rake was smiling into Petra's eyes and her shameless body wouldn't fight. She waited to see what he would do next. Admit it. She waited in hope that he would kiss her again. The smile in his eyes deepened—then he kissed the fisted knuckles of her right hand and let her go. "You'd better go out, or he'll be back."

Damn you, damn you, damn you.

"You first," she said, rubbing her hands as if he'd hurt her.

He lay back down, hands behind his head. "No, no, ladies first. I insist."

"Mr. Bonchurch, I am *not* going to give you the pleasure of crawling over you."

"I'd think you'd need to piss soon."

"Make way or I'll piss on you."

Petra wondered if she was going to have to do it, whether she could do it, but then he laughed and curled up in that same effortless way. Her mind marked it. Marked the catlike strength of him. Her strong and agile ally—but her opponent, as well.

He swung to sit on the boxes facing out. "Powick," he called, "find me some clean stockings and pass up my boots, if you please."

Petra glared at his back, but despite the loose cut of his shirt, every long line of him was clear. She felt starved. *You are,* she told herself. *When you have some decent food in you, you'll be yourself again. You'll remember men are nothing but trouble, especially the young gorgeous ones. Women fall for them so easily, they have no concept of fidelity.*

Clean stockings were passed up and then clean boots, but by the valet, not the groom. The slender man looked gray but resolute. "I did my best to remove the mud, sir."

"Fontaine, you fool, I'm only going to get them muddy again." Robin's tone was fond, however, and he added, "Thank you. I'm devilish glad you're well enough to fuss. How are you?"

"I will survive, sir. If you'll pass out your coat, I will attempt to restore that, too."

When Robin twisted to pick up his jacket, Petra saw his wry expression. As he turned back and handed it down she had to appreciate his concern about his servant. His valet seemed to have been badly affected by the drugs, but he'd be better for routine.

She leaned forward to say, "I, too, am glad you're recovered, sir." Fontaine only sniffed before walking away.

"I warned you," Robin said, rolling on a stocking. He had remarkably elegant feet, even dirty. "When in doubt, blame the woman."

Petra looked away from his foot. "He's right. This is all my fault."

"You are an associate of Madame Goulart, after all?"

"Of course not. But if you'd not encountered me, you wouldn't have left Abbeville."

"I chose to stop here."

"The storm gave us no choice."

He twisted to look at her, blue eyes serious. "There's always choice, Petra *mia*. Remember that."

"I am *not* your Petra, and there is no choice when it comes to sin. Or duty. My duty was to stay with Lady Sodworth."

"I can't imagine why. Did she cherish you?"

"No."

"Did she even pay you?"

"No, but—"

He turned away again. "If you're intent on a deep examination of your conscience, I'll leave you to it. But make it fast, because we're leaving as soon as possible."

He tugged on a second boot and then jumped down and walked out into the muddy farmyard. In just breeches and rumpled shirt he managed to look lordly. Glaring after him, Petra knew that he'd walk into a royal court dressed in satin and lace in exactly the same graceful, casual way. She desperately wanted to see his confidence exploded, but that could only rebound on her. Their fates were entangled for now.

She spotted his crumpled waistcoat among the tapestry cover and pulled it free to straighten it. When she realized she was stroking it, she put it aside and dropped her sandals out of the chaise. Then she climbed down the steps barefoot. Her feet were dirty, anyway. She inspected the sandals and used the skirt of her habit to clean off as much mud as possible. All in all, she was in a disgusting state. When would she have an opportunity to bathe and change?

She checked on the women, but they were still secure, huddled under quilts, apparently asleep. What were they going to do with them?

She squeezed behind the coach to relieve herself, struggling to protect her skirt. She could do nothing about the sounds and felt as if she'd sunk to new depths. *And all due to your folly and impetuousness, Petra. When will you learn?*

When she was neat again she walked back into the open, realizing that it was a surprisingly lovely morning. Surprising, she supposed, because after the night it seemed this place should never be bright.

The sky beyond the walls glowed pink and pearl, and the wall itself was softened by tufts of wildflowers. There was even a small kitchen garden. She saw a sage bush and grimaced. She thought she also saw henbane and hemlock.

The chickens were small but busy. There were probably eggs somewhere, but she'd eat nothing else here.

The cock stalked majestically despite his size, beady eye on the invaders. Coquette went over, curious and friendly. He threw back his head and crowed a challenge.

Petra snatched up the dog. "There are altogether too many cocks in this barnyard, and some are dangerous."

Where was Cock Robin? She saw him helping his groom to open the sagging gates. "Are we leaving already?" she called.

"Not quite. There's a small field out here, so we'll let the horses graze."

True enough. Beyond the lane, a small, fenced field held a few goats. Everything else nearby seemed to be under crops. There had to be other farms nearby, then, because the Goulart women wouldn't be responsible for those.

She looked back at the bound, huddled women. What if the cunning Mère Goulart claimed that Robin and his men had attacked her? Even if the people around here knew her business—and who but local men would be her customers?—they might believe her. When traveling with Lady Sodworth, she'd learned that the French regarded the English as old enemies and vile heretics. Then, her presence as a nun had helped, but here in such scandalous company it might only make things worse. Would the story they'd concocted earlier satisfy a magistrate?

At best, they could end up stuck in this area for hours or even days, snarled in legal complications. At worst, they could be thrown into prison. Either way, she'd be trapped if Varzi truly was in pursuit. She shivered, but it really was in part because of the damp morning air. She put the dog down and went looking for her cloak. She found it, but it was damp and thick with mud around the hem. She spread it over a wheel to dry and wrapped her arms around herself.

"May I warm you?"

She turned sharply, but found Robin was merely offering a golden brown velvet jacket braided in black and gold. It was always dangerous to accept gifts, but Petra didn't resist when he helped her into it, the silk lining sliding over the coarse cloth of her habit. It held his smell, both him and a trace of court perfume. She could picture him in this fine garment and matching breeches, embroidered waistcoat, and red-heeled shoes, strolling into a court like Versailles, jewels on fingers, delicate lace at his throat.

She looked at him to cover illusion with reality, but it remained vivid, and her movement brushed the silky edge of the collar against her cheek.

"Thank you," she said as coolly as she could.

The postilion returned then to say the road was firm enough. "Though there could be deep places still, monsieur." The man's eyes flickered to the bound women. "Begging your pardon, monsieur, but what do you intend to do with them?"

"We must deliver them to the law."

"If you say so, monsieur."

"They tried to kill us all."

The man shrugged. "I was asleep."

"A natural sleep?" Robin asked.

The man's eyes shifted. "Can't say, sir." He must be a local man. A customer here? Whether that was true or not, he clearly wanted no part of arresting the women.

"Why would I lie about it?" Robin demanded.

The man's jaw worked as if he were chewing very

tough meat. Eventually, he said, "No reason, I suppose. But . . ."

Robin's eyes met Petra's, and he completed it in English. "But you are a cursed English heretic and probably mad."

Petra frowned a warning. Speaking English then was the worst thing to do.

"They truly did try to kill us," she said to the man in French. "*I* would not lie."

But clearly her sharing the coach with a man, even as supposed brother and sister, had tarnished her halo.

"We take them," Robin said firmly. "In their cart. Harness their horse."

The postilion went off muttering.

"Take them where?" Petra asked.

"To Nouvion, I assume. Or back to Abbeville."

"No!" It escaped sharply.

"Ah yes. The screeching Sodworth."

Ah yes, the vile Varzi. But they must not be delayed by this. "What if the women claim that we attacked them?" she asked. "They might be believed."

"You want to leave them to prey on others?"

"I don't want to be delayed. What if Lady Sodworth catches up?"

"Stay out of sight. She can't know you're with me." He turned and walked away.

Petra ungritted her teeth and hurried after. "We could simply report the crime and continue our journey."

"Leave them tied up here? Not very charitable, Sister."

"More charitable than hauling them bound to justice."

"Which they deserve."

"They are local people and we are strangers," she pointed out, "and the postilion doesn't seem likely to support the story. We could be held here for days or even arrested ourselves."

"I know people around here. The Guise, the Montaigne. Leave this to me, Petra. I promise, we won't end up in prison."

"But we'll be *delayed*."

"At least it'll be in decent lodgings. Of course, if you told me why you're in such a hurry . . ."

He'd switched like a conjurer from light to serious, leaving Petra off balance. Her troubles had driven secrecy deep into her bones. She'd survived by the code "Tell no one, trust no one," but she had to change his mind, so she had to tell him some of the truth.

"Someone might be pursuing me," she said.

Chapter 10

"Who?" he asked.

"It doesn't matter. I might be wrong."

"Why, then?" he asked patiently.

It felt like pulling out one of her own teeth. "Because someone in Milan didn't want me to leave."

"The convent?"

"Why do Protestants think like that? No." Reluctantly, she added, "A man."

"Ah." The knowing word made her want to hit him, but at least he was taking her seriously now. "A dangerous man?"

"Yes."

He considered that a moment. "Then we had best make all speed. I can write letters to make sure these wretches don't harm anyone in the future." He turned to tell the postilion to forget the cart and bring in the post horses, and his men to help ready the chaise. Petra was left mutely staring at crisp efficiency.

She had her way, however, and hurried to fold her cloak, muddy as it was, and stuff it into the boot. Did she have time to change into her cleaner habit? Or privacy in which to do it?

Robin came over. "If you're pursued, we should change your appearance."

"Out of the habit?" Petra felt the old reluctance to leave its concealment, but it might confuse Varzi. "How?"

"We could look in the house."

"Steal?"

"We'll leave money."

"Anything in there will be dirty."

"A nun is a very easy trail to follow."

Indeed. Why hadn't she thought of that back in Milan? She'd not thought anyone would pursue her beyond the Alps, however.

"The old woman's in there," she warned.

"Is she likely to have a gun?"

"I don't think so. Wouldn't they have used a gun last night if they had one?"

"Then we can handle her." He took his own pistol out of his pocket, saying, "What do you think she *has* done?"

"Drunk herself silly, if she has the means."

"Very well. Come on."

The yard was still muddy, but not deep enough to cause trouble, even for her sandals. Robin opened the door and they stepped inside. There was no sign of the old woman, but something—rats or mice—leapt off the table to scurry away. The fire was dead, the candle merely a puddled lump.

"Could she have run away?" Robin wondered.

"Impossible." Petra pulled back the curtain into the sleeping area. "She's in bed. Or on the bed." He joined her and they went to where the crooked woman lay, slack mouthed. Petra leaned to check for a pulse, but was already sure. "Dead."

"How?"

Unwillingly disturbed, Petra drew one side of the coverlet over the body, then straightened. "Shock, rage—who can tell? We should have checked on her."

"And possibly been stabbed for our trouble." He plucked a wicked-looking knife from among the covers. "You thought her as bad as the rest."

Petra pulled herself together. "She was. She poisoned the soup. But . . ."

"It doesn't change anything," he pointed out.

"Except that we can be accused of murder as well as assault and theft."

"True. Let's get out of here." He threw back the lids of chests to inspect their contents. He pulled out a skirt striped in green and red and a bodice of shiny scarlet. "These look to be the cleanest."

"They look like whore's clothes." Petra searched the chests herself, but her choice seemed to be between grubby and gaudy.

"It's only for a little while," he said. "We'll buy you better as soon as possible, but if your pursuers are looking for a nun, they won't find you in these sorts of clothes."

Petra looked at the horrible clothes, but said, "Wait in the kitchen."

It didn't take long to strip down to her shift and put on the striped skirt and satin bodice. They smelled, but mostly of a cheap perfume. The skirt was too short, however, and the bodice too small. This must be an outfit of Solette's. Something of Jizzy's would be loose, but she couldn't bear the thought of more searching here, especially with the crone's corpse on the bed.

She laced up the front of the bodice but it still

gaped, showing two inches of her shift. The bodice was also very low, but at least her shift wasn't.

The only spare footwear was some backless, heeled slippers that would be ridiculous and impractical. If she was willing to try wearing clogs, she'd have to take them off their prisoners' feet.

She had to take off her veil and cap. She bundled them, her belt, pouch, cross, and rosary in her habit, wishing she had something for her head. She saw a mobcap hanging on a hook and took that, praying it held no nits. At least the floppy frill would hide her face. She felt like a thief, but they'd pay for everything. Or rather, Robin would. She couldn't afford to use any of her small store of coins with the future so uncertain.

Uncertain and dangerous.

She unwrapped her bundle and took the dagger out of her pouch. It was in a leather sheath that had straps to fasten it around her leg. She put it on. It felt strange there, but she wanted it at hand, and her pouch didn't fit this outfit at all.

She put Robin's velvet coat back on to hide some of her outfit and returned briskly to the kitchen. His brows rose in a humorous way, but there was another type of look in his eyes. Petra tugged the edges of the coat together and wished her ankles weren't exposed. "I'm ready."

"So, my pet, am I." He pulled her into his arms and kissed her.

Petra tried to resist, tried to make herself resist, but this seemed as inevitable as thunder after lightning, and the lightning had been sizzling for a long time.

It had begun when he'd kissed her in the storm. Or perhaps at first sight. It exploded now, after danger of death, with a searing passion that had her gripping his face and exploring deep in his mouth as his hands pressed her hard against him.

He still wore only his breeches and shirt, and she felt almost skin to skin. She slid a hand down inside his shirt, to truly touch his flesh, firm, strong, hot beneath her fingers. . . .

"Sir?" A voice out in the farmyard.

They sprang apart, staring, wild-eyed, and breathless.

"You all right, lad?" That was Powick, coming closer.

Petra turned, pressing hands to her cheeks. "That should not have happened and must not again. Never, never, never!"

He shushed her. "Everything's in order," he called. "We're just borrowing some clothes."

See how quickly he recovers. He's kissed a hundred women, a thousand. You've kissed only one other man.

"Remember to leave some money for the clothes," she said briskly and went outside. Powick's jaw dropped at the sight of her.

"At least I don't look like a nun," she said to him.

"I'll give you that, lass, but is there any reason not to look like a nun?"

Clearly Robin hadn't told him, but he needed some explanation. "Someone might be looking for me."

He pulled a face. "What did you do, then?"

"Nothing wrong," she assured him.

"Some man fell in love with her," Robin said, "and didn't accept rejection well."

"Not a nun, then?" the groom asked, still not happy.

"I had every right to wear that habit, but I'm willing to disguise myself for now."

"Right you are," Powick said, "but don't go wandering the streets unless you want to live up to expectations." He seemed resigned to odd adventures. Another indication of the sort of man Robin Bonchurch was.

The horses were already in place and the postilion mounted. Robin went to speak to him, and Petra headed for the chaise. Robin's valet stepped into her way. "The coat, ma'am."

His tone was even more sneering than usual, but she shrugged out of it and passed it over. He clutched it as if it were a stolen babe. Petra didn't want to part from her prayer book and what it contained, so she carried her bundled-up habit into the carriage with her. Robin scooped up Coquette and put her in the carriage, closing the door.

Petra watched him go to the women. He said something and then slit their bonds. The younger ones scrambled up, clearly stiff. Mère Goulart didn't try, but a sudden thrusting of her lower lip might be in response to him telling her about the old woman.

A mother was a mother, Petra supposed.

He walked back to the coach and let Fontaine help him with waistcoat and jacket. He fastened the waistcoat buttons, but refused a neckcloth. Petra heard him say, "No point in trying to look respectable with our female companion in such a state."

He came to the chaise, but when he opened the door, he said, "I'm riding. Fontaine will travel in here."

He left before she could argue, and Petra supposed

he was wise. Given what had just happened, privacy in close quarters was the last thing they needed. She bit her lip, however, to stop stupid tears.

The valet entered, taking his seat as if he wished to be anywhere else in the world. Did he dislike all women? Did he hold her responsible for their misfortunes? Or was it simply because she'd caused him to have to ride in the rain? Certainly her present appearance couldn't help.

He slammed the door shut, and the chaise rolled out through the gates to lurch back to the Boulogne road.

Once they reached the road their way was smoother, though the road had obviously suffered in the storm. With the rising sun shining on flourishing fields, the macabre night seemed like a nightmare. It would be easy to pretend that it had never happened, and Petra wished she could. Instead her mind worried over how to avoid further disaster.

If she'd imagined Varzi, all should be well as long as her willpower was strong enough to resist Cock Robin's seductive wiles. But what if she hadn't imagined him?

He would probably have searched the inn and Abbeville before deciding she'd left, and by then the storm would have stopped him. He'd set off early today, however, assuming she was continuing to Boulogne. She thanked God that she was now about five miles ahead and also getting a very early start. Better still, since she'd told Robin the reason for her urgency, he'd travel as fast as possible.

Even if Varzi caught up, he couldn't know who she was; she looked nothing like Sister Immaculata. As long as she concealed her face, he'd never recognize her. Yes, perhaps she would reach England after all.

To begin with they saw no other travelers, but after

about an hour, they passed a group of young people walking to a harvesting job. A little later they worked around a slow cart loaded with vegetables and sacks, probably going from a local farm to Nouvion.

Nouvion, where they'd change horses, which meant a new postilion. During a slow maneuver round a hole in the road, Petra let down the window and called to Robin. When he came over, she asked, "Won't the postilion tell everyone about the events last night?"

"Not with the bribe I've paid him, or not immediately, at least. Stop worrying."

Petra raised the window, knowing it was wrong to be irritated by his self-assurance, but she was sure he'd never been involved in true danger before. And she hadn't truly explained the nature of the pursuit.

They arrived in Nouvion as the town was just stirring, though a bakery spilled a stomach-tormenting aroma of fresh bread. Petra would have been willing to delay there long enough to buy some food, but they sped by and stopped at the posting house on the far side of town. It was a long, low building amid fields full of horses.

As soon as the chaise stopped, Fontaine climbed out. Coquette jumped down, too, before Petra had a chance to stop her, but she raced to Robin. Petra stayed in the coach, out of sight.

A short, sinewy man hurried out of the house, still tucking his shirt into his breeches, and she heard him exclaiming at their early arrival, and at the hour they must have left Abbeville. Robin spoke to him, and then came to the chaise.

"We're too early. He hasn't brought the morning's horses in from the fields, and the postilions are still abed. He offers breakfast as we wait."

There was no help for it, so Petra climbed down. "A decent breakfast would be very welcome. I'm going to get my cloak, however, muddy as it is, to hide these clothes a little."

He helped her find it and helped her put it on, which caused a warning frisson. Every moment, every touch made the effect more powerful.

"How long to Boulogne?" she asked, swallowing.

"If God provides good roads, we can make it for tonight's sailing."

"Then I'll try prayers, but dressed like this I fear they'll be even less effective than they were before."

"I can't imagine a rational God caring. Come along."

The posting house was a two-story building, but the ground floor was laid out much like the Goulart place. It resembled it in no other way, however, being clean and fresh, with a cat, a dog, and a baby in a cradle. The smell of grinding coffee already filled the air. Petra thanked the pretty young matron for her hospitality. She knew that the smaller staging posts didn't normally offer food or lodging.

"Such a storm!" Madame Crespin exclaimed. "And Madame Goulart's! Ai, ai, ai! No wonder you left so early." All the same, she was looking askance at Petra's clothes. Petra couldn't clutch the cloak around her without looking extremely strange.

"Is there anywhere I could wash, madame?"

"I've no hot water yet, but you can take this bowl out to the pump in the back." She gave Petra a metal bowl, a pot of soap, and a thin towel.

Petra thanked her, followed directions to a fenced yard where hens pecked and some piglets ran around squealing, and was soon scrubbing her hands and face. The soap had a harsh smell, but it got rid of Goulart grime. She wished she could wash all over, especially her feet, and that she'd taken the time to change her shift. No point in that, however, with everything else so soiled. She poured the water onto the ground, rinsed out the bowl, and returned it to the kitchen.

A short, sinewy man came into the room from another direction, yawning, his shirt hanging loose, muttering about early travelers. Madame Crespin shot a warning look at Petra and he turned. Then leered.

Petra did clutch her cloak around herself then, and went in search of her protector. Robin was talking to their old postilion, probably impressing again the need for secrecy.

A lad came running with a basket of bread and soon everyone was around the kitchen table, enjoying warm bread rolls and raspberry preserves. The postilions got thick slices of ham, as well, and flagons of something. It was probably part of their pay.

Petra was happy with the big bowls of café au lait. Coffee, at last.

While he ate, Robin was talking easily with the new postilion about the storm, the road, and travel to the coast. He'd said he spoke French like a native, and it seemed to be true. She didn't have the ear to be sure, but she suspected he was even roughening his accent a bit for the comfort of these country people.

Soon their old postilion went off to his quarters and the new one went out to help bring horses. Powick went along, too. Madame Crespin began to clear the table, and Robin sent Fontaine for his writing desk.

"As we still have a short wait," he said to Petra in English, "I might as well write a letter about the events of the night."

Fontaine returned to tenderly place a traveling desk

on the table. It was small and shallow, but a work of art, its sides covered with marquetry designs of birds and flowers all done in exotic woods and mother-of-pearl. As Robin sat, the valet slid open a drawer in the side to remove a pen and a small container of ink. He inspected both, then passed them over. Robin took out a sheet of paper and laid it on the sloped top.

He began to write in a strong, purposeful hand, each letter beautifully formed, each line as straight as if he followed a guide. Petra was so struck by the neatness that she leaned closer to see if there were faint lines drawn to guide him, but no. She'd have expected careless handwriting with an excess of loops and squiggles. What did such writing say about this mystery of a man?

He completed his account, and then hesitated. Petra wondered what was wrong, and wished he'd hurry. She heard horses being led by the house. They'd soon be able to leave.

He dipped the pen again and scrawled. It was completely at variance with the rest of his writing. The "Robin" was rough but legible; the rest was not. It might be "Bonchurch," but it might well not. He sanded it, shook off the sand, and folded it quickly, but still with every crease just where it should be. Then he took a ring out of his pocket. Fontaine dripped wax. Robin impressed a seal into it.

Petra stared at the ring and its impression. The ring had the patina of old, well-used gold. The design in the impression it left was curlicued, but mainly a letter. It might be an B, but she doubted it. An A? An H? Perhaps a K or an R? Didn't she have trouble enough without having to wonder who this man really was?

He stood, pocketing the ring and handing the document to Madame Crespin with some coins and instructions about delivery to Monsieur de Guise. That impressed madame greatly, as it should. They were one of the great families of France. He had mentioned them, Petra remembered. She shouldn't be surprised. Despite informality he admitted that he was part of the English nobility and that he had just visited Versailles.

He turned to her. "Are you ready?"

Petra returned practicalities and hurried to the privy. She returned to hear Madame Crespin exclaim, "Another early one!"

Petra's heart jolted, but through the front window she saw part of a large carriage, loaded with luggage. Varzi would never travel like that. She relaxed, but then a strident voice told her who had arrived—Lady Sodworth. The woman must have left Abbeville at first light!

Petra went to the window and peered out from one side. The grooms were leading horses to Robin's chaise, but how could she get into it unobserved? She remembered her disguise and went to the door.

Lady Sodworth stormed out of the coach, her strident voice slicing the air as she demanded horses *immediately*. The postmaster promised only a short delay.

She marched toward the house, but then she whirled to scream, "Arabella, Georgie, get back in the coach!"

Of course the little monsters paid no attention, and Lady Sodworth continued on to the house, ignoring them.

The back way, Petra thought and turned, but it was too late. Lady Sodworth swept in, blinking in the darker room, still complaining. But then her eyes widened. "You!"

Petra took the only possible route. "Me?" she asked as if confused.

Lady Sodworth carried on in English. "How dare you abandon me, you ungrateful wretch! The night I had with the storm and the children. I didn't sleep a wink. The sooner I'm out of this horrible country, the better."

She seemed blind to her two children grabbing bread off the table and running out through the back door. Petra turned to do something about that, but Lady Sodworth grasped her arm.

"Oh, no. You're coming with me!"

Petra twisted free and dodged behind a chair. "I don't know who you are," she cried, "but you are clearly mad. Robin! Help me!"

Lady Sodworth stared, and Robin ran in.

"This woman," Petra cried, pointing, "she imagines I am someone she knows and is trying to drag me away."

Lady Sodworth stared at him. "You!" she exclaimed, not much given to originality. "You were in Abbeville." Though not original or clever, she wasn't stupid, and she looked, narrow-eyed, between the two of them. "So the nun is not so virtuous after all."

Petra thanked God the woman had spoken in English, though she feared Madame Crespin was interpreting tone all too well.

Robin faced her calmly and bowed. "I'm afraid you've made some mistake, ma'am. This is my sister."

"But . . ." The first trace of uncertainty crinkled Lady Sodworth's brow. That air of authority was working again.

"Powick!" he called.

The groom came in.

"Powick, this lady is under an extraordinary misapprehension. Kindly assure her that my sister is my sister."

Powick's face twitched, but he must be used to such demands. "Of course, sir."

Robin waved him away, and looked a polite question at the baffled lady.

"And who are *you*?" she demanded.

He bowed in an elegant but moderate manner. "Robin Bonchurch of Derby. And you, ma'am?"

"Lady Sodworth." When she added, "Of Bristol," it didn't come naturally. That only confirmed Petra's belief that the Sodworths were nouveau riche at best.

Lady Sodworth studied Petra again, not swallowing the nonsense, but not knowing what to do. She turned her anger elsewhere. "What is happening here?" she demanded of Madame Crespin. "Why are there no horses for my carriage? I insist that you provide some immediately, or I shall lodge a most serious complaint."

Madame Crespin snatched up her baby and rushed out to chivvy her husband to his work—or perhaps she simply escaped.

Lady Sodworth glared between Petra and Bonchurch. "What, then, is your sister's name, sir?"

He answered with a relaxed courtesy that managed to be dismissive. "Maria Bonchurch, ma'am."

Lady Sodworth's sharp eyes turned on Petra. "You do not dress your sister well, Mr. Bonchurch."

"I do not dress my sister at all. Most improper."

"Then where is her maid?"

"Absconded with Gypsies, taking my sister's entire wardrobe with her. If you were a little larger, ma'am, I'd ask your charity for her."

Lady Sodworth came close to snarling, baffled by his light, polite nonsense.

"Horses are being brought now, ma'am," Madame Crespin announced from the door, adding coldly, "and your children are chasing my hens."

"They'll not hurt them," Lady Sodworth said, reaching for some bread. "I'll have coffee, woman."

Madame Crespin moved the plate away. "They will put them off their laying, ma'am. Kindly stop them, or I will."

Lady Sodworth's arm rose to slap the woman, but then she spat, "I will report your insolence, you . . . you ugly trull!"

In her fury she'd abandoned French, but the meaning was clear. After a fraught moment, Lady Sodworth caved, turned, and swept out into the backyard to scream at her brats.

Robin beckoned, and Petra was only too glad to hurry outside. But Lady Sodworth caught up with them, literally dragging her infants. "So, Maria Bonchurch of Derbyshire," she screamed, "how is it that you speak English with an Italian accent?"

Petra turned to face her. Again, the woman had used English, but the post keeper, postilions, outriders, and even Madame Crespin were all watching this show.

"You're mistaken," Petra said, trying to imitate Robin's manner. "It's a Derbyshire accent."

Lady Sodworth laughed. "Oh, you're a bold piece. I always suspected it, but that won't wash. I wondered why the nuns were so eager to get rid of you. With child?"

"No!"

"Spend much time with that 'brother' of yours and you will be. Come with me now, and I won't tell all these people the truth." The predatory woman would do anything to get her own children off her hands.

Robin stepped between them, and this time his tone was icy. "Your horses are ready, ma'am. I suggest you get on your way."

Color flared in Lady Sodworth's cheeks. "Didn't you hear what I said?"

"It is hard not to hear you, but create trouble here and I will repay you tenfold in England. Do not doubt that I can."

"Who do you think you are?"

"I know perfectly well who I am, though I have no idea who you are."

"Lady Sodworth," the woman said, but even she knew that wasn't what he meant. Her face pinched to ugliness with the need to carry out her threat, but it would take a braver woman to face down Robin Bonchurch in this mood. She threw her children into the Berlin, and in moments it rolled on its way in a cloud of dust.

"She'll make trouble," Petra said, sick with dread.

"Let her try." He offered his arm. "I believe we can now depart, sister."

He was trying to be at ease, but some residue of the confrontation with Lady Sodworth lingered. Petra took his taut arm, wondering again who this man was. At times his arrogant certainty was fit for a prince.

He rode again, and she was glad of it. She couldn't stop teasing at the puzzle that was Robin Bonchurch. *He* should be called Riddlesome. His dress was ordinary, and he sometimes seemed a lightweight in all the worst ways. He'd been effective against Mère Goulart, however, and against Lady Sodworth, in an entirely different way.

He confessed to being highborn, but was he hiding a great title?

She considered Coquette, with her fringed butterfly ears, gold-tipped fur, and jeweled collar, and the haughty valet Fontaine. She remembered that writing desk and old signet ring.

"Who is your master?" she asked the valet.

"Who he says he is," he replied in a pinched-nosed tone that said he'd give her nothing more.

Petra turned to watch the passing countryside, frustrated by confusion. But it didn't really matter. Once they were in England, he could go his mysterious way and she would go hers. She'd never see him again.

And any pang that caused was proof that it would be a good thing.

They passed Lady Sodworth's lumbering Berlin, but the heavy carriage with its big wheels was probably giving a smoother ride on the storm-damaged road than the speeding chaise. Petra was soon aching from bumps and the strain of resisting jerks and jolts, but she had no intention of asking that they go slower. If it were possible, she'd demand more speed. As before, she clung to the strap for balance, and she couldn't help remembering the wildness of the storm.

The security of his arms.

The shameless way he'd touched her.

The thunder, the lightning, the kiss.

They changed horses in Bernay and found the road better thereafter. At Nampont they learned the storm had never touched there. The post keeper complained that the water carts should be out to keep down the dust. But no, the officials were penny-pinchers. . . .

There was certainly plenty of dust. The road ran close to the coast and the ground was sandy. Traffic became heavier with people traveling to or from the Channel ports. Hooves and wheels whipped dust into fog in places. That probably caused the accident. There was a great bang, splintering, then shrieks. Their chaise didn't hit anything, but it veered sharply left and jerked to a halt at a tilt.

Petra watched Robin dismount and give his reins to Powick. He shouted, "Stay inside," at Petra and went to the wrecks.

Fontaine left through the door on the other side, probably simply to escape. Petra swooped to stop Coquette from following, then tried to see what was happening ahead.

Two chaises going in opposite directions had locked wheels, creating a splintered jumble. Those horses were panicked, and all the others were restive. The chaise jolted and juddered as their horses fidgeted.

Servants and gentlemen were running about, yelling for help, giving orders, or simply complaining. Petra couldn't see or hear Robin, but one thing was clear. The road was impassable, and likely to remain so for a while.

"Truly, God does not favor my cause," Petra muttered to Coquette. "If we had been ahead of this, any pursuit would have been delayed."

A new vehicle stopped behind. Petra twisted to look out, fearing to see Varzi, but the head that poked out of a window was round and red. The man began to bellow in French, demanding that someone clear the way.

"Stupid creature," Petra muttered, "and so are you, trying to go out there amid wild horse hooves."

Another vehicle pulled up behind—a coach with coachman driving. Perhaps it was the diligence, the public coach. Surely Varzi would use transportation under his own command, but she'd heard so many stories about him. One of his strengths was to do the unpredictable.

She was safely out of sight and would stay that way, but then their chaise jolted and slid to a steeper angle. She wriggled to the other side and saw they were close to a ditch. She pulled up the hood of the cloak and managed the tricky business of climbing out of the safe side, flinching at the swirling dust and noise. She moved quickly to the edge of the road, farther from both. "Stop wriggling to get to him, you stupid creature," she told the dog.

There were three carriages behind them now. The most recent was disgorging two purposeful men in blue uniforms. Perhaps they'd bring order to chaos. She couldn't see Robin—until she realized he was the dusty, shirt-clad man helping to break apart the two locked wheels by brute force, Powick by his side.

"Who is he?" Petra demanded of the dog. "Or are all Englishmen in truth mad?"

Coquette had also spotted her beloved master and was more desperate to be let free. Why on earth didn't she have a leash? And where were the horses, or Fontaine? She saw both at the side of the road behind her, along with others who'd chosen only to watch far from the dust.

Petra joined him. "Does Coquette not have a leash?"

"She has a number," the valet replied, with the usual suggestion of a sniff. "One to match each suit. Some are jeweled."

Petra had known precious elegants who carried pets as accessories, but Cock Robin, who couldn't be bothered with a neckcloth?

"Where's the leash that matches his current attire?" she asked. "The stupid creature wants to be trampled."

"Let her be. He would be relieved of a burden."

"I don't believe that."

"No?" The valet smirked. "He acquired her only to impress a Versailles beauty. Once he had his way, the bitch was of no use to him."

Which bitch? Petra wondered, disgusted but fascinated.

"Yet the silly creature pesters him still," he sighed. "They so often do, much to his disgust."

"Is that a warning for me, Fontaine?" When he merely smirked, she said, "Forget these clothes and remember my habit. And even if I were an ordinary lady I'd have no interest in a man like him."

"Then you'd be unique among females."

"Lady Sodworth wasn't swooning. Nor were the Goulart women. Where is Coquette's leash?"

"In his coat pocket, I assume."

And his coat was heaven knew where.

Petra watched chaos, her mind sifting through details. "If he's coming from court," she asked, "where are his court garments?"

"He sends those by cart in order to travel faster. I warn him that one day they will be lost or stolen, but he pays no heed. As it is, we arrive in London ahead of them, and if a grand event occurs I am obliged to cobble together something from his older clothes." The valet actually shuddered.

"Mr. Bonchurch enjoys fashion and court elegance?" she asked, watching the dust-caked man heave, joking with his fellow laborers.

"When the mood takes him."

And that, thought Petra, was probably the truth of the man. He was a creature of whim and mood, and as reliable as a weathercock. Another cock!

Coquette was still wriggling to get to her adored one, so Petra picked her way along the rough verge until they were out of sight. As they went, she expressed her frustration.

"Jeweled collars and ribbon leashes to match each outfit. And you, you're as bad. He used you. Don't you mind? He used you, but now he'd give you to a passing stranger if anyone would take you. It's shameful to worship someone like that."

Coquette merely tilted her butterfly head as if considering a puzzling concept.

"You can't stop, though, can you? A female in love has no sense of dignity. I know it all too well. There were so many signs of the truth with Ludo, but did I pay any attention? Of course not."

She sighed, but then spotted raspberries. Long canes rambled through the fence, offering both a treat and escape from troubling memories. Petra tucked Coquette firmly under one arm and enjoyed them, suppressing any thought of taking some back to share. As she ate, she lectured the dog at length on dignity, prudence, and the wicked ways of devastatingly attractive men.

She knew it would do no good at all.

Chapter 11

"Maria!"

Petra started, and turned to see Robin staring at her, hands on hips.

She hurried back to the chaise, looking quickly down the queue. It was now up to six vehicles, but no sign of Varzi, which was as well since she'd let her hood slip.

"There's no need to bellow," she said.

He took the dog. "The name 'Maria' didn't seem to penetrate. Get in. We can be off."

The wrecks were off to the verge, and their chaise was on level ground again.

Once inside, Petra said, "I'm sorry. It's not my familiar name." She reached to take back the dog, but Robin climbed in and slammed the door.

"It didn't seem wise to be shouting 'Petra.' "

So he, too, had been thinking about pursuit.

As the coach moved slowly forward, Petra shook her head at how dusty Robin was. His skin was caked with it because of sweat, which might be why he hadn't put his coat or waistcoat back on. A jagged tear in the sleeve of his grubby shirt would take genius to mend. He was certainly no angel now, but the sweat-flattened hair and dusty skin made clear his stronger side.

Another English nursery rhyme came to her.

> *Rich man or debtor*
> *High court judge or a thief*
> *Admiral or scrubber*
> *Dry bread or beef?*

That was to teach children that they had paths in life and that their choices would have consequences. It didn't allow for a man being a dozen things in one.

Rich man or adventurer?

Courtier or laborer?

Fribble or hero?

Sane man or lunatic . . .

Coquette jumped down and shook herself.

"Too dirty for her taste," he said with a grin. "Too dirty for you to kiss?"

"Dirt has nothing to do with it."

"Still, I must bathe. We'll be in Montreuil soon and will stop there."

"There's no need—"

"I must bathe. Forgive me for the indelicacy, but you should, too."

A wave of embarrassment flowed through Petra, but she said, "I will wash, but I have no clean clothes to change into unless I revert to nun. . . ."

"Ah yes, clothes. Those, too, Montreuil can provide. Petra, we would have halted there, anyway. It's the last chance for decent food before Boulogne."

"Can't we get something to eat on the road?"

"Do you expect my men to eat on horseback? They deserve a rest."

That was unanswerable, but how long would a bath and a fine meal take? How far behind were Lady Sodworth and Varzi? What use had speed been if they stopped for hours in this pretentious Inn of the Court of France?

"Behold Montreuil," he said.

Through the front window, above the working rumps of the horses, Petra saw a hill crowned with gray fortifications. "We have to go up there? It will take forever!"

"Not all the way, and the coach will take its time while we walk the faster route. It's a charming town offering magnificent views."

"Mr. Bonchurch, we are not on a pleasure trip."

"I was, or as near as made no difference, until I met you." He smiled, however. "I'm not complaining, and yes, we have some urgency, but the boats in Boulogne leave on the tide, which will be in the late evening. Haste will only have us kicking our heels in a very inferior town."

"You're not taking this seriously."

He shrugged. " 'Tis my nature. I think you've seen I can be serious when called upon."

Petra couldn't deny that, but every instinct longed to race onward.

Robin observed his dark conundrum ruefully. His tone had offended her, but it truly was his nature to take things as lightly as possible. She, on the other hand, seemed to seek the dark. Was she truly pursued by an evil Milanese lover, or did she imagine such things? She hadn't imagined the danger last night, but he'd told her the truth. Haste would only mean more time in Boulogne, and she'd be safer here, in the luxurious Inn of the Court of France.

The horses labored up the incline toward the town until it met the steeper but faster footpath.

"Here's where we walk," he said, pulling a thin leather leash from his pocket and clipping it to Coquette's collar.

"I needed that during the wreck," she complained. "I had to hold her the whole time."

"You should have asked."

"You were ripping a wheel off a coach at the time, enveloped in a cloud of dust."

"How improvident of me." He climbed down and turned to offer her a hand, trying to soothe her with a smile. She accepted his help, but released him as soon as possible, looking almost afraid. If she were fearful, it was because of the spark that had jolted between them when skin contacted skin. It almost terrified him, too.

He put down the dog and began the walk, allowing Coquette to dart here and there and sometimes stop to explore. His maybe-nun walked ahead steadily, dark cloak concealing her gaudy, provocative outfit. Clothing had nothing to do with it, however. She'd sent lightning through him when in her dull habit.

Eventually she stopped and turned a frown at him. "Do you mean to take all day for this stroll?"

"I'm enjoying it. Consider the view."

"Magnificent," she agreed flatly, "but we do not have time."

Robin picked up Coquette and joined her. "To business, then. What sort of clothes will you want?"

"We don't have time," she said, setting off again.

"We've been over that, and after a bath, do you really want to put that lot back on?"

"I'm not taking a bath."

"I am, and then I intend to wear clean garments from the skin out."

"I have a clean habit in my box."

"To dress as a nun again will provide a beacon for your pursuers. I'll buy you something suitable."

"I will not be even more in your debt. . . ."

"We're talking shillings."

". . . Because I know the return you'll demand."

Robin held on to his temper. "I never demand such favors."

"No, you seduce them with gifts like ridiculous dogs."

Robin looked down at Coquette. "You were just insulted. A pity you don't bite." He looked up and saw Petra's tight, pale face.

"I'm sorry," she said. "I'm sorry, but you're so . . . you never *listen* to me. You must have everything your own way."

"I want you in my bed, Petra, and all indications are that it will be magnificent, but I don't expect to get my own way about that. If I do, it won't be in payment, or even out of gratitude, but only driven by true, pure desire."

Did she shiver? He hoped so, because she was driving him mad. He risked a touch on her elbow to turn her onward, to resume their climb, and felt the tingle again.

"You can't return to wearing your habit, and you need respectable clothing before we arrive in England."

"There you go again."

"But I'm right."

She halted for a moment, rigid, and then marched on.

"Assuredly," Robin murmured to the dog, "I am a fool."

He could be a fool for women, but only with his eyes open. He would allow them to use him or deceive him, but only to a point, and only as long as it amused. Where lay the reward in this tight-wound, secretive wench? If he had any sense, he'd get her to Dover, let her escape, and forget about her. But he couldn't. Like Coquette, Petra was his now to take care of until he was assured of her safety.

They entered through the town gate and Robin indicated the direction. She took it, but said, "Perhaps I could dress as a young man. My hair is short, and that would be an even better disguise."

" 'Struth, woman, no one but a half-wit would believe you male. And if they did, you'd be in dire danger."

"I can use pistol and sword. You saw that."

She might actually try to do this insane thing. "Some men lust after beautiful young men more than they do after beautiful young women."

She flipped a glance at him. "You must live a dangerous life, then."

He stared, then laughed, shaking his head. "Come inside. The sun has turned your wits."

Petra went into the dauntingly grand inn, wishing that last comment unsaid. He was right. She must be losing her wits. If so it was entirely his fault. He was beautiful. Sparks flew when they touched. And he always wanted his own way.

The inn was busy, but clearly accustomed to it—though not, perhaps, to women dressed as Petra was. The servants were too well trained to act badly, however, and they were soon in a handsome suite of rooms. Fruit, wine, and small cakes awaited, and jugs of warm washing water arrived only moments after they did. Robin ordered a meal and two baths.

Petra wanted to protest on principle, but if he was going to bathe, why should she resist such a pleasure?

He was speaking to a maidservant. "You see that my sister has suffered on the journey. Her trunk was lost and the clothes she was wearing ruined. Would it be possible to acquire something more suitable for her? You see her size."

The maid was blushing and fidgeting under his handsome charm. "I don't know, monsieur. I wish to oblige, but I have my duties. . . ."

"I will pay all the charges, including the innkeeper for the loss of your time."

She bobbed a curtsy. "I'll go and ask, monsieur. I'll do my best!"

Petra ate a cake, and perhaps that sweetened her mood. "Thank you. I apologize for being tiresome."

"Oh, dear, you must be in a bad way if you're beaten down to submissiveness."

"I am not—"

"Pax!" He poured golden wine into two glasses and brought one to her. "It is less than a day since we met, Petra. Given events, I'm all admiration that you're still on your feet."

She sipped the sweet wine and suddenly her knees

felt weak with exhaustion. She sat on one of two chairs by the window. "Sometimes, so am I."

The double casement window stood open, giving a small breeze and an extensive view. She could see the road they'd traveled, busy with vehicles traveling in both directions. She couldn't help searching for signs of Varzi and his men, even though she knew she could tell nothing at this distance.

Robin came to lounge in the seat beside her, sun catching light in his dusty hair, his eyes a clearer blue in dirty skin. "Tell me about your pursuers."

Petra sipped her wine. She should, but it was so wild a tale and would mean she'd have to tell him about her folly and sin with Ludo. "Someone didn't want me to leave Milan."

"A man, you said. You took a lover?"

She wanted to deny that, but the truth should crush any romantic notions he might have. She met his eyes and said, "Yes."

No visible response. "And he is now what? Desperate? Vengeful? Angry?"

Petra thought about that and then said, "Possessive."

"Ah."

"I'm glad you understand it, for I can't, especially now he's married."

"Irrelevant, I'm afraid. Though his wife can't be happy if he's chasing you across Europe. He doesn't fear her wrath?"

"He fears no one."

"His name?"

"Ludovico."

"The rest of his name?" He was interrupted by a knock on the door.

"Enter," he called, his thoughtful eyes never leaving Petra's face.

A manservant announced that their baths were ready. Robin rose and thanked him with a small coin. He turned back to offer his hand, like a gentleman leading a lady into a dance. Petra didn't need assistance, but she put her hand in his and allowed a slight upward pressure as she rose. Unwise. He stepped closer and raised her hand to his lips.

She dragged her hand free. "Because I had a lover," she said harshly, "doesn't make me easy prey."

His eyes sparkled with mirth. "My dearest Petra, only a dolt would imagine you easy prey. You are well named—'the rock.'"

"Petronilla. The 'little rock.'"

"A pebble can be torture in a shoe."

Torture. "I don't want to cause you hurt. . . ."

He laughed. "Petra, Petra, I was teasing. You won't hurt me."

"Oh, you are so *infuriating*. A smug, comfortable Englishman with his silly dog and ridiculous leashes who knows *nothing* of the world. You cannot begin to imagine that danger might ever touch you!"

"Danger touched us both last night."

"Peasant women," she spat. "And we were properly armed whilst they had only a kitchen knife."

"And poison," he said soberly. "Never, ever forget poison. Kings and mighty warriors have been brought low by poison. And by beautiful women they trusted too well."

Petra stared at him, wounded by that truth.

He opened the door to her bedroom, where the cloth-lined bath steamed and a mobcapped maid awaited. "At the moment, our only danger is expiring from pleasure. Come, sister dear, and drown in it."

Petra marched through and closed the door in his face, leaning back on it for an exhausted, tearful moment. She shouldn't have weakened to confess pursuit or danger. But she'd had to prevent delay, and she'd had to try to warn him. She was putting innocent, charming Robin Bonchurch in danger. . . .

"Madame?" the puzzled maid prompted. Petra straightened, the bath calling to her like a siren. She walked forward, pulling off her mobcap and then unlacing her bodice.

"Louise has gone to find you better clothing, madame," the maid said, eyes flickering curiously to Petra's hair. "With Monsieur Belmartin's permission, of course."

"That's very kind." Petra dropped the bodice and untied her skirt. "And you are?"

The girl bobbed another curtsy. "Nanette, madame."

Baths in the convent had been stingy things, taken while wearing a shift. Petra d'Averio had reveled in luxurious baths, and always naked. She was almost salivating at the thought of doing it again—but she wore a knife strapped to her thigh.

"Please," she said, "take those clothes out of my sight."

The maid gathered up skirt, bodice, and cap. "What shall I do with them, madame?"

"Anything you want."

The maid left and Petra quickly unstrapped the knife, then took off her shift and bundled the knife into it. She hoped the maid would bring clean underwear, because she'd hardly be able to bear putting that shift on again.

She stepped into the bath. It was exactly the right temperature, and the steam carried a hint of soothing rosemary. She sat down and relaxed back with a blissful sigh. Drowning in pleasure. Oh yes, indeed.

As was he, she assumed, naked in his bath in a nearby room. What did he look like naked? She'd have thought him on the soft side, like the Apollo in the loggia at home. Ludovico was like that—handsome but sleek. Just a little fleshy in the belly, which Robin, she was sure, was not. Not after seeing him in action last night, after seeing a little of his chest this morning. And especially not after seeing him struggle with that wheel, sleeves rolled up to reveal lean, muscular arms.

The statue of Saint Michael, then. Broad of shoulder, narrow of hips, rippling muscles down his long abdomen. In the statue, the saint wore Roman armor that molded every contour, but hid the interesting bits. There were religious debates, anyway, about whether angels had those bits, or those hungers.

Which only proved that Robin Bonchurch was no angel . . .

"The soap, Sister?"

Petra sat up with a start, grateful the warmth of the water would explain her blush. She hadn't even heard the maid return. "Was I falling asleep? You're right, there's no time for that."

She took the washcloth and soap and started to scrub every inch, getting rid of Goulart grime. The water was soon dirty and scummed, but she'd be able to rinse off, and at least the dirt was no longer on her. She had the maid scrub her back and then wash her hair in a basin of clean water. As Petra lay back for this wonderful ministration she remembered her maid,

Maria Rosa, doing it. It had taken a long time then, when her hair had hung thick down to her hips.

Dear Maria Rosa. She'd been as much friend as servant. How they'd chattered and laughed. She'd acted the friend, or so she'd thought, when she'd helped arrange the meetings with Ludovico.

The delicious, secret courtship, as Petra had seen it. The clever, secret seduction from his point of view. Her mother's warnings had been true—men are all deceivers, and once they conquer, they abandon. She must remember that. Even her English father, whom her mother trusted to help his misbegotten daughter, had been a seducer and deserter.

Some men were all too constant, though. Only consider Ludo, who refused to accept rejection.

The maid wound a cloth around Petra's head. "There, madame. If you'll just stand, I'll rinse you off."

Petra obeyed and the maid hefted a large jug and stood on a stool to pour the lukewarm water to rinse away any lingering scum. Then Petra stepped out of the tub and into a large towel. She was drying herself when someone knocked on the door. She couldn't help a jerk of alarm, as well as a glance toward her shift and the knife it held.

A screen had been set in front of the door and Nanette disappeared behind it. She spoke quickly and quietly, then came back smiling, a bundle in her hands. "Clothing, madame. I was concerned you'd have to eat wrapped in a sheet!"

She laid out a clean shift, a pale petticoat, and a gown of green cloth sprigged with flowers. Petra immediately thought, *Too pretty*. Was it guilt at abandoning nunlike sobriety, or concern about Cock

Robin's reaction? Whichever it was, she had no alternative.

She put on the shift and petticoat.

"Oh, madame. We forgot stays for you!"

"No matter," Petra said, picking up the gown. There was also a pair of pockets to wear beneath her gown, accessible through slits. That was good, very good. She'd have a place to carry her precious prayer book. She regretted leaving that in the chaise.

She dressed quickly. The gown was snug across her breasts, but that compensated for the lack of stays. It fit well enough and was about the right length.

But when Petra turned to the mirror, she knew her earlier concerns were valid. It was too pretty. The bodice was quite low and its tightness pushed up her breasts. The color suited her too well. It was years since she'd worn anything other than the habit—leaving aside the Goulart clothes. To her surprise, she felt vulnerable.

"Is something the matter, madame?" the maid asked.

"My hair," Petra said as excuse, touching it.

It did look peculiar. When long, it had waved, but now, short and newly washed, it rioted in curls. On a cherub it could be charming; on a grown woman it was ridiculous. But more than that, her head felt naked.

"It is unusual, ma'am, but pretty. Is that the fashion where you come from?"

Petra said yes. It was easier than finding an explanation.

"There's a cap came with the dress, ma'am."

Petra took it eagerly, astonished at how nerve-racking this change of clothing was. The cap was similar to the one that was part of her habit, but looser

and much more frivolous. The frill around the front
was deep and lacy and there was no widow's peak. It
tied beneath her chin, but with a wide silk ribbon.
Petra saw a hat, too, if a disk of straw deserved the
name. Ribbons to match the dress formed a knot on
top of the hat and there was a good yard, in addition,
to hang down the wearer's back.

"This must have been someone's favorite outfit,"
she said, wondering if tragedy lurked behind.

"Louise's sister's, madame. She was proud of it, but
she's carrying her second now and doesn't expect to
get that sort of figure back. Don't worry, madame.
Your brother paid well."

"All the same, I'm grateful." Petra smoothed cloth
over her hips nervously. No hoops or stiffened under-
skirts. "I won't wear the hat yet, but do I have shoes?"

"Oh! I'm sorry. Louise took those strange sandals
for size. I'll go and see what she's found. Stockings,
too. How could she forget them?"

*Because any ordinary lady would be wearing her
own,* Petra thought.

There was a knock on the parlor door and Robin
spoke through it. "Are you ready, Maria? Our meal
is here."

"Coming!" Petra called, waving the maid on her
way. She quickly dug her knife from her shift and
strapped it back on. Somewhat armored, she went to
the door, only realizing as she opened it that she
was barefoot.

He stared, but not at her feet. "My apologies. I
haven't seen you dressed in anything like that. . . .
For so long," he added, clearly remembering their relationship as brother and sister. Then he saw her feet

and smiled in a way that probably made her toes
blush. She hurried into the parlor where their table
was set, curling her toes as if that might conceal them.

"Ah," he said. "At last I can satisfy some of your
desires. . . ."

Warm, crusty bread tantalized her nose. Butter,
wine, and a basket of ripe fruit made her mouth water.
An inn servant stood ready to ladle soup into bowls,
and this soup smelled wonderful. Petra sat and ate.

"Oh, this is very good." She sighed and smiled at
Robin before she remembered what he'd said.

His dimples showed.

"You're in fine feather," she said to break the moment. "I assume the chaise has arrived."

He poured white wine into her glass. "Only a quarter hour behind us."

Valuable lace flowed over his long-fingered hands.
More foamed at his neck. For the first time since she'd
encountered him, he was wearing a neckcloth, and a
beautiful one.

His suit was not suitable for court, but it was very
fine, of deep blue cloth with gilt buttons, worn over a
waistcoat of beige brocade. No jewelry, however—but
then she noticed a pearl-headed pin fixed in his cravat.
White on white. She wouldn't have expected such sub-
tlety, but it looked perfect.

"I'm glad my plumage pleases you," he said, his
eyes still smiling.

Caught, Petra blushed and attended to her soup
again.

Rake or protector?

Beau or common man?

Swordsman, wastrel?

Seducer, courtier . . . ?

She couldn't make a rhyme of it, but he truly was an ever-changing conundrum.

When she'd finished her soup, she had to look at him again. His hair was tied back, but that didn't explain its tameness. Ah, it was still damp. He met her eyes, raising his brows.

"Hair," she said. "Yours is still wet."

"Yours isn't?"

"Short hair dries quickly."

"Even so, should you cover it damp? I'm sure that's unhealthy."

He was teasing, and when Petra said, "It's dry enough," she added, *"Brother,"* to remind him of their pretense. Inn servants here, so close to the coast, might know some English, but in any case, the language of flirtation was universal.

Petra concentrated on the dishes being laid out between them, all smelling delicious. Robin told the servant that they'd serve themselves and summon him again later.

Suddenly they were alone and his hair was drying, springing free and catching sunlight. The pure white neckcloth somehow heightened his radiant good looks.

He put food on her plate. "Sole, I think, with mushrooms. I don't see any reason for this inn to poison us."

"So you thought of that, too," she said, taking a taste. It was perfectly cooked. "What do you think Mère Goulart has done?"

"Fled, if she has any sense."

"Her mother died. She might blame us." At his skeptical, overconfident look, she said, "It's another

reason to race to the coast. We shouldn't be dallying
here."

"We need to eat, the men need to eat and rest, and
you, I point out, don't even have shoes. But as I said,
rushing away from here would only leave us kicking
our heels in Boulogne, which is a much less pleasant
place."

"Kicking heels?" she asked. "Dancing?"

He laughed. "Having nothing to do. I'm going to
enjoy teaching you idioms. Eat."

Petra didn't try to argue. She ate.

"Good. Now, as we eat, tell me who objected to
you leaving Milan and why."

Petra's appetite fled, but she knew she must tell
him something.

Chapter 12

"His name is il conte di Purieri, and he desires me."

"A man of good taste. A conte. A rich and powerful man?"

"Very."

"And your lover?" He put more fish in his mouth as if the question meant nothing.

Petra glared at him. She'd like to hide so many aspects of this story, but she couldn't lie about this. "Yes."

"Was this after you became a nun?" he asked, still as if they discussed fish.

"Of course not."

"Not impossible. But then, you must have been very young for such a liaison."

"You can put away your inquisitor's implements, sir. I'm willing to tell you everything. At least, as much as you need to know. What are you smiling at now?"

"Your hands," he said. "You speak with your hands. You didn't do that so much before."

"In the convent, it was disapproved."

"But now the real Petra d'Averio emerges. Like a butterfly." He snapped his fingers and his little dog

came over to be fed a morsel. "They call this breed
the butterfly because of their large ears and the mark
down the center of their face."

"I am no butterfly," she objected.

"You're not a stone, either. Eat. If you're in danger,
that's even more reason to need your strength."

Petra obeyed, amazed by his ability to irritate her
even with food. It was very good, however, and she
was very hungry. She ate all her fish without realizing it.

He changed the plates and served her some sort of
meat fricassee and vegetables, but then prompted, "Il
conte di Purieri?"

She sighed. "I've known him most of my life. He's
a friend of my brother's. I fancied myself in love with
him. We met clandestinely. I was foolish. That's the
whole story."

"Eat," he said again. When she'd finished one
mouthful, he said, "An heir to a title was not an approved match for you?"

Here they came to some parts she'd rather hide. "*I*
was not considered a suitable match for *him*. Being
young and foolish, I thought that a minor problem,
but of course it wasn't."

"So you were packed off to a nunnery."

"I *chose* to go to the nunnery, but yes, one reason
was to escape Ludovico's persistence. He could not
marry me, so he wanted me as his mistress."

He paused in eating. "Your family offered no
protection?"

"My father was dead. My brother is a friend of
his."

"And is also—my apologies if I offend—a cur."

"A dog?" she translated, puzzling over that.

"A dog can be a noble animal. A cur is the lowest, vicious sort, fit only for shooting."

"Ah." Petra ate more of the tender meat, savoring the thought of her brother Cesare as a cur.

"But the convent walls did not protect you," Robin said.

"They did for a while. Or, more precisely, my mother did. Look, this may all be nothing. If I imagined Varzi . . ."

"Varzi?" he asked, and she realized that she'd not mentioned the name before.

"He is Purieri's minion. His hunting dog. The one he would send after me."

"Let's assume you didn't imagine him. If we're in danger, I prefer to know. Go on."

Petra ate a little more. "I thought I saw Varzi as we entered Abbeville, but you know how it is. We call out to a friend, but when they turn, it isn't them at all. It must have been so, for if it was him, why didn't he seize me?"

"Perhaps because you speedily fled with me."

Petra wanted to believe that she'd imagined Varzi, but that made more sense.

"Expect the best, but prepare for the worst," he said. "Explain Varzi by explaining Purieri. Tell me about Milan."

Petra contemplated walking out, but Robin was owed some of the truth. She made herself eat a little more as she thought.

"It's complicated. There was my folly with Ludovico. Then my father died. As a widow, my mother wished to enter a convent—it is often done so—and I asked to go with her, because I knew that my brother, who had inherited, would be difficult."

"A rather drastic solution, surely?"

She shrugged. "I saw no choice, and it is not uncommon for unmarried ladies of good family to live in a convent."

"Why?"

"They are often a liability. They are not allowed to marry beneath their station, but the young men of similar families want larger dowries. The sons are not prevented from marrying low as long as there's money. Why marry the sister of a friend when one can become rich by marrying the daughter of a Venetian silk merchant?"

"That's what Ludovico did?" he asked.

"The daughter of a Genoa spice merchant, but . . ." She caught herself gesturing with knife and fork and stopped it. "It is not that way in England?"

"No, probably because we don't have convents to take our languishing ladies. How improvident of Henry VIII. A houseful of generations of spinsters would be the very devil."

"Truth?" she asked, studying him. "You would marry a lady of your own station, even if a rich merchant's daughter was available?"

"Are you a rich merchant's daughter?"

"No."

"Alas."

"Why?" When she saw his meaning, she said, "I am virtually penniless, sir."

He shrugged. "I assume I'll marry a lady of my own station who also has a handsome dowry."

"So money is not irrelevant."

"Money is never irrelevant, but there are other dowries. Powerful connections and influence can also be valuable."

"Does no one in the world marry for love?" she demanded.

"My dear Petra, never say you're a romantic."

She looked with distaste at the remains of her food. "Not any longer."

"I have nothing against love," he said, "but with good management it coincides with other benefits."

"And if not, there is a less holy arrangement."

"Which your Ludovico wanted. Such permanent liaisons are not always without honor."

"For a married man?" she objected. "It is wrong in any situation, but for a man to so betray his wife, and for a woman to so betray another woman and the holy vows. I could never do such a thing. And in any case, why trust such a man? He who cannot be faithful to one will be faithful to none."

She hadn't intended a personal attack, but his lips tightened.

"You are not married," she said, making it worse.

He pushed aside his plate. "So you preferred the cold convent to a hot lover, but it did not solve your problems?"

Petra restrained the urge to fight. "I was content in the convent, and Ludovico married. I thought the problem over, but when my mother sickened . . ." He filled her wineglass and she sipped. "Mama was sure that once she was dead Cesare would find a way to force me out, so she came up with a plan."

"Your brother could give you to be his friend's whore, and Milanese society would not object?"

No wonder he was astonished. They'd come to the point she wished to conceal, as much for her mother's honor as her own. She contemplated the wine, but saw no alternative. "I'm a bastard," she said.

"Ah. Hold your story there a moment. We'll refortify ourselves."

He rang the bell on the table, and the servant returned to clear away dishes and replace them with sweets and a coffee tray. Robin dismissed him with a generous coin and poured the coffee himself. Petra watched, inhaling the aroma, knowing it was of the finest quality and perfectly made.

He passed her a cup. "Is it possible? Do we share an indulgence?"

No point in lying. "I do have a weakness for good coffee."

She added three sugar lumps and plenty of cream, then sipped, eyes closed, letting perfection fill her senses and slide down to satisfy her body.

"My dear Petra, I pray I can one day bring that look to your face."

Her eyes flew open and her face went hot. "I'm sorry! It's just that I haven't . . . this is the best I've tasted since leaving Italy. Since before the convent, in fact. There we only had it on the most celebrated holidays, and it was never very good."

He was watching her. "I have someone in all my houses who knows how to make coffee even better than this," he said softly, clearly meaning to tempt her.

Instead he'd startled her. "*All* your houses?"

A blink. Did it mean that he'd lied? Or that he'd told a revealing truth?

But then he explained, seeming at ease. "My place in Huntingdonshire and one in London. I confessed to being a courtier, did I not? I also have a small property in Vienne that came with my mother."

"I see. Are all younger sons so well endowed?" She sipped again, then licked cream off her lip.

He stared for a moment, then seemed to shake himself. "We were talking about your family. I assume you are your mother's love child?"

"Yes." She fixed him with a look. "She was a good woman. Do not think for a moment she was not. She was very young when it happened. Younger than I am now, even though she was already married, and mother to two sons."

He put a fruit tart on her plate—golden pastry filled with something red and topped with rich cream. "Married too young, then."

"At fifteen. It's not surprising. . . ." She let her hands complete the sentence. "A Venetian masquerade. A brief folly. Consequences she could not disguise. She had borne two sons, and I gather my father had other pleasures. He forgave her, but at a price. If the baby turned out to be a boy, it would be sent away, but if it was a girl, my mother would be allowed to keep me, and he would accept me. But in return, she had to be a docile wife who never objected to anything he did."

"Presumably that wasn't her true nature."

Petra said only, "He was a difficult man."

"None of this was your fault," he said gently.

"I was born. It would have been much better not so. My father kept his word, but as he lay dying, he told my brother the truth about me. So you see, that explains his behavior."

"No. But go on."

She frowned at him. "You wouldn't mind one of your sisters being a bastard?"

"I certainly wouldn't set her up to be the whore of a friend."

"You forget my folly. Cesare had reason to think I desired Ludo."

He merely shook his head. "So you enter the protection of the convent, but then your mother becomes ill. She must still have been a young woman."

"Yes, but something caused her to weaken and fail. She was determined that I be safe, however, and developed her plan."

"This journey to England? Why?" he asked. "There was no refuge closer to home? No supportive relatives?"

"None who could oppose Cesare. He is also a difficult man. And my mother was always an outsider."

"What of her family?"

"They are Austrian. My father, il conte, married my mother to gain favor at the Austrian court, but times have changed. Her family has trouble of their own and hardly know me. She was unwilling to entrust my safety to them."

"So instead she entrusted you to whom?" Then he said, "Your true father? Riddlesome?"

"Yes."

" 'Struth. But then why is he not assisting with your journey?" When she didn't answer, he said, "He is aware of your existence, is he not?" At yet more silence, he shook his head. "My dearest Petra, you truly will need me."

"No! I mean, you have to understand. My father—il conte—would never have allowed my mother to contact him, but also she didn't try. She knew it had been a passing thing for him. He was very young, younger even than she, touring Italy, as young English gentlemen do for their education. She assumed he would take other lovers and forget them all. Even so," she remembered, "she smiled when she spoke of him. She said he was so beautiful, and glowed with energy and enthusiasm. That he was tender and kind. So strange to hear such words from her."

"We are all young once," he said.

"Do we all let beauty tempt us to destruction? I mean Ludovico," she said quickly, though in truth she'd been thinking of Robin Bonchurch, with his halo of bright hair, his sapphire eyes, and his lean cheeks showing dimples now with the hint of a knowing smile.

"But why not contact him with this plan in mind?"

"There wasn't a great deal of time, and we feared we were watched. If a letter was intercepted, it would tell Cesare too much."

"He doesn't know who your father is?"

"My mother told no one until she told me. She told my father that he was masked and that it happened only once. In fact, the affair lasted for over a week. I still wonder how she could . . ."

He picked up the tart and held it to her lips. "Eat. It's too good to waste."

She took it, but only licked a little cream.

He hummed. "Do that again."

Petra blushed and took a full bite, then sighed in pleasure. The pastry flaked with butter, and the tangy fruit was the perfect complement for the rich cream. She licked some off her lips without thinking, then saw him watching her again. "It's very good," she excused. "I haven't tasted the like in ages."

"Not in the convent, I can understand, but were there no sweet indulgences with Lady Sodworth?"

"She's frantic about her tiny waist and won't allow any such foods in sight."

"No wonder she's peevish."

Laughter escaped her. He scooped some cream from another tart and held it to her lips. She licked before she could help herself, but then pushed her chair back so she was out of reach.

He licked off the remains of the cream himself. Slowly. "But that, my sweet Petra, is how she could when even younger than you, with less cause to be cautious. I can't imagine your English father's reaction. Are you even sure he's still alive?"

Petra pulled herself together, dropping the remains of her tart on her plate. "We're not idiots. My mother had always cherished mention of him, and we found ways to hear the latest news."

"Not a nobody, then. His name?"

When she stayed silent, he said, "Even now you can't trust me?"

"Exactly. But I will trust no one with his name. I know much about him, and some is worrying. He has the reputation of being a harsh man. My mother was sure he would accept me and be good and gentle, but I must be sure before I put myself in another man's power."

"Perhaps wise, but how could telling me be a threat?"

"A secret broken is no longer a secret. The truth might slip out."

"Stubborn again."

"Persistent again. But it will do you no good."

"If your father is vile, you will do what?"

Go to a convent, but that part of the plan was no use. For the first time Petra realized what poor options she might have.

"Petra, I will compel you to nothing except to remain within my protection until you find some other. Anything else would be madness."

Petra controlled her fear and anger. He couldn't prevent her leaving him if she was resolute, any more than Cesare and Ludo had been able to stop her leaving Milan.

He consulted a gold pocket watch. "We have time. Complete your story. You were in danger of being torn from the convent. I'm astonished that the Church would allow it."

"The Community of Saint Veronica is not exactly a convent. The order's ancient mission is to offer aid in the street, which they cannot do when living in cloister. They exist by the tolerance of the archbishop, but he, alas, is a Morcini, a member of Ludo's family. Pressure was applied—return me to my family, or cloister would be imposed, ruining our work.

"Mother Superior stalled him with talk of my being prostrate with grief because of my mother's death, but we had to act immediately. To cross Europe alone, however, that was impossible. Then we heard about this Lady Sodworth, who was about to journey home and was making a great fuss about it. We asked her to escort me to a convent in England, tempting her with free service. She swallowed it whole, and even agreed to keep the arrangement secret. I slipped out and joined her party just before she left the city. I hoped it would be a long time before Ludovico realized I had left, and that then he would give up his folly."

"How long since you left Milan. A month?"

"A little under," she said, disturbed. "But . . ."

"He'll have learned about your absence fairly

quickly. As you implied, there would be spies in the convent. But would he really send men after you?"

"You don't believe me?" She threw her hands up. "It's insane, I know it! That's why I've said nothing, why I was reluctant to speak now. My mind is clearly disordered by my ordeal. Il conte di Purieri has probably washed his hands of me and no one in the world cares where Petra d'Averio has gone."

"Let's assume your lover's hunting dog did track you to Abbeville."

"Hunting cur," Petra corrected with satisfaction.

"No. Curs are vile, and one merely shoots them. This, I assume, is a dangerous beast."

"How could you know what sort of man Varzi is?"

"Because you fear him, and il conte di Purieri employs him. What sort of man is *he*?"

"Ludovico? Hotheaded, spoiled, and unable to accept rejection. Ever. Once I found his arrogance thrilling."

"Alas, for we more modest men."

"This is no time for jokes."

"Even the darkest dramas demand humor. Otherwise we embrace hell. So, let's assume Purieri did send Varzi after you. He'd soon discover you'd left with Lady Sodworth and followed her trail. Not a difficult one, with the Berlin, the children, and the screeching, so he's confident and plays a little game. Would he do that?"

"If it were a cruel one, yes."

"He comes up close behind you and then travels ahead to Abbeville and stations himself in the street where you will see him. Thus he throws you into terror for a while before snatching you away. How he must have relished that."

"But instead I left with you," she said, smiling as she savored that. "I wish I'd been able to see his reaction when he realized."

"I wish I could grant your wish. Let's see, what does he do then? Wastes some time searching the inn. Perhaps searches the town, inquires at any convents. By the time he suspects you've traveled on, the storm is too close. He's furious, but still sure of his quarry. He knows your destination."

"How?" she asked, but then answered herself. "Because I went with Lady Sodworth, thus I am en route to England." She stood. "He could be here now. We must leave!"

"We're as safe here as in the Tower. The danger will be on the road. He could hold up the chaise and steal you, or think he could. I assume he doesn't work alone."

"No."

"So tell me more about him. He is formidable?"

"Oh yes. How to explain? Politics and intrigue in Milan are treacherous. Currently it is ruled from Vienna, but the old families vie for power. Despite regulations, they all have their private armies, their spies, and their . . . ruthless ones. The ones who will make people disappear, or return, or who will torture information out of them. The Morcini have Varzi."

"What does he look like?"

"If I were to point him out to you, you'd think me demented. He's quite old now, at least fifty, and round. He has beard-darkened jowls and a rather sorrowful look, and he dresses like a shopkeeper. His hair is grizzled and thin, but he never wears a wig. He simply ties it back."

"I'm sure he finds it useful to appear harmless. I assume his henchmen are a little more frightening?"

"Yes, but when I think about it, they, too, don't draw excessive attention."

"A clever and effective man."

"It's as if you admire him."

"I appreciate people who are good at what they do."

"You won't if he catches us. His men will kill you."

"At least you'll be safe. Your Ludovico won't want the treasure returned damaged."

"There are ways to hurt that leave few marks."

"And others that would heal in the time it takes to travel to Milan," he agreed soberly. "We'd better stay one step ahead. He'll have to assume you've found a way to travel on to Boulogne or Calais. If you're in Abbeville, you see, he can return and search. But if you've found a way to go on, you could reach England, and there you could disappear."

Petra muttered a curse.

Robin smiled. "I think that's where we came in. 'She wooed me with a curse,/And it's gone bad to worse. . . .' "

"Stop that!"

He raised a hand. "Ignore my whimsy. How bad would it be for Varzi if you reach England? Very bad. If your secret really is a secret, they have no idea where you will go."

"Also, we hoped they would assume another destination there."

"What?"

Another piece of information, but Petra surrendered it. "My mother had a friend. A Venetian opera singer. Perhaps it's more accurate to say my mother was her patron, but they were friends when young and have corresponded. She is now in London. If all else fails, I am to go to her, but my mother warned that she is not respectable and also not reliable. Not to be trusted with secrets."

"Who is this woman?"

"Teresa Imer, Signora Pompeati. But I understand that in England she is known as Mistress Cornelys."

He laughed in disbelief. "You know Teresa Cornelys?"

"You do?" Petra asked, equally surprised.

"My dear, the whole world knows Cornelys. Her Venetian assemblies are all the rage. But your mother was right. That's not a nest for you. If signor Varzi believes you are going there, however, it could be a useful distraction."

"I'm hoping he won't follow me to England at all."

"That, like a rat, he won't cross water? Don't count on it. But once there, he won't have a clear trail to follow, and we have many more resources."

Petra was thinking. "He'll know I'm with you, and your name. Perhaps—"

"No," he said, before she could complete her suggestion of separating. "How can he know?"

"Lady Sodworth. If he asks for news along the road, he'll hear about her behavior in Nouvion, probably including her attempt to drag me away."

"My turn to curse. Very unfortunate, but we only have to be careful. The wreck was probably fortunate, you know. He might have been hurrying after, intending to seize you on the road, but that created too much congestion. Perhaps your prayers are answered, after all."

"I hope so. How are we to prevent him from attacking us between here and Boulogne?"

"I'll think of something. I wonder if he's here now. I'd like a word with signor Varzi."

Petra rose and leaned forward, hands on table. "You want *nothing* to do with signor Varzi. He's dangerous, I tell you. He and his men. Beautiful eyes and dimples won't impress them."

"My eyes again. You really do adore them, don't you?"

Petra straightened, throwing her hands up. "Why you? Why did you have to be the person leaving Abbeville?"

"Perhaps it's destiny."

She swung and stormed to the window to look out, to search for Varzi, to try to think what to do.

"I'd stand back a little. If he's out there, better that he not see you."

Petra stepped back and to the side, but tears stung her eyes. Varzi might be here, and this idiot was going to get himself killed with his overconfidence and flippancy. "Is there a public coach? He couldn't hold up a public coach."

"You may not leave me until you're safe. Trust me."

She whirled, but he was at the door, shouting for a servant. One came running and was sent for Powick and Fontaine. When the men came, Robin said, "Danger. Fontaine, get the pistols and my sword and bring them here. Powick, find what parties are nearly ready to set out. We want company on the road."

Both men looked surprised but asked no questions. In minutes, Fontaine was back. Robin checked both pistols. Petra watched, frustrated but reluctantly impressed, remembering the pale warrior who'd emerged at Mère Goulart's. Yes, like a butterfly out of a cocoon of whimsy. But then again, his butterfly dog was prancing around as if this were all a game.

Powick came back quickly. "Two naval officers are about to leave, sir. Same ones as was at the wreck. And there's a French couple in a coach. Saw no sign of anyone of this Varzi's appearance."

"Right. Tell those parties that there's rumor of brigands on the road and suggest we travel together. Fontaine, get my jewel box."

When both men had gone, Petra said, "You think to bribe Varzi with a trinket? It will not work."

"Of course not."

She gave up trying to make sense of him. "If we make it safely to Boulogne, what then?"

"If Varzi is the sort of man I believe he is, he'll not want to attract attention by open violence in a town."

"But he will definitely want to stop me boarding the ship."

"That's his dilemma. You will be well guarded in a locked room while I hire a private vessel with a trustworthy crew. Getting you from room to vessel will be the most difficult part, but I'll hire extra guards if necessary."

Petra gaped at him. She had to admit that his plans sounded effective. Except for jewelry. What on earth could he want with jewelry at a time like this?

The valet returned with a plain, cloth-covered box. Robin unlocked it and raised the lid to reveal the spines of very old books. Had she misunderstood? He took out the end volume on the left and opened it to reveal a tray of glitter. "Nothing truly suitable for a lady," he said, "but I think these will do." He took out a pin and a brooch.

Petra backed away. "I will take no gifts from you."

"My dearest Petra, if I try to buy your body, I won't insult you with trinkets." He showed her a cravat pin headed with seed pearls and a pale green stone, and a cameo brooch of a bird. "We're about to travel in company, and you are my sister. The gown is not of the best quality, but some ornaments will help."

He fixed the pin in the center of her bodice, slipping his fingers behind the cloth before she realized his intention and had a chance to object. By the time she pushed at him, he was already stepping back. "You have a hat?"

Breasts still tingling from that casual contact, she wanted to deny it on principle, but went into her room to find it. It lay on the bed beside plain stockings and garters. Simple black shoes sat on the floor. "Wait a moment," she called, and sat to pull on the first stocking, tying it above her knee.

She sensed something and looked up. "Go away!"

He smiled. "I'm on guard. Varzi might sneak in here."

"Look at the door, then, rather than at my legs." He did, and she quickly pulled on the second. "You're peeping." She couldn't make it serious, however, and he grinned at her.

She stood, shaking her skirts back into line, and slipped on the shoes. "A little loose, but they'll do."

"Then you stand guard while I improve your hat."

She took the pistol and watched as he pinned the brooch into the knot of ribbons.

"There, rather stylish, don't you think?"

She exchanged pistol for hat and tried it on. It came with its own plain hat pin to fix it to the cap, and settled securely enough. "It will do," she said, and returned to the parlor, aware of the flirtatious ribbons fluttering behind. Oh, for the sobriety of her habit. Being in a bedroom with Robin Bonchurch in this mood was more than her nerves could bear.

She looked at his jewelry box. "Wouldn't a thief check the books?"

He slid the "book" back in place and said, "Play the thief."

Petra tried to remove the book, but couldn't get a finger around it anywhere. She tried other books and one, a slightly smaller one, did come out. She opened it triumphantly—to find browned, musty pages and a heavy, old style of print.

That useless success didn't help her get any others out, because they each had their slot. "Very well," she said, returning the book, "unless you encounter a book thief."

"That," he admitted, "would spoil the show."

"How did you get that one out?"

He took her left hand. She'd have resisted except that she'd asked to know. He put her fingers on the near edge of the box. "Press down lightly, then press down on the top of the spine of the book."

She did so, choosing the third book in from the left. It sprang up a little, but she still couldn't pull it out.

"Release the pressure with your hand."

When she did that, the book surrendered and she could draw it out. She opened it and gasped. She knew jewels, she'd worn jewels, but these were extraordinary. There was a set of buttons, each centered by a large sapphire and surrounded by diamonds and pearls. In the center of the tray sat a spray of flowers formed entirely of brilliantly cut jewels.

"Versailles," he said apologetically. "One must, or be completely disregarded."

Petra began to close the box, but he touched the spray. "Now, that might come close to doing you justice, my dark mystery."

"My price, you mean?" She looked him in the eye. "It doesn't even come close."

"Care to bargain?"

"This isn't a game! I'm putting you in danger."

"My dear pebble, I wanted relief from boredom on the journey. You're fulfilling your part to perfection."

Chapter 13

Robin watched this tormenting woman whirl back to the window to watch for her Varzi, who might or might not be pursuing her. He observed, too, but mostly her.

Was her story true?

It was fit for a dark and murderous play. *The Duchess of Malfi,* perhaps, with its evil brothers oppressing and in the end murdering the virtuous sister. Or the plot of an opera. Petra came from Milan, after all, famous for that art.

England, prosaic England, did not do opera. Repeated declarations of passion might sound well enough in a foreign tongue, but they sounded damn stupid in English.

Such stories occurred in England, however. His friend, the Duke of Ithorne, had stopped a similar tale. In that case the lustful man had owned a livery stable and the reluctant beauty had been the fifteen-year-old daughter of farm laborers, but the passions and pressures had been the same.

In higher circles there was Lady Annabella Rathbury, who'd been forced into marriage with mangy old Viscount Curzwell last year. No one had raised a finger over that, for after all, marriage made all right even if the bride wept at the altar. Robin had danced a time or two with Bella Rathbury, who'd been pretty, good-natured, naive and just sixteen.

There had been nothing he could have done, of course, short of offering to marry her himself. As she had no dowry to speak of, his mother would have had fits and it would have been pointless, anyway. Bella's story wasn't unique, and he could only donate himself in marriage once. Unless he took to murdering his wives. . . .

His mind was spinning into fancy again, and Petra's situation—if true—was deadly serious. He went to put his hand on her shoulder for encouragement, but felt the slight tremor. He turned her face and saw pale terror. He took her into his arms.

She clung there for a moment, but then tried to push away. "Don't, don't. I'm wicked to have brought this on you. It's all my fault. I should never have been so silly over Ludovico—"

He covered her mouth with his fingers. "Hush. He's a bully, that's all, used to always having his own way."

"A vicious, deadly bully."

"Served by vicious dogs, I know. But he won't harm you or me."

Her lips parted to argue, so he kissed them. This time, through longing or fear, she surrendered. He was wound tight, too, keyed up for action, and was whirled into fever by the softness of her lips, the sweet heat of her mouth, and the deep, true aroma of Petra d'Averio.

He sat in the nearby chair, pulling her onto his lap, the better to hold her close, to feel again her firm, luscious body. The hat pin came free. The ribbons of her cap slid loose at a tug, allowing his fingers to shed it and plunge into thick, silky curls. She pulled her lips free, but only to stretch back, gasping for air, giving delicious access to her slender neck, her rapid pulse. . . .

Beneath his hand, beneath thin cloth, her nipple peaked. His slightest touch there sent a shudder through her. No stays, my God, no barrier but a couple of layers of cloth. He played with her, hard and aching himself, moving beneath her, capturing her lips again, her willing, hot, and hungry lips. Her hooks were undone, his hand in her shift now, on her full breast that heaved with her breathing.

She pulled free again, but this time on the brink of protesting, her eyes huge, her lips red, her beauty stunning in daylight, perfect features haloed by dark curls. . . .

"My God, whoever thought long hair the epitome of beauty?" he murmured, stroking to pleasure her.

"A woman, seeing yours?" she breathed, grabbing his loosened hair and pulling him to her for a kiss.

He took her nipple between finger and thumb. Her kiss faltered, she shifted, then her lids fluttered with surrender as a delicious, needful noise escaped her throat. He echoed it, but this wasn't the place. This would be madness.

He sank deeper into the kiss, anyway, the most intoxicating kiss he'd ever known, and his hand found stocking, found hot naked thigh. . . .

A knock.

Perhaps a repeated one, for Powick called, "Sir? Are you all right?"

Devil, a bit of me's all right, Robin snarled silently, warring for control, wanting to send the man away.

But Petra was struggling free of him now, clasping her clothing together in front, face flaming.

"Yes," Robin called. "Are we ready to leave?"

"*We* are," said Powick in a disapproving tone that suggested he knew, damn his eyes.

Petra turned away, fumbling to refasten her gown. He'd offer to help, but wasn't capable of it in his state of arousal.

"Stay there," he said, and went into his bathroom to get rid of his clothes prop. He leant there, gasping for breath and sanity. When had he last slid into such an ill-planned disaster? How had he allowed himself to be swept beyond all sanity like that?

His mind seized up.

Not love. Oh, no, that fiery lust had nothing to do with love. Love was sweet, love was tender, love was reverent and respectful. This spicy creature had simply been too tempting, too willing at a wound-tight moment. She'd admitted to having taken a lover. No surprise if she was hot for it, especially after years in a convent.

No wonder that puerile Ludovico couldn't bear to let her go, however. Robin could almost imagine scouring Europe for her himself.

Oh, no. Not him. He'd not scour a village for a woman who wanted free of him. Any woman.

He pulled himself together and checked his appearance in the mirror. He tied back his hair again, rearranged his neckcloth, and anchored it firmly with the pin. Then he returned to the parlor, braced for trouble, only to be annoyed by her neat composure. She was fully dressed, even to her frivolous hat.

"A good thing we were interrupted," he said, putting one pistol in his coat pocket and picking up his scabbarded sword. "No time for that sort of thing now."

"Definitely not," she said coolly. Damn her.

"Ready?" he asked.

"Of course. May I carry the other pistol?"

"Better not. Demure sister, remember. Carry Coquette instead."

Petra picked up the dog, muttering, "Much use you would be against Varzi."

Disastrously tempted to laugh, Robin picked up the other pistol, cocked it, and opened the door. Powick was there, also armed to escort them down, and impassive in the way he always was when he disapproved. *Nothing happened,* Robin thought at him. Damn it.

But that wasn't true. He felt shaken to his soul and wanted nothing more than to drag the woman to bed and burn through this passion and be rid of it.

Petra went downstairs, feeling hot and icy at the same time, and aching in deep, deprived places. How could she have let him do that? How could she have been so weak?

She'd never expected, never known, such passion, however. Never realized how it could roll over a person like a storm, flare like fire touching oiled cloth. Nothing with Ludovico had come close to what had just happened.

She should have known a rake would have skills, that she'd be oiled silk in his flaming hands. She must never be alone with him again. Never. She'd escaped Ludovico more fortunately than her mother had fared with her lover. She'd not quickened with a child. It would be even more disastrous to become pregnant now.

In the innyard they greeted the parties they'd travel with for safety. The two naval officers carried an air of reliable authority. They assured Robin they were armed.

"Excellent," Robin said. "Truth is, sirs, my sister entered a French convent, but then changed her mind, but her convent doesn't allow that. She had to sneak out, but now they've sent men to drag her back."

Petra wanted to roll her eyes. Was there a scrap of truth in the man? But as usual, his story had the right effect on these Protestant gentlemen.

"Dastardly," declared fine-boned Captain Galliard, standing even straighter.

"We'll have none of that," said Captain Worsley, color high despite his weather-beaten face. "You can depend on us, Miss Bonchurch."

Robin thanked them and led Petra to their coach, putting the spare pistol and his sword on the floor by Coquette's cushion.

Petra halted before entering. "I need some things from the boot," she said. "My prayer book. And rosary," she said, to lessen the significance. When he hesitated, she said, "Just because your sister's fled a convent doesn't mean she has to give up her faith."

"Very well," he said, leading the way to the boot. "But don't make too much of a show of it."

More evidence of the English attitude toward Catholics.

Petra unrolled her habit and put the prayer book, rosary, and cross in her pockets, then entered the coach. He joined her a moment later, and the dog promptly leapt into his adored lap. Foolish females everywhere.

"I thought we were dedicated to truth," Petra said as they set off.

"Are we?" He was settled in his corner again, legs stretched, watching her, damnably stroking the dog.

"As best I can remember, every word I've told you is true. You, however, spin a story for every occasion."

"Only in your service, my lady."

Service. That was how they talked of animals mating, wasn't it? A bull serving a cow. That was how it would have been between them if they hadn't been interrupted.

Petra looked away, abandoning conversation, as did he.

At the next stage, he switched with his valet despite his fine clothing and rode. Fontaine was no more interested in conversation, which should have suited Petra, but it left her alone with her thoughts. Even Coquette ignored her, choosing her cushion and sleep. Petra watched for Varzi, but they were passed by few vehicles, and none contained him.

Nothing interfered with their journey and they reached Boulogne as a mellow evening softened the busy town. The French couple called thanks for escort and split off to enter a grand hostelry called the Coq d'Or. The naval men came along to a much smaller inn called the Renard.

As Robin was clearly rich, Petra wondered why he'd chosen the Fox over the Golden Cock, but it couldn't matter. The four of them alighted and gathered in the innyard, but the officers wanted to go immediately to ensure passage on the packet ship, the mail ship that

provided most passenger service to Dover. Robin asked
if they'd be willing to book places for his party, and
they agreed. He gave them money, and they departed.

Petra almost asked about the private vessel, but
stopped herself. Not here, where she could be
overheard.

"Come along," he said, and steered her into the inn
with his left hand, leaving his right free to draw his
sword. Powick and Fontaine stayed with them, abandoning the luggage for now. Petra was beginning to
feel foolish, to be sure she'd imagined seeing Varzi,
but she still stayed alert. She was the only one who'd
know him on sight.

"Monsieur Bonchurch!" declared a thin but potbel-
lied innkeeper, bowing low. "A pleasure, a pleasure."

"A pleasure to be here, Lemans. I need an inside
room until the sailing. An upper floor with limited
access."

The man's bushy eyebrows shot high. "But it will
be very small, monsieur, very dark. . . ."

"Even so. If you please."

With a shrug, the innkeeper led the way upstairs.

Here, as in most inns, most rooms would open onto
a gallery around the innyard, so Petra understood the
innkeeper's surprise. She saw Robin's plan, however.
The narrow, dead-end corridor they entered would be
easy to defend.

The room truly was small and contained only a narrow bed, a small table, and one hard chair. The window was almost too small for anyone to enter. Robin
opened the casement and leaned out. "Blank wall,
kitchen garden with people coming and going. This
should do. Go and see to the luggage," he told the

men, "but put out some plain clothes somewhere. I'm not traveling in this." He locked the door behind them, then put his pistols on the table, close to hand.

Oh, no. Alone again. Petra sat down, braced to resist.

He stayed standing, perhaps even stiff. "It's rude accommodation, but you'll be safe here."

"It's all that's required. Thank you."

"When the men come back, I'm going to have to leave you in order to find us a suitable ship. Powick will guard the corridor, and Fontaine will be in here. I won't be gone long."

"So berths on the packet are a diversion. Clever."

"Let's hope Varzi is fooled."

Silence began to press on her, so Petra asked, "Do people often hire a ship for themselves?"

"It's not peculiar. But I want a captain who'll take us to Folkestone."

"Folkestone?" she asked, wary. "Where is that?"

"A few miles west of Dover. A small fishing town without a good harbor, but smaller boats can put in. Smugglers do so all the time."

And how would you know that? Despite expensive jewelry, she knew in her bones that Robin Bonchurch was not what he seemed, yet she had to trust him, at least until England.

"I leave it all to you, then."

"This nunlike docility worries me."

"Most nuns are not at all docile." She spread her hands. "I have nothing to offer at this point—no knowledge, no experience, and no money."

He seemed to find that unsatisfactory, but then Powick knocked and announced himself. Robin unlocked the door, opened it, and gave the men their instructions.

"You know I'm not good in dangerous situations, sir," Fontaine said, eyeing the pistols.

They often encounter dangerous situations?

"You need only watch the window, and not unlock the door." Robin put one pistol back in his pocket and gave the other one to the valet. "No matter what happens, don't unlock the door."

He made to leave, but he'd forgotten Coquette. She'd been patient, but now she clung to his heels so tightly he nearly stepped on her. He picked her up, dumped her on Petra's lap, and escaped, ignoring the dog's yapping complaints.

"You never learn, do you?" Petra said to the dog. "Do any of us?

Robin suppressed guilt over the dog and went to the room where Fontaine had put out plainer clothing. Why the devil had he dressed up in the Court of France? To impress Petra d'Averio, that was why, and only see where it had led.

In boots, buckskin breeches, and a plain coat and waistcoat, he blended with the crowds of Boulogne, scrutinizing everyone who might be Varzi or a Milanese bravo. There were villainous types everywhere in Boulogne, but none that fit the bill.

It was not one of his favorite towns, and the less time he spent here the happier he always was. It was ancient and dirty with all the flotsam and jetsam to be expected of a seaport, but he'd passed through often enough to know it.

In case he was being watched, he went to the packet office and checked his booking. Only as he was leaving did he think about papers and passports. Did Petra have any? If so they certainly wouldn't be under the name Maria Bonchurch. Devil take it, he had no practice at this sort of subterfuge. All the more reason to find a ship to take them to Folkestone and land them on the sly.

Robin strolled down the wharf, where luggage was piling up under the eyes of passengers or servants. A few people were already boarding the packet ship, but most preferred to spend the next hour or two in the comfort of an inn, enjoying a good meal.

He chose his spot and ducked into a low-beamed tavern that seemed likely to be patronized by captains as well as crew, hoping his ability to sound like an ordinary Frenchman would work. He made his curiosity idle at first. Would the crossing be smooth? Was the town especially busy? Anyone peculiar seeking passage?

He soon heard about the screeching lady with monstrous children and a mountain of luggage. She'd booked the *Jeanne d'Arc* for a price named with a snigger.

"No man to do her business for her," said a squint-eyed salt with broken teeth. "Even her outriders are hired men and end their service here."

Robin sighed to himself. "I heard tell of this lady along the road," he said, in the manner of one sharing juicy gossip. "A foolish woman, as you say, and thus has suffered many mishaps, including losing the protectors provided by her husband."

The others nodded, looking even more hopeful.

"But I heard from one of her servants, one who fled her service in Amiens, that her husband, who she says is a merchant, is more of a pirate. That he has fought hand to hand with corsairs and with buccaneers in the West Indies. That he will hunt down and torture any who harm his wife and children."

The men shifted, shooting glances around.

"Thanks for the warning, monsieur," said one at last. "And what is it you want in return?"

Robin ordered a round. "Passage to Folkestone."

Eyes shifted again. "Why not Dover?" asked the one with broken teeth.

Robin took a risk. "I have something I'd rather not pass through customs."

"Ah."

After a moment, a dark, wiry man with a big nose said, "Costs extra, that. Harbor's poor there."

"Not in good weather," Robin countered, "and the weather seems fine."

"Never can tell, monsieur. And, of course, it's against the British law to avoid their custom house."

"That," said Robin, "is definitely worth a little extra on the fare. Perhaps I might look at your boat, sir?"

The man nodded and rose. As they walked down the wharf the man said, "How many would be traveling, monsieur?"

"Just two. Myself and my sister. And no luggage."

"Not much for a whole ship." When Robin didn't respond to that, he asked, "Was it true about the pirate husband?"

"I don't know, but unfortunately I have enough connection to the lady to perhaps feel obliged to retaliate myself if she were harmed."

"And who might you be, monsieur?"

"Name's Robin Bonchurch, but I'm a friend of the *Black Swan*."

"Ah," said the man, and clearly that settled things.

The *Black Swan* was the name of a boat, not a person, but it was sailed by Robin's friend the Duke of Ithorne. It was a pleasure yacht, but during the past war, Thorn had undertaken a few missions for the government that had involved smugglers from both sides of the Channel, and some of his friends as crew.

Thorn sailed as Captain Rose and Robin as Lieutenant Sparrow. A third friend, Christian, had joined them once as Pagan the Pirate. Thorn had declared it damn odd to take the name of Cock Robin's murderer, to which Robin had retorted that it was even odder to take the name of a flower. They'd all agreed that for Christian to take the name "Pagan" had been inspired. Good times, and he hoped Thorn was at Ithorne Abbey when they landed, because it wasn't many miles north of Folkestone.

"Here she is, monsieur," the man said, stopping by a fishing smack with *Courlis* on her bow. "Sound and seaworthy, and with a small cabin to shelter your sister."

Robin dropped down into the single-masted ship and gave it a quick inspection. "Been to Folkestone before?"

"Once or twice," the man said blandly.

"I want no one to know I've hired the *Courlis* or where we sail."

"What business is it of anyone else, monsieur? But you'll need to go in by boat at the other end. I'll have to signal."

Robin knew what sort of people would come to a nighttime signal. "I'll pay for their help."

"They'll be happier if I'm bringing them something, monsieur."

Robin smiled. "By all means. Let everyone be happy, and all will be well."

They haggled for the form of it, but quickly came to an agreement. Robin had to return to the tavern to seal the bargain even though he'd rather hurry back to the Renard and bring Petra here, where he could keep her safe.

He managed to get away in under a quarter of an hour.

Chapter 14

Petra didn't attempt conversation with the nervous valet, and Coquette sulked by the door. Unable to bear her thoughts, Petra took out her rosary and sought true, deep prayer. She succeeded, and was a second late in responding to voices in the corridor.

She met Fontaine's frightened eyes and wished she, not he, had the pistol. At least the door was locked and he'd be too terrified to open it. They both watched the handle press down and the door move slightly against the lock.

Petra went quickly to the window. Outside everything looked normal. Should she call for help? No. The crucial thing was not to open the door.

A knock. Petra gestured to Fontaine to answer.

"Yes?" he asked, his voice pitched high.

"You will open this door," a male voice said with such calm certainty that even Petra felt a twitch to obey. He spoke French with an Italian accent. She didn't know Varzi's voice, but she was sure it was him.

She went quickly to Fontaine's side and whispered in his ear. "Tell him he has the wrong room. You're sick. Tell him to go away."

The valet obeyed, and in his terror sounded convincing. Petra relieved him of the pistol and cocked it.

"You will open this door," the man said in the same level tone, "or I will castrate this man out here."

Powick!

"Blessed Virgin!" Fontaine exclaimed, hands to his head, then to his crotch.

"Devil incarnate," Petra muttered, suddenly short of breath. But she knew, she knew instantly, her only choice. She put down the gun and went toward the door.

Fontaine grabbed her and dragged her back. "You must not! Milord said you must not!"

"Idiot!" she spat, fighting to get free. "You think he will not do it?"

"Of course he won't. No one would!"

"Damn you!" She made a fist and struck at him as hard as she could.

He let her go, howling and clutching his bloody nose. Petra raced to the door, crying, "I'm coming, I'm coming. Don't hurt him!" Her trembling, sweating hands fumbled the key and she kept calling, "I'm coming, I'm coming!"

She swung the door open, and there was Varzi, looking, if anything, politely bored at having been kept waiting. Powick sprawled on the floor, a long, lean man standing over him, sword drawn and pressing on his throat.

"What have you done to him?" Petra asked, moving to kneel beside the man.

Varzi grasped her arm and pulled her up. "Nothing too serious, *contessina,* and he will regain consciousness soon. If we are still here, Marco will need to be more violent." He turned back toward the room, where Fontaine was whimpering, and said, "Be silent, or Marco will castrate you."

Fontaine became silent.

"What did you do to him?" Varzi asked, perhaps amused.

Petra answered the deeper question. "He didn't believe you."

"A reputation is an invaluable thing."

The man Marco knelt beside Powick.

Petra wrenched against Varzi's grip. "Don't you dare!"

"He is forcing a little potion down him, that is all. To delay pursuit. So much better for everyone, don't you think? As long as you behave, *contessina,* there will be no further hurt."

Marco went into the bedroom. Fontaine objected, but then no doubt drank the potion. Varzi was already drawing Petra down the narrow corridor, and she had no choice but to go.

But white fur raced out of the room, yapping. Petra tried to turn, but not in time. Varzi swung the tip of his cane, flipping Coquette against the wall. Yaps turned to yelps, and Petra knew that in a second the dog would be killed for making noise.

She broke free and gathered her, saying, "Hush, hush . . ."

To her astonishment the trembling little creature went silent. Petra held her close, murmuring reassurance, wishing someone could do the same for her. She tried to return the dog to the room, but Varzi grabbed her again and forced her down the corridor, around a corner and into another room. Another man waited there; a bulkier man with a leering face. There was also a large trunk, its lid open.

"Inside, if you please, *contessina*," Varzi said.

Pointless to quip, *And if I don't please?*

Petra couldn't leave Coquette with these men. The dog would bark again, and Varzi would kill her without a thought. She had no choice but to take the dog with her as she climbed in and lay, curled on her side. *Lucky Cock Robin,* she thought sadly. *Rid of two bothersome females at once.* And surely, she told herself as the lid came down, there will be an opportunity between here and Milan to escape. She rubbed the hard shape of the blade strapped to her thigh.

Or opportunity to kill herself. Yes, she really would kill herself before allowing Ludovico Morcini to touch her again.

Robin walked quickly back to the Renard, going over his plans. Powick and Fontaine would travel on the packet with the luggage, and he'd see if he could hire a couple to impersonate himself and Petra, at least as far as boarding. With any luck, the Milanese wouldn't realize they weren't there until the ship sailed. In Dover, they'd look for them in vain. He'd have to give his men careful instructions to avoid retribution. So many things to consider, so many dependents.

He entered the Renard and saw Powick on the bottom of the stairs, head in hand, a cluster of people around him.

Robin strode over. "What's happened?"

His man looked up, then staggered to his feet, clinging to the post. "Sir, sorry, sir . . ."

Robin grabbed his arm to support him. "Where's . . . my sister?"

"Gone, sir. Poison . . . don't know . . . threats.

Fontaine . . ." His words were slurred and barely un-
derstandable. "Opened door . . ."

Robin sat him back down again and raced upstairs,
cursing himself every way possible. He should have
set more guards. He should have stayed. Or taken her
with him. Or . . .

The door stood open and Fontaine lay on the bed,
pressing a bloody cloth to his face. A wide-eyed maidservant stood by.

"Punched on the nose, sir," she said to Robin.
"Might be broken."

Thank God it wasn't worse. "Why did you open the
door?" Robin demanded.

The valet's eyes shot open and he tried to rise.
Robin pressed him back down.

"Tried not to," he moaned. "She hit me!"

Ice tightened Robin's back. "She did this?"

The valet nodded. "Insisted on opening the door."

Robin saw his pistol on the table. When he picked
it up he saw it was cocked, and quickly uncocked it.
It hadn't been fired. Her story had all been lies? But
why? And if Varzi were imaginary, who had attacked
Powick? He'd damn well find her and find out.

"Powick?" Fontaine asked. "He is . . . all right?"

"They drugged him in some way, but he's
recovering."

"Not injured?" Fontaine persisted strangely.

"No."

The man sagged back. "They drugged me, too.
Forced it down me. I feel sick."

"Will you be able to travel? If not, you can stay
here."

He surged up again. "No, no, milord! I will manage
with God's help."

He'd slipped into calling him my lord, but Robin couldn't take him to task for it now. He looked around. "Where's Coquette?"

"I don't know, sir. She must have run away."

"Rest for a while," Robin said, and went back downstairs, feeling infuriatingly impotent. He wanted to rip the town apart with his bare hands to find Petra d'Averio, if that was her true name, but it wasn't a job for one man.

In the entrance hall he found the innkeeper. "Lemans, send for a doctor for my men."

"I have, monsieur. He should be here at any moment. I have moved your man onto the chaise in the ladies' parlor. I have never known such scandal!"

Robin found Powick also being ministered to by a maid, and recovering. He turned back to the innkeeper. "When did all this happen?"

"Just minutes ago, monsieur. Your man here staggered downstairs, crying abduction. That the lady, your sister, had been snatched away."

"Did anyone see her taken?"

"No, monsieur, but now I hear that two men carried a chest out through the side door not long ago. It is possible she was in it. No one thought anything of it then."

"Yes, I understand," Robin said. So she might truly have been captured. Absurd to feel comforted by that, especially with no explanation for her opening the door.

"Take care of my people," he told Lemans. "Someone show me this side door."

It didn't tell him much. The door led from the stairs out into the innyard, and it wouldn't be unusual for luggage to be carried down that way. He questioned some people who were gossiping there, but learned nothing new. Some thought the chest had been loaded on a cart. Some into a carriage. Some that it had been carried out. With the ships loading, there had been many chests in motion.

Then the two naval men rushed in. "What's this I hear?" demanded Captain Galliard, eyes wild with outrage.

"They have her," said Robin, thinking quickly. "It's over an hour yet till anyone can sail. Can I trouble you to alert the harbormaster that a woman has been abducted and might be smuggled onto a boat in a chest? And also to ask the officials here to barricade the roads so that they cannot carry her away?"

"Consider it done," said Galliard.

"Assuredly," said Worsley, and the two men hurried away.

Robin turned to a gossiping maidservant. "Pass the word that I'll pay a handsome reward for news of my sister."

The woman hurried off, too, and Robin returned to the inn. "Can you find me some people to search through the town for these blackguards, Lemans?"

"I can give you some of my men, and they'll know others."

Robin nodded. "They're to report back here."

He went to Powick, who glared up, furious with himself. "Hit me, sir," he said, making a great effort to talk clearly. "But after, when I was coming round, they made me drink something. Woke up all wobbly."

A brisk young doctor came in, exclaiming rather excitedly at events. He examined Powick, murmured various erudite things, and declared that he'd been forced to consume some noxious compound but would probably recover. Robin rolled his eyes and sent him to Fontaine, but knew he'd return to report a bloody nose in complicated terms, designed to raise the bill.

Robin dismissed the maid, then asked, "Was it Varzi?"

"Like as not. Right sort. Him an' a tall, wiry sort. Swordsman, I'd say."

"What about Petra?"

"She was there. When they made me drink . . ."

"She helped them?"

"No, no, sir. She tried to help me, but then they dragged her away."

Thank God. Whatever the reason for her opening the door, it hadn't been some plan of hers.

"Take care," he told Powick. "If you can, board the packet, and bribe a couple of servants to imitate me and Petra. They can slip back off later. I'll be traveling another way."

"You be careful, lad. These aren't easy people. That tall one, he'd have spitted me as easily as he'd have spitted a chicken."

"So I gather," Robin said and went out into the hall. "No news yet?" he asked the innkeeper.

"Not yet, monsieur, but they can't have gone far."

"These are very cunning men."

"Who are they, monsieur? And why abduct your sister?"

Robin repeated the story of the fleeing nun. Lemans, being Catholic, wasn't so completely outraged, but he agreed that nothing justified vicious attacks.

Then a young lad burst into the inn and skidded to a halt before them. "At the Mouton Gris, m'sieur!" he gasped. "A man dying, and they say as a woman did it!"

Chapter 15

Robin had to bully his way through the mob outside the Grey Sheep, but once inside his authoritative manner got the innkeeper's attention.

"Monsieur, such horrors! Here we have a guest most foully stabbed. A fainting maidservant. A puking manservant. A full inn—"

Robin cut this off. "Who stabbed whom?"

The man threw his hands wide. "Monsieur, I have no idea! The man, he says nothing but curses in a foreign tongue. I think it is Italian. The other, he has disappeared. Some, they say it was a woman. This I cannot believe."

He turned to snap frantic directions to chaotic servants while attempting answers to questions from alarmed guests.

Robin grabbed one servant. "Where's the victim?"

The man jabbed a finger. "There." He looked green.

Robin pushed into a ground-floor room where people gawked at a man on the ground. The stink of blood, shit, and vomit made Robin want to back out. When he saw where the man was clutching, where the blood came from, he understood why a manservant had puked. He really must be careful not to make Petra d'Averio too angry, but a kind of laughter was bubbling up.

No, she hadn't gone willingly. Not willingly at all.

Shame the victim wasn't Varzi, but the bleeding man was tall, muscular, and in his twenties. How, exactly, had she managed to land any sort of blow on a man like that?

A sallow-faced, middle-aged maid was standing in attendance, but not attempting any aid. If anything, she looked as if she were thinking sour, satisfied thoughts about the whole tribe of men.

Robin went on one knee by the man and summoned his weak Italian. "My poor man, how can I help you?"

Scrunched-up eyes opened a crack. "Kill the bitch," he hissed.

"A *woman* did this to you?" he asked in innocent astonishment.

Presumably the string of words that came next was yet more abuse of women.

"Quietly, my friend, quietly. A doctor has been summoned. All will be well. But do you have friends here? May I find them for you?"

The man perhaps relaxed a little. Alas, the wound wasn't as serious as it looked.

"Signor Varzi," the man muttered. "My master. Signor Varzi."

"He is staying here?"

"Yes."

"The room number?"

But then a doctor rushed in—gray-haired this time—exclaiming in masculine horror. Robin had to retreat, shooed out with the rest. He saw the innkeeper knocking back a glass of brandy and went over. "Nasty business."

The man shuddered. He snapped his fingers, and another glass of brandy was brought.

Robin sipped. "Where is signor Varzi?"

"Probably out booking his passage, monsieur."

"Did he travel with just this man?"

"There is another, monsieur."

"And a woman, I gather."

"No, monsieur. Who she was, I cannot tell. A maid saw a woman in green running out just after the man started to yell. She said she carried a white cat." He shrugged, hands spread again. "Perhaps she was a witch. . . ."

Coquette. Why on earth had Petra taken the dog? But at least it sounded as if they had both been more or less all right when they'd escaped here. Very soon, however, there'd be a hue and cry for her.

Robin tried to plant a seed. "Perhaps signor Varzi attacked his servant, and the woman merely glimpsed it and fled in horror. Foreigners," he added, in his most Gallic manner. "Italians are notoriously violent."

The innkeeper nodded. "Indeed, indeed."

Where would she run to? The Renard? Not when she'd been snatched from there. But she knew nowhere else in Boulogne.

"The guard has been summoned," the innkeeper said, and as if triggered by his words, marching feet, then an order to halt, sounded in the street.

Robin slipped into the innyard to blend into a chattering group. He didn't have to ask about the lady in green, for everyone was talking about her. Fortunately, the stories were garbled.

In blue. No, green. With a hat. No, a cap. With a cat. No, a rat. Beautiful. A hag. Frightened. Demented. Cackling with evil.

No one seemed sure which way she'd gone. One woman was convinced she'd turned into a crow and flown away. Robin left thinking, *Petra, you astonish me as always. But where the devil are you?*

He entered the street, alert for other gossip, but then froze. At the door of the Mouton Gris, the innkeeper was talking with much gesticulation to a swarthy, middle-aged man. The plainly dressed man looked concerned and alarmed—just as he would be to find his servant cruelly assaulted.

As Petra had said, signor Varzi looked ordinary. Swarthy looks were often perceived as villainous, especially in England, where they were uncommon, but the man's roundness and jowls suggested a prosperous merchant, and his anxiously spread hands seemed soft. He even had sorrowful bloodhound eyes.

He was a hound with razor-sharp teeth, however, and part of his teeth stood behind him—a lean, soberly dressed swordsman. Robin touched his own blade. That man had threatened Powick. No time for that—for now, at least. He had to find Petra before they did.

He set off back to the Renard in hope of news, but searched for her every step of the way. Instead, he saw a rag shop, heralded by bits of clothing hanging around the open door. An old woman sat knitting in the doorway, but she gave him a gap-toothed smile.

"Come in, come in, milord! I have fine garments here, fit enough for court, some of them!"

Robin didn't bother to argue. He entered the dingy, smelly place, scanning for what Petra would need—a concealing cloak. The women of Boulogne seemed to wear shawls and cloaks most of the time, so it wouldn't look out of the way.

He found a dark red one. It was stained down one side, but of quite good quality. It even had a hood. "How much?" he asked the woman. "Don't try to overcharge, for I've no time to play games."

She looked suitably affronted at this unsportsmanlike announcement, but named a price that was tolerable. Robin paid, bundled it up, and left.

He decided to risk some questions and asked two gossiping women if they'd seen his sister's dog. "A silly little thing. All white fluff and wearing a fancy collar."

No, they hadn't, and they warned that the collar, at least, might not last long around here.

Then a shopkeeper overseeing trays of fruit remembered the dog with the huge, feathery ears. "Had a fancy collar, sir, so I knew she'd stolen it. The thief went that way."

Robin passed over a coin and hurried on. "That way" was not toward the Renard.

Then a group of children told him about the pretty dog who'd escaped to play with them and had been snatched back by an angry woman. She'd asked directions to the Coq d'Or.

Of course. The one place other than the Renard that she knew. Robin stopped himself from running, but he hurried, telling himself that these stories indicated that Petra was whole and well, and Coquette, too. But both must be terrified.

The grand inn was busy, but seemed undisturbed by dramas elsewhere as yet. Robin avoided the main door, as Petra surely would have, and went to the innyard at the back. It was a frantic bustle of late arrivals, all anxious to secure passage for that night, so no one paid any attention to him. But he saw no sign of Petra or Coquette.

She'd be hiding, in shock over so grievously injuring a man. But wouldn't Coquette's misplaced devotion cause her to run to him, or at least bark? He circled the yard, poking his head into stables and carriage houses, ostler rooms and grain storage, but found no sign of them. Should he ask people? The soldiers would be here soon, so that would be dangerous.

Perhaps she wasn't here, or perhaps she was inside. Might she have sought refuge with the French couple in their convoy? He was turning to enter the inn when he spotted a wooden gate in an arch. He opened it and found a small walled garden, presumably for the use of guests. At the moment it was deserted, but overlooked by the inn. He saw no one in the windows.

He scanned for hiding places. It contained a small lawn with a wide white path around it. Between path and wall were beds of shrubs and small trees, but how could he search them?

Was that a yip?

He walked along the path, listening, wishing his boots didn't crunch so loudly on the gravel. A rustle? Over in that corner where a bay shrub nestled against a small tree? A branch fluttered. He went that way, calling a soft "Coquette." The dog flew out of the shrub and raced to leap into his arms, trembling in every delicate bone. His hand touched something sticky. Blood. Murmuring to her, he told himself that her race to him meant she wasn't badly hurt, but Varzi had another bill to pay.

"Where's Petra, then, my sweet? Petra?" he called

softly. Could the dog be here alone? Or was Petra injured?

Coquette was struggling to be put down, and he did so. She raced back to the motionless shrub. Robin followed and slipped behind it to find Petra huddled down in the corner of the wall, hugging herself, eyes huge, a smear of blood down one cheek. For a moment she shrank back as if she didn't recognize him, but then she scrambled up and she, too, threw herself into his arms.

Robin held her close. "What an excess of amusement you're providing me, my dear. Can we please stop now?"

She burst into a mix of laughter and tears, fortunately smothering them in his coat. He turned so he could see through the leaves and watch for any approach.

When she'd calmed a bit, he touched her face. "Did Varzi hurt you?"

She shook her head, but her eyes were swollen and red, and skin blotchy from being pressed against his coat. He kissed her forehead gently, a wave of disconcerting tenderness rushing through him. It was far removed from excitement or lust—and thus much more dangerous.

Petra leaned against Robin, wonderful Cock Robin, in danger of bursting into tears again for many reasons. She was so glad to see him, so distressed by what had happened, what she'd done. So terrified of consequences.

"Did I kill that man?"

"I don't think so."

"Thank God, thank God." She looked up at him as if he was her judge. "I had to do it. I had to escape!"

"Assuredly. Calmly, calmly. . . . Is that his blood?" he asked, touching her face again.

"Oh!" She looked at her right hand, which had been so very bloody. "I wiped it as best I could. . . ."

"Shades of Macbeth," he said, and spat into his handkerchief to wipe at her face. "There, the damned spot is out." Then he kissed her. It was gentle and tender and probably intended only to be comforting, but it poured life into her in a painful, burning torrent. She pressed closer and hooked her hand behind his head to make the kiss deeper, to drink down more of him.

To live.

He held her tight and his mouth responded, but she sensed resistance. *Of course,* she thought, going still. He understood now the danger she represented. His men and his dog were all injured because of her.

She pushed away. "I'm sorry. . . ."

"No more apologies. But Coquette is decidedly de trop."

The little dog was dancing around their feet, demanding his attention. He picked her up to gently explore the wound.

"That's not her blood. My hand. I'm sorry. I'm sorry for saying I'm sorry." She began to wipe away tears but smelled the blood on her hand. "Are Fontaine and Powick all right?"

"I believe they'll survive, but you might have broken Fontaine's nose."

"I'm sorry. But he would not let me go!"

He gently tucked the tiny dog into his pocket. "The question is, Why did you want to?"

"I should have let them castrate Powick?" she demanded.

He stared at her. "Varzi really would have done that?"

"Of course. Then move on to other bits."

" 'Struth."

"You see what risk I've put you in. I never should have—"

He captured her waving hands. "All will be well now."

"Oh, *you*!"

"Yes, me." He pressed her hands, smiling, but then stepped away, looking around the ground. "Ah, there it is." He scooped up a bundle from the ground and shook out a dark red cloak. "Behold my having forethought for once." He swirled it around her and fastened the tie at her throat. "It gapes. Can you wear your petticoat on the outside?"

His light manner that had irritated her so much now soothed her like balm. "Yes, yes, of course." She turned her back and untied the cream garment, then tied it on again on top. When she turned back, he said, "Better."

He unpinned her forgotten hat, took out the cameo, and gave it to her. "Tuck that away somewhere and pull up the hood of the cloak." He stepped back to look her over. "That'll do, I think. Let us depart this leafy glade."

Petra hesitated, but then gathered her courage and brushed through the shrubs to the path. He followed, saying, "Coquette's likely to give us away." He moved the dog under his coat, holding her in place with his arm and saying, "Hush." He pulled a wry face. "Being court trained, occasionally she obeys that."

"She did for me. It probably saved her life."

"Truly Varzi has many debts to pay." He offered her his other arm, and they strolled toward the gate.

She could only pray Robin never encountered Varzi at all. She glanced nervously at the inn windows. "I suppose if anyone sees us from the windows they'll assume a tryst."

"Of course. How did Coquette get injured?"

It came so suddenly it felt like an attack. "I'm sorry about that."

"Was it your fault, then?"

"This is *all* my fault," she said fiercely. "Powick, Fontaine . . . Coquette yapped at Varzi, so he hit her off with his cane."

"Haven't you sense enough to know that you're pure decoration?"

"What?" Petra gasped.

"Coquette, not you."

"She's a little warrior. She tried to bite the other one. My guard. He was so startled, I managed to land a blow."

"Diamonds in your next collar, my valiant butterfly, but of your kindness don't take such risks."

Petra almost felt he was addressing her, too. Another burden to be protected, stroked, and tolerated because Robin Bonchurch was unable to shrug off inconvenient responsibilities.

He unlinked their arms and opened the gate. They walked into the innyard, but then she halted. "There are soldiers there, asking questions."

He forced her onward. "We're just a respectable couple, taking the evening air."

As they passed, Petra heard one soldier ask about a woman in green with a white cat. The other was looking around. Robin wished him a good evening, adding something about a smooth passage tonight. The soldier agreed and turned his attention elsewhere.

Petra's heart was racing and her legs felt weak, but she did her best to play her part. When Robin began idle chatter about the voyage and how delighted everyone would be to see her home, Petra responded mindlessly, grateful not to have to make sense of his words.

She expected to return to the Renard, but noise, bustle, and the stink of seaweed woke her to the fact that they were near the ships.

"Do try to look completely at ease," he said to her, smiling. "I set up a hue and cry for any woman being forced aboard a ship."

Petra put on a smile and even managed a light laugh, as if he'd said something witty.

He led her to a single-masted ship where a hard-faced man with a strong nose said, "There you are, monsieur. Thought you'd changed your mind."

"I became entangled in an incident," Robin said.

"The man who had his balls sliced? He a friend of yours?"

"Don't know him at all," Robin said, and assisted Petra onto the ship and into a sort of shed in the middle. He joined her and closed the door. "Again, poor accommodation, I'm afraid, but you must stay inside, out of sight."

"Of course."

It was a space about eight feet long and six wide, with wide wooden benches on either side covered with a thin pad. She supposed they could serve as beds if necessary. Robin and she in here at night in beds?

The small windows were still unshuttered, so they let in some light but also stole privacy. That was good.

But then he began to undress, stripping off coat, then waistcoat, then neckcloth and sword belt.

"What are you doing?" Petra protested.

"Becoming a common man. I'm going on deck to talk to Merien, but I don't want to be recognized, either. Will I pass as a common sailor?"

She had to smile. "No, but I don't suppose Varzi has a good idea of what you look like."

"Pray for that. Keep out of sight, and make sure Coquette doesn't escape. She's like a flag. I'll urge Merien to leave as soon as the tide allows."

As usual, Coquette tried to follow him. Petra held her small body tightly until the door closed, thanking her again for her part in the rescue. When she let the dog go, Coquette sniffed sadly at the door, then curled up on Robin's coat. Petra was alarmed by a temptation to do something similar herself.

Suddenly overwhelmed by events, she sat on a bench so as to be invisible from outside. Varzi really was here and as ruthless as ever. He had almost succeeded in capturing her. She had wounded that man. . . .

She covered her mouth with her hand, then almost gagged at the smell of blood. She must wash! She rose to demand water, but then sat down again. Varzi would be searching furiously, and now he'd want revenge.

When the door opened she started, but then she recognized Robin, his hair tied back beneath a long knitted hat of some sort, a blue-and-yellow cloth knotted around his neck.

"Seawater," he said, offering a tin bowl. "Best I can do at the moment."

Petra took it, close to tears. "You are the most wonderful man."

He shook his head. "You are astonishingly easy to please. Unlike this one." He picked up the yapping dog. "Hush." Coquette did go quiet, but somehow managed to look reproachful. "I'm sorry, little one," he said, gave the dog to Petra, and left.

Petra put Coquette down on his coat again, where the dog laid her head on her paws in a grieving pose. Petra was sure a good half of it was acting, so she said, "He's not here to see."

She rubbed her hands together in cold salt water until no trace of blood remained. She couldn't wipe away the memory of her blade thrusting into flesh, however, or of hot blood gushing. Or of the man's choked cry. She didn't know why he hadn't screamed, but it had been a choke as he clutched himself. *There.*

She'd not meant to do that. He'd been a big man, and when Coquette had distracted him, she'd simply thrust upward with her dagger and that's where it had hit. She'd abandoned knife and victim, grabbed Coquette, and fled.

She remembered the empty scabbard for the dagger and took it off. It was useless now and might even be incriminating evidence. She stuffed it under one of the seats. She studied her gown beneath the cream petticoat. Yes, there was blood, but among the sprigs of spring flowers it didn't show.

It might always stain her mind, however. Shakespeare had known of what he wrote.

Chapter 16

Robin helped prepare the ship, keeping a sharp eye out for Varzi or his men. He hated leaving Petra alone when she was so distressed, but he couldn't rely on the sailors as lookout. In any case, the less they were alone together, the better. Tension, danger, and action seemed to create strange impulses and wreck self-control.

The sun was almost down and the sea was rising. Passengers were moving steadily onto the packet ship, but boxes, chests, and other luggage were still being loaded into the hold. Closer by, people were boarding smaller, privately hired vessels. He saw one that already held a coach, and another that was being loaded with casks under a man's careful supervision. Burgundy? Port? Cognac?

"You are escaping villains, monsieur?"

Robin looked to see a fresh-faced lad looking up at him. The long face and nose said he was the captain's son.

"Of a sort," he said. "Are you free to help me keep watch?"

"Yes, monsieur!"

"Then climb higher and watch for anyone who's

behaving strangely. Not going aboard a ship, for example."

"Yes, monsieur," the boy said, and climbed nimbly up the sheets, clearly enjoying the mission. A lad after Robin's heart, but this wasn't a game, alas. Nor were his feelings for Petra d'Averio. They could shape, perhaps destroy, his life.

He leaned against a rope, enjoying a fresh breeze and golden evening light, watching the quay settle. But he was thinking about family, duty, and his mother, still grieving for her husband and expecting Robin to be his image as Earl of Huntersdown.

His parents had been warm and attentive, but much of their attention had focused on training him for his future. All his attendants and tutors had been carefully selected, and his progress closely observed. He'd been trained as intensely in elegance, wit, and charm as in Greek, Latin, and the sciences. He knew music and all the arts, and had been encouraged from youth to be a patron according to his tastes. He had no particular talent for any such thing, but no one could be perfect.

His parents had been held up as role models, and he'd seen them that way—people of intelligence, grace, and civility. Nothing was less elegant and civil than excess emotions, especially those connected with romantic love—and romantic love had no place in the business of marriage, especially for a future earl. There one chose a person of congenial nature, correct behavior, suitable family, and handsome property. Robin's parents had expected to select an ideal bride for him, and Robin had not objected, knowing they would choose wisely. He'd asked only to wait until he was thirty. As he had two younger brothers, they'd agreed, but only upon his promise not to marry without their approval.

He supposed that promise still held, and his mother would never approve of Petra d'Averio. He shook himself. He didn't even know why he was thinking such things. He'd known her only days, and what he knew wasn't promising. She was a penniless bastard, perhaps of an English lord who would probably deny her when confronted.

And perhaps not even that. He didn't think Petra was lying, but her mother might not have been entirely truthful. If she'd had an affair with an actor, mercenary, or even a nobleman's footman, might she not have preferred to say it was the nobleman himself?

Would she then send her daughter in search of him?

Alas, it was possible for lies to turn into truth in some people's minds, especially over twenty difficult years.

Petra would make a perfect mistress, of course, perhaps even for life, but she was fleeing across Europe at great risk to avoid exactly that.

So he would let her go. He would see her safe somewhere, give her money if she'd take it, but then walk away and forget about her. He realized his hand was tight on a rough rope and relaxed it.

Petra d'Averio was nothing but trouble, and it would be a good day when she left his life forever.

Petra sat on a bench, listening to the bustle of the wharf and watching the light change as the sun set. The ship began to bob a little more, which she assumed meant the tide was rising. She'd never been on the sea before, unless one counted the canals and lagoon of Venice. Surely after all this, God would spare her seasickness.

Then she heard a screeching voice. Lady Sodworth! She turned and knelt to peer out. Yes, there she was, late apparently, harrying her children toward a nearby ship. Georgie broke free to run—too close to the wharf edge. Petra started as if to capture him, but a sailor grabbed him, tucked him screaming under his arm, and carried him on board. Perhaps that was the sort of nursemaid the children needed.

She remembered caution and slipped back quickly out of sight, but she smiled ruefully at what might have been. If Ludo had been the slightest bit sensible, he would have washed his hands of her. She would have endured the journey in Lady Sodworth's party, and would arrive in Dover tomorrow with only simple cares. She would never have encountered Robin Bonchurch, never have suffered this tormenting conflict of the heart.

Tomorrow she would have gone with Lady Sodworth to London and . . . and somehow managed from there. At worst, she could have sought refuge with Teresa Imer. Surely she wouldn't turn away her patroness's daughter.

Petra straightened, thinking. If Teresa was now so famous a hostess, wouldn't she know her father? When she escaped Robin, perhaps she should go to her address in Soho Square. Unwise to trust such a woman with her secret, but surely she could steer gossip.

After all, her mother's beautiful, gentle young lover, the one of the dark, somehow smiling eye, was now a great man, but a dangerous one. He was sometimes referred to as the Dark Marquess or even the Eminence Noir—the dark power behind the throne.

They'd heard other things, as well. That he was a duelist of great skill who'd killed a man who insulted his sister. That his mother had gone mad and that her blood had tainted him. Petra's mother had dismissed that possibility, but . . .

Petra had promised her mother that she would go directly to her father, but she couldn't put herself into the power of the formidable Marquess of Rothgar until she was sure at the very least of safety.

Robin saw Powick and Fontaine go aboard the packet ship, along with a cloaked man and woman. He watched for Varzi but didn't see him. Merien began to call orders, and his crew sprang into action. The same thing was happening on other ships. The tide was right and the journey had begun.

Had Varzi decided not to continue his hunt into England?

Robin turned to go into the cabin, but the lad called to him. Robin turned and saw a man running down the quay, shouting up to the readying ships. Varzi's swordsman.

Damnation!

Robin ducked into the cabin to lie on the empty bench, saying, "Stay down," to Petra. Coquette, damn her, leapt onto him with a yip of greeting. He said, "Hush," covering her muzzle with his hand, and she obeyed.

The running man was shouting a question to each ship. Booted footsteps clattered to a stop at the *Courlis*.

"Captain!" An Italian accent. "I've mislaid my

party. A young couple, he with golden brown hair; she with dark, very short. They have a small white dog."

Petra gasped, and Robin shook his head at her.

"Not here, m'sieur," Merien called back. "Got two finicky older gentlemen and their servants threatening to be sick before we even cast off."

Footsteps ran on.

"Varzi knows!" she gasped.

Robin rolled onto his side and tried a calming smile. "I did hope to keep them fooled a little longer, but no matter. There, we're off and free of them. No, no looking yet, tempting though it is."

She settled back, staring upward, and he saw the rosary move through her fingers.

Nun. Now she was out of her habit, he kept forgetting that detail. His mother was Catholic. Did that make it more or less likely that she'd approve of a nun? As a bride? *Don't be an idiot.*

"Varzi won't stop," she whispered.

"Don't worry. In England he'll be on my territory."

She rolled her head to look at him. "King George in disguise, are you?"

He sat up, feeling the welcome roll of the *Courlis* catching the wind. He pulled out a coin and gave it to her. "No resemblance at all."

She studied the profile in the fading light. "I grant you that, so why think yourself immune to Varzi there?"

"Trust me. If he takes one step outside of the law in England, I can crush him."

She sighed, and he knew he'd exasperated her again. Perhaps he should tell her his rank, but with all these shady goings-on he might prefer to keep his identity a secret. He could settle her somewhere, and Robin Bonchurch could disappear.

"Robin," she said patiently, "Varzi will follow your men to London. When he doesn't find me, he will capture them and torture them."

Her certainty chilled him, but he said, "No, he won't. They'll travel on the public coach, then go to my house. Then they'll alert a friend of mine, a major in the Horse Guards, who'll make sure no one can touch them. As for us, we go from Folkestone to a friend nearby, where we'll be equally safe."

And that's going to explode any secrets, Robin thought, *unless I can forewarn Thorn.* Why did this all have to be so complicated?

"Or where we'll put your friend in danger," she protested. "Why will you not understand?"

He put Coquette aside and slid to sit cross-legged on the floor by her. He turned Petra's face to him and saw evidence of recent tears. "Why can you not trust me? I will keep you safe."

"I know you'll try."

"I'm getting better at it," he teased. "This rescuing of damsels business is new to me, you know."

"Please stop *joking*!" She rolled sharply onto her side to face him. "Don't you understand Varzi yet? His diabolical way of knowing everything, his ruthlessness?"

"Don't you understand me?" he retorted. " 'Tis my nature to joke, Petra, but I can act seriously in season. Yes, I misjudged the situation at the Renard, but I know better now. Are we not here? Have we not escaped?"

"I want to believe that."

"Believe."

She rested her face on his hand for a blessed moment, but then pulled back. "But if he asks about alternative ports, won't someone tell him about Folkestone?"

"Do all Italians think in knots? Yes," he conceded, "but there are other harbors. Hythe, Deal, even Ramsgate or Hastings. He'll have to follow my men and we'll be safe, though . . ." He didn't want to confess another mistake. "I don't suppose you have any money, do you?"

"You don't?" she asked, eyes widening.

"A slight lapse in planning, I confess. When traveling, I split the ready money between the three of us. There's more concealed in various places, but all the luggage is on the packet. No ducats sewn into your clothing, my sweet?"

"As every stitch I have on is new . . ."

"True enough. Ah, well, I have enough to pay Captain Merien and the smugglers—"

"Smugglers?"

He explained the necessities of landing in Folkestone.

She rolled onto her back. "When supposedly ordinary farm women turn out to be murderers, and villains stalk us, you will entrust us to known criminals?"

He took her hand and found it chilled, so he held it for warmth. "Most smugglers are ordinary fishermen and farmers, just earning a little extra by night. Perhaps you really did live a life of virtue and propriety until recently."

"On the contrary, I was a wild and willful girl."

"Ah yes, with Lousy Ludovico."

She turned her head to frown at him. "He didn't have lice."

"Your translations again. It also means 'disgusting.'"

"He's not even that. Remember, I would have married him."

The spear that went through Robin was undoubtedly jealousy, the most forbidden of forbidden emotions. He rose to his feet. "I'm going out again."

"Don't."

It was almost a whisper, but stopped him dead.

"Did that disgust you?" she asked, looking upward. "I'm only trying to be truthful. How can you imagine that I wanted to marry a disgusting man?" She looked at him again. "Please. I'm so afraid. . . ."

The dim light caught tears on her dark lashes and the quiver of her lips. Robin hesitated, then lay down beside her, taking her into his arms. She stiffened and pushed him away, but he said, "Merely an anodyne for fear. Don't we all need comfort in the dark?"

"It's not quite dark," she said, but she relaxed against him.

The bench was narrow, so he readjusted their positions so she lay half on top of him, her head in the hollow of his shoulder. She sighed and settled there, her arm across his chest, one leg over his thighs. Dangerous, but he'd been trained in self-control. He'd also been trained to offer protection and comfort to those in need, and that he could do.

He didn't attempt conversation. It would strain his truthfulness to tell her more about himself, and therefore didn't seem right to pry more information from her. They rolled on the sea as flaming sunset settled into moonlit night. And he, too, relaxed, sure of his purpose and his ability to achieve it.

He would keep Petra safe.

Petra absorbed his warmth and inhaled his smell, varied now by sea air and a touch of tar. She knew she shouldn't indulge in this intimacy, but there was no easy way to reject it and it might be her last chance to lie so close to Robin. Only his open-necked shirt covered his chest, and the rolled-up sleeves exposed his forearms. Only his breeches covered his lower body, and she regretted her skirt and petticoat that added to layers there.

It could be just this once, because she was going to have to flee him soon. It was partly to keep her secrets, but also in the hope that Varzi would ignore him and his men once they were apart. There was a selfish part, however. Varzi knew she was with Robin, so leaving him would make her safer.

It would be hard, though, perhaps the hardest thing she'd ever done. She'd never imagined that a heart could be snared almost instantly, that a stranger could become precious overnight. Her mother's attempts to explain her liaison had made no sense, but now Petra could begin to understand. If it had been like this . . .

Even now, simply lying here, danger stirred.

He was stroking her back, doubtless in the same meaningless way that he stroked Coquette, but heat began to flicker along her skin and below where her thighs were open against his leg. She pulsed with the same kind of hunger an empty stomach might feel and perhaps had done so since Montreuil. Her body remembered and ached to complete what had been interrupted.

No, no, no. What a disaster that would have been.

But she couldn't make herself tear away from him. Couldn't ask him to stop his gentle, tormenting stroking of her shoulder.

A sudden sharp toss made him tighten his arm and pushed her harder against his thigh. "We're well under way," he said.

Too far, too fast. "How long?" she asked.

"We could arrive by two in the morning."

Arrive where? Petra tried to be practical. "We can travel on to your friend's house at that time?"

"There's always a way, and there's a moon."

"Who is this friend?" she asked, unable to resist moving her hand to cover his naked arm, to feel his firm muscles there, and fine springy hair.

"Captain Rose of the *Black Swan*. A smuggler of sorts."

She stirred to look at him in the increasingly dim light. "Now we have the truth. You, too, are a smuggler. Your wealth comes from brandy and lace."

He grinned. "Not me. I'm a respectable fellow."

She made a disbelieving noise, and he looked hurt. "I just hope Captain Rose is at his place in Stowting."

"And if not?"

"I have free run of his house. We're by way of being related." He pulled her close. "Once there we'll be safe."

"I hope so."

"It will be so. Forget Vile Varzi." Had he moved his hand lower, or had she only just become aware of its heat in the small of her back?

"Mind you," he said, breath warm in her hair, "I'm wondering if I should introduce you to Rose. He seems to appeal to the women, even though he's a dark-visaged fellow."

"Is he rich?" she asked, realizing she was stroking him. She stopped.

"Are you mercenary?"

"A penniless lady has to think of these things," she murmured into his chest, slipping helplessly into flirtation that had once been so natural to her. And so very dangerous.

"He's rich," he said. "All that smuggling, you know."

"Richer than you?"

"Alas, yes."

"Then perhaps I *will* woo him and win him."

"Then perhaps I shall be jealous," he murmured with a bit of a growl in it, playing the game.

"Not you," she teased.

He raised her head so she had to meet his eyes. "Why not me?"

"Because you have more hens than you know what to do with, Cock Robin."

"Cock?" His eyes lit with laughter. "Do you resemble your mother?"

"Why?" she asked, startled.

"Because if you do, I understand Riddlesome entirely." His lips met hers, but only in a teasing brush. She should leave it like that, but her tongue flickered out to play. The tingle in her skin ran hot now, and her breasts felt tight. She was moist and hungry between her thighs, but she couldn't go as far as that.

They played, a joust of tongues and hot breath, then came together for the unavoidable kiss. Petra sank into it with despairing relief, like a starving woman grabbing poisoned bread, not caring for anything as long as she ate. The boat rocked and tossed, adding tumult to a tumultuous blending of mouths and more than mouths.

Men talked on the deck. They might hear. Perhaps that's why she and Robin were being so very, very quiet. That taut control drove Petra wildly beyond hope of resistance. She tugged his loose shirt completely free so she could explore his body, so lean, so strong, so perfectly vibrant. She stretched her leg around his, wanting, needing.

He gripped her stocking-covered calf, then her uncovered thigh, widening her still more as he slid fingers to the inner side and up.

"No!" she gasped.

He went still, rigid. She heard the silent plea. And surrendered. "Not no," she whispered in helpless, trembling surrender. "Yes, yes, please. Yes."

He slid a finger deeper, catching her gasp in a kiss, shifting them both again and exploring more deeply. She should fight, she should, but all willpower, all thought incinerated in the flaming desire roaring through her, arching her.

Cool air brushed her naked thighs. He'd pulled her skirts up high. "Open your bodice for me," he whispered as his clever fingers stroked in gentle torment.

Fighting to suppress gasps, her hips moving against his hand, Petra fumbled with the hooks, cursing the way they resisted. But then the gown fell open, so she was covered only by her shift above, her bunched-up petticoat below. She fumbled with the tie that gathered the neck of her shift, but her fingers wouldn't work.

He nuzzled his way to her linen-covered breasts. They were already aching, and when he found a nipple with his teeth she let out a soft cry.

"Hush," he said, as he had to the dog, but with bright laughter in his voice.

Petra turned her head into his shoulder to smother other noises as he started to stroke again, faster now, driving and demanding her, as Ludo—

Don't think about Ludo!

But, oh, how she'd missed this, this soaring, tightening, tormenting surrender to a man's hot, hard body, his spicy man scent drowning all. And this man was tormenting her, playing her with hand and mouth. She wanted to demand, to scream, but instead sank her teeth and felt him jerk. He gave up his games and she exploded again and again, her mind going blind white with pleasure.

He captured her lips and she poured desire back into him, still wanting, still needing, deep in her throbbing, cavernous core. She pushed her hand down between them, tugging at the buttons of his flap.

"No," he said, struggling to control her, but she had his hot, hard length now. He wanted her as much as she wanted him. She wriggled under him. "Please, please . . ." And he broke. He moved between her wide, hungry thighs and plunged deep.

It had been so long it shocked her, and he was big, almost too big. . . . But then he slid on thick moisture and was perfect, filling her perfectly, joining to the hard-hitting hilt again and again so it seemed almost too much, but never too much, as their sweat ran together and her heart raced fit for bursting.

He stopped, still deeply seated, breathing in deep gasps. He couldn't stop now, could he? Just in case, she wrapped legs and arms around him, pushed her hips against him, and he pumped into her again, pounded against her, and the sailors were probably hearing everything but she didn't care as she exploded again more blindingly than before, and again moments later when he went rigid with the same burning, arching ecstasy.

Lax on her back, sucking in air, Petra finally felt astonishingly, perfectly complete.

"Hell," he said, and moved out of and off her.

Chapter 17

Petra lay there, still against him, sweat cooling, abruptly hollow with empty dread.

Hell?

What did one do or say? Ludo had said sweet things, flattering things. She was going to be sick. . . .

A touch startled her. Robin's fingers in her hair, playing gently. She could interpret it as loving and satisfied, but she thought of his fingers in Coquette's fur—offering dutiful kindness to a burdensome devotee.

She longed to thrust away from him, to run. But where was there to go? This room offered only a few feet of escape, and outside lay the deck, the sailors, and the deep, dark sea. If she stayed very still and silent, perhaps this would all go away.

The boat tossed more wildly, and cold spray shocked her skin.

" 'Struth," Robin said, scrambling over her to close and fasten the shutters.

Petra sat up, hastily rearranging her clothing, thanking God for rescue. But she was surrounded by the smell of him, of them both, of what they'd done. The last shutter thumped closed, dropping pitch darkness over them. *Hell.*

She sensed him sit on the opposite bench. *Please don't say anything.*

"You honor me," he said.

She swallowed and tried to make her voice practical. "You know I wasn't a virgin, so that was of no great moment. Though pleasant, of course."

Silence suffocated and Petra struggled not to gasp for breath, wishing that by some magic she could be sucked somewhere far, far from here.

"You could conceive."

"A common risk. I won't expect you to marry me." Practical was becoming brittle.

"Don't you think I might wish to make a child of mine legitimate?"

Petra wished she could see his expression. "Why? This can hardly be a new risk for you."

"There are ways to lessen the risks, none of which we used."

Petra rested her head back against hard wood and closed her eyes. "I don't want to talk about this."

After another long silence he said, "I need to check on our journey." He fumbled around for clothing. Perhaps he stepped on Coquette, for there was a yelp, then some soothing. Soothing another inconvenient female. The door opened, letting in some moonlight and a blast of damp air, then shut again.

Petra sat where she was for a while, then lay down wearily on the pad still warm from their passion, still scented in that musky, mysterious way. She fought it, but began to weep. She wept until she hurt, she wept until she ached, and then until she slipped mercifully into sleep.

* * *

"Petra . . ."

Petra stirred out of sleep and squinted against light. Daylight? No, someone had brought a lantern, but the boat was tossing sharply, with creaks and cracks and howling wind.

Robin was looking down at her, made macabre by the wild candle flame. She flung her arm over her eyes, but not before seeing that he was fully dressed even to the cravat.

Was that armor?

Hell.

"I thought it time to wake you," he said. "We'll be off Folkestone soon."

His exquisite care was painfully wrong for the man she'd come to know, but she tried to match his tone. "Can we land in this weather?"

"It'll be calmer close to shore."

"No other trouble?"

"Signor Varzi bearing down on us like Blackbeard the pirate? No."

He left, letting in a blast of air and spray that almost touched her. Struggling in the tossing ship, she scrambled for her cloak and pulled it close against the weather and against a deeper cold. She'd soon be alone in a strange land without a guide, for she would have to flee Robin Bonchurch at the very first moment. At least now he'd be pleased to see her go.

"Coquette?" she said softly, needing comfort, but Robin must have taken the dog with him. She was truly alone.

He returned. "It's time."

"We're there?"

"The smuggler's boat is coming alongside."

There was a bump, and Petra heard voices calling against the wind. She pulled the strings of her cloak tight at her throat, and one broke. She simply looked at it, helpless.

"Where's the brooch?" he asked.

She fumbled in her pocket, then was tossed by the ship's movement and would have fallen if he hadn't grasped her, his other hand braced on a wall. She dragged out the cameo, and sat for safety. He fastened her cloak, apparently unaffected by their closeness, by contact, when she thought she might choke from his touch on her throat.

He stepped away. She touched the brooch as she rose. "I'll mend the strings, return this to you. . . ."

"It's a trinket. It's yours."

Petra hit him. It wasn't a slap. She swung her fist and caught him on the side of his jaw. He staggered and a curse escaped. She cursed more, cradling her hand.

"Good God, woman, did you break it?"

"No, may you rot in the deepest depths of hell."

He froze in the action of rubbing his jaw. "Don't dare to accuse me of rape."

"*What?* This is not about that!"

"Isn't it?"

She knew it probably was, but not the way he seemed to think.

"It's because everything's a trinket to you! Because you can treat what happened as nothing! You—"

"Nothing!" He dragged her into his arms and kissed her. Petra fought him, because not to struggle was to die. He suddenly went still, then shoved her away from him. "I apologize."

Petra closed her eyes. "There you go again."

When she dared to look, he was in complete control. "It must be because I'm English. I don't think I have a temperament in me—carefree or sober—that you could like."

It would be so easy to deny that, and fatal.

Someone knocked on the door. "Monsieur, you must come."

Petra thanked God again. Robin picked up Coquette and tucked her into his pocket. "Getting crowded in there with two pistols to carry. Try not to wet the powder, no matter how nervous you get."

He opened the door and stood back for Petra, saying, "Keep hold of something as you go." Not surprising if that something wasn't him, but as Petra staggered into the rolling, wind-tossed night, she wished it was. Instead the captain gave her his hand to help her to the side.

They were close to shore and a longboat lay alongside, knocking against the side now and then as barrels and boxes were passed down in the dark. Petra held on to a rope as Robin paid the captain, taking in the moon riding high among clouds, and the dark, turbulent sea laced by its silver light. She suddenly saw beauty amid the violence, and inhaled the sharp, intoxicating air.

Robin came up beside her and she asked, "What's that white to our right? Mist?"

"No. That's the chalk cliffs. The end of them. The cliffs on the other side of the town are darker. Ready? I'll go first so I can help you into the boat."

He climbed over the side of the boat and disappeared. Petra leaned over to watch him climb down a rope ladder, and thought she'd finally come across something she couldn't do. She'd evaded Ludo, endured Lady Sodworth, joined her fate to a rake, fought off evil women and Varzi's henchman, but she couldn't climb down that rope.

She was given no choice. The captain hoisted her over and dangled her until she grabbed the sides of the ladder. Someone, probably Robin, guided her feet onto rungs. The prickly, wet rope stung her palms, but his hands on her ankles stung more. If she fell into the sea and died, perhaps it would be a blessed escape. She was about to give up when he grasped her around the waist and swung her onto a narrow, hard bench. He sat beside her, bracing her in place, just as the boat bucked waves toward shore under the power of urgent oars.

He held her close of necessity, but as soon as the boat jarred and scrunched up onto land he let her go. He leapt out into shallow water, then turned. Again she had no choice but to let him carry her onto dry land. No slipping this time, and no teasing, either. Just aching memories and tears that sea air might explain.

The eight smugglers were working with swift practice to unload their cargo. Everything went into sacks, and the boat was hauled up to join a row of them. Then all the men but one moved with remarkable swiftness up the beach toward the town above, disappearing into the dark. Out on the water, there was no sign of the *Courlis*.

Petra saw some cottages nearby, but no sign of life. If anyone was awake, they'd know not to interfere with smuggling matters.

"Who be you, then?" the remaining man asked, in an accent so rough Petra had to guess the meaning.

"Robin Bonchurch, sir, and glad of your assistance. And this is my sister, Maria." He held out some money, which clinked into the smuggler's pocket. "Any chance of a vehicle?" Robin asked.

"Not this time of night, sir, not without questions asked." After a contemplative moment, he said, "You'd best come up to my place till morning, sir. Doesn't do to have strangers turn up in the night." He set off, surefooted in only moonlight.

Robin extended a hand and again Petra felt she had no choice but to take it. A broken ankle would be one disaster too many.

"Can we trust him?" she murmured in French.

"Thus far," he replied. He didn't say *Don't worry,* but she heard it.

The shifting pebbles became a kind of ramp that became a rough street between narrow houses. Rushing water suggested a stream had cut this valley.

"You live nearby, sir?" Robin asked.

The man twitched his head. "Just up the town a bit. Best not talk."

Soon after, he stopped at a door that looked to be in an ordinary house, but something shrieked above. Petra flinched, but when she looked up she saw a swinging sign.

"It's an inn or tavern," Robin said quietly. "Should be all right."

"Goulart," Petra reminded him, shivering.

They were ushered into a gloomy space with a sour smell. The smuggler opened a lantern to shed more light, showing five rough tables surrounded by chairs and benches, and some huge casks against the wall. A tavern, as Robin had said, serving not wine but beer. She knew the English drank a lot of beer. Would she be expected to?

"Want something to drink?" the man asked. "Or

some baccy?" He took a long clay pipe from a rack over the fireplace.

"No, thank you," Robin said. "In fact, we'd like to leave the town as soon as possible. With a few directions from you, or better, a lantern, we could walk."

The man crushed aromatic tobacco into the pipe bowl with a thumb. "You can if you want, sir, but it threatens rain tonight, and come first light my brother Dan'll be driving into Ashford to pick up an order of rope and deliver a few things, if you know what I mean."

Robin turned to Petra. "Which do you prefer? It'll be hard going in the dark."

Petra felt hopelessly undecided. Why had she imagined that being in England would make things simpler? Her instinct told her the smuggler was in his way an honest man, however, so she said, "It will be wiser to stay, I think."

The man nodded. "I sleep in the kitchen, but there's a bedroom upstairs if you want it. I'll wake you come morning." He put down the pipe and went to a door. "Name's Josh Fletcher, by the way." He went through the door, leaving them alone.

Petra stared at that pipe as if it were a dark mystery. "Why did he fill it and then leave it?"

"Some do as a nervous habit. Remember, he's probably wondering if we're a danger to him."

"That's what I thought about Mère Goulart, and see how that turned out." Petra knew, however, that she was more concerned about the bedroom upstairs than danger.

"We can leave if you wish," he said patiently. "I suppose we can't lose the road."

Silence fell around and between them, threatening to suffocate her again. "Let's go upstairs," he said.

There seemed no argument to make, but Petra was sick at the thought. She felt as sexual as a marble statue, but he might think he had a right to her now. She'd have to fight. She couldn't imagine the outcome.

He'd picked up the lantern and was waiting to light her way up the wooden steps that were almost steep enough to be a ladder. She climbed it with her skirts bunched up, aware of her legs being visible, although they were no secret to him now.

He followed, bringing the light to illuminate a large space under the bare, sloping roof and one enormous low bed.

"Probably sleeps six in a pinch," Robin said, putting the lantern on the floor and taking Coquette out. "Lie down and get some sleep."

Petra studied him and realized he meant it. Of course. He wouldn't want to repeat a hellish experience. She pushed that word out of her mind. If she could, she'd forget the whole thing herself. Remembering Mère Goulart's, she pulled back the patchwork quilt, but though the sheet wasn't fresh, it wasn't unbearable. She'd not be taking off any clothes, after all.

It really was large enough to sleep six, and she could prove to him that his rutting had meant little to her. "We can take a side each," she said. "I slept a little on the ship, but I doubt you did."

Avoiding eye contact, she took off her shoes and lay down close to one edge, pulling the quilt over herself. The mattress was lumpy and probably supported by ropes, which needed tightening. It sagged toward the middle, pulling at her, but she could cling to the edge.

She heard Robin taking off some things—his boots, she supposed, his sword, perhaps his coat with a pistol in each pocket. Coquette was still exploring the room, her nails clicking on wood like rat's feet. What would happen if she met a rat? The dog was Robin Bonchurch's problem, not hers.

He blew out the candle and it became dark except for clouded moonlight coming through the one unglazed window in the end wall. She felt the bed shift as he lay down on the far side. Probably five feet separated them, but her every sense knew he was there.

Say nothing, say nothing, say nothing, she told herself. But sleep wouldn't come, and the question wouldn't go away.

"Why 'hell'?" she asked softly. Perhaps he was asleep and wouldn't hear.

She thought that was the case, but then he said, "I apologize. That was unforgivable, but I could have planted a child in you."

"And every other time you've been with a woman, I assume."

"As I said, there are ways to avoid problems. Do you really want to talk about this?"

"Yes," she said fiercely to the dark ceiling. "Why did you not use these ways?"

The silence lasted so long that she might imagine he'd left if she didn't know he was there, just out of reach.

"I lost control," he said at last.

"Isn't that the point?"

"Only by intent. When I said 'hell,' it was also a lapse of control. Unpardonable, but I do ask your pardon."

Instant forgiveness rose to her lips, but she said, "If you felt that way, it's better I know."

"Petra . . ." He sighed it. "It's not your fault. It's nothing to do with you. No, that's nonsense." He stirred, and when he spoke again, she knew he'd turned to her. "You are a very beautiful, very desirable woman, but I chose to be your protector, almost your guardian. What I did, it was not appropriate."

"Appropriate," she echoed, unable to hold back a touch of wry humor. "No one would think it appropriate, but I did as much as you."

He didn't reply.

"I don't expect you to marry me. I mean that."

"I don't expect me to abandon you if you're with child."

"It will be *my* choice."

"We'll see."

She rolled to face him, to look into half-seen eyes. "I haven't come so far and striven so hard to be commanded and imprisoned here."

"Marriage isn't usually considered a prison."

"It was for my mother."

"I am hardly a man like your father. The Italian one."

"I don't know what sort of man you are. I felt sure at least that you were a libertine, but here you are preaching a sermon at me."

"I have my code."

"As do I." She turned over again. "Good night."

"Petra, please, allow me to be your protector until you're safe. I will ask no more than that."

She couldn't reply, because she would make no false promise.

She thought that was the end of it, even though she couldn't imagine sleeping, but then he said, "Will you lie with me?"

She couldn't believe it. "Of course not."

"I mean, together. This bed dips so much that gravity will pull us together, anyway, if we sleep, but I'd like to hold you. In the hope it might comfort us both, but also to show you can trust me."

"Said the lion, opening its jaws," she muttered. But the pull of gravity and him made her turn and slide down into the dip, where he met her and took her into his arms.

A scrabbling brought an eager third party.

"Down," Robin said.

A whine.

"I have never allowed a dog in my bed, you little pest, and will not start now. Get down."

Petra thought reason couldn't work, but perhaps it was tone. She heard a rustling of the quilt, then claws on the wooden floor.

"She's probably sleeping in my coat, damn her," he said, but without heat.

She loves you, Petra thought, but managed to keep that to herself. But, oh, she shouldn't be here in his arms. He might be able to control himself, but she wasn't sure she could.

"Wasn't this where we were on the ship?" she asked, inhaling his smell, absorbing his warmth.

"Trust me."

Petra sent up a prayer that she could trust herself. Again she tried to sleep. Again she failed.

"Are you awake?" she asked softly.

"Yes."

"If not for me, where would you be going now?"

"To London," he said. "You see, you've only taken me a little out of my way."

"That dirty place everyone escapes in summer?"

"It's also the hub of all roads. I have to go through it to get to Huntingdon, but I have a few small matters to take care of there. If you think Riddlesome is there or at Richmond Lodge, it will be easy to check."

"From what you said, I doubt it."

His hand moved on her shoulder. She knew it was his instinct to stroke, to comfort. He instantly stopped. His careful control could break her heart.

"I know you're even less likely to trust me with your father's name now," he said, "but there are some very bad men among the peerage."

"I know. In Italy, too."

"If he's vile or doesn't acknowledge you, what will you do?"

"Go to Teresa Imer. To Mistress Cornelys. Perhaps I can be of some use to her."

"I shudder to think. Please, Petra, allow me to find you a safe place. My mother would take you under her wing, for your religion if for no other reason."

Petra might have truly shuddered. Live on the fringes of Robin's life as he went on his way, enjoying loose ladies and eventually marrying a tight one. Tight? That didn't seem quite the right word.

"Petra?"

"We'll see," she said, deliberately echoing him.

"I see," he replied wryly.

"Robin, why should your mother welcome a young woman of scandalous background who's dragged her son into mishap and danger? I'm Cock Robin's sparrow, aren't I?"

"I'll keep bows and arrows out of reach. Go to sleep. All will be well. I'll make sure of it."

He fell asleep, but Petra lay a little longer, pressed close to him, before easing apart and back to her safer edge. She tried to stay awake, to be on guard, but sleep sucked her down.

Robin wasn't asleep, so he knew when she moved apart. Was he imagining reluctance? At least she hadn't wanted lovemaking. He hadn't thought it likely, but the prospect had worried him. He knew no gracious way to handle a situation like this. He wanted to blow his brains out over that one word.

Coquette tried her luck again, leaping up and wriggling under his hand. He let her stay. He needed some loving comfort. But then he remembered stroking Petra after that disaster. The elegant pleasuring of women had been part of his education, and it included attention to their feelings and their dignity. "A gentleman should be a gentleman in every part of life" had been his father's dictum. Whore, duchess, or merry widow, there must be courtesy and mutual delights—and a disciplined avoidance of disasters.

"Disaster" was too tame a word for his current predicament. He was tempted to avoid Thorn for fear of his opinion, but he needed to get Petra into protection as soon as possible. He could leave her at Ithorne, however, on the excuse of racing up to London to make sure Powick and Fontaine were safe. And everyone else at his London house, he supposed.

Yes, he'd do that, and now he'd stay awake to be sure Josh Fletcher didn't creep up here with a bread knife. Or Varzi appear, torture implements in hand . . .

"Mr. Bonchurch?"

It took Robin a moment to realize that was him, and that, plague take it, he'd fallen asleep after all. But it was morning and they'd survived. And Josh Fletcher was calling him from downstairs.

"Yes," Robin called back, sitting up, easing an ache in his back.

"You need to be down, sir, if you want a bite before setting off."

"Thank you."

Robin turned, but Petra was already out of bed, her back to him. She, too, stretched, arching with her hands in her back. Robin's mouth dried at the sinuous beauty of her in morning light. Her simple gown did nothing to hide the lines of her body, and above the neckline he could see the fine bones of her neck and the beginning of the long indent of her spine.

She bent to pick up her shoes, and his mouth watered at her natural grace. . . .

He dragged his eyes and mind away, turned, and pulled on his boots, forcing his mind to practical matters—ways to persuade her to let him help her.

He wanted her, though, in more ways than the physical. He'd fight armies to possess her.

But a part of him wanted to escape the chaos she brought, to get back to carefree days. It had been a terrible year. The shock of his father's death had crushed the whole family—his mother, his two brothers and two sisters, aunts and uncles, servants, tenants. . . . A vital, respected, beloved man gone in a week from a neglected gash from a bull he'd been admiring at the local fair.

He realized he was just sitting there and rose to stamp his boots into place. He'd pulled everything together again. The world was more or less turning in the right direction. He'd played the earl at court and in parliament, and then plunged into summer amusements.

And now this.

Coquette was quivering at the edge of the ladder, impatient to go outside and piss. That was a simple matter, easily solved. He put on his sword and heavy coat and found Petra ready, too. Why had he bought her a dark red cloak? Because he'd known how magnificently it would suit her.

He scooped up the dog and went down, turning at the bottom to offer assistance. She was already following without help. Wise woman. That's the way it should be.

Chapter 18

They followed noises to the room at the back—a beam-ceilinged kitchen with a bed alcove at one side. When asked, the pipe-smoking Fletcher directed them outside to a privy. When they returned, Robin asked for a bowl of water for his dog, and some scraps of meat if there were any.

Fletcher's jaw dropped at the sight of Coquette, and Robin knew he'd mutated from puzzling to a proper strange 'un. He and Petra shared a simple breakfast of ale, bread, and pickled herring. Robin offended his own code by not assisting Petra to sit, but when she sipped from her pot and pulled a face, he said, "Do you have any small beer, sir? My sister doesn't care for ale."

Fletcher looked at her with disapproval, but he took a tankard into the taproom and came back with some. Petra gave the man one of her smiles, and the smuggler might even have blushed.

"Well, then, strong ale's not to everyone's taste," he said. "I hope that suits you better, Miss Bonchurch."

"Yes, thank you."

She bewitched every man she met. That, too, would make a devilish wife.

"Have to be off," Fletcher said. "Dan wants an

early start." Because he was transporting the illegal cargo from the *Courlis,* Robin assumed. It would crown all to be taken up for smuggling, but at least here he had only to wave his title to get off most hooks.

Fletcher led the way out by a back door that led to a lane. "You be going all the way to Ashford, sir?"

"I don't think so," Robin said. "I'm for Stowting. I've a friend there."

"Dan can only take you partway, then."

They were climbing, for the town was built up a hill. Robin looked back at the sea, softly magical in the misty, predawn light. The town still slept, but some fishermen were active in the harbor, preparing boats and nets.

They turned down another lane to where a man as sinewy and ruddy-faced as his brother waited by a plain cart holding only a few sacks and drawn by a swaybacked horse. Words were apparently rationed between the brothers, for the exchange went:

"Stowting."

"Westerhanger, then. Why Stowting?"

"Friend."

"What's the animal?"

"Dog. He says."

"Rum 'un. I'll be off, then."

Dan Fletcher climbed into the seat and merely waited.

Robin helped Petra up into the empty back and joined her, putting Coquette down to run around. She sniffed along a plank, doubtless smelling something interesting beneath the false bottom. They both thanked Josh Fletcher, and the cart rattled off out of town.

They soon passed a signpost: ASHFORD 11 MILES, LONDON 70. Another finger pointed to CANTERBURY, 10 MILES, and another to DOVER, 8.

"Powick and Fontaine should be well on their way to London by now," he said. "There are coaches that meet the packet."

"With Varzi and his man in pursuit," she said.

"They'll be all right in public. I'd forgotten how rough a ride one gets in a cart, though. I promise you the comfort of springs soon."

"Promises," she said, "always promises." Then she looked surprised at herself for making a joke. She blushed a little and looked around. "It's a pretty morning."

"Kent's a pretty county."

"The light is beautiful, and the birds seem to be caroling it."

The sun had risen, turning the sky pink and red, and from the high ground they had a grand view. The dawn chorus wasn't deafening now as it would be in spring, but enough songbirds greeted the day to provide a show, and gulls were calling as they swooped over the sea.

"Welcome to England," he said, wanting to be her guide to every part of it.

The best he could do was identify some birdsong and some trees that were strange to her, and share her delight in a couple of rabbits hopping across the road as they rolled along.

"Halt."

Robin looked around, astonished. Yes, a rider really had just emerged from a stand of trees to point two pistols at them. A highwayman in broad daylight?

"What the . . . ?" Dan Fletcher said, stopping the cart and staring, too.

For a moment Robin thought it might be Thorn playing some trick, but then he recognized Varzi's man.

"What th'hell do you think you're doing?" Dan Fletcher shouted, shaking a fist. "Get on with you!"

"I am relieving you of your passengers," the Italian said. "Make no difficulty."

Petra seemed frozen, but beneath the concealment of the side of the cart she'd pulled one of Robin's pistols out of his pocket.

Where was Varzi?

Heart pounding, Robin calculated the odds, knowing he faced likely death. Hell and damnation, but he had no choice. He turned to kneel as if simply facing the man, taking out his other pistol to put on the cart floor. He could only hope Petra had the courage to use them.

"Us?" he asked blankly, loosening his sword. "What do you want?"

Cold, dark eyes fixed on him. "Play no games, sir. I will take the *contessina* and leave you in peace."

Contessina.

Robin put that aside for now. His only advantage was surprise, so he surged up and vaulted out of the cart, drawing his sword as soon as his feet hit the ground. He ducked to his left, hearing a pistol crack and then the ball splintering into the cart behind him. Damn, he should have told Petra to stay down.

Dan Fletcher yelled something, but Robin was sprinting straight for the horse.

An explosion hammered from behind. Petra had

fired. God alone knew where the ball went, but it startled the Italian enough that his second shot went wild. The man leapt off his wild-eyed horse, his rapier screaming out of its scabbard to send a thrust right at Robin's heart.

Robin parried it easily, but everything was clear now.

This was to the death.

A light, almost a fire, in the man's eyes said he was a true swordsman who loved to fight and doubtless did it frequently. Robin loved it, too, but he'd never fought other than for sport.

The Italian knew it. He drew back, showing big white teeth between red lips. "You don't have to die for this, signor. What is she to you?"

Robin attacked with a classic pattern to disarm. It was countered, but the man stopped smiling.

"What is she to *you*?" Robin asked, then tried another pattern. He had to think of this as a bout at Angelo's. It was the only way.

"A rich prize," the man said, again countering in an equally classic way. "Give her up."

Robin was sure the man knew many ways to fight outside the rules and would use them. For now he was giving Robin time to think, to accept defeat. Varzi's way seemed to be "Create no more of a problem than one must."

Robin also knew some ways to fight outside the rules. He enjoyed training with a man called Fitzroger, an interesting friend of a friend, and had learned a lot, but he didn't fool himself that he was in this man's class. He was good; among his friends, he was considered very good, but he wasn't a professional.

He had no damn choice, however. "She goes nowhere unwillingly," he said, and attacked suddenly with an unconventional move, and was rewarded by his opponent's switch to deadly seriousness. They fought fast and furiously then, and he held his own.

But he wasn't good enough.

He knew it.

Chapter 19

Petra crouched in the cart, the second pistol in hand, praying for a clear shot. Her first had been wild, a distraction, but this time she'd kill the monster dead, dead, dead—if only she had a clear shot. She wasn't good enough to risk firing with Robin partly in the way or even close by.

She was shaking, too. She'd never seen a serious swordfight before. The weapons clashed and whirled in the rising sunlight. Hard bodies lunged and twisted in moves she was sure weren't found in any book of duello. Varzi's man tried to trip Robin. Robin recovered and hammered at the man's face with his pommel. It was only just avoided.

Death was often only an inch away.

Robin, sweet Robin, Cock Robin, was fighting well, but he didn't have the skill and experience of Varzi's man, and she didn't have a clear shot. Coquette was at the back edge of the cart, yapping in distress. Heaven knows where Dan Fletcher was. Perhaps the attacker's second shot had struck him.

It was up to her.

Saint Peter and Saint Veronica, aid us both. This isn't fair!

She gasped when a blade slashed Robin's coat
sleeve. Had it slashed flesh? No, he didn't seem affected. Varzi's man had a swelling bruise on his temple, but had escaped the worst of Robin's blow. Both
were breathing hard and probably hampered by boots
and coats. They drove each other up and down the
road. Petra braced the pistol on the rim of the cart,
sighting carefully, but they moved so fast and she
couldn't risk wasting her only shot. At one point the
Italian twirled, slashing backward, almost catching
Robin unawares.

White flashed.

Coquette! How had she managed the jump down?
But there she was, yapping and snapping at the boots
of the man who attacked her beloved master. With an
evil grin, the man moved to spear her.

Robin beat his blade aside and thrust—right
through the man's shoulder.

Petra leapt up with a cry of victory, but even as
Robin wrenched his blade free and the blood ran, the
man tossed his sword into his left hand and slashed
Robin's thigh.

Robin staggered, his leg buckling. The Italian
jabbed at his shoulder as if trying to repay the wound.
Robin caught the blade on his hilt and pushed it aside,
but he was unsteady now. Petra remembered her pistol and raised it two-handed, knowing she had to fire.

But Dan Fletcher appeared then, running up behind
the Italian with a bludgeon in his hand. He smashed
it into the man's head and the Italian cried out, then
crumpled to the ground.

Petra simply stared for a moment, but then she remembered to uncock her pistol before discarding it
and running to support Robin, whose leg was pouring

blood. "Sit down, sit down!" she cried, arm around him. "How bad is it?"

"If I sit, I'll never get up," Robin muttered, pale and heaving for breath. "Damn Varzi to the lowest depths of hell. Is he the devil incarnate? Where is he? Where?"

He was trying to stay on guard.

"Not here, I'm sure of it, or you'd be dead. Come lean on the cart, then. Mr. Fletcher, your help, please." Coquette was frantic, so Petra scooped her up one-handed and exchanged her for the bloody sword. Robin, despite pain and exhaustion, found strength to soothe and praise the little creature.

Oh, sweet saints in heaven, how could she bear to leave this man? He'd fought for her, risked death for her, been wounded for her. She helped support him to the back of the cart and put the sword on the cart bed. Then she knelt to press her hand over the bleeding wound. "It's not gushing, thank God, so you won't die of it, but I need a bandage. I can't use my petticoat with an open gown."

"My shirt," he said. "But someone should tie up that man before he comes round."

"Likely he's dead," Dan Fletcher said. "I bloody well hope so. But I'll check."

Robin put Coquette in the cart and took off his coat. Petra watched Dan Fletcher go to the fallen man, cudgel in hand, and stir him with his boot. "Dead all right," he said, and came back.

Petra had seen death before, but not so suddenly and violently.

"Petra?"

She looked up to see that Robin was naked from

the waist up, which did nothing for her spinning head. She hastily took the shirt and tried to tear it, but the hems and seams were too strong and there were no weak spots in the expensive linen.

"Knife," she muttered, raising her skirt, trying to keep up the pressure on the wound. But of course both knife and sheath were gone. She caught Robin staring and let her skirt drop. "Mr. Fletcher! I need you to cut up this shirt."

The man appeared, a big knife in his hand, and made short work of it. "Nasty furrin' type," he muttered.

Petra hoped he didn't think her foreign, and pressed a pad of cloth over the wound. She used long lengths of sleeve to bind it tightly. How to fix it? She wiped her hands on the bandage, then pulled out the sapphire-and-pearl pin and used that. She watched the wound for a minute or two, but the bandages didn't soak with blood.

She rose, blowing out a breath. "It will be all right for now, I think, but you need a bed and a doctor. How far to Stowting?" she asked Mr. Fletcher.

"Eight miles or so."

"He shouldn't be bounced along that far."

"You'd be right there, ma'am. My niece Sarey's place b'ain't far."

"I am here," Robin said in a teeth-gritted tone, "and freezing. Pass me my coat, if you please."

Fletcher did, and Robin put it on, but a long, lean, muscular stretch of chest still sucked at Petra's attention. She gave in to temptation and touched him there. "I need to see whether you're really cold," she said. "No, but your heart's fast."

"Hardly surprising," he murmured. Their eyes met, and perhaps he was capable of lust even when wounded, the impossible rake.

Petra took her hand away. "Are we still in danger here?" she asked softly in French.

He replied in English. "No point in keeping secrets from Mr. Fletcher, my dear. My apologies for putting you in danger, sir, but I had no idea they would find us here."

"They?" the man asked, looking around, but he didn't sound afraid so much as alert. A smuggler's brother, after all.

"Only one here, I think." Robin quickly gave Fletcher the sister-nun story.

But the man eyed them. "Begging your pardon, sir, but it don't seem to me as you two treat one another as sister and brother. Wouldn't say as the lady was even English, if it comes to that."

Robin looked at Petra, seeming at a loss for once.

"You're correct," she said with a rueful smile. "In truth, I am Italian, and Robin and I eloped. My family has sent people after us. Ruthless people, as you see."

"Ah," the man said. "And you're a *contessina,* are you? Sounds important, that."

Always a mistake to think country people stupid.

"It is," Robin said. "Are you still willing to help us?"

"Don't see why not, sir. Just like to know what I'm dealing with. So you reckon that 'un was alone?"

"Yes."

"Then let's get you up into the cart."

When Robin, pale and breathing hard, was in the cart, his bandaged leg straight out, he said, "What about the body?"

"I'll just roll it out of sight for now," Dan Fletcher

said and did so, scuffing away any blood at the same time. He climbed back onto the seat and clicked the horse into motion. "Be a rough few minutes, sir."

They jolted off. Robin gritted his teeth and endured.

"I'm sorry for not firing," Petra said. "I was afraid I'd hit you."

"Your first shot startled him."

"But you're wounded."

"It's a scratch."

"It is not. It could fester—"

He closed his eyes. "Petra, that doesn't help."

He was so pale now. "Very well, very well. Don't worry about anything. I'll take care of you."

His lips twitched. "Isn't that my part in this play?"

"Be quiet."

He hissed at a particularly sharp jolt, and she checked the bandage again. Some red blood showed.

"They must have split forces," he muttered. "I should have anticipated that. Varzi had time to think on the voyage. If we'd taken another ship, we wouldn't have to go to Dover, so he sent his man to watch the road out of the nearest alternative port. Plague take it, I feel so stupid."

She squeezed his hand. "I didn't think of it, either."

"But you're the damsel and I'm the knight errant."

"Robin!" But then she said, "I know, I know, it's your way." She had to say it, though she knew she shouldn't. "You do have a temperament that I could like."

He smiled ruefully into her eyes until another jolt made him wince. "Fencing is much more enjoyable at Angelo's."

She didn't know exactly what he meant, but knew it was a joke of sorts.

"I have a very sorry record," he said. "Thus far, you've saved me from having my throat cut, rescued yourself from Varzi's man, and are now stopping me from bleeding to death. I only survived that encounter back there with Coquette and Fletcher's help."

"Nonsense. Without you I'd be that man's prisoner, and without you neither Coquette nor Fletcher could have done anything. The way you leapt out of the cart was brilliant. You took him completely unawares. Now be quiet and let me take care of you."

"As my lady commands," he said, and shut his eyes.

The last bit, down a rough lane, was the worst, and Petra breathed a prayer of thanks when they lurched into a farmyard and stopped. The bandage was now mostly red, and she was applying pressure again.

A black-and-white dog raced out barking. A trim young woman grasped its collar and called, "What're you doing here, Uncle Dan?"

"On my way to Ashford," he said, climbing down. "Had a bit of bother."

"There's a surprise. Custom's men?"

"Nay. Taking this couple to Westerhanger and we was held up by a highwayman."

"Dan Fletcher, talk sense!"

"I am. Clear as day, he was. Furriner, too."

"Where is he, then?"

"Dead. I tucked him out of sight."

The woman rolled her eyes, but didn't seem shocked.

A young man came to the door of a shed in shirt-sleeves. "What's up, Sarey? Uncle Dan?" he added in surprise.

Dan gave the story again, then introduced Robin

and Petra to Tom and Sarah Gainer. Two young children came to the farmhouse door to gape, soon joined by an older girl. A lad of about twelve ran from somewhere, excited by a change from routine. The whole family was brown-haired, fair-skinned, and robust.

Mistress Gainer had come over to the cart. When she saw the bandage on Robin's leg, she exclaimed, "Lawks! Get him inside, you dolts. Kit, ride Maisie to the doctor."

"No doctor," Robin said sharply.

"But, sir—"

"He's likely right, lass," Dan Fletcher said. "Don't want questions asked."

Certainly the smugglers wouldn't want scrutiny, nor did Robin. He and Petra had just landed illegally, after all.

"It's a simple wound," Robin said.

Petra didn't argue at this point. When she'd seen it, she'd decide.

The two men carried Robin into the house in a hand cradle. He was silent, but it clearly hurt. All the way Mistress Gaines exclaimed, "Highwaymen? In broad daylight? Well, I never! What's the world coming to?"

Inside the house she rushed ahead to throw a rough cloth over a bed, and then Robin was eased onto it with bolsters behind so he could sit up. He was still carrying Coquette, who now wriggled free to sniff at his bloody bandage.

"What on earth is that?" the farmer's wife cried, reaching for a stick.

"A heroine," Robin said, stroking her. Always stroking.

"A what?"

"A dog," he said. "Small but brave. She risked her life for me."

"A rat could eat that," Mistress Gainer said, unimpressed.

The farmhouse dog had come with them and was staring at Coquette as if recognizing something that called itself dog, and even female dog, without the slightest idea what to do about it.

Mistress Gainer shooed her dog out. "So you fought a highwayman, sir. What a turn."

"Not quite a highwayman," said Dan Fletcher, standing hat off by the door. "Seems as these two are eloping, and he was one as wanted her back. Back to Italy."

"Italy! Well, I never. Proper wicked that be, coming over here to make trouble."

"I'm sorry," Petra said.

"Oh, not you, ma'am. But are you Papist, then?"

She might as well have said *Might you be carrying the plague?* "Not now," Petra lied.

"Ah, that's good. You off, then, Dan?"

"Can't linger. Seems as if there was only one, but tell Tom to keep an eye out."

Robin asked, "Will there be trouble with the magistrates? I've no mind to be delayed here, and I've no wish to make trouble for you."

"No need for them to know anything about it, sir." The man touched his head in a kind of salute.

"Wait," Robin said, and twisted to dig out money, gritting his teeth.

"Stop that." Petra hurried to his side, but she hadn't thought what sliding her hand into his deep pocket would mean. Heat rushed to her cheeks as she dug for the coins there, and his breeches bulged. She heard their hostess choke on a laugh.

Robin might even be blushing as he took the coins she found. He offered Fletcher a guinea. "Poor payment for my life, sir. Thank you."

"Thank you, sir, but you held your own. Never seen fighting like that before, I ain't. Don't care if I never see the like again. God save you, sir." He touched his head again and left. Soon hooves plodded away.

"I have to help with the milking," Mistress Gainer said. Her husband had already left. "Can you see to his leg, ma'am?"

"Yes, of course."

"I'll get you some rags, hot water, and salve, then."

"Thank you for your kindness, ma'am," Robin said, showing dimples. The woman went pink. She might be a decent wife and mother, but she wasn't immune to his charm.

"Go on with you," she said, and bustled off.

Petra soon had a bowl of hot water, some clean rags, and a pot of green salve. She took out the jeweled pin, set it aside, and then unwound the bloody bandages, but the pad was stuck. She soaked it, but had to rip the last bit off.

"Plague take it!" he cursed.

"The wound has to be opened," she said, peering at it and watching the new flow of blood. She pressed the pad down again, and the bleeding slowed. "Good." She straightened. "Now to get your breeches off so I can dress it properly."

"Saucy wench."

Their eyes met and a humor danced between them that was miraculous. The dark, tumultuous night seemed like a different world to this sunlit room, and they different people. Desire still wove around them, but now it was decent, civilized, and under control.

First they managed the tricky business of removing his boots. When that was done, Petra helped him to his feet, where he used the head of the bed for balance. She knelt to unfasten the buttons at the knees of his breeches while he undid the top, so she could then ease the breeches down. Thank heavens he was wearing drawers, but even so her hands tingled and felt hot. Perhaps not so perfectly under control.

She rolled down his stockings and tossed them aside, refusing to admire his legs and feet, and settled him on the bed again so she could check the wound. It oozed blood, but not too badly. He was pale, but when he looked at her from under heavy lids, heat wavered in the air.

She picked up the big pair of shears that Mistress Gainer had provided. "Your drawers are blood soaked."

He smiled. "This could get interesting."

"I'll just cut them on one side."

"I don't mind being naked for the cause."

"Behave yourself."

"I never have yet." But she saw him remember, remember disaster and the necessity of control. He turned his head to look at a wall.

Chapter 20

Petra blinked away tears and set to snipping up the bloody side of his underwear, trying to ignore the way his perfectly formed body was gilded by warm morning sunshine. Outside a cow lowed, crows called their harsh cries, but nearer, sweeter birds sang. Petra could easily imagine dropping the shears and lying down on the bed with him, cuddling close against that chest to simply enjoy country peace.

Coquette leapt back up onto Robin. The dog wasn't capable of a glare, but was trying.

"The butterfly of wisdom are you?" Petra murmured.

Robin turned. "What?"

"Nothing." She completed the destruction of his drawers and focused on the wound.

The sword had been sharp, which was good. The long cut was clean edged, but she couldn't tell if a muscle had been badly affected. She began to clean the cut carefully. "It does need a doctor, I think."

"Not here. We need to move on."

Mistress Gainer returned with a tray. "We're sitting to breakfast and I've brought you tea and eggs, sir." She stopped dead. "My, you're a fine one."

"Thank you," Robin said, laughing. "And you're both pretty and kind, Mistress Gainer."

"Go on with you," she said, putting the tray down beside him on the bed, still enjoying the view without a trace of shame.

"Of your kindness, ma'am, can a message be sent to my friend?"

"The one at Stowting?"

"That's right. At the Black Swan Inn there. He'll take us off your hands."

"You're no trouble, I'm sure, sir, but after breakfast, Kit can ride there. As good as a holiday, this is to him."

She left, and while Robin ate, Petra washed his leg, clinging to sanity by a thread. When she'd finished, the bowl was a dark brown.

"You lost a lot of blood."

"Perhaps that's why I'm lightheaded."

She looked at him sharply, but his face went blank. She stretched the wound open a little. He inhaled and tensed, but didn't protest.

"The blade was sharp," she said, "so chances are good that nothing went in. Blunt weapons and pistol balls are far worse." She decided not to use the unfamiliar salve and bound the wound up again using the cleaner parts of his shirt and Mistress Gainer's rags.

She rose and frowned at his expression. "Are you in a lot of pain?"

"No."

"Are you wounded anywhere else?"

He spread his hands, a teacup in one. "Do you see any other wounds?"

She made herself look. She even dug her fingers into his hair to feel his scalp.

He suddenly relaxed. "That's very soothing."

She knew it was, so she massaged his head, looking down at him, able to relax herself now she was out of his line of sight. She could show her love through the gentle work of her hands.

She loved him. She'd suspected it earlier, but it had become absolute during the fight, because he'd been outmatched but fought to defend her, anyway, and fought well. He was so different from the man she'd first thought him to be.

She laughed softly. His silly dog was on his lap, being lovingly caressed.

"What?" he asked, unstirring.

"I stroke you, you stroke Coquette."

"Come lie in my lap and I'll stroke you instead."

She closed her eyes for a moment and then drew back. "Coquette, remind him of all the reasons that would be a very bad idea. I'm going to get rid of the dirty water and enjoy some fresh air."

She passed through the kitchen, where the family ate, and tossed the water onto the ground, and then simply stood, firming her resolve. He was not for her.

She returned to the house to find the husband and lad had gone about their business. Mistress Gainer and her older daughter were washing dishes, and the two littler ones were playing with a cat. This was a pleasant reminder that happy homes existed. Petra could wish to live like this, but even after her years as a sister, she didn't feel part of this simple world.

"Sit you down, ma'am," Mistress Gainer said, drying her hands on her apron. "Take a bite of breakfast."

Petra sat, knowing it was best to avoid Robin for a while.

"Beer, ma'am? Or there's fresh milk."

"Milk, please."

"Help yourself to the rest."

The rest was a brown country loaf, butter, and plum jam. It was delicious.

"That's a fine, handsome man you have," Mistress Gaines said with a grin. "No wonder you ran off with him."

Petra could only say, "Yes," knowing she was blushing.

"A cocky sort, though. You'll have your hands full, that's for sure."

"Cocky?" Petra asked, wondering if the woman knew Robin's name.

"Like a cock. Full of himself. Ruling the roost." She took down a big pottery bowl and began scooping in flour from a bin.

"Yes, that is how he is," Petra said, remembering when she had thought that about him. Now Robin Bonchurch was much more than that to her.

"And a terrible flirt, I'll be bound."

"He's a very good flirt," Petra protested, and the woman laughed.

"You're a one." A foaming bowl was tipped into the flour along with more water. She was making bread. "Where did you meet him, then?"

If she was going to lie, she might as well lie grandly. "At a masquerade in Venice."

"Oooh, you mean people all in costumes, like a mummers' play?"

Petra had no idea what a mummers' play was, but she said, "Yes. Your closest friend could pass by and you'd not know them."

As Mistress Gainer worked her dough, she and

Petra talked about men and courtship as if they were two ordinary women. When talk turned to where she and Robin would live, however, Petra stood. If she followed this fancy too far she could tumble right into it.

"I must see how he is. And he will be wanting to send a message to his friend."

"Oh, right. Sukey, go and find Kit."

Her daughter ran off, and Petra hurried into the bedroom, but there she found Robin fast asleep on his bolsters. She paused to delight in his elegance, even in complete relaxation. And in his beauty, as he was almost entirely naked. His hand rested on Coquette, who lay on guard.

"Papillon couche," Petra said with a smile.

There was a spare quilt on a chest. She picked it up and spread it over him, leaving hand and dog uncovered, but then she touched his cheek with the back of her fingers to be sure he wasn't fevered. He wasn't, but he rolled his head toward her touch and murmured something. She left her hand there for another moment, then found the strength to step away.

She had the perfect opportunity to escape. She would send the note to Captain Rose and then leave. But she needed paper. Robin had a leather notebook. She found it in his left coat pocket, a pencil attached in a slender sheath. When she opened it, however, she found it wasn't simply a journal or a source of paper for hasty letters; it was a kind of keepsake in which people had written notes to him.

On the first page she read: *To my darling Robin. Fly, my dear, but not too high. Maman.* The writing was elaborately decorative, and the page was illustrated with flying birds. Petra felt some sympathy with the worried mother of such a bird. She probably shouldn't read more, but she couldn't resist. Contributors had chosen whatever page they wished, so she had to go partway through the book to find the next.

My prayers go with you always. Lacy. She wondered who'd contributed that message, decorated with ribbons and flowers. Perhaps he had a sister. It hurt that she didn't know.

On another page someone had simply scrawled, *Magnifique! Clarisse.*

That wasn't from a family member.

You're a monster. I hate you. Return to me soon or I will die! That was signed only *L.*

She shot a dark look at the rake on the bed, but any glower melted into a sigh. No wonder women desired him so, and no wonder some simply cared. He was such a kind and generous man.

Too generous with his favors, she told herself, and looked for a blank page. Any number had been cut out, so she wouldn't feel guilty for doing the same. Then another page of writing caught her attention. No illustrations here, but a lot of words.

Dated, the third day of January, the year of the Lord, 1760.

Be it resolved that young men should never marry. Therefore, we stalwart bachelors do hereby decree a penalty to be paid by any of us who succumbs to that unholy state from this day forth until he achieve the age of thirty. The penalty for failure shall be one thousand guineas donated to Lady Fowler's Fund for the Moral Reform of Society.

This was signed in three different hands: Sparrow, Rose, and Pagan. Petra recognized Robin's neat, elegant writing in Sparrow. Cock Robin's murderer. Why take that name?

Rose? That was the smuggler. Not surprising if he wished to conceal his real name.

Pagan? She couldn't imagine how anyone came to be called that, even in fun.

Here, however, was proof of Robin Bonchurch's determination not to marry. If she should turn out to be carrying his child?

Perhaps she'd never let him know. She'd have no marriage of obligation, and, heavens, she wasn't even sure who he was or how he made his living. She did know he was an inveterate philanderer who'd make a terrible husband, especially if forced to it.

She chose a blank page and wrote to Captain Rose, emphasizing the urgent need of care. She tore out that sheet, folded it, and wrote the address Robin had mentioned—the Black Swan Inn, Stowting. She had no scaling wax, but nothing in the note was private.

She stared at the next blank page, then gave in and wrote, *Thank you, Cock Robin. May God bless you always, P.* Despairing at herself, she added, *Please listen to your mother and stay safe.*

She put the book on the little table by the bed, the pencil marking that page, then picked up her cloak. She saw the cameo at the neck. She should leave it, but she needed a means to fasten the cloak. She considered the pearl-and-sapphire pin. One day soon she might need the price of it, but it was too fine a piece. It would raise suspicions.

Money. Apart from her concealed guineas, she had little. She hardened herself and went through his breeches' pocket, remembering the last time, then pushing the memory away. She took out some coins and chose the smaller ones. A venal sin rather than a mortal?

Among the coins was that ring. She studied it again in the light. The complex letter certainly wasn't a B. An A or an H. Just possibly an N. It was, however, the sort of signet passed down through a family of importance.

He was a man of substance and had done his best to hide it from her. That was yet more proof that for all his charms, Robin Bonchurch wasn't a man to truly trust.

When she put the stolen coins into her right-hand pocket, she touched her cross and rosary. She took them out, considered them, and then put them in Robin's coat pocket. A strange and probably unwanted gift, but it was all she had to give.

Coquette was still watching alertly, but made no objection to larceny. Petra would miss the pretty creature and blew a kiss to the dog. If it went just a little off target . . . well, what of it?

Now all she needed to do was give the note to the boy, who'd take it to Stowting, and then she would slip away and disappear.

She went to the door but halted. What if Rose wasn't there? Or what if something went amiss with the note? She'd be abandoning Robin here, defenseless, for why should these people put themselves at risk? By tomorrow Varzi could be here, searching for his man, seeking news of stray travelers. If he found Robin here and her gone, he might kill him in vicious reparation.

Yet she *must* escape. If she stayed she was in great

peril of sinning again. What was more, she couldn't
imagine her father's reaction if she turned up at his
door in the company of an out-and-out rake. No matter who Robin really was, she was sure his nature
was well known. Robin, however, would never let her
go alone.

She considered and came up with a plan.

She sent the note with the lad, Kit, who rode off
happily on the round-barreled horse. Then she waited
for the right moment and slipped out of the farmhouse. She walked to the road and looked for a hiding
place. She found a stile nearby and settled on the
other side of the hedge to wait, praying that Robin
wouldn't wake up before his friend arrived.

Then, with any luck, they'd assume she'd left long
before, and if they searched, they'd search onward.
She was going to set off along the footpath marked
by the stile and hope to be well out of their way. It
would break her heart, but it would be for the best.

Chapter 21

R obin woke to a deep voice drawling, "What have you been up to now, you madman?"

"Thorn?" he asked, opening his eyes, but only slowly recollecting events. He moved, winced as pain shot up his leg, but then grinned. "Thank heaven and hell. Help has arrived."

"It certainly has," the Duke of Ithorne said, sinking onto a chair that an awestruck Mistress Gainer had just pushed up to the bed. He turned and thanked her, which made her blush. Presumably he was here as plain Captain Rose, but still they swooned.

He was dark-haired and his love of sailing meant his skin was always brown. In addition, his features were strong rather than fine, so he was never described as handsome, but somehow women never noticed. Like Robin he wore his own hair, but Thorn's was neatly confined and staying there, and his buckskin breeches, plain brown coat, and neckcloth were impeccably neat. It was most annoying, but now he was a blessing.

"How did you get here?" Robin asked.

"By coach?"

"I mean, how did you know?"

"Captain Rose received a letter. How did you get wounded?" But then Thorn stared. "What," he asked, "is *that*?"

Coquette had risen from her place by Robin's arm to stare at him.

"The latest thing in guard dogs."

"It certainly scares me." Thorn took out a gold quizzing glass to inspect the dog, then shook his head. "No wonder someone got away with sticking a sword into you. Will it grow?"

"I fear not."

Thorn tucked away the glass. "I thought not. She's one of those idiotic papillons they favor at the French court. What possessed you?"

"A whim—what else?" Robin said, hitching himself up to a sitting position, cursing as his leg pulled. "How long have you been here? Has Petra told the tale?"

"Petra?"

"Mrs. Bonchurch, then."

"My dear Robin, did you suffer a blow to the head?"

Robin looked over at the hovering woman. "Where's my wife?"

"Wife?" echoed Thorn.

"Why, I'm not sure, sir. We was just wondering that. She seems to have wandered off somewhere."

Robin began to struggle off the bed, cursing women and pain. Thorn stopped him. "Decency, old fellow."

Robin realized he wore only his drawers, and they weren't whole. He looked at Mistress Gainer. "Please, ma'am, can you find me something to wear? Anything."

The woman hurried off, while Thorn rose to pick up the bloody, slashed breeches between finger and thumb. He dropped them again and asked, "It truly is only a slash?"

"So I gather."

"May I inspect?"

"Please do."

Behind the laconic words lurked the fact that Robin's father had died of a minor wound turned poisonous. A gash from a farm animal, and thus dirtier, but he'd received the best treatment. And died.

Thorn folded back the quilt and leaned closer. "It looks well bandaged. No sign of redness or smell."

"It's early for that."

"True." He flipped the quilt back. "We'll have the doctor see to it at Ithorne. What happened to your shirt?"

"Bandage."

"Ah. The absent Petra?"

"Yes. Damnation, get off after her, will you?"

"Where? And no. I'm getting you to Ithorne and a doctor first."

Robin cursed him, but he knew Thorn in this mood. "Are my waistcoat and coat wearable?"

Thorn tossed over the waistcoat, but when he picked up the coat he paused and pulled a pistol out of each pocket. He checked each to be sure it wasn't cocked. "One discharged? I thought it was a sword wound."

"Petra fired."

"Robin, Robin . . ." Thorn shook his head and passed over the coat. Robin felt something else in one pocket. He pulled out a rosary.

"Never say you've turned Papist!"

"No." Robin found a wooden cross, as well. After a moment, he pushed them back, but he'd seen his notebook. "Pass me that."

Thorn did, and Robin read the marked page. "The woman is insane. She can't possibly survive alone in England." He struggled into his waistcoat, then his coat.

Thorn read the few words. "Perhaps you should tell me who she is?"

"Not sure I know. Sister Immaculata of the order of Saint Veronica. Petra d'Averio . . . no, I forget. *Contessina* Petra d'Averio." Stifling a curse at the pain, he swung his leg so he could sit on the side of the bed. "Or *contessina* someone-else-entirely, but she's mine to take care of. Until she finds her mythical father, that is. Plague take it, where's that woman with some clothes?"

Thorn put his hand on Robin's forehead as if checking for fever. Robin dashed it away so Thorn said, "Toga," and helped Robin to his feet. He pulled the sheet free and wrapped it around him.

"Wife?" he asked again.

"We merely pretended to be married."

"Bonchurch?" But then Thorn said, "I suppose it was your name du jour. Good and holy?" He rolled his eyes.

"You've been known to travel as Captain Rose."

"But I, my dear fellow, am a duke."

Mistress Gainer returned then, some garments in her arms. Robin didn't want to delay even long enough to put them on. He sent her his most charming smile. "No need to deprive your husband, ma'am. If you will just allow me to purchase this sheet. A guinea, my friend?"

Thorn produced one. Mistress Gainer protested the amount. Robin assured her it was a pittance for her kindness, and then limped with Thorn's support to the waiting coach, toga clad and attended by a fluffy butterfly.

"Somewhat grand for a captain?" he murmured at sight of the ducal traveling chariot.

"The note said 'comfortable accommodations.' "

It hurt like blazes to get into the luxurious vehicle and settle sideways on a seat, his leg outstretched, and Robin felt shaky and glad of the offer of brandy. He found a smile as he thanked the Gainers, however, and managed a wave. Then he gritted his teeth because even the well-sprung coach lurched as it made its way back to the road.

Coquette tried to comfort him by licking his hand.

Thorn was studying him in that way he had. "When you're ready, I'll have the whole story. But don't worry, we'll get your other bit of fluff back, word of a duke."

Petra watched the coach leave and knew it was time to go on her way. She was surprised by the grandeur of the vehicle, but that merely confirmed her belief that Robin had told her a parcel of lies. She supposed it was a rake's nature to conceal who he truly was.

There'd been no immediate search other than some calling by the Gainers. Perhaps he'd be relieved to be rid of her, but all the same, she'd do her best to cover her tracks. She also had to consider that Varzi might come to this area. She suspected that the Fletchers would make the dead man disappear, but if Varzi heard about the wounded man at the Gainer farm he would be intrigued. Some questions there, and she'd have him on her trail.

She headed off down the footpath, not worrying for now about direction. She simply wanted to be far from the Gainer farm and not leave a trail that could be followed.

She tried to avoid people, but this area was dotted with farms and she heard signs all around—a dog barking, a woman calling a child, and a clock chiming the hour. One man passed her on the path, merely nodding a good day, but he might remember a woman in a red cloak. She took it off and made a tight bundle of it. She should discard it, but she might need it.

Of course, she was now in the green sprigged dress that Robin knew well, and he also knew she was wearing the pale petticoat on top. She remembered his gentle caring in the garden of the Coq d'Or. . . .

How could a couple of chaotic days have dug so deeply into her heart? She walked on, facing the fact that absence from Robin Bonchurch was eating at her like a wild beast. He was beautiful, but she'd known beautiful men. He was feckless, he took everything too lightly, he lived only for pleasure and seduction. . . .

He'd fought for her, been wounded for her, and if he sought her now, it would be because his honor would not let her be at risk.

She tried to push all thoughts of him out of her head and focus on evasion.

She was young and active, but not accustomed to walking such long distances. Her legs began to ache, and her thirst became intolerable. When she saw an isolated cottage or what was perhaps a small farm, she took the risk. After all, this was one farm among hundreds. What chance that any hunters would find it soon enough to matter?

A brown dog ran out snarling, and Petra was truly afraid until a young woman appeared and called it off. Young, but hard-faced and suspicious. Petra supposed she wasn't exactly a picture of respectability. The woman let Petra dip water from a well, but she kept the dog by her side and watched every move.

Petra would like to rest, but now she had to distance herself from the farm. She headed north, where the ground rose and might be less populated, but when clouds drifted in to cover the sun, it turned chilly. She put on the cloak again, but it didn't fight a deeper chill.

As the cloudy day began to sink into evening, Petra desperately wished she knew where she was and where she would sleep this night.

Robin arrived at Ithorne Castle with his leg throbbing and the bandage wet beneath the sheet. As soon as the coach stopped, he said, "Get the hunt started."

"I'm getting you to bed and sending for the doctor. A few minutes isn't going to matter at this stage."

"Damn it all to Hades."

Robin had told the story. Thorn had been as incredulous as Robin at Petra's quixotic quest for a father who had no idea she existed, and was inclined to believe it all a lie. Robin had argued for truth, but even so, it was no help. She'd never said where this father might be other than her idea he was at court, and that was little help. The summer court was Richmond Lodge, an unpretentious house at Kew, and the king kept few of his household in attendance there. Riddlesome, if he existed, could be anywhere.

Thorn forced him into a hand-chair made by two footmen, to be carried up to a bedchamber. "Plague take you, anything could be happening to her. I can't take to my bed like a dowager!"

"What can be done, will be done," Thorn said as they reached the bedchamber. "Your presence isn't needed."

"At least cover that bedspread with something that can be bloodstained."

This bit of household efficiency made Thorn raise his brows, but a footman was sent off with the task, and Robin took the chance to limp to the window to look out. Impossible that Petra appear, walking across the lush park toward him, but he had to look.

A black-clad housekeeper came in, attended by a maid bearing a large cloth. They spread it over the bed and Robin was forced to lie down, propped up on pillows, but at least he could see the park by turning his head.

When the servants left, Robin said, "She doesn't know the country. She looks like a vagrant. She speaks English with an accent. What if people think she's French? It's not long since we were at war. . . ."

"You seemed to think she could take care of herself."

Robin pounded the bed with his fists. "She thinks she can take care of herself. She's a demented idiot!"

Thorn leaned against one of the bedposts, arms folded. Unlike Robin, who often looked lighthearted when he wasn't, the Duke of Ithorne often looked in a dark mood when he wasn't, but he was somewhat somber now.

"The question is, why has she fled you?"

"Secrets."

"What secrets?"

Robin reared up. "Devil take you! If I knew—"

Thorn spread his hands. "Sorry, sorry."

Robin fell back. "She's probably a spy."

"From Italy?"

"Milan's controlled by Austria."

"So it is," Thorn said, suddenly thoughtful.

"Oh, pay no attention to me. It's all wrapped up in this mad idea of finding her father. She doesn't want me to know who he is in case she decides not to claim the relationship. In effect, she doesn't trust me."

"You have given her a false name," Thorn pointed out.

"It didn't seem important at the time." Robin cursed again. "Powick and Fontaine! I need to send instructions. Get me some writing materials and a messenger."

Coquette yapped a demand to be lifted onto the high bed. Thorn rather gingerly obliged.

Robin petted her, but said, "It's a damned nuisance having so many people to take care of."

"You're an earl," Thorn said, using the bellpull by the fireplace. "Responsible for hundreds."

"Who all seem hell-bent on taking care of me. Don't give me that look. You know they'd all faint and die if I demanded changes."

"It'll happen one day."

"They'll faint and die?" But Robin pulled a face. "I know, but the earldom works like a perfect clock."

"Then you should enjoy this bit of chaos."

"This," said Robin, "isn't chaos, it's torture. Of your kindness, send for some coffee," Robin begged.

"Coffee, always coffee. I think you love it more than women." But Thorn sent the order. He drank only tea, but he kept a cook able to make coffee well especially for Robin's sake. For his part, Robin kept stores of Thorn's favorite teas, even though he disliked the stuff.

Robin's mind turned to Petra, and her almost ecstatic delight at the coffee in Montreuil. He'd supply her with the best coffee she'd ever tasted. They'd explore all its variations together. He'd sampled a new recipe in Paris, with chocolate, brandy liqueur, nutmeg, and whipped cream that might carry her halfway to orgasm before he even kissed her. . . .

"The desk?" Thorn said.

Robin started and found it on his lap. He took out paper and the pen Thorn had prepared for him and pulled his mind back to business. "Powick and Fontaine were to wait for me at the London house, but they'll be sitting ducks for Varzi."

"You think he'll attack them out of spite?"

"He's capable of it, but he might think they can tell him where Petra is."

"How positively medieval."

"It sounds as if Milan still is, beneath opera and gloss. Where will they be safe but not connected to you or me? Is Christian in London?"

"Doing his stint at court, and thus at Kew." Christian, Major Lord Grandiston, was in the Guards.

"Damn, though that could be useful. He'll know if strange Italians turn up there. I need to write to him, too."

"I believe I have paper enough."

"Rathbone?" Robin asked. "I suppose he's in Derbyshire. Ashart?"

"Working like a busy bee on restoration of the moldering Surrey pile. Marriage," Thorn said with a sad shake of his head.

"Perfect," Robin said. "He can use another pair of hands."

"I'm sure he'll be delighted. As will you—here is your vile potion."

"No man with a soul can dislike coffee," Robin said as the footman poured coffee into a cup, added sugar and cream, and delivered it to Robin. They all knew how he liked it. Robin inhaled, sighed, and sipped.

"I have no idea why I indulge you in that vice."

Robin fluttered his lashes. "For love." But he turned serious. "Any news yet?"

"Hardly. We'll hear as soon as anyone returns."

Though seething inside, Robin settled to drinking coffee and writing letters. It was the only useful thing he could do. He asked Christian to be alert for Italians, especially a man of Varzi's description or a woman of Petra's. He sent to the Marquess of Ashart at Cheynings, Surrey, alerting him to the arrival of Powick and Fontaine. He wrote extensive instructions to his secretary, Trevelyan, about the security of his people in London, and included instructions to Powick for removal to Surrey.

All in all, it was exhausting.

The arrival of a Dr. Brown, middle-aged, authoritative, and very Scottish, gave some hope that he'd soon be able to take action. As Robin watched the man unwrap the bandage, however, fear stirred. Surely he'd feel something if it was already putrefying?

"Satisfactory," Dr. Brown eventually declared.

"Excellent. Stitch it up, sir, so I can get about my business."

"By no means, my lord! There is nothing more dangerous than trapping the poison inside."

"I need to get up, to be able to ride."

"You need to kill yourself, then."

They glared at one another, but the doctor was master of this domain and Robin had good reason to know he was correct. Damn it all to Hades.

"Tomorrow, my lord, if the wound still looks well and shows signs of good healing, I will consider the stitches. Until then, keep that leg as still as possible. Keep it still, or I take no responsibility for the consequences. None at all."

When Brown left, Thorn said, "Anyone would think you've never been wounded before."

"Don't think I have, since boyhood, anyway."

"A charmed life. Let's hope it holds."

"Petra's the one in danger, not me."

"Completely of her own choosing."

"No," Robin said. "If I'd managed things better, she wouldn't have felt she had to go."

Thorn's brow twitched, but he wisely didn't comment. Instead he went to collect maps of the area, and they tried to work out what route Petra might have taken. The only result was to show the infinite number of them.

As the long day passed, inactivity became torment.

Reports came in of glimpses of a woman in a red cloak, and Petra had almost certainly begged for a drink at one small farm. Men were sent to scour that area, but only hours after the sighting. Robin studied that part of the map, even though he knew it was pointless.

Where was she going? A watch on the main roads had turned up nothing, as had inquiries at coaching inns. Was she walking every step of the way? The scraps they received showed no firm direction, and every hour that passed expanded the places where she could be.

Evening began to pale the view outside the window, signaling night, with all its dangers. Robin felt sick with fear for her, but also because he was coming to think that she truly could disappear into England, never to be seen again. He picked up the rosary lying on the table beside his bed. Did it work for those who had no faith in the beads? He fingered them anyway, attempting prayer.

Petra's stomach was cramping, so in a small village, she risked buying some bread and cheese and some of the thin beer the English drank. She said she was walking to seek work in London, and that was accepted so easily she felt she'd found a story to tell in other places.

Heartened, she set out again, but had to take more frequent rests, and it was harder and harder to start up again. But then, as she leaned on a tree trunk, wondering which of two paths to take, a young man ran by. She was off the path and in dappled shade, and perhaps her dress blended with nature. For whatever reason, he didn't notice her.

She heard him call out to someone, however, and risked looking out. A man was coming down the path with a bundle of sticks on his back, and the lad was asking something about a woman in a red cloak. The man shook his head and the lad ran on, but Petra swallowed. So Robin was indeed searching, and if men were hunting her here, the search must be extensive. How could they have any idea where she was? She didn't know. But then she remembered the place she'd begged for water. Perhaps they'd also found the inn where she'd bought food. With regret, she stuffed the red cloak deep beneath a hedge.

Warily, she retraced her steps, then took another path across a cow field and into nowhere. The day was paling into evening now, so she had to face the prospect of sleeping outdoors at night. She didn't think she could do it, but she couldn't risk seeking a room at an inn. In any case, it was unlikely they'd let her in, looking such a vagrant. Would she be breaking some law if she slept in a barn or crept into a farm outbuilding?

She was trudging along a footpath, feeling close to despair, when the hedge to her right shrank lower. A church spire not far ahead told her she was coming into a village. She heard a woman call a child and a dog bark. She halted, knowing she should turn, but to go where? At the end of her resources, she walked on, half hoping to be caught, to be gathered back into Robin Bonchurch's protection.

"Good evening."

Petra started, her heart pounding madly. The hedge was chest high now, and an elderly woman was looking over it at her. Brown, leathery skin was topped by an enormously wide straw hat with steel gray hair escaping in all directions. She was leaning on some tool, but Petra could only see the long handle.

"Good evening, ma'am," Petra said, and hurried on.

"Where you off to, then?" the woman called.

To run away would make her look like a thief, so Petra turned back. "London," she said.

"Long way, that be, Lunnon."

"I fear so."

"Not that way, either. Lunnon be north of 'ere."

"Then I'll turn north when I can." Petra tried to speak without an accent, but knew she was failing. She smiled and moved on again.

"Why you going there?" the woman called.

Her interest drew Petra like a warm fire. She turned back. "I'm looking for work."

The woman wiped her sweaty forehead with the back of her dirty, knotty hand, leaving a streak. "You can weed 'ere for supper if you want."

Petra looked past her at rows of neat plants and had to confess, "I wouldn't know the weeds."

The woman nodded. "Thought you sounded a bit of a lady."

"Sometimes ladies have to find work."

"Suppose so. Where you from, then, with dark eyes like that? Abroad?"

Petra suddenly wanted honesty, and it could make no difference. "Italy," she said.

"Fancy that! I'll give you supper for some stories. It'd be grand to hear about Italy."

It might be wiser to go on, but Petra ached for food and simple kindness and gave in. "Then thank you."

"Come in through the gate," the woman said, and stumped off toward the house with a gait that suggested sore hips.

Petra followed and found herself in yet another kitchen. She smiled sadly at the thought of her many kitchen adventures, all shared with Robin. This was a tiny room, however, with a small hearth built into the wall. An open door showed a small parlor beyond, with only a few bits of simple furniture.

"I'm Mistress Waddle," the woman said, swinging a pot over the fire.

If any of Petra's pursuers tracked her here, petty lies wouldn't serve. "Miss d'Averio," she said. "Can I help in some way?"

"No, sit you down. You look as if you've walked a ways today. I've some soup 'ere, and bread. Simple fare." She might be embarrassed about it.

"That sounds wonderful. It smells wonderful, too."

Unlike the crone's foul brew. *Don't think of that, because all such thoughts lead to Robin.*

"There's a bit of 'am 'ock in it," Mistress Waddle said proudly. "Are you thirsty? There's water in that pitcher there."

Petra stood, alarmed by the effort it took, filled a chipped cup, and drank.

"Italy," Mistress Waddle said, standing sideways as she watched her pot. "I suppose that means you're a Papist."

"I'm afraid so." Would that get her thrown out?

"Takes all sorts, that's what I always say. Why're you tramping England, then, dear? For I can tell you're not used to it."

Petra agreed ruefully, wondering what to say. She didn't want to lie, but the truth was complicated. She learned from Cock Robin and adapted it.

"I was a lady's maid," she said, sitting down again, "hired by an English lady in Milan. But she only wanted my services until she reached home, so when we arrived in Dover, she cast me off."

"Wicked cruel, that be. Why go up to Lunnon, though? Fearsome big place, they say, Lunnon, and full of sin."

"I have family there. That's why I was willing to leave Italy." Petra suddenly thought of a useful twist. "In truth, ma'am, my lady's husband took an attraction to me. Of course, I wanted nothing to do with him, but she could not bear it. That is why I don't even know where I am. I was afraid to take the direct route to London for fear he would pursue me. Please, if a gentleman comes this way asking for me, do not betray me."

"Be sure I won't, dearie, but pretty as you are, you'll have that problem again and again."

"I know," Petra said, and didn't have to invent a sigh. "My looks are my ruin."

"Need a good man, you do."

"As do all women."

"Not me," the woman said with a gap-toothed laugh. "I've buried two and I'm done with 'em. I've three daughters married well and two sons who don't forget their mother, so I've no need of a man as old as me, expecting to be cared for like another baby."

Petra had to laugh, too, but sadness was welling up and might produce tears soon. She'd found a small haven here, but it could be no more permanent than any other haven she'd found in recent years. Soon she'd have to leave, to go out again into the wild. To be hunted in the night.

"Do you have somewhere to stop tonight, dearie?"

Petra studied Mistress Waddle's kind face and said, "No."

"Then stay here. No arguing. I can't do with you wandering the roads in the dark, and you could maybe use a few bits of extra clothing, as well. I've nothing suitable for the likes of you, of course, but there's some old things of me daughters' as might fit. That way you can save your better stuff. You don't want to turn up at your London relatives' with days of dirt on you."

Petra stared at the generous woman. "I'd be very grateful, Mistress Waddle. I can pay—"

"No, no, none of that! I'm enjoying the company. You just tell me about Italy, and the clothes and jewels the fine ladies wear, and I'll be in your debt."

Petra had to fight tears, and perhaps Mistress Waddle knew, for she turned tactfully to her pot.

So Petra spent a pleasant evening. She accepted the

old clothes with true gratitude, even though they were indeed worn and mended almost to death. They were clean and had been stored in lavender. Once in them, she brushed and damp-wiped her gown and petticoat and hung them on the line outside to frcshen. She lingered in the sunset, allowing some sweet thoughts and memories before burying them deep in her mind.

She turned to admire the tiny garden, utilized to the full with rows of vegetables and beans growing on tall stakes. A small structure of bits of wood was a henhouse, and three hens pecked around the garden. Herbs grew by the doorstep—lavender, mint, savory, dill, and others—and heavily perfumed sweet peas wound through some dead sticks up against the back window.

Heavenly in one sense, but she saw the sagging lines of the cottage and the ill-fitting doors and windows that probably let in icy drafts in winter. She would leave some coins for Mistress Waddle and send more if she were ever settled.

A cat slunk into the garden, paused, and then streaked into the house. When Petra entered, she found it curled by the kitchen hearth at Mistress Waddle's feet. So the woman had some company, at least.

They ate the nourishing food, and then spent the rest of the evening in the little parlor. Petra shared some mending tasks while entertaining her hostess with stories. In return, she learned that Mistress Waddle wasn't at all lonely. Most of her family lived in the village of Speenhurst and were generally in and out all the time.

Eventually, Mistress Waddle lit a tallow candle, but it gave too little light for needlework, and in any case, Petra was very tired. She suspected the lady usually went to bed with the sun, so asked to retire. She went up to the attic, where she'd already made up one of the four narrow beds. She stripped down to her threadbare shift and settled under the colorful quilt.

A clean, well-aired bed will do, in a clean room. In a room entirely for myself.

That's what she'd asked from Robin, oh, so long ago, and this was as close as she'd come. She prayed that his leg was healing well and that soon he'd feel he'd done his duty and could get on with his life.

Chapter 22

Petra woke to a cock crowing, pulled out of a dream in which she and Robin had been searching for each other at a masked ball, with masked enemies constantly intervening. She lay there in the morning light, letting the frantic urgency fade. She knew where he was—Stowting, being cared for by his friend "Captain Rose." But he would be worried.

She remembered how kind he was to Coquette, even though he didn't really want the dog, and how genuinely he'd been concerned for his servants at Mère Goulart's. Men were trained to be protective of women, and some took that seriously. She supposed he did.

She sat up. There was nothing for it. She must find a way to get a message to him to assure him she was all right. She got out of bed, wincing at some stiffness, and dressed in her new clothes. Over her shift, she tied on a linen skirt that had probably once been brown, but which had been washed and faded to a motley beige. She added a rust-colored sleeveless bodice that laced up the front, grateful that this one was a little large rather than in danger of popping. The plain, elbow-length sleeves of the shift covered her arms. There was also a floppy-frilled mob-cap that hid her face, and a brown knitted shawl.

She went downstairs and the old woman beamed at her. "Sleep well, dear?"

"Very well, thank you. You've been so kind."

"Not at all. It's been a treat for me. Sit you down and have an egg."

There was only coarse bread and water on the table, but the woman cooked an egg for each of them, and put out a bowl of plums from her tree. As they ate the simple food, Mistress Waddle said, "Are you sure you want to go on, dear?"

Petra smiled at her. "I can't stay here. No, I have a destination, but it isn't London."

"Ah. Then where do you go?"

Even now, an instinct for secrecy made Petra name only a town en route. After all, one of Robin's searchers might find this place. "Guildford. It's southwest of London."

"Never heard of it," the old woman said, "but Thad Hythe at the Three Cocks likely has."

Cocks. Robin. An omen? Coquette. Cock Robin. The Coq d'Or. The Three Cocks.

"I'd also like to send a letter, but I have no idea how it is done in England." Or whether she could conceal its origins.

"A letter," Mistress Waddle echoed, as if Petra had said, "I would like to catch a unicorn." "Parson would have pen and paper, and Squire, and probably Mistress Kershaw as lives near the church, but . . ."

"Please don't concern yourself," Petra said quickly. "I wouldn't want to send it from here, anyway."

Mistress Waddle nodded, but Petra knew that she'd ruined any illusion that her problems were minor. "Thad'll likely have paper and pen. Has to do a bit of writing and reckoning, running the tavern. We'll walk down after we've eaten."

As they walked into the small village, however, Petra knew this was unwise. Any hunters coming through here would learn all about Mistress Waddle's foreign guest. Everyone gave them a cheery greeting. Often it was Ellie, twice it was Ma, and once Gran. Everyone asked, "Who's that with you?"

To each Mistress Waddle said, "Nice young lady from abroad. Helping her on her way."

The Three Cocks was merely a cottage that did its business in the front room, and the inn sign was crudely painted on the front wall. They went around the back, where Mistress Waddle called a cheery "Good morning" as she walked in through the open door.

After a surprised but welcoming flurry of greetings, the story was told.

"Lawks!" exclaimed Mistress Hythe, stocky and high colored. "I'll get paper and things, though Lord knows when it was last used."

"Guildford, eh?" said Thad Hythe, who was tall and thin. "Sit a while, Auntie. And you, ma'am."

Petra sat, smiling at her hostess. "Is the whole village related to you?"

The woman chuckled. "Not quite, dearie. Thad's my cousin Megsy's boy, but I suppose that counts."

Speenhurst was a close community of friends and family and Petra envied them, but then she thought how poor most of them seemed to be. Poor, but not complaining, and they did seem to have tolerable houses and enough food, even if it was all simple. Happiness and security came in many forms.

Mistress Hythe came back with two sheets of cheap paper, a few quills, and a little pot. "Ink's dry," she said, "but a bit of water'll fix that."

Petra inspected a quill, asked for a sharp knife, and

mended the point. When the ink was ready she dipped
and then thought to ask, "What day and date is it?"
How strange not to know.

"It's Friday, ma'am. The twentieth of July."

Petra wrote that at the top, trying to decide what
to say. The ink was thin and the paper rough, so this
was going to be a sorry piece of work, but it was the
words that mattered. She must avoid expressions of
fondness, but she didn't want it to be cold.

> *To my admired protector,*

That was unsatisfactory, but it would have to do.

> *I know you must be concerned, which is poor re-
> ward for your kindness, but please know that I am
> well and with friends. I hope the same is true of you.*

She knew what she had to include.

> *I promise you that I will keep my word. If I
> am in need or distress, I will send to you for help,
> so if you do not hear from me, you'll know all
> is well. Farewell, my friend. You will dance more
> lightly through life without a pebble in your shoe.*

"There, see," said Mistress Waddle with pride,
"doesn't that look pretty?"

Petra looked up to see the others watching, as if
she were performing some remarkable feat. As she
folded the note, she resolved that one day she'd send
the kind lady a piece of perfect penmanship on thick,
smooth paper. She wouldn't be able to read it for
herself, but Petra knew she'd enjoy it.

"I have a bit of sealing wax," Mr. Hythe said with pride and produced it and a candle. He carefully dripped red wax onto the flap, and Petra pressed it down with the handle of a knife that lay on the table. To settle it, she pressed again with her finger, remembering Robin's signet. That had been proof of a lie, however—that he had lied in some way about his identity.

She turned the letter, and dipped her pen again and wrote:

> To Robin Bonchurch, Esquire,
> By kindness of Captain Rose,
> The Black Swan Inn,
> Stowting, Kent.

She rose and thanked them. "I'll find a way to send it farther down the road."

Mr. Hythe had been thinking. "Guildford, eh? You want the Maidstone to Guildford Road, then. Good road, that is, and just up north of here."

"There would be coaches? How much would a seat on a coach cost?" She was sure she couldn't walk another full day.

"That'd be costly, miss, but you can travel cheap by wagon."

"Wagon?"

"Lots of wagons on the Guildford Road, carrying goods, see? Travels slow, no faster than walking, but cheap. Saves your soles," he added with a chuckle that meant nothing to Petra.

"Soles on your shoes, dear," Mistress Waddle said. "And your eternal soul. I suppose it's different when English isn't your own language."

"Yes, it is," Petra said with a smile, but again her

thoughts turned back to Robin. What had it been? Kicking heels.

She made herself think about her journey. She wanted to travel as fast as possible, but if she depleted her money she would be in a desperate situation if Lord Rothgar rejected her, or if she decided it was wisest to flee. A few extra days now would do no harm.

"I think I would like to travel by wagon," she said.

"Then we can help you on your way. Alice is off to visit her sister near Micklebury. That's almost to the Guildford Road. And," said Mr. Hythe, clearly delighted to be the guide, "she could put your letter in the post there."

Petra thanked him warmly. "How much will it cost to send the letter?"

"Nothing if you reckon the person getting it'll pay."

Petra considered that, but surely "Captain Rose" would pay for this letter. He was clearly not short of money, whereas she was.

She returned to the cottage to put her other clothing into a bundle made of the better half of a worn-out sheet. She accepted some bread from Mistress Waddle and tucked a silver sixpence behind a pot where her hostess wouldn't find it for a while. Later she'd find a way to properly repay this astonishing kindness, but for now, she simply hugged the woman before hurrying back to the Three Cocks.

Mistress Hythe was waiting in a small, two-wheeled vehicle drawn by a donkey. She called farewell to her husband and clicked the animal into action. Thus Petra bounced off into her second day on the road, giving thanks for being well rested, well fed, and having a fairly clear plan for her journey. What's more, her appearance was so changed that any hounds still on her trail would fail entirely.

Chapter 23

Robin ate breakfast, feeling useless. There'd been no good news yesterday and he couldn't see why there'd be any today, and he wanted to be galloping around the country, seeking her. But Petra was working hard at not being caught, and she was succeeding. Strangely, he was proud of her. If only he could be sure she was safe.

Thorn sat by his bed, drinking tea and studying a map. "I wish we knew her destination."

"That would be entirely too easy."

"This isn't a game."

"No, of course not. Do I make it seem . . . I probably do. Petra berated me for it. It's just my way."

"I know, I know." Thorn tossed aside the map. "I suppose I'm worried about her, too. But she chose to leave, and you met her only a few days ago."

"Unless my nursemaid popped me in her cradle. Sorry. Flippant again. Some days are a lot longer than others, I find. Was I ever the lighthearted Earl of Huntersdown, who knew not Petra d'Averio?"

"There you go again."

"I'm a hopeless case."

A footman entered then with a letter. Thorn opened

it and said, "Some good news. The man I sent to Dover reports that a man of Varzi's description followed your men. They took the coach; he rode."

"So he's not gone to the Folkestone area. Right, then. Let's follow him to London. Petra's greatest danger is from Varzi. If I can stop him, her situation is improved, and your people can continue the search down here."

"That's actually an excellent and surprisingly sane idea. If the doctor approves."

Robin suppressed his opinion of the doctor. "She might well be going there anyway, to seek help of Teresa Cornelys. That could be disastrous. The woman would give her up for some pieces of silver."

"Gold, Robin, gold," said Thorn, and sent to hurry the doctor.

Once he'd arrived, Doctor Brown pulled a face, but Robin knew that when the physician agreed to stitch the wound and permit travel—gentle travel—he was healing. The man had even muttered something about healthy young flesh, shaking his head.

Soon Robin was hobbling out to the traveling chariot with the aid of a footman and a sturdy walking stick. He knew Thorn would insist on careful travel to favor his leg, but even so, he was out of his damned bed and they'd be in London by evening.

"London," he said as they set off, "and something useful to do."

Petra parted from Alice Hythe and walked north. It was only a few miles to Maidstone, and she felt comfortably anonymous in her shabby clothing. In any case, she doubted anyone was looking for her this far afield.

Having been trained all her life that men were dangerous and that a woman alone was indecent, she was nervous about walking the open road. Most, however, were simply polite, and the few who smiled too broadly or even made lewd suggestions didn't persist when she walked by. Perhaps it was simply that country people were busy. Idleness is the devil's garden, as they said. Or perhaps her shabby clothing concealed her attractions. That would be a very pleasant change.

She arrived in Maidstone to find a market in the street and wandered it in hope of cheap food. When she saw a place selling used clothing, however, she checked the goods. Two brown pennies purchased a battered, wide-brimmed straw hat. It would help shield her from the sun, but it also reminded her pleasantly of Mistress Waddle.

"Welsh, then, are you?" the man asked.

Petra agreed, and he nodded, pleased. "Thought so."

Very well. If anyone asked where she was from, she would say Wales. Unfortunately her knowledge of Wales was almost nonexistent, but she thought Monmouth was there, connected to the tragic Duke of Monmouth, bastard son of King Charles II. She hoped that would do.

A man came by with a tray on his head, shouting, "Hot pies!" Petra bought one and sat on a wall to eat it. It was delicious, filled with potatoes, meat, and thick, rich gravy. With some plums and water from the town pump, she felt she'd dined well. She ached for coffee, but that only made her think of Robin, so she closed that door in her mind.

She explored the market a little more, finding that her clean but poor clothing and a mention of Wales seemed to make her acceptable and unremarkable. She indulged in a currant bun and then bought some more plums to take with her, and a piece of hard cheese that would keep. She was content until she heard, ". . . Woman in a green flowered dress beneath a red cloak. Foreign. Lost her wits . . ."

Petra peered from under her straw hat and saw a young man in brown coat and breeches and a three-cornered hat weaving his way through the market, asking all the stallholders. Would Robin never give up? She hated that he be so worried, and prayed he'd accept the message of her letter.

Feeling safe in her disguise, she decided it was better not to try to slip away. The searcher looked around and his gaze went right over her. She was safe. She turned away casually and strolled onward in search of a place where she could buy a seat on a wagon.

It was easy, and within an hour she climbed into the back of the enormous cart. It was covered by canvas stretched on big hoops and fully loaded with boxes and sacks, but at the very back end benches on either side would hold about ten people. At the moment Petra greeted a young woman with two small children, an ancient couple, and a peg-legged sailor. She saw that wagon travel was mostly for those unable to walk, and hoped she wouldn't be conspicuous.

No one seemed surprised by her, however, and when they asked her name, she said Monmouth. They seemed to accept that and her being Welsh. The team of eight huge horses started their steady plod, and she was on her way. A short distance out of town, Robin's hound rode past with only a cursory glance, off to ask questions at the next place. It didn't matter. Petra d'Averio of the green dress and red cloak had completely disappeared.

In London, Robin went to Thorn's house rather than his own, because he'd realized Varzi might be watching Hastings Street. One of Thorn's men was sent to visit the house and get news. He returned as Robin and Thorn ate a late meal.

"Your man and valet have left as ordered, my lord," he told Robin. "A couple of people have called at the back door who might have been suspicious, but they might have been seeking employment or directions as they claimed."

"No one lurking?" Thorn asked.

"Not as I could see, your grace."

When the man had gone, Thorn said, "Seems to me it's going to be as hard or harder to find Varzi as to find your Petra." Robin glared at him, and Thorn raised a hand. "Pax!"

"I need a good fight."

"You're still recovering from the last one."

"Yes, plague take it. I want to fight Varzi, but he's an old man."

On the journey, they'd discussed what to do with the villain and come to no good conclusion. Neither could swallow coldblooded murder, but if Petra was correct, nothing short of death would deter him from his task.

"I remember boasting to Petra that in England I could deal with Varzi, but now . . ."

"The difficulty is finding him. You'll deal with him then."

Robin speared a piece of roast chicken. "Don't patronize me." After a moment, he said, "You know, we're playing the game on his terms. I've no need of secrecy now. The Earl of Huntersdown can get away with landing without due process, and I can protect the smugglers if necessary. I can accuse Varzi of complicity in that attack on me," he said with relish. "In fact, I don't see why I can't advertise."

"Advertise what?" Thorn asked.

"For Varzi. Reward to be given, man of this description, et cetera et cetera . . ."

"On what grounds?"

"Complicity in the attack, as aforementioned. If I catch him, I can have him before the courts for an attack on a peer of the realm. Heinous."

" 'Struth, you're showing terrifying depths. I assume one simply sends the notice to the papers. Overstone will know."

His plump, dull, but extremely efficient Town secretary did know. He showed no reaction to his instruction, but did say, "If you will excuse me, Your Grace, I will suggest that if you do not wish to draw attention to this house or any involvement of Lord Huntersdown, perhaps any responses should be directed to a discreet third party?"

"Overstone, you are invaluable. See to it, there's a good fellow."

Robin went early to bed and this night he quickly fell asleep. It might be exhaustion, but it was probably because he finally felt he was doing something to keep Petra safe.

Chapter 24

Petra woke to Saturday in a common inn room close to a place called Sevenoaks. She was relieved not to be itching, for she'd discovered the unpleasant side of this form of travel. The wagon passengers had all slept together, each on a narrow mattress on the floor, along with four other travelers. There'd been a baby who'd woken twice, and the old man had snored. All the same, she'd had some fairly decent sleep.

She ate a simple breakfast with the rest and then climbed back into the wagon for her second day. She wouldn't reach Guildford today, but she'd be there tomorrow, Sunday. It began to rain, proving that England wasn't always idyllic, but she was dry and safe inside the wagon and counted her blessings.

By now, Robin would have her message, so she could stop worrying about him. That didn't quite happen, but she managed not to think about him at least part of the time.

Robin woke to anxiety fueled by vaguely remembered dreams of struggling to reach Petra, who was crying out for help amid dancers wearing Venetian masks. Chasing Varzi wasn't easing him when there was no sniff of the man yet, and his own doctor was coming soon to inspect his wound. Every sense said it was healing, but he still broke into a cold sweat when he remembered his father's suffering.

He got out of bed to test his leg again. It was sore and the stitches pulled, but he could move around reasonably well with the stick. It had to be all right, but when Dr. Wright was announced, his heart pumped. Wright was his family's London physician and knew the story. He looked both grave and disapproving.

I can't wrap myself in flannel, Robin wanted to protest as the man unbandaged his leg, but he knew there was a lot of ground between swaddling and dueling.

He sat up to look for himself, trying to persuade himself that the ugly, sewn gash was in good shape. He wasn't sure until Wright muttered, "Better than you deserve, sir."

"Perhaps actually good?"

The man looked at him sternly, but then relaxed into a smile. "Very good, my lord, but you're demmed lucky. You, above all, should know . . ."

"I know life is chancy and might as well be enjoyed."

The doctor sighed and rebandaged the wound, leaving strict instructions to take things gently and alert him at any sign of increased pain or fever. Having thus diluted his optimistic opinion, he took his leave.

Robin decided to take the positive point of view and celebrate by hobbling downstairs for breakfast. Thorn was equally delighted by the assessment, and they ate with some merriment as they pored over the newspapers. There was the advertisement, responses to be sent to a legal office not previously connected to him or the Duke of Ithorne.

"I can't wait to see Varzi locked up for highway robbery."

"It won't stick," Thorn warned.

"I'll make it stick for a while," Robin said, "and then think of some other reason to hold him. Why haven't we heard from Christian about Italians at Richmond Lodge?"

"Because the whole world hasn't stopped to attend to your business. Eat!"

Robin picked up his café au lait and sipped. "No news from the watch on the coaching roads?"

"None. Coffee isn't food."

Robin took a bun and buttered it. "It's as if she's not traveled by coach, but . . ."

Thorn spoke gently. "If she were dead, someone would have found her body."

"Perhaps."

"She's merely disappeared efficiently. Perhaps she's an old hand at it."

Robin wanted to object, but the same idea was growing in his mind. Petra had slipped away from Lady Sodworth without much of a qualm. Perhaps she'd found another protector. Perhaps she was behaving with him as she had at Montreuil and on the *Courlis*. After all, she hadn't been a virgin, and how could a gently raised foreign lady evade his search without help?

"I doubt she ever was a nun," he said. "Consider how she left her rosary and cross behind without a twitch. Perhaps she thought that funny."

Thorn, wisely, didn't attempt a response.

"She used claws, pistols, swords—"

"Claws?" Thorn queried.

Robin almost scratched at the healing scabs on his shoulder. "And wounded Varzi's man in an unthinkable spot."

"I thought that gave you some satisfaction."

Robin swigged coffee without tasting it. "She probably discarded that cloak within a furlong of the farm and got rid of the gown shortly after."

"To wander naked?"

"Quite likely. No, but she'd find something else easily enough. After all, I'm not the first protector she used and abandoned."

"Lady Sodworth?" Thorn said. "The intolerable harpy with a voice like a screeching peacock?"

"A commitment is a commitment."

"Which, according to you, the Sodworth woman broke in many ways."

Robin pounded the table. "If I only knew what she was really up to! Then I could put her out of my mind."

"As you don't, put her out of your mind, anyway."

Thorn didn't expect him to agree to that, so Robin did out of sheer perversity. "Excellent advice. I'll hold a card party tonight."

"Here?" Thorn asked. "Is my house available for rent, then?"

"No, at my house. It's time for me to go home. *I'm* not the fugitive, after all."

Thorn leaned back, mouth tight. "I don't suppose Varzi—you do remember Varzi?—will really attempt to kidnap you and torture the wayward *contessina*'s whereabouts out of you."

"I only wish he'd try."

" 'Struth, you madman! But if that's the way of it,
I demand a return of hospitality. I want to be in at
the kill."

"Done. Just to make sure of it, I'll let the papers
know of my entertainment. How? Ah yes." He
snapped his fingers, and Coquette danced over to be
fed a tidbit. "I'm sure it will amuse the world that
I've acquired such a dog."

Petra approached the end of her second day in the
wagon bored and prey to many doubts.

In Milan, full of her mother's substantial memories
of her lover and spurred on by very real fear, it had
seemed reasonable to seek out her English father.
Now, with endless time to think, all the unlikely aspects grew in her mind.

Why should any man remember an impetuous liaison during a wild Venetian festival twenty-two years
ago? In her mother's memories it had been a unique
event, but to that merry young man the naughty
contessa di Baldino would have been only a passing
amusement.

He'd probably been very like Robin Bonchurch.
Had he been as appalled by impetuous loving? Had
he been as courteous afterward, trying to conceal the
truth? When she thought back to Robin after the ship,
she couldn't help seeing only kindness and courtesy
and obligation. He'd be hunting her under the same
pressures, that was all.

She completely understood his position, for she'd
been raised under the same code. There were people
one married and people one did not, and any marriage
was to serve the family, not personal taste.

She was thinking about Robin again! She turned

her mind to Lord Rothgar, troublesome though that was. If he remembered, even if he remembered with fondness, why should he believe that she was his child? Hidden in the spine of her prayer book was a short letter from her mother attesting to the fact, but would that impress? Showing him that picture of his eye would mean nothing. Her mother had said she resembled him, but similarities between a young woman and a mature man couldn't be so marked. Did she have any absolute proof to offer?

No. She even began to wonder if her mother had been correct. She couldn't believe that she'd lie, but over time, might she have become mistaken? Had there only been the one lover when she'd been so very unhappy in her marriage, or were there more? After all, her best friend had been Teresa Imer, who had never been quite respectable.

Could a woman shift the truth over time to suit romantic notions or a guilty conscience?

When they stopped for the night in Dorking, Petra found the common bedroom intolerably crowded and noisy, and went out after supper to find some peace. That wasn't easy, because the White Horse was a busy coaching inn, so she walked a little way down the road, tussling with her future.

She was learning much about herself, including that she enjoyed company, but would choose solitude over some people. It would be horrible not to have choice. If her father rejected her she would need to find work. She might find a position as a lady's companion if she were lucky, but the lady might be someone like Lady Sodworth. She'd likely hang for murder before the year was out.

She'd survive in a convent, but she'd learned by

now that Robin had told the truth. There were no monasteries or convents here, and the English were wary of Papists, as they called Catholics. She said her prayers silently and never crossed herself.

She wasn't afraid of menial work, but she wasn't trained for anything except the elementary nursing of the poor.

There was always Robin, and she had promised to ask his help if she needed it, but she didn't know what to expect from him or what she could endure. She could not be his whore, but it would be almost as intolerable to be in his orbit with nothing.

Shadows were lengthening, so she turned back toward the inn. The words of the psalm invaded her mind. *Si ambulem in medio umbrae mortis, non timebo mala.* . . . Though I walk in the shadow of death, I will not be afraid. . . .

She had to step back sharply to avoid a speeding coach that halted at the White Horse, and the dangerous moment made her laugh. There were practical reasons to be afraid of walking in shadows. She watched the public coach disgorge passengers and their luggage and consume others. All people with purpose in their lives.

She asked an ostler what vehicle it was.

"Why, that's the Guildford Flyer, that is, miss, and with Mighty Mike Cockcroft on the box. Be there inside two hours tonight, it will."

Cock. Petra looked from the dusty, laden coach to a short, burly man downing a huge tankard of something while flirting with an adoring maid. Two hours to Guildford?

"Would I still be able to buy a seat on it?" she asked.

"Aren't you from the wagon?"

"Yes, but I have some money."

"I'll ask, but you'll have to be quick, though, miss. Mighty Mike won't wait."

Petra ran in and up to the sleeping room, where she grabbed her bundle, giving a quick explanation to her fellow travelers. She ran back down to find the coachman on the box, reins in hand.

"Up on top for a shilling," the ostler said. "Hurry up. You can pay 'im at the other end."

Petra scrambled up the ladder to squeeze in between two men. The coach immediately jerked into action, and she was glad to be jammed in so tight. The Flyer turned onto the Guildford Road and picked up speed, the groom on the box blasting a long note on his horn to celebrate the fact. She grabbed onto the sleeve of the man to her right. He didn't seem to mind.

Petra, Petra, only think what happened last time you acted on impulse!

I escaped, she told her protesting mind. *If I'd stayed with Lady Sodworth I'd be back in Milan by now, or more likely dead in an effort to escape.*

And cocks were her good luck symbol.

She saw a weathercock on a clock tower, pointing west. *Follow the cock.*

Ride a cock horse to Banbury Cross.

Wherever that was, if all else failed she'd go there to seek her fortune.

Robin had forgotten that a return to his house would mean a return to duties, but as soon as his secretary, Trevelyan, expressed his delight with his good health he began to mention correspondence and documents to be signed, as well as something Robin should read about the situation between Austria and Prussia.

Austria ruled Milan, Robin instantly thought, but pushed the connection aside. He'd deal with Varzi, but wouldn't waste any more time on Petra. She'd made her choice. He, on the other hand, had no choice. Trevelyan could be as demanding as a tutor— probably because he'd been Robin's tutor, but also because he was always right.

After going through the most urgent matters, Robin lost control of one impulse. "If anything comes that mentions Italy, I want to see it."

Trevelyan was at a nearby table, applying Robin's seal with precision to correspondence already dealt with. "Italy, sir?"

"Italy. You know, that long country that looks like a boot?"

"Yes, sir."

Damn. Robin never sank to sarcasm, and Trevelyan had probably picked up some of his ridiculous adventures. He still considered it his duty to keep informed about all Robin's affairs. Were they done?

Trevelyan brought over one remaining letter, the seal unbroken. Robin saw at a glance that it was from his mother. "Why didn't you give me this first?"

His secretary was staring at the far wall, his face rather pink. "I, er . . . I took the liberty of informing the countess of your wound, my lord."

Rare anger flared. "Damn your black heart! It's a mere jab, but you know how she'll worry. I should dismiss you on the spot."

Trevelyan went from pink to white, his face pinching. "Her ladyship particularly requested that I inform her of any wounds, sir."

And a man could hardly dismiss his mother. "Oh, go away," Robin growled, and snapped the seal on the heavy paper. She'd be worrying herself sick. . . .

" 'Struth," he muttered, then shouted, "Trevelyan. Get back here!"

The man returned immediately, alarmed in a new way.

"Mother's arriving tomorrow. Traveling on Sunday, even. Tell Mistress Dunscape to prepare her rooms and . . . oh, do whatever else is needed."

"Yes, sir. My apologies, sir."

"Oh, hell. If I were in a bad way she'd want to be here, and I suppose she'll be delighted to see me well."

When the secretary had left, Robin rose to pace the room, but halted at the pain. A knock at the door brought the well-scrubbed kitchen boy who'd just been elevated to dog care. He put Coquette down and she ran to Robin in her usual fervor of devotion.

"Not you again," Robin muttered, but picked up the dog. "Petra was right. I'm a heartless monster, aren't I? Who has so much devotion they can afford to toss some away?"

He knew the dog's sin was to remind him of Petra. He'd only had Coquette for a week when he'd met Sister Immaculata, and after that, they'd shared some remarkable adventures, all three of them. He remembered to send the lad off to his other duties, and sat back at his desk, putting Coquette on the surface, something she seemed to love.

"Pet and Petra," he said, tilting the dog's head up

as if there might be an intelligent response in the
bright eyes. "Is she, unlike you, a faithless bitch?"

The dog tilted her head as if thinking, but offered
no wisdom.

"You're finally going to be useful, though, my little
nothing. With any luck, you'll alert signor Varzi to my
presence in London, and he'll emerge from hiding.
Then we can pay him back for his cruelty to you."

Petra did indeed arrive in Guildford in less than two
hours, and paid Mighty Mike Cockcroft his shilling.

"What you going to do now?" he asked gruffly.

Petra hesitated. He was a weather-beaten rock of a
man but had a kindly look in his eye.

"Take a bed here, sir, then continue my journey in
the morning."

"Not back to Maidstone, I assume."

What point in concealment now? "No. To
Farnham."

"There's a slow coach to Farnham. Shamleigh, the
innkeeper here, will put you right for it, but it won't
run tomorrow, love, it being Sunday." He touched his
big hat and shambled off.

Petra had no trouble getting a bed in another common room, but her spirits were low. She was stuck
here until Monday, so she'd wasted her shilling, and
by now she was desperate to know her fate and be
able to make some sort of plan.

There were only two other travelers in this room—
a middle-aged woman traveling with a slow-witted
daughter. When the woman struck up a conversation,
Petra took part lackadaisically.

"You look troubled, dear," Mistress Culler said.

Wryly, Petra adapted an old story. "My mother's

sick near Farnham and I'm rushing to her side, but with Sunday, I'll be stuck here."

"But I thought you were Welsh, dear."

Petra invented quickly. "My father was. When he died, my mother came back here to look after her mother, but I stayed in my position. Near Monmouth."

That seemed to satisfy. "No one could blame you for traveling in such a cause, dear, but it'd have to be Shanks's pony." Petra's puzzlement must have shown, for the woman added, "On foot, dear. It's not much more than ten miles, and likely you'll get a ride here and there from people going to church and visiting family."

Heartened, Petra lay down to sleep, resolved to walk the ten miles and complete her journey the next day.

Robin hadn't expected many attendees in July in London, but his house was soon crowded. Those in Town had sent alerts to others whose country residences were nearby. Everyone wanted details of the duel with a highwayman in broad daylight.

Some men brought beautiful women of obliging natures, all of whom seemed eager to oblige him. Robin felt an alarming lack of enthusiasm and used his leg as an excuse. That didn't deter them all, and a few began to tease him about where the wound actually was.

He greeted the sight of a strapping blond gentleman in a spectacularly braided uniform as escape. "Christian!" Robin declared with true enthusiasm, but not rising from his place. His leg was giving him hell.

"What news of court, my friend? Damme, that sounds like a line from Shakespeare."

"No, that would be *'that shrewd and knavish sprite called Robin Goodfellow,'* " said Major Lord Grandiston. "How did a fribble like you acquire a wound?"

"Ask rather how anyone got past my impenetrable guard. You've never managed it."

Christian laughed. "Very well. How?"

"He was rather good."

"And dead?"

"Yes, but I can't take credit. The story's been in the papers."

"Never read 'em. Anything really interesting is all the buzz at court." Christian accepted wine from a servant, but said, "Good God, what's that?" He was looking at Coquette, who had danced out to be adored.

"Fluff," said Thorn dryly. "Someone sweep it up."

"Princess Coquette," said Robin. "I swear that her ears grow larger with admiration. She was the heroine of the hour."

"How?" Christian asked in disbelief.

"Startled my opponent at a crucial moment."

"That, I can believe."

Robin summoned a hovering footman to help him up out of his chair, then grasped his walking stick. "Let's find a quiet corner and I'll tell the tale."

"Is a quiet corner possible?" Christian asked, already bombarded with greetings and teasing about braid from all sides.

It took time to work out of the room, but then it was a short distance to the parlor that was part of the earl's suite of rooms. Robin still thought of them as his father's. Thorn had come with them and, of course, Coquette. Robin gave his friend the true account of his Kentish adventures.

Christian whistled. "Only you, Robin. Only you."

"Why does everyone say that?" Robin scooped up Coquette and put her on his lap. "You take me seriously, don't you, my little papillon?"

"The dog makes you ridiculous," said Thorn.

"You have no appreciation of the art of frivolity."

"Thank God."

"One day merely being a duke won't be enough to charm people."

"Evidence says otherwise," Thorn said dryly.

"Children," Christian chided. "Back to matters of moment. Robin, you wrote to ask about Italians at Richmond Lodge. The reply is, none in the past week."

"No one fitting the descriptions?"

"No. We live very quietly."

Robin hesitated about the next question, because Petra's story was probably all lies, but he lost the struggle. "Can you think of anyone attached to the court who would have been in Italy about twenty-two years ago? If he really was young, then we're talking about a man close to forty now."

Christian thought for a moment. "In London, court would be crawling with them. Nearly every peer visited Italy as a youth."

"What about permanent court officers?"

"Not offhand. I've finished my stint at court, by the way, but I know people there I can ask."

"Thank you," Robin said. "I doubt there's anything in it. It was all a story made up to amuse me. I did,"

he recollected, stroking Coquette, "demand amusement. As always, beware what you ask for."

"Good advice," Christian said, but added, "Is there
any danger of Lady Fowler's Fund increasing?"

"That idiotic vow we took? 'Struth, no," said Robin,
hoping he'd put the right degree of amused disbelief
on it. As he hobbled back down the corridor he heard
one of the men behind him murmur, "A side bet that
the Foul Fund will be a thousand richer by year's
end?"

That must have been Christian, because it was definitely Thorn who replied, "Done. He'd never be such
a fool."

Chapter 25

Petra walked through placid countryside, along a high ridge that spread patchwork fields around her. The land looked so prosperous and well tended, and bells pealed from many churches. When she passed through villages, some people gave her good morning, but most eyed her warily, seeing a vagrant.

Why hadn't she thought of that? She'd not even get close to a marquess in Mistress Waddle's donations. As the woman had said, she needed her better clothing to meet her relations.

Once she got to Farnham, she went into a small inn to ask to pay for a room and soap and water. She told the suspicious woman that she was going to apply for a position and wanted to look her best. Three pennies bought her use of a small room and a generous jug of hot water, soap, and a towel. She stripped to her shift, washed, and then changed into the green sprigged dress. It was still a simple garment, but much more respectable. She put the mobcap and wide hat back on, but she'd discard the battered hat before requesting admittance to Rothgar Abbey.

How precisely was she to do that? She'd be driven from the front door, but how to explain her mission at the servants' entrance? Perhaps she should ask for employment, but that would only take her to the house-keeper at best. Was she then to sneak around the house, seeking an opportunity to accost the marquess? That would get her thrown out, without doubt. Some servants never saw the family side of the house at all. All she could do was put her faith in God and her mother.

She looked in the small mirror, hoping for an appearance that would penetrate the barriers, but knew it wasn't there. The only comfort she found was the minor reassessment in the innkeeper's eyes. Up from vagrant to respectable peasant, Petra assumed.

She set off again, now only a couple of miles from Rothgar Abbey. She found a signpost to ALTON, 10 MILES. That was her road. But she smiled at the other fingerposts nailed beneath it. BENTLEY, 5 MILES. CUCK-OO'S CORNER, 8 MILES.

"Cuckoo" was close to "cock." She hoped it was another good omen that she was heading that way.

Robin didn't suffer the aftereffects of drink, but for some reason he awoke on Sunday feeling stale, foul-mouthed, and fuzzy headed. He listened to a clock chime ten, wished a glass of water would miraculously appear and someone would raise him to drink it, and went back to sleep again.

He felt a cool hand on his forehead and opened his eyes, only just managing to change "Petra?" to *"Maman?"* at the last moment.

"How could you, you careless wretch?" his mother demanded furiously in French. "They say you have had no doctor here. How *could* you?"

She was still in black, and it didn't suit her delicate skin and brown hair.

"Wright checked my leg at Thorn's house," Robin said in the same language, struggling to sit up. "I'm perfectly well."

"Do not seek to deceive me, me who bore you and raised you—"

With the help of about twenty servants, Robin thought.

"—and suffers terrors whenever you are out of my sight." She used her hands like Petra. Why had he never thought of that? "And now," she exclaimed, "and now, you get into a duel. You get a wound! You are a monstrously ungrateful child!"

He managed to capture a sharply gesticulating hand. "My dearest mother, my wound is small and healing. I am perfectly well except from revelries last night."

She stilled, assessing him with fierce blue eyes. "Truth?"

"Truth." He would not think of Petra, or of Powick marking similarities. They were nothing alike.

She sat on the edge of the bed, sagging with relief, and he kissed her plump, perfectly manicured hand. "I almost dismissed Trevelyan for worrying you. I should have."

"I would have rehired him. I hired him to begin with."

"To be my tutor, *Maman.* I believe I may dismiss my secretary."

"You would not do anything so dishonorable. He only obeyed me."

Pointless to suggest just now that her interests and his might sometimes split.

"You are truly healing well?" she asked, cradling his face. "You do not lie?"

"On my honor. But if you came to minister to me, I would be grateful if you brought me a glass of water."

She laughed and went to the carafe, a well-rounded woman with strength and grace in her movements. No, his mother had never used sword or pistol as best he knew, but she was active morn till night in the ruling of her domain, and fierce in fighting for her chicks.

What would she do when he took over the reins, which he feared he'd have to do soon, if only to hold on to his self-respect?

She returned with the water, smiling now.

"Ma belle," he said, toasting her.

It was flattery designed to amuse, but also true, or had been when she wore colors that suited her. Would she ever do so again?

"Why is Fontaine not attending to such things as water?" she demanded.

"I sent him on holiday."

"To Cheynings?"

"If you know everything, why ask?"

"But I don't know everything. I don't know *why.*"

"It's a long story, but he is well. Powick is well." *All your lovingly chosen attendants and watchdogs are well.* As if on cue, Coquette wriggled up from under the sheets, tail wagging.

She stared. "What is that?"

"A papillon dog. You've seen them at the French court."

"Then *why* is that? In your bed, even!"

"She begs most effectively. But to be precise, she's in her bed in my bed." He flipped back the covers to show Coquette's new basket, complete with pink velvet cushion.

"But you like big dogs. You have described my spaniels as fribbles."

"I've been seduced."

She reached to feel his skin again. He caught her hand and kissed it. "My dearest, darling mother, I'm not fevered. I will tell all." *Almost all.* "It will entertain, it will amuse, it will even thrill you, for any dangers are past and survived. But I pray you, let me rise, bathe, dress, and breakfast. I assume you have just arrived?"

"Would I delay in coming to you?"

"Absolutely not. So you will appreciate some time to recover from the journey."

"Oh, will I?"

He didn't reply.

"You've changed," she said, startling him.

"I assure you—"

She waved him to silence. "Definitely. A woman?"

Robin very much feared he blushed.

"For marriage or pleasure?" she demanded, all business now. "You haven't done anything foolish, have you?"

Robin crushed a flustered response and said, "I'll tell you all when I am bathed, shaved, and dressed."

She straightened as if challenged. Which, he realized, she was. When he didn't quail, she said, "Very well. I will summon a servant for you." At the door, she fired a parting shot. "I told you you should have bellpulls put in here."

Once she'd gone, Robin felt an alarming temptation to wriggle down under the covers, like a child attempting to hide. Coquette, ever sympathetic to mood, licked his hand. He stroked her. "She's not going to be happy." But then he corrected it. "No, nothing will distress my mother, for Petra d'Averio is a deceptive adventuress and I'll probably never see her again."

Robin's temporary valet entered and was sent to prepare a bath. Since the wound, Robin had only washed, but now he removed the bandage and sank down into hot water—and tumbled right back to Montreuil.

He'd lain in the bath there imagining Petra so very nearby, soaping her lovely body. He'd gone hard and had to relieve himself, but he'd still roared into that insane passion an hour later. . . .

Petra d'Averio. He'd known some of the most beautiful women of his world, and some of the most alluring, and definitely some of the most skilled at the seductive arts, but with her, it had been madness from the first. She'd caught him at first sight in the innyard of the Tête de Boeuf. No, at first word. *Maledizione*. A warning, that, for anyone with wit enough to realize it.

Her power had sizzled in the coach and then burned at Mère Goulart's under the extra fuel of danger. It had flared out of control in Montreuil, but reached its full, wildfire power on the *Courlis*.

Now she was gone—but not from his mind.

Petra in the smuggler's house, stretching in morning light. In the Gainer bedroom, tending to his wound with serious attention. A Sister of Saint Veronica, dedicated to aiding the wounded in the streets?

He surged out of the tub and swore at the strain on his wound. The alarmed footman supported him to a chair and helped him dress. He had things to do today, and the most difficult would be dealing with his mother. He replaced the bandage and dressed in plain breeches, shirt, and waistcoat. Instead of a coat, however, he wore his blue silk banyan on top—a touch of the invalid to soften her.

She was right. He had changed, perhaps because of a brush with death, or perhaps, as she'd implied, because of Petra. Whatever the cause, it was time to put his father's spirit to rest and assume full responsibility for his earldom. Strangely, he was even looking forward to it, but he didn't expect to achieve it without a battle.

He went to his mother's rooms, which wasn't a long journey, as she still used the ones next to the earl's suite. She should vacate them. She'd have to when he married.

Marriage. Despite their agreement, she probably had a list ready. A list of well-bred, well-mannered young ladies of excellent family and fortune. Young ladies raised to understand the ton, and understand how to be discreet and pragmatic in marriage. Not an adventurous, Italian sword-wielding nun among them.

He found his mother changed out of her traveling clothes and refreshed, but she frowned to see his limp and stick.

"The wound is fine," he assured her, kissing her hand and cheek. "There was some muscle damage and I'm pampering it. Truly, *Maman*."

"I suppose I shall have to trust you. I don't see why you brought that with you," she said, turning her annoyance on Coquette. "It's a mockery."

"She was a means to an end," he said, and related the story of the reluctant comtesse because he knew she would approve of that.

"Wicked boy," she said, but smiled.

How nice to live up to someone's expectations.

"May I summon my breakfast here, *Maman*? Then I can tell you my misadventures as I eat."

"Of course. Felice, see to it."

"Plain coffee," Robin told the diminutive maid, who'd come with his mother to England thirty years ago. "I need intense restoration."

The woman's wrinkled face creased with a wide smile as she curtsied and left.

"Now," said his mother, pacing restlessly. "Who is she?"

"Coquette?" he asked, deliberately misunderstanding. "I don't know her antecedents."

"The woman in this! I know there is one. Trevelyan said something before becoming difficult."

"*Maman*, I truly will have to dismiss him if you make him your spy."

She actually flushed, a bright, rather beautiful flare of color high in her cheeks. "What could you want to hide from me?"

He just stroked Coquette.

"Who is she, Robin? Italian, I gather."

"I don't know why you say it like that. It means she's Catholic."

"Which is a great trouble in this country. Consider me, who has had to watch my children raised without the sacraments."

He gave her a look. Her devotion to her religion was weak at best.

"You will not put me off," she snapped. "Is she your mistress? That is no big thing, a mistress. I see no reason for you to conceal that. Which is why I demand, who is she? What is she to you? Where is she?"

He answered the last. "I have no idea. That, at least, should make you happy. I encountered a lady in distress and aided her. You would not wish me ungallant."

"Fah!" Her favorite exclamation. "She caused you to be wounded."

"She was pursued by some Milanese determined to drag her back to service their master. You would not want me to have permitted that." He suspected she disagreed. "We crossed to England, but one of them caught up with us near Folkestone. There was a sword fight, I was injured, but am now recovering well."

"And your opponent? He is dead?"

"Yes."

"That is good. Very good. I do not like to think of you fighting with swords, but if you fight, you must win, and an enemy is better dead. Otherwise, they could seek revenge."

"Pragmatic, and completely correct, as usual."

The coffee came along with a loaded tray. Robin dismissed the servants and served himself. He sipped and shuddered with relief, his mind coming more alert.

His mother was drinking café au lait. "Strong coffee in the morning," she said, frowning. "It will weaken you. Felice!"

"I prefer it this way," Robin said, smiling at the maid who'd hurried in. "But to please you, *Maman,* I will choose a weak bun over strong beef."

"Fah!"

He ate a mouthful. He knew he shouldn't revive the topic of Petra, but felt compelled to ask, "If I find my damsel in distress, will you be kind to her?"

"If she is to be your mistress, yes. If you think to marry her, no."

"You know nothing of her," he protested.

"On the contrary. I know everything. She fled Milan, so she has no powerful family there to assist her. She was in distress, so she has no money. She chose to travel with a young man like you, so she has no discretion, or perhaps worse, no morals. She is probably a whore."

"No."

"You failed with her?"

"*Maman,* you are in danger of becoming vulgar."

She jerked as if he'd hit her. "Perhaps, but . . ." She exhaled. "Very well. You have never disappointed me in these matters before. I will trust you to do what is right."

"What I *believe* is right," he said, and took another bite.

She didn't respond, which was, he supposed, a victory of sorts, but he knew her vigilance would be extreme from now on.

Petra had left the Alton Road, but not found the turn to Rothgar Abbey and began to wonder if she had misunderstood the directions. She paused by the side of the road to rest and think, but then she heard a vehicle approaching and wished she wasn't quite so exposed. A sort of open coach appeared, pulled by two steady horses, and seeming to hold a whole family from grandmother to baby on side seats in the back. A sparely built middle-aged couple rode in the driver's seat.

"We can take one more," the cheerful gray-haired man said.

Petra was bemused. "But you don't know where I'm going, sir."

He smiled, making cherry cheeks. "Ahead or behind. If ahead, we'll take you to wherever our ways part."

This simple logic had Petra climbing into the cart to squeeze between a young woman and a girl. She found a few young children sitting on the floor among the legs, but in their modest way everyone was well dressed. "You are going to church?" Petra guessed.

"No, miss," a young woman said, with her father's smile. "We went this morning. We're off to Rothgar Abbey."

Petra gasped, "Why?" before she could stop herself. Had there been some great disaster?

"His lordship's fete," the woman replied, bouncing a toddler on her knee. "You're not from these parts, are you?"

"No. From Wales. What is this fete?"

The man on the box called back the answer. "The Marquess of Rothgar, he who owns the Abbey, opens his estate to his people now and then."

From her seat, Petra could see a bit more of the countryside, which seemed to be farmland. "We are already on his estate?"

"Lord no, dear," said the woman, twisting to smile at Petra. "We're from Aldershot, but my Tom is one of his lordship's bookbinders, and all the local people he does business with are welcome. It's a grand day out for us all, and does the young ones good to see such lovely things."

"You are allowed in the house, too?" Petra asked, ideas stirring.

"Not on the public day, no. But," the woman said with pride, "people like us, ones he trusts, can ask to visit when his lordship's not in residence. We take the children to see the library now and then, so they can

see their father's work in its place. One of the servants
takes us round the pictures and statues and things.
Ever so lovely, some of them are."

One of the lads broke in to mention a battle painting, and a girl some furniture decorated with birds
and flowers.

"He seems to be a very kindly lord," Petra said,
her spirits rising.

"To those who deal honestly with him," the man
said in a tone that lowered her spirits a little. "I'm
Tom Harstead, ma'am, and this is my wife, Abigail.
You just say when you want to be put down."

Petra tried to decide how to handle this. It seemed
she might be able to go right into the Rothgar Abbey
estate today, but perhaps she'd need to be with people
who had an invitation.

Mistress Harstead said, "Warmer a bit now, Tom,
after marrying."

The weather?

"We was all invited to the wedding celebration,"
said the young woman opposite, flushing bright at the
memory. "Now, that was a feast to remember."

They all began to chatter about it. Petra wanted to
cry for everything to stop while she thought. The
woman had meant that the marquess had been cold
and now was warm? But a recent marriage?

"He only married last year?" she asked when she
could get a word in. "Or is it a second marriage?"

"No, dear, his first."

"He is a young man, then?" Petra asked, feeling sick.
Could her Marquess of Rothgar be dead and his son
have the title? Why had they never thought of that? But
no, a son would have to be even younger than she. A
brother could have inherited, however, or even a cousin.

"Nay," Mr. Harstead called back. "Nigh on forty, he is, but a fine, handsome man still."

Petra breathed again, but said, "Strange that he not marry until so old."

"Forty's not old," Mistress Harstead protested, "but he had his reasons."

Petra knew she'd hit something Mrs. Harstead didn't think fit to tell a stranger. What? She couldn't see how to ask.

"So what brings you to these parts, dear?" the woman asked, clearly changing the subject.

Petra spun a variation on her story about a cruel mistress and being cast off.

"That's wicked, that is. Do you have a particular destination? If not, you might want to try your luck at the Abbey. Good employment there."

"Perhaps I will."

The cart stopped and Mr. Harstead twisted in his seat. "This is where we turn off. Do you wish to continue with us and try your luck at the Abbey?"

"Yes, please. And thank you."

The man turned the vehicle and they rumbled on their way. "Likely you'll not find anyone to talk to right now, mind," Mistress Harstead said, "for nearly every servant'll be out in the grounds. But later on."

The cart slowly became part of a steady stream of vehicles and pedestrians, with everyone dressed in their best. They passed one party who were pushing a shawl-wrapped ancient in a wheelbarrow, and finally stopped because of the jam of traffic entering the estate.

Petra was tempted to laugh. However she'd imagined this momentous moment, it had been nothing like this.

Chapter 26

Feeling alarmingly as if his world were turning up-side down, Robin went to deal with his secretary, to insist on no more tattling. The man looked as if he were going to protest, but at least kept his mouth shut.

"I *will* dismiss you," Robin warned. "I'm sure that's hard to believe of the lad you birched for not learning his Greek, but I am no longer that boy."

Trevelyan frowned. "You are still not wise."

Robin held on to his temper. "Then I will have to learn faster, won't I? But you are to obey my orders and keep my privacy, even from my mother. If you cannot, leave now and I'll give you glowing recom-mendations. Fail me, and I'll throw you out. Reluc-tantly, but I will do it."

For a horrible moment, Robin thought the man was going to cry, but then he said, "Perhaps you're readier than I thought. But . . . yes, then, I'll take your first offer. I don't believe I'm best suited for the new role."

Robin almost protested, but said, "Very well." He held out his hand, and after a hesitation Trevelyan took it. "You've served me well, but it's hard for all of us to metamorphose into new roles. Where will you go?"

They broke hands and Trevelyan took out a handkerchief and dabbed at his eyes. "I believe I will return to tutoring, sir. It was very satisfying with a mind such as yours."

"Mine?" Robin asked with a laugh. "You berated me every inch of the way."

"For laziness, for taking the easy way. And it galled me that you could excel at everything even so."

"Ah, is that the secret of it? Sweat and grit teeth, and the whole world will applaud the results, even if they be dismal. Doesn't the Bible recommend that every valley shall be exalted and every mountain made low?"

"The crooked straight and the rough places plain," Trevelyan completed with a slight smile. "Yes, that is your nature, isn't it, sir?"

"Whether people want it or not. But I'm coming to see that a grimmer style is sometimes required. God go with you."

Thorn crossed with Trevelyan as he came in. "Bad news?" he asked, putting gloves, riding crop, and hat on a small table.

"As always, that depends. Any news?"

"No useful responses, no unaccounted-for Italians."

"Varzi the Clever. I should have expected nothing less, but it makes it interesting." He caught himself. "I'm done with games."

"Alas, poor world."

"Haven't you often complained of my levity?"

"Only out of jealousy. Don't change too much."

"If I can find the way out of this maze, I promise a jig every Tuesday and a revel on Saturday."

"At least news of your Town revel is out as

planned," Thorn said. "I was asked about your 'pretty
new bitch' on the way here. It'll be in all the papers
tomorrow, along with details about your card party,
so if Varzi was in any doubt about your whereabouts,
he won't be now."

Robin pulled a face, but said, "There's something
else. What?"

"Might be nothing," Thorn said, taking a somewhat
battered letter out of his pocket. "Came up from
Ithorne yesterday, but wasn't drawn to my attention
immediately because of its shabby appearance."

Robin took the poor-quality paper and read the
blotchy inscription with a pattering heart. He turned
it to inspect the seal. Wax simply squished down. He
snapped it and fumbled the paper open.

To my admired protector,

Oh, God.

I know you must be concerned . . .

"Damn her," he muttered.

*. . . which is poor reward for your kindness, but
please know that I am well and with friends. I hope
the same is true of you.*

"Friends? What friends? When was this written?"
He looked back at the top. "Friday. Where was it
sent from?" Robin turned the sheet and studied the
smudged writing of the postmaster. "What does this
say? Mickly?"

"Micklebury. I've already sent an inquiry there
posthaste, but she won't have lingered, of course. Can
you share what it says?"

Robin read the rest aloud. " '*I promise you, on my
honor, that if I am in need or distress, I will send to
you for help . . .*' If you're able, you idiot. '*So if you*

*do not hear from me, you'll know all is well. Farewell,
my friend. You will dance better through life without
a pebble in your shoe.'* "

Robin threw down the note. " 'Dance through life.'
I'm not dancing with a carved-up leg, am I? Or with
concern for her a millstone around my neck."

"Pebble in your shoe?" Thorn asked.

"Petra, 'rock.' Petronilla, 'little rock.' We might find
a trail to follow. But no. She wants to escape me."

He picked up the letter as if a second reading would
reveal new information. All it revealed was Petra. He
could hear her saying those words in her lilting accent.

"She doesn't write an elegant hand," Thorn
pointed out.

"Lowborn after all?" But Robin studied the letter.
The writing was plain and perhaps even effortful, but
then he saw how she'd begun by trying to write with
complex loops on the rough paper. She'd written
sparely by necessity.

"Whoever these friends are, they're impoverished,"
he said. "I suppose it makes no sense to hurtle
down there."

"And could play havoc with your leg."

"God rot my leg!" But then Robin thought how
literally that could be true. "No, not that. Very well,
I'll play the wise man and send someone on the er-
rand. I must do something, however," Robin said, rising. "I'm going to visit Mistress Cornelys."

"I'm sure she has fine-quality writing paper."

"But it's somewhere I can go. It is also somewhere
signor Varzi might check if he knows of the connection between Teresa Cornelys and Petra's mother.
And," he said in sudden excitement, "why didn't I

think of this? La Cornelys might know who her father is."

"Might she, by gad? But I'm coming, too. Armed."

"Varzi might be there?" Robin said. "That would
be delightful, but she'd never permit attack on a titled
guest in her house."

"Would he ask her permission?"

"A point. I'll go armed and with armed men. I'll
have to use my damned sedan chair, anyway. If you'll
oblige, I'd like you and some men to keep a watch
outside. First to see if anyone else is watching, and
then to see if Cornelys sends a message after I leave."

"Glad of some action. Do you take your fluffy
guard dog?"

Coquette was frisking around Thorn as usual, trying
to win him over.

"Tempting, but she'd probably bite the woman on
principle and die of poisoning."

Petra tried to look like a comfortable part of the
cheerful Harsteads, but she noted two footmen in
blue and gold livery and powdered hair watching everyone stream in. They might partly be for show,
for everyone loved their gilded elegance, but Petra
guessed they were local men able to spot who
didn't belong.

One passing couple riding a single horse called,
"Ain't you grand, Jimmie!" and got a grin and a teasing reply.

The other footman, who was closer to Petra, said,
"Good day to you, Mr. Harstead," a mark of respect
that made Mistress Harstead preen. Petra passed by
unnoticed.

"Isn't it lovely?" Mistress Harstead said, looking around.

The estate was obviously designed by an expert hand to simulate countryside at its most perfect. Petra saw a lake in the distance upon which swans glided, and some sort of white temple.

"There's deer normally," Mistress Harstead said as her husband turned the cart into an area set aside for vehicles. "But for these big events they put them somewhere. There's lovely gardens up near the house, and peacocks. Such a noise as they make. Wouldn't want them outside my bedroom window."

The cart stopped and everyone climbed out. The older boys unhitched the horses and led them into a roped-off paddock. Mistress Harstead and her older daughters cleaned and tidied everyone. Petra took off her hat, but that was the best she could do. When no one was looking, she stuffed it and her bundle under one of the seats. It contained nothing but Mistress Waddle's donated clothes, and though she'd liked to keep them for sentimental reasons, she'd look too out of place carrying it here.

She was as ready as she'd ever be, but when she surveyed the park and the distant, majestic house, her courage leaked out through her worn-out shoes.

The baby was put into her arms as the young mother ran to capture an escaping toddler. It was plump and drooling but happy, and Petra had to smile at it. She instantly felt better and wondered if the mother had truly needed help or had sensed her need. She made silly noises at the infant, who obligingly chuckled, showing the beginnings of one tooth.

But then the party was ready. The mother reclaimed her baby and Mr. Harstead pointed toward the house.

"You might as well ask, but if everyone's busy, I'm sure they'll let you wait."

It was a dismissal of sorts, so Petra said, "Thank you," and set off across grass scattered with people.

"Watch the ha-ha!" he called after her.

She turned back. "The what?"

"A deep ditch around the house. Keeps the deer out of the garden. There are bridges."

Petra thanked them again and watched as they went off along a wide path, the younger children running here and there and everywhere around the slower older people. She'd met all kinds of people in her English journey, and all, old to young, had homes, families, and a place in the world. Unlike her.

She joined a stream of people ambling toward the house, knowing she stood out by being solitary, but there was nothing she could do about that. She walked at the same pace as most, trying to look as if she belonged, eyes alert for a man who could be her father.

Was she to approach him in public, though? Perhaps it would be better to go straight to the house and wait nearby until this event was over.

She crossed a bridge over the grassy trench and then more smooth lawn to enter some formal gardens closer to the house. There she found more footmen. All looked pleasant and were chatting to visitors, but they were clearly stationed to prevent people from entering the house.

Petra halted and looked around, wondering where she could wait without seeming suspicious, but then she spotted a dark-haired gentleman. An ignorant eye might think him one of the better sort of guest, and his manner was relaxed and amiable, but Petra knew he was an aristocrat. Her father?

He was dark-haired and could be dark-eyed, but something didn't feel right. How peculiar. Had she really thought she'd feel some deep instinct of the blood?

There were too many people for an encounter, so she moved on, but she'd already paused too long. A hand grabbed her arm. "Who're you, then?" demanded a heavy-jawed woman in an alarming hat. "Never seen you afore." The woman was bolstered in front and wide of hip, and had the manner of one who loved to command.

Petra tugged. "Let go of me," she said, but a crowd was gathering.

"Let's have your name first."

"Maria Monmouth."

"Never 'eard of you. Anyone else 'eard of 'er?"

The murmur of denials sounded ugly. Where had all the good cheer gone?

"I have a right to be here," Petra protested, cursing her foreign accent.

"Dressed like that?" the inquisitor sneered. "A vagrant, that's what you are, and up to no good, I'll be bound. What's more," she said, narrow eyed, "you're a furriner. What if you're a spy? Or out to kill his lordship?"

She'd relaxed her grip so Petra wrenched free and pushed her away. "You're mad. Leave me alone!"

She was encircled, however, and the mood was nasty.

"Doesn't she sound like a furriner to you?" the woman demanded of all, loving the furor she'd started.

"Looks foreign, too," a man said. "Where you from, then?"

"Wales," Petra said.

"Ah, well," he said. "That explains it, Mistress Digby. Even speak a forcign language in Wales, I 'ear tell."

"Then what's a Welsh woman doing 'ere?" the woman demanded. "She's no right. This is for his lord-ship's people, this is—"

"What's going on here?"

At the calm, authoritative voice the circle melted into a formless cluster. It was the dark-haired man, seeming relaxed and at ease, but his eyes were taking in every detail.

Not dark eyes. A kind of hazel.

"This 'ere's a spy, milord!" the woman exclaimed, swelling with importance. "No business 'ere, unless it be wicked business."

Petra's arm was taken again, but more gently. "Thank you, Mistress Digby. I'll deal with her. Please, everyone, go along and enjoy yourselves."

The crowd dispersed, but part of it went with Mistress Digby, who was expounding on her suspicions and sagacity.

His lordship drew Petra along a crushed stone path between low flower beds, and she had no choice but to go. He was a lord, but not her father unless the portrait of the eye lied. He stopped in a new spot with no one close by. "Well?" he asked in a neutral way. "Your story, ma'am?"

Petra studied him. "My Lord Rothgar?"

His brows rose a little. "No. You seek him?"

Perhaps she wavered, for he touched her arm again, just enough to offer support. At the end of her re-sources, Petra simply said, "Yes."

"Why?"

"It's a personal matter."

He looked her over. "With child? You'll not foist it on him."

"I would never—"

His raised hand stopped her. After a moment, he shrugged. "Come along, then. This could be amusing."

At that echo of Robin, Petra was tempted to flee, but she'd come this far and would see it through. She went with him, asking, "May I know your name, my lord?"

"Lord Arcenbryght Malloren. Lord Rothgar's brother. One of them."

Such a simple explanation, but what a strange name.

Lord Arcenbryght asked a servant for the marquess and was told he'd recently been demonstrating the workings of a fountain. Was the marquess eccentric? Hadn't she heard that he might be mad? When they arrived at the fountain it was playing merrily without assistance, and someone said his lordship had gone to the topiary garden.

Her escort strolled along the trail of his busy brother, stopping frequently to talk to people. Petra did her best to ignore the strange looks sent her way, but she wished to heaven they'd reach the marquess and have done with this.

Then a petite lady joined them. "What's happening?" she asked, with a bright-eyed look at Petra. She wore a hat as wide as Mistress Waddle's, but a great deal more stylish.

"I'm taking a conundrum to the master of them. Any idea where he is?"

"I think I saw him going to the pineapple house."

Lord Arcenbryght switched directions. The lady fell in beside Petra. "I'm Lady Bryght."

"Lady Bright?" Petra queried, dazed.

"No one can be bothered with Arcenbryght. An ancient English prince. They often had unpronounce-able names. So he's Lord Bryght, and as I'm his wife I'm Lady Bryght. May I know your name?"

"I don't know." It escaped because of weariness and confusion, but it wasn't surprising that both her hosts looked skeptical.

"I'm not mad. Truly."

"Perhaps we should find Diana," Lady Bryght said.

"Rothgar she wants, so Rothgar she gets."

"Perhaps you should check her for a knife, then."

"She'd probably cry rape. You could feel her all over."

"I'm not dangerous!" Petra protested.

Lord Bryght turned to her and said something rapidly in French. After a heartbeat's thought, Petra pretended not to understand. He smiled slightly but coldly, not fooled at all.

"A conundrum within a maze. Bey should be delighted, and I *am* armed."

Not entirely careless, then, on this public occasion.

A long glasshouse came into view. The wooden parts were made in a lacy design that was quite beautiful, and the glass panes shone like diamonds in the sunlight, but Petra's attention was fixed on it as the place where perhaps she might finally have the encounter she'd come so far to make. She studied all the males near the hothouse, but saw none that were likely.

Lord Bryght said, "Bey. An unexpected guest."

Chapter 27

Petra turned so quickly she cricked her neck and found herself meeting eyes with another tall, dark gentleman, but this one was different. His features were harsher. He was older. Perhaps, just perhaps, something did twang deep inside her, but if so, it could have been fear, or a reaction to the sudden attention in the Marquess of Rothgar's dark eyes.

Why was he looking at her like that?

He took a graceful farewell of his companions and came toward them. Like his brother, he was dressed plainly, dark hair simply tied back. Like his brother, no one would mistake him for an ordinary man. He said nothing, so Lord Bryght explained.

"I found this lady being harassed by the officious Mistress Digby, and she said she wished to speak to you. I haven't searched her for weapons."

"We haven't searched anyone here for weapons. It would be unfair to single out one, and I do believe no one's tried to assassinate me for at least a year." He bowed slightly. "Ma'am?"

Petra was unable to speak. Though everything else was casual, his gaze was not, and she'd never imagined this moment taking place with so many people nearby.

"Perhaps you would care to visit the house?" he said, gesturing. "I have a number of items that might interest you."

She was frozen again, wildly imagining dungeons, or her disappearing entirely. Who would ever know?

"Bey . . ." said Lady Bryght anxiously.

The marquess smiled a little. "Am I being terrifying? I mean you no harm at all, my dear, but if you would prefer, Lady Bryght can accompany us. *Forse dovremmo andare in un luogo un po' più appartato per discuterne.*"

At the Italian, Petra's breath caught. He had simply said that they should discuss matters in private, but it showed that he knew or at least suspected who she was. She couldn't read his emotions, but she didn't see rage or fear and this was the encounter she'd come so far to achieve, so when he held out his arm, she put her hand on it and allowed him to lead her away.

Robin dressed grandly because Teresa Cornelys valued such things, and his chairmen would carry him right into the richly decorated entrance hall, so there'd be no chance of being seen in finery at this time of day. He climbed out, looking around. He'd been to Carlisle House on a number of occasions for her assemblies, but the place seemed strange now, empty and echoing like a theater set.

Teresa Cornelys swept downstairs to greet him, dressed like a duchess and with an equally grand manner, but her eyes were sharp as a hawk's. If Petra had found refuge here Robin would be grateful, but he'd also remove her as soon as possible. He followed the woman to a reception room and declined refreshments. He sat and asked his question.

"Petra d'Averio, my lord?" she said, painted brows rising with what looked like honest astonishment. Her Italian accent was stronger than Petra's, but achingly reminiscent. "I haven't seen her since she was a child."

"You do know her, though?"

She shrugged with a typical spreading of the hands that also reminded him of Petra. "Does one know the daughter of a patroness? I saw her playing with her dolls. A pretty child. Very dark." Slyly, she added, "Neither *il conte* nor her mother were so dark."

Robin was momentarily stunned. The woman had casually confirmed Petra's story. She was the contessina Petra d'Averio, and he was awed by her courage and resilience when tossed out into the harsh world.

"You knew her mother well, I understand," he said.

Another shrug. "She wished to improve her voice and was kind enough to hire me, but yes, a warmth developed. We were close in age."

"Then I'm sorry to have to tell you that she recently died, ma'am."

"Ah." Her face pinched, but she said, "It was all long ago, and I haven't seen her for over a decade."

"Did you correspond?"

"Occasionally. I'm a busy woman, my lord. Things linger undone."

And that might be the root of her business problems. Despite the popularity of her entertainments and the high prices she charged, she teetered constantly on the edge of bankruptcy.

"I gather the contessina was not, in fact, her husband's child," Robin said.

Her painted face became even more masklike.
"Who would say that?"

"You implied it, ma'am, and her brother has confirmed it, now that his mother is dead."

She made a moue of disgust, but no other comment.

"Did the contessa tell you who Petra's father was?"

"Why does that concern you, Lord Huntersdown?"

"For my own good reasons."

He could almost see her calculating profit and loss.
"Amalia never mentioned his name, only that he was
young and English. And, of course, perfection in every
way. She fell foolishly in love, my lord, a sad affliction
of the young. She was fortunate that it did not end
in disaster."

There seemed to be some fondness there, so Robin
decided to tell her a bit of the truth. "It may still harm
Petra. Now the contessina's mother is dead and her
brother has shamed her, she has fled to England. I
hoped she had contacted you."

"Me?" No doubting the astonishment. "Of course,
I would welcome my old friend's daughter if she came
to me, but . . . but this is extraordinary."

Robin lost any lingering hope that the woman was
concealing Petra. He rose, hating having to still use
the stick to take the weight off his leg. "If she should
come here, ma'am, I would be grateful for word of it."

She rose, too, studying him. "Pardon me, my Lord
Huntersdown, but what are your attentions to little
Petra?"

He replied coolly. "I encountered her in France and
was able to do her a small service. I was concerned
by her lack of firm plans and hoped to hear good news
of her."

"She promised to become a beautiful young woman," she remarked.

"And has fulfilled that promise, but I wish her no ill, ma'am."

"Young gentlemen like you, my lord, think no ill of ruining women."

"Mistress Cornelys, you would not want to make me your enemy."

Her cheeks reddened beneath the rouge, but she said, "Would you marry her?"

"That is none of your business."

"As I seem to be in place of her mother, I must disagree."

Perhaps this woman had good intentions after all. "I rejoice that you will stand her friend, ma'am. If she comes to you, will you send me word?"

Every inch the grand lady, she said, "That, my lord, shall be up to her."

Robin's jaw tensed with frustration, but he said, "I would be generous to anyone who relieved my anxiety."

He noted the flash of greed in her eyes before she masked it and accompanied him to his chair. As one of his men opened the door, she said, "I have seen advertisements for a man called Varzi."

Robin halted. "Yes?"

"He came here. He, too, seemed to think Petra might seek refuge with me."

"You gave him the same answer?"

"It is the truth, my lord."

Robin settled in his sedan and was carried outside. He'd achieved nothing except confirmations. Petra's story was true and Varzi was in London, seeking her. He had to capture the man, but the advertisement was doing no good. He returned home and went to his study to make new plans.

He'd left Petra's splotchily written letter on his desk and picked it up to read it through for perhaps the tenth time. This time he noticed that the rough wax seal held traces of a fingerprint and wasted time studying it. Contessina Petra d'Averio. Still the misbegotten daughter of a careless Englishman. Still penniless and highly unlikely to be a discreet, pragmatic wife, but he was sliding down a slope without hope of reverse.

His mother was going to rage, but at least Petra was aristocratically born and raised. He was certain she'd acquit herself perfectly in drawing room and ballroom, and execute the tricky court curtsy with ease.

Was he actually imagining her presented at court?

Of course, for as his wife, his countess, she must be.

Smiling wryly at his own folly, he kissed the broken wax, then tucked the letter under his waistcoat, close to his heart. For the first time in an age, part of his way was clear. He would stop Varzi but also find Petra and convince her to give him a second chance.

Thorn arrived with no news, however. No one appeared to the watching Carlisle House, and no one had left with a message. He'd left one man observing the place just in case.

Robin reported what Mistress Cornelys had said.

"She spoke the truth?" Thorn said.

"That's my assessment."

"So your Petra's extraordinary story is true."

"And I need to find her, but in God's name, at this point, where do I start?"

"Why not insert another advertisement?"

"Much good the last one has done me."

Robin grabbed the map that sat open on his desk,

marked with the Gainer farm and possible sightings. No amount of study revealed anything new, and Petra could be anywhere by now.

The marquess didn't speak, so neither did Petra. Like his brother, he moved without haste, exchanging words with his guests, pleasant to all. He did not, however, introduce Petra, which won her some strange looks. But how could he? She realized now that she'd not given Lord Bryght a name, and Lord Rothgar hadn't asked.

They entered the house from a patio that led into a glasshouse, which led into a room whose walls were decorated with paintings of plant-twined trellises, as if to make a transition from the outside to within. Then they were in a wood-paneled corridor inside a great house that seemed very weighty and eerily quiet. Petra couldn't help but shiver.

"You have nothing to fear from me," he said as he took her down the corridor and into a gilded marble hall with a huge, empty fireplace and a sweeping staircase. A solitary footman stood impassively by the closed front door. "But I do have something to show you."

He led her down another corridor into a small room lined with cupboards and drawers, and with a table and chairs in the center.

"This is where we keep our surplus ornaments," he said, pulling open one shallow drawer, then another. "Ah." He removed something and turned to offer it to her.

Petra took the small, oval miniature of a young man against sketchy Italian ruins. The picture had not been executed by a great artist, but it caught the luminous beauty some youths possess before they truly become men. He was dark-eyed, and his dark hair hung loose around his collar.

He looked astonishingly like her.

"Sit," he said, moving a chair for her.

Petra did so. Otherwise she might have crumpled to the floor. "So it's true."

"You doubted it? I'm sorry if that little performance shocked you. I have a lamentable taste for theatrics. Do you need something? Tea, wine?"

Petra breathed deeply a few times. "Perhaps I do. I don't think I've eaten enough recently."

He left and she studied the picture, seeing the young man who'd enraptured her mother. Beautiful but so very young, but then her mother had been only twenty, though married for five years.

He returned and moved a chair to face hers. As he sat, he said, "Don't feel you have to talk. We have time."

"You have guests. Many guests."

"And family to fill the breach. Bryght and Portia, Brand and Rosa, even my sister Hilda and her brood." She must have looked glazed, for he added, "Don't feel you need to remember anything. I'm filling a silence for fear you'll disappear, like a genie from an Arabian tale."

She studied him. "I don't think you fear anything."

"Fear is not shameful, only cowardice."

Petra looked down at her grubby hands on her cheap and dusty skirt, then looked up again. "Did you know?"

"That you existed? No. Foolish of me not to wonder, but I was very young. I suppose I assumed that Amalia would tell me, but why should she? Her husband accepted you?"

"Yes," Petra said, not ready to get into the complexities.

"Your name?" he asked.

She laughed with embarrassment at not having supplied it. "Petra Maria d'Averio."

He nodded, but there was a knock at the door. He went to open it and take a tray. Preferring that a servant not see her? But the footman already had. The Dark Marquess was taking this very calmly, but she couldn't read him at all. He still might want to make the embarrassment disappear.

He placed the tray on the table and poured. "Highhandedly, I ordered coffee, for few Italians like tea. Was I wrong?"

"No," she said, shivering slightly as the rich aroma reached her. How long had it been?

Montreuil. She squashed down that thought. Her father must never learn about Montreuil, and especially not about what had happened on the *Courlis*. If she had any hope here she needed her virtue.

"Cream, sugar?" he asked.

"Both, please." Warily she added, "Generously."

He smiled and complied, then put the cup and saucer into her hands. She sipped and sighed, then drank some more, savoring. She knew, however, that he was waiting for her story.

"I . . . I don't know where to begin, my lord."

"There's no hurry." He placed a small plate by her, offering meat between slices of bread. "They're called sandwiches, after the Earl of Sandwich, who invented them because he wouldn't leave the gaming table to eat. Useful at a time like this." When she took one, he smiled. "How delightfully novel, to feed a hungry child of my own."

"You have no other?" But then she blushed and hastily took a bite. He'd only married last year and one did not refer to bastards, even if one was one.

"None."

The sandwich was tasty and she was hungry, but she put it aside. "I must tell you that I could be bringing danger here, my lord."

His brows rose, but he didn't seem alarmed. "Danger from whom?"

She didn't want to tell him, because it all led back to her folly, but she'd have no more people harmed over her. "A man called Varzi, who works for the conte di Purieri. Ludovico—il conte—wants me, and has sent Varzi to drag me back."

He snapped his fingers. "That for Varzi, but it's good that you told me. What has he done so far? Has he hurt you?"

He spoke without heat, but Petra felt as if she'd suddenly been surrounded by high walls and an army. She could almost weep for relief, but for fear, too. These were cold walls and a ruthless army. Her father must never learn about Robin, or he might turn his army on him—on the man he'd see as having violated his daughter.

Her father.

Her mother had been correct about the resemblance, but she couldn't have known he'd have a picture in which he looked so much the same, so she'd still trusted to remembered kindness. But the harsher-featured man before her had doubled his age and become the Dark Marquess, the Eminence Noir, the duelist. When all Petra wanted was to collapse into someone's strong protection, she would have to dredge up a little more strength and stay on guard.

"Varzi seized me in Boulogne," she said, choosing each word. "I escaped, but he injured two men who were trying to help me. I must confess to injuring one of Varzi's men when I escaped. There may be trouble over that."

"No French legal matter can affect you here. As for this Varzi, now that I know, he will not bother you further."

Do all Englishmen think themselves invulnerable? "Don't underestimate him, my lord."

"I try never to underestimate people, especially enemies. Do you think he has followed you here?"

"I took great pains to lose any pursuers."

"Good. He need not worry you any longer, my dear."

Irritation sparked. She might have wanted a father, but she didn't want to be patted on the head and told not to worry.

Perhaps he read her thoughts, for he smiled slightly. "You must allow me a father's right to protect."

That was exactly what she was afraid of.

He rose. "I am delighted you've found me, Petra, but I must return to my guests. May I assume you would like to rest, bathe, and change?"

Petra rose, too, remembering her sorry state. "I'm sorry. And I have no other clothes. . . ."

"No matter. Clothes can be found. I believe you're of a size with my wife."

She'd forgotten his wife. "She will not mind?"

"Lending you a gown? No."

"My existence."

"Mind a love affair over twenty years ago? She's much too wise, and, in fact, you bring a precious gift. But that, too, must wait." He hesitated then, in a way that seemed unusual for him. "I will not pressure you, but it would please me if you could eventually call me Father or Papa."

She stared at him. "You wish to openly acknowledge me?"

"With such a striking resemblance," he said, amused, "I see no choice."

He went to the door to speak to the footman again, then returned to lead her out of the room, up the grand staircase, and into a warren of corridors. What sort of remote room did a bastard daughter warrant?

"This place is a maze," he said. "Too many piecemeal renovations over the centuries. Summon a footman to guide you if you don't wish to wander. Most rooms have bellpulls."

He opened a door into a lovely, sunlit bedchamber, decorated in deep pink and creams. "You may choose another later, but this is recently vacated and thus aired. The pull is there, by the fireplace. Request anything you wish, my dear. This is now your home. I'll station a footman outside your door to serve as guide, and in case you're wrong about signor Varzi. The abbey is more vulnerable than usual today."

Vulnerable. Petra glanced outside, seeing the crowded estate with a new eye. "He is ruthless," she warned. "In Boulogne, he overpowered one guard and threatened to mutilate him unless I went with him. But he had two henchmen then."

"How many does he have now?"

"None of those. One I wounded. The other . . . was killed by a smuggler."

"I'm all admiration. But don't fear. My own position and activities demand a certain amount of security. He will not threaten you here."

He left, and Petra sat on a chaise upholstered in deep pink velvet, weakened by relief, confusion, exhaustion, and fear, especially for Robin. Thank God she hadn't let him bring her here. She'd recognized the sort of man he was at first sight. The Marquess of Rothgar would surely do the same. He did not seem to be a man who'd look kindly on a rake who'd fornicated with his daughter, no matter how protective he'd been.

Of course, she didn't need to reveal that. Unless she turned out to be with child. That was a disaster she refused to contemplate.

But many fathers would insist on marriage if their daughter was merely alone with a man in an intimate situation, never mind if she shared a bed with him. Three times, if one counted the coach.

A forced marriage. What a horrible thing to do to Robin, and she didn't want it herself. She was in such turmoil now, too raw and unsettled in this life to take steps that could not be reversed. She needed time to grow accustomed, to understand, to discover what opportunities she had and which she wanted.

She would have to make sense of her story without mentioning Robin. . . .

No, that was impossible.

Then she'd invent someone to play his part. She hated to start her new life with lies, but she must. She wiped tears from her face with her hands. First, she needed a name.

She'd keep "Robin" because she knew she'd make

a mistake there sooner or later. Or . . . Robert. That was more common, she thought.

If anything he'd told her was true. She realized that she wasn't sure of anything. Ridiculous after their adventures, but she couldn't be sure even of "Robin." She searched back to their first day when they'd been playing that truth game, and she'd been concealing facts. No doubt he had, too, and largely because he didn't want a suspect adventuress to know too much. She wished he'd trusted her with the truth before they'd parted. . . .

But why should he? She hadn't revealed her secrets to him.

But "Robin." She had to believe that, or she had nothing, nothing at all.

She had to come up with a surname that sounded realistic for an Englishman, and she knew such things were full of traps in a foreign language. She remembered Mighty Mike Cockcroft. Robert Cockcroft, then. Yes, that should work.

What other details? Derbyshire might be true. In fact, Huntingdonshire probably was, so Robert Cockcroft must be from somewhere far from there. She envisioned a map of England and picked the toe that stuck out into the Atlantic. Cornwall. Robert Cockcroft, a quiet gentleman of impeccable virtue. Older, but not too old for adventures. About forty.

Yes, that would do.

She built Robert Cockcroft in her mind—a little gray, a little stocky. Kind and dependable, with no hint of cockiness.

Next she thought of protecting herself. She would have to admit to folly over Ludo to try to explain his mad pursuit, but not the extent of it. One day rumors would reach here from Milan, but rumors could be denied.

Or she'd prove to be with child, showing she'd made not one mistake but two.

That made her cry again, but she pulled herself together. She was here. She had fulfilled her promise to her mother, and her mother's predictions had come true. Her father was willing to accept her, provide for her, and protect her, and if anyone could protect her it was the Marquess of Rothgar.

He would pursue Varzi, and that would help keep Robin and his men safe, too.

Possibly, just possibly, with luck and her wits, she would soon have again an orderly, secure life. First she would have to tell her story, however, and she'd feel stronger and braver if she was clean and decent.

She looked at the bellpull, but instead the lovely bed called to her. It was hung with cream cloth scattered with embroidered wildflowers, the mattress covered with a cloth of the same design. Not now. Perhaps later, when she was clean . . .

But then she couldn't resist. She stripped down to her shift, toed off her battered shoes, dragged down the covers, and climbed the short steps up onto fresh, white sheets. She pulled the covers back up over herself, inhaling the sunshine in which the sheets had hung to dry, looking up at the gathered silk on the underside of the bed's canopy. *A clean, well-aired bed will do, in a clean room. In a room entirely for myself.*

Oh, Robin. I hope you are in as good a state as I right now.

With that, she fell fast asleep.

Chapter 28

Petra opened her eyes to dimness and rubbed them. Had she dreamt it all? Was she still in some inn bedroom? No. Pleated silk lined the canopy above her bed, and when she sat up she saw the pretty room to which the Marquess of Rothgar had brought her. Someone had drawn the thick curtains, that was all, cutting the light, but chinks at either side showed it was still daylight outside.

How could she have simply gone to bed? What sort of behavior was that?

She climbed out of bed and saw a glass pitcher of water, which made her aware of how thirsty she was. She poured and drank. Then did so again until the jug was empty.

That prompted another need. There was no chamber pot beneath the bed, but she found a privy chair behind a silk screen and used it. There was no washing water on the stand, however, and she was still dirty. She blushed to see her feet had left smears of dirt on the pristine sheets.

Then she noticed that her clothing was gone. She remembered shedding it and letting it lie where it fell, and winced. Now some servant knew that the mar-

quess's bastard daughter was a slut. This was not the
entrance she'd hoped to make.

If she'd stayed with Lady Sodworth she would probably have arrived here in her habit. It wouldn't have
been particularly clean, but there would have been
some dignity in that. Except that the English disliked
Papists. She shook her head at the memory of leaving
her cross and rosary in Robin's pocket. What use
could they be to him?

Robert Cockcroft, she reminded herself, *sober man
of Cornwall.*

She raised the curtains to let in light but still didn't
see her clothing. A brown robe lay over a chair, however, so she stripped off her threadbare shift and put
that on, then went to the fireplace and resolutely
tugged the pull.

That was when she saw a folded sheet of paper on
the mantelpiece with *Petra* written on it.

She reached for it, but then saw it lay beside the
cameo brooch, her prayer book, and some coins—the
simple contents of her pockets. What had a servant
made of them?

She touched the raised design of a robin, wondering
if it would betray him, but surely that was far-fetched.
To anyone else it would merely be a bird. She picked
up the letter, knowing it had to be from her father
before she saw the seal, with its clear impression of
an R.

R for "Rothgar." R for "Robin."

Had the design on Robin's ring been an R?

She shook that away. A seal would not be a person's first name.

She unfolded the sheet of heavy paper, remembering the poor stuff she'd used in Speenhurst. Robin

should have received that yesterday. Had he done as requested and given up his search?

Clear, straight writing, like Robin's, but forming darker lines.

> *My dear daughter,*
> *On fete day the family eats in the evening and informally, as the household has been busy all day. If you feel able to join us at half past six we will be delighted, but if you prefer to spend the evening quietly in your room, we will hear your adventures tomorrow.*
>
> *Remember, you are to command anything you desire. Some garments have been provided, which we hope will suffice for now.*

It was signed simply *Rothgar.*

Petra read it through again, seeking some deeper understanding. It was somewhat formal, but this was a situation without social guidelines. Half past six. She looked around, but there was no clock.

The prayer book contained her evidence—the picture of an eye and the letter from her mother. It seemed they might not be needed, but she took the book, looking around for something with which to cut out the pieces of paper.

There was a knock on the door.

Petra had only just put the prayer book back in place when a maid entered and curtsied.

"What time is it?" Petra asked.

"Nearly six of the evening, miss."

She had the rosy cheeks and robust look of the Gainers, but blond hair showed at the front of a neat, frilled cap. Petra felt her own head. Her mobcap was gone, exposing her short hair. Perhaps that was why the maid looked curious. "Miss," she'd said. What name had the servants been given? She'd look mad for asking.

"I need to wash and change," she said hesitantly. Despite the marquess's note, she was unsure of her privileges. "Bathe, if possible." That might be too great an imposition at short notice.

"Yes, miss."

"Quickly?"

"Yes, miss." The maid curtsied again and left. Petra threw her hands up. She should have said she must be ready in half an hour. What was the matter with her? She'd been raised with servants to provide every want, so why not make clear demands here?

The maid returned very quickly, entering through a side door Petra hadn't noticed because it blended with the white-paneled walls.

"Your bath's ready, miss."

"Already?"

"Yes, miss."

"Your name?" Petra asked.

"Susanna, miss."

"Then take me to my bath, Susanna."

"In here, miss."

"Next door is a bathing room?"

"Your dressing room, miss."

Petra entered a small chamber, easily warmed by a fire and containing a clothes press and two chests of drawers. The bath sat in the center, but it was not a tub to be carried in for the occasion, but a piece of furniture in a glossy wooden box.

Steam rose from it, and Petra asked, "How is this done so fast?"

"There's always hot water, miss, and the marquess devised a way to feed it to the dressing rooms."

Petra was astonished, but didn't hesitate in shedding her robe and climbing up the steps. When she eased down into the just-right water, she sighed with pleasure. "This is lovely." Then she realized she'd said it in Italian. Ah, well, the maid probably understood the meaning.

The inside of the bath was decorated with painted flowers, but as Petra scrubbed away days of travel they were soon clouded by dirty water.

As in Montreuil.

Don't think about Montreuil.

Robin bathing nearby. She'd imagined his naked body. Later she'd been his lover, but all she remembered was taut muscles, intense life, and blinding pleasure. *Oh, God, don't remember that pleasure.*

"Are you cold, miss? Do you want me to draw more hot?"

Had she shivered?

"No, no, thank you, but I must hurry. Wash my hair, please. It's short and doesn't take long to dry."

Don't remember. Don't remember anything. Robert Cockcroft, quiet man of Cornwall.

Petra soon rose to step into the towel the maid held. She would think of this bath as a baptism, a transition into a new life, the new life her mother had wanted for her.

She quickly put on the clean shift—one of finest lawn and trimmed with lace. She tied on a new pair of pockets, and then the maid laced her into stays, which she hadn't worn for years but which encompassed her like a hug of conformity. These were pretty, too, being covered in striped material and trimmed with lace. The stockings were plain, practical cotton, however, held on by simple garters of brown braid. Lastly, she put on something else she hadn't worn for years—cane hoops to hold out her skirt.

She was changing, remembering. Embroidered silken skirts, floating and bobbing as she danced and flirted. A young girl so sure of her place in her world and her charms . . .

She turned her mind to choosing between the three gowns laid out for her. One of green reminded her too much of Robin. A red one seemed too dramatic. She chose the gown of sky blue with a thin white stripe. It seemed demure.

She put on the white petticoat and then the gown, which was closed on top but open at the bottom. *Like the gown Robin bought for me . . .*

She shook that away and studied herself in the long mirror. At last, she looked a lady—except for her hair. A clock somewhere chimed the half hour, and she started.

"I must go down. Shoes?" Wherever her own were, they weren't suitable for this outfit.

Dining with Robin in my stockinged feet . . .

"I think these slippers will fit, miss."

The maid offered backless shoes with a small heel, the front made of blue silk. Petra put her feet into them. "Yes, they do. Thank you. I will need a guide down to . . . to wherever the family is eating."

"A footman's waiting outside, miss."

"Oh yes. Thank you."

Petra checked her appearance again in the mirror, but then realized she was delaying. She had to do one thing, wise or not. She had no time now to retrieve her evidence, but she hurried into the bedroom and pinned the cameo to the middle of the bodice for courage.

A robin for courage? As likely as a butterfly.

She remembered when he'd told her his name. "Robin."

She'd said, "The small bird with the red breast?"

He'd said, "Cheerful and friendly," and continued with a challenge about having stood her friend. That was when he'd teased her about being his sparrow, the one who killed Cock Robin.

That prediction had almost come true outside Folkestone. She'd make sure nothing like that happened again.

She straightened her spine and left the room. A liveried footman stood there, pretending to be a statue. For a moment, Petra couldn't think of magic words to animate him, but then she said, "I'm ready."

He inclined his head and set off. She followed, trying to revive the contessina Petra d'Averio, who'd taken servants and fine clothing so for granted that she'd hardly been aware of them.

She was led back down the grand staircase to the marble hall and across it to a door, which the footman opened. He didn't announce her, so Petra still didn't know who the servants thought she was.

She saw a relatively small room filled with a large number of people, and faltered. They'd all turned to look at her. She summoned the contessina and walked in to curtsy to the room.

Lord Rothgar was already coming to her, seeming warm and relaxed. He took her hand and presented her. "A delightful addition to our family—my daughter Petra."

Everyone smiled and welcomed her.

Lord Bryght said, "Now you've shown us the picture, I can see why you didn't doubt, Bey.'

Bey?

No one seemed shocked by her, but which was his wife?

A brown-haired woman approached and kissed Petra's cheek. "My dear! This must all be quite alarming, but you are very welcome. I'm not sure I'm ready to be a stepmother, however, especially to someone only a little younger than I. I hope you'll call me Diana. Let me introduce you to the family."

Petra knew the kind stream of words was meant to soothe her, but she couldn't stop seeking hidden hostility and traps. For all the charming informality, Lady Rothgar was a grand lady who would be well skilled in sugaring poison.

"I believe you met Lord and Lady Bryght. . . ."

"Portia," said the smiling, petite woman whom Petra had met in the garden.

"And this is Lord and Lady Steen. Hilda is Rothgar's sister."

Petra dipped a curtsy to a russet-haired woman and a brown-haired man who had none of the aura of the high aristocracy. Lady Steen, who seemed to be mending a child's stocking, said, "Welcome to the madhouse, my dear."

Mad.

"Hilda," Diana chided with a smile, and led Petra on. "Lord and Lady Brand Malloren. Brand is another of Lord Rothgar's brothers, and Rosa is my cousin. You'll see there are dark Mallorens and reddish ones."

Lord Bryght and Lord Rothgar being dark, and Lady Steen and this man being reddish.

Petra smiled, but she felt shaken. Lord Brand didn't actually look much like Robin, but a well-formed face, loose burnished hair, and smiling blue eyes had been enough for a moment of shock and longing.

"Hilda's correct," Rosa said. "It takes time to adjust to the Mallorens." She was plump and pretty except for a sad scar down one cheek that distorted her face a little. It didn't seem to bother her, and her smile was warm.

"Doesn't it just!" said Portia. "With a Malloren . . ."

The women all completed it: ". . . *all things are possible.*"

"But of course, it's really Bey," Portia completed.

Bey? Petra wondered again.

"Petra is already a Malloren," Lord Rothgar said with a mock frown, "and lives up to the motto, for she has made all things possible in coming here. Her adventures seem remarkable."

Petra thought perhaps Lord Steen groaned, but when she looked around, she could see only good humor and welcome.

She risked a question. "Bey?"

"Our names are all from before the Conquest," her father said. "Being first, I received the name Beowulf."

"Sometimes I threaten to call him Wolf," his wife teased.

"I am not a predator."

"No," said Lord Bryght, "but try denying that you're a potentate."

"Has it not served you all well? Ignore this irreverent lot," Lord Rothgar said, and steered Petra toward a table. "I found a few more pictures."

Petra saw the miniature he'd shown her earlier, but

also a painting about eighteen inches high from the same period, and a skillful pencil sketch that was perhaps most true to life. It captured youthful self-assurance and a touch of haughtiness that went deeper, and a bright-eyed enthusiasm for life. There was more, however—a suggestion of powerful intelligence in the eyes and high forehead. No wonder her mother had been swept into insanity.

As she herself had been by another magical young man.

"I, too, have a picture," she said. "But only of an eye."

"Ah yes," he said with a rueful smile. "I had one in return. I have to confess to not knowing what became of it."

Whereas her mother had treasured hers. Love was not always reciprocated, and she must remember that.

A footman entered to announce supper. Lord Rothgar took Petra's hand to lead her from the room. "We'll be delighted to hear your story as we eat, my dear, but if you wish to wait, simply say so."

"I'd be happy to tell you," Petra said to the room. "But you must tell me if you're bored."

"Impossible to imagine."

The dining room was of moderate size, which made her think there must be a grand one, as well. Even so, it could have held twice their number. Lord Rothgar seated her on his right hand, but she realized she made an uncomfortable ninth. Then an empty chair was taken by a middle-aged man.

"This is Mr. Carruthers, Petra," the marquess said. "He's my invaluable secretary, and I'd only have to relate every detail to him later, especially if action is required."

Petra greeted the gray-haired man, but warily. Was this her father's Varzi?

The secretary smiled. "And to think, we were growing somewhat dull."

As her father had said, there were no servants in attendance. The cold food was spread on the table and a sideboard, and they served each other. Once they all had a cold soup, Petra was invited to tell her story.

She began with Ludovico, admitting some folly, but not the whole of it. She told of her father's death and her removal to the convent.

"You were a nun?" Portia asked, astonished.

Petra tried to explain about the Sisters of Saint Veronica, but these Protestants seemed mostly bemused.

"Is this your calling?" Lord Rothgar asked, and Petra sensed shielded regret.

"To be a nun? No, sir. But I think I will always concern myself with the welfare of the poor. It is needed."

He nodded. "Go on."

As cold pies and salads were passed around, she related her mother's illness and the frantic plans for escape. When she mentioned Lady Sodworth, she saw the same lack of recognition that Robin had shown. But then the marquess said, "Ah. An ill-mannered couple? He's in trade? She's young and strident?"

"Omniscient," groaned Lord Bryght, adding to Petra, "He does have that reputation."

Petra sincerely hoped it was overrated.

"He's Bristol based but has been at Court," her father said as wry explanation of his knowledge. "If Lady Sodworth helped you, Petra, she deserves our goodwill."

With a sick feeling in her stomach, Petra remembered the encounter at Nouvion. What if Lord Rothgar brought about a meeting? The woman would mention Robin Bonchurch of Derby.

So many traps beneath her feet.

That was a hypothetical danger, however, and one she could do nothing about. For now, she tried not to give her father reason to feel ill will toward the Sodworths, and presented her flight with Mr. Cockcroft entirely because of Varzi.

"Cockcroft?" Lord Bryght said. "Can't think of anyone by that name."

"Nor can I," said Rothgar. "But if he was traveling post with two servants, he must be of some wealth. Would you say he was a gentleman, Petra, or a rich merchant?"

Petra would have liked to make Robert Cockcroft a merchant, but she was sure it would trip her up later. "A gentleman, I think."

"A nobleman?"

She hesitated. There was that old signet ring and his familiarity with important French families like the Guise, and he'd said he was highly born. But the nobility of any country knew one another, so that presented particular dangers.

By way of answer, she said, "He explained that in England a person could be a plain mister but highly born."

"True. So he gave that impression, did he? Cockcroft? A conundrum."

"What a treat for you, Bey," said his sister Hilda in a wry tone. To Petra, she added, "He so delights in solving intricate puzzles. You could have brought him nothing better."

Petra wanted to grip her head and scream.

"Perhaps he used a false name," Lord Brand said, entering the game.

"Being up to no good?" Rothgar speculated.

"Not necessarily. I know a few titled men who prefer to travel simply—the sort to find the fuss not worth the candle. Ashart's one. Huntersdown's another. Done it myself a time or two."

"Very well. We'll hold judgment on his identity and rank. Carry on, my dear."

She was failing, but Petra told the rest of her adventures, careful of every word while trying to sound believable. The adventures at Mère Goulart's caused amazement and admiration, especially of her part.

"You really are skilled with pistols and sword?" Diana asked.

"Slightly," Petra said. "I'm grateful I didn't have to actually use them."

After that, she skipped quickly to Boulogne.

"These men seized you at an inn, Petra?" Lady Steen said. "How appalling."

"It was terrifying, but I escaped"—*don't mention Coquette*—"and Mr. Cockcroft found me. We went on board the ship he'd hired—"

"Name?" Lord Rothgar asked.

"I'm sorry?" Petra asked, staring.

"The name of the ship."

"Oh." She was flustered beyond invention here. "The *Courlis*."

He nodded. "The 'Curlew.'" He didn't say that the ship could be found, but she knew that was the fact—unless Robin had thought to bribe Captain Merien to silence. She was making a mess of this, but couldn't find a better way. She proceeded to Folkestone and the smugglers, pretending not to know their names.

"Don't worry," her father said with a twinkle in his eye, "we won't bring down the law on them."

Petra smiled her thanks. "I would like to reward them, for they were all kind."

She couldn't mention "Captain Rose," for even though that was surely a false name, it might lead directly to Robin. Sharing the address—the Black Swan Inn, Stowting—would be fatal. She couldn't mention the fight, for these people might know about one of their own who'd been wounded recently.

Trying to hide panic, she said, "Once we were out of Folkestone, our routes parted, for Mr. Cockcroft had urgent business in Cornwall. His mother is ill. He explained the coaches and such, and gave me money for the journey. I had to walk at the end because it was Sunday."

"An astonishing story, Petra," said Lord Steen, with perhaps a hint of skepticism. "You are to be congratulated on your enterprise."

"Or, speaking as a father, to be chastised for impulsive folly," said Lord Rothgar.

Petra twitched, but he seemed to be teasing.

"That's unfair, Bey," Portia said. "If Petra hadn't gone with this Cockcroft, the horrible Varzi would have won."

"My wife," said Lord Bryght, "is somewhat impetuous herself." His wife swatted his arm.

"And Petra managed to extricate herself when captured," Rosa said. "How brave of you."

But Lord Rothgar looked at Petra. "You said one of Varzi's men died in England."

Petra went cold. Had she? Yes, she had, earlier in the day. "Oh, did I miss that? He was watching the road out of Folkestone and tried to stop us, but one of the smugglers hit him over the head."

"A very careless type of villain," Lord Brand remarked.

"And a strange thing to forget," Lord Bryght said.

Petra knew she was red. "It happened so quickly. R-"—*maledizione!*—"Mr. Cockcroft tried to fight him, but he was losing. It was lucky that the smuggler had a cudgel."

"Very," said her father, showing no sign of doubting her. "I do hope to be able to find this Mr. Cockcroft and reward him."

Petra wondered if she could believe that. There was something not quite true in the tone.

"You must give Carruthers as much detail as you can, my dear. Such as the gentleman's first name, perhaps?"

Of course he'd caught her slip.

Striving for an innocent tone, Petra said, "Robert, I think."

"Excellent. Now we must turn our attention to the unpleasant signor Varzi. He must be stopped."

"Bey," said Rosa. "I know you don't read the lighter parts of the newspapers, but I could swear that in one of yesterday's I saw an advertisement that mentioned that name. I wasn't paying much attention, but the name struck me as odd. Someone offering a reward for news of the man, I think, with something about an attack."

"A lesson to me to read every word," said Lord Rothgar. "Carruthers?"

The secretary was already leaving the room.

"So who," asked the marquess, "is seeking our villain?"

"Cockcroft, I assume," said Lord Steen flatly, in the manner of one cutting short a game.

"Cockcroft," agreed the marquess. "My dear Petra, it seems your protector didn't entirely abandon you." There was clear speculation in his eyes now.

"He didn't abandon me at all," she said. "A sick mother must take precedence. I can't imagine why he'd take the time to do this."

She could, though, she could. *Oh, Robin, faithful protector to the end, but you're ruining everything.*

"We'll deal with this Varzi," said Lady Rothgar, as if the man's arrest was unquestionable, "but we must also decide how to establish Petra in her new life with as little disturbance as possible."

"I don't wish to be any trouble to you," Petra said.

"Rothgar feeds on trouble," Steen said. "You may as well surrender."

"Would you be willing to take my name?" the marquess asked.

Petra stared at him. "Become a Malloren?"

"You *are* a Malloren, but if I present you to the world as Miss Petra Malloren there will be no doubt as to my feelings on the matter. That also acknowledges the truth of your origins, which you may not like, but the resemblance between us is marked. Not so much now, of course, but there are enough people who remember my wild youth."

"There is an alternative, Petra," said Diana. "You could remain the contessina Petra d'Averio, and we would sponsor you into our world as friends of your family." She smiled. "Whichever you choose, I doubt your name will remain unchanged for long."

Marriage? At the moment, Petra couldn't face the thought.

"I'm not sure," she said. "The truth is known in Milan, which means it will arrive here eventually. Not my father's identity, but that I am not the true child of il conte di Baldino, so my mother's reputation is lost in any case." She fought tears.

Lord Rothgar said, "It seems your brother has disowned you, but if you take my name it will ensure he has no ability to disturb you ever again."

Petra inhaled. "Then I choose to be Petra Malloren, sir, and I thank you."

"You honor me," he said. Innocuous words, but Petra's eyes suddenly filled with tears at memories of Robin, of heaven and hell.

"Oh, my dear!" Diana rushed over to embrace her and offer a handkerchief.

Petra was saved from complete embarrassment by the secretary's return with a number of rather battered newspapers.

"We pass them to the servants' hall," her father explained, opening one and scanning it. Other family members were doing the same, simply pushing aside plates and wineglasses with no ceremony at all.

"Here it is!" Portia exclaimed. " *Reward. For any information leading to the location of a signor Varzi of Milan, lately come to London and suspected of involvement in a broad-daylight attack on a gentleman in Kent. He is of middling height, round build, and with thin, graying hair. . . .* ' I must say, he doesn't sound dangerous. This is your terrible villain, Petra?"

"Yes, I assure you."

Portia shrugged. " *Information will be received and rewarded at Messrs. Grice and Hucklethwait, Chancery Lane.* ' "

"Excellent," Lord Rothgar said. He didn't say that

tomorrow someone would be seeking information of Messrs. Grice and Hucklethwait; it didn't need saying. But they were probably Robin's lawyers and would lead right to him.

Robin, I'm sorry. I tried.

Others had been finding the identical advertisement, which provided no new information. Lively speculation was interrupted by Diana saying, "The masquerade at Cheynings."

"Oh yes," said Portia.

"Intriguing," said her father.

Petra waited warily to be enlightened.

Diana did so. "Bey's cousin, the Marquess of Ashart, has been feverishly refurbishing his family home. To celebrate completion he's holding a Venetian masquerade. When? Two weeks or thereabouts? I believe he has Mistress Cornelys arranging it for him so it will be correct in every detail. She is Venetian, you see. She was an opera singer to begin with, but now hosts such events in London in the season."

Teresa Cornelys? Could things become more tangled?

"The timing is perfect," Diana said. "Just long enough for you to become comfortable with the family and English ways, but not so long that it would be difficult for you to avoid society's attention. If we can keep your arrival secret, the masquerade will be the perfect occasion to present you to the world."

"And keeping secrets," said Lord Steen, "is another of Rothgar's talents."

Perhaps he wasn't as fond of his brother-in-law as the rest of the family.

"And you can advise us, Petra," Portia said brightly. "Have you attended a masquerade in Venice? Bey has, and Bryght, but none of us ladies."

"Yes, of course," Petra said, carefully not looking at her father.

It had been at a Venetian masquerade that he'd met her mother, and where she had been conceived.

Chapter 29

On Monday afternoon, Thorn visited Robin and said, "Something, perhaps."

"About Petra?" Robin asked. "At last!"

"About Varzi. From Grice and Hucklethwait. A customer at a coffeehouse in Fernleigh Street—the Arabian—reports that a gentleman who's taken rooms there might be our quarry. He claims to be a Spanish scholar by name of Garza, but the respondent has spoken to him and doesn't think his accent is Spanish."

"And 'Garza' is close to 'Varzi.'"

"Which may be misleading," Thorn warned. "But Garza wears a bob wig, which was knocked askew one day when he was jostled. The hair beneath was thin and graying. Hardly, I must point out, unlikely."

"Except that most men wearing that sort of wig are bald or shave their heads. It has to be investigated."

"There's more," Thorn said. "The coffeehouse also serves as a receiving point for post, but the letters are merely left out on a side table. The man thinks—only thinks—he might have seen Garza pick up a letter there. But he asked, and the owner of the place said he'd seen none for that name."

"It may be nothing, but it must be checked," Robin said, excitement building. "How do we arrange this?"

"Report him to the authorities as discussed earlier?"

"I know the man. I can make sure."

"He's dangerous."

"I'll be careful." Robin sat down to write a hasty note.

"I don't know how you can scribble so neatly."

"My only talent."

"Who's the blessed recipient?"

"Christian. Once I confirm his identity, we'll give the military the honor of arresting him on suspicion of espionage. That'll work around the normal forms for a while."

"Only a temporary solution."

"Then I try to nail him for that attack outside Folkestone and see him hang."

Men were sent to the Arabian to find out if Senor Garza was there. If so, they were to watch and follow him if he left. By the time a message came back to say he was in his room, Christian had arrived.

"I'll arrest him," he said, "but you'd better hope he doesn't have some sort of diplomatic credentials. And I'd rather you stayed out of it."

"I can recognize him," Robin repeated. "Don't worry, I'll be armed."

"You're hoping for an excuse to shoot him," Christian said.

Robin's jaw tightened. "Unreasonable?"

"No, but have you ever shot anyone?"

Robin had to admit he hadn't.

"It isn't as easy as you might think, even if the

opponent is thoroughly evil. When he's old enough to be your father . . . remember he's a bad man, Robin.''

Robin remembered Petra and Coquette and the attack on his men. "Oh, I won't forget that.''

Less than an hour later, Robin limped into the coffeehouse, his heart beating faster. Thorn would follow shortly, and Christian was already placing his men at front and back. The clientele seemed a normal collection, from clerks to gentlemen, young to ancient, merry to quiet. Many were reading the newspapers provided, but some were simply talking. He wondered which was the informant.

A servant came to take his order, but Robin said, "Senor Garza? Which room?''

The man hesitated. "Shall I get him for you, sir?''

"I prefer to go up.''

Robin saw some coffee drinkers look behind him and turned, but it was only Thorn entering and strolling over to look at the letters on the table. He was attempting to look ordinary, but, as usual, it didn't work.

Robin turned back and found the waiter gone. He saw him disappearing upstairs and followed, cursing his leg. It made stairs particularly difficult.

As he neared the top the waiter appeared, hurrying back down. The man stopped, eyes going wide.

"Which room?" Robin asked.

"Don't know . . .''

Robin pulled out his pistol. "Don't be foolish.''

The man swallowed. "First on the right, but . . .''

"But he's going out the back way," Robin completed, hearing noises as he pushed past the man. He yelled back to Thorn, "It's him!" and turned right into a corridor to see a man's back—a man in a dark suit and a bob wig.

"Halt," he said, unable to resist adding, "Your money or your life, signor Varzi."

The man turned, pistol already aimed, and fired. Robin fell to his knees by instinct, cursing searing pain in his leg, deafened by the gun roar, feeling the ball slam into wood by his head.

He shot the man.

Varzi clutched his chest, huddling in as if in self-protection, looking more surprised than anything, but then his eyes filled with pure malevolence before glazing over as he crumpled.

Robin stayed where he was, his ears ringing, his mind numb until pain shot through his leg again and he clutched it. A mass of soldiers burst from the back stairs, hiding Varzi; then Thorn knelt at Robin's side. "Did he hit you? Leg again?"

Robin could hardly hear him, but his sense of smell was working. The stink of Varzi's blood and excretion was joining acrid powder in the narrow space.

"Is he dead?" he asked, not even hearing himself clearly.

"Definitely. Are you hurt, Robin?" Thorn shouted.

"Not shot. My leg . . ." He moved his leg slowly with his hands so he could sit at the top of the stairs and stretch it out, but that meant he faced the crowd trying to come up to see what was happening.

"Help me up," he said to Thorn, "and get me out of here."

Thorn did so, but the stairs were blocked by now. "Back way," he said, turning and taking Robin's limping weight.

"Why didn't I expect him to shoot without warning?"

"Because he was old and looked harmless," Thorn

said. "Christian warned you. Take the lesson to heart."

Robin's ears were clearing, but that made the cacophony of voices worse. They were nearing the corpse. "Have you witnessed violent death before?"

"Not unless you count a hanging," Thorn said.

Robin caught a glimpse of the body as they squeezed past. Varzi's limbs splayed and his wig had fallen off, revealing straggly graying hair. Death had no dignity. "There was Varzi's man outside Folkestone," he said, "but I didn't actually do the deed. Perhaps one becomes accustomed."

A hand gripped his shoulder. Christian. Christian, who'd fought in battles and presumably become used to killing. "You did what you had to do, and a damned good shot, too. Right to the heart."

"Blind instinct."

"Then you have good instincts. The man was a cold-hearted villain, a cur."

"And a cur one merely shoots," Robin said wryly.

Christian slapped him on the back, hard. "Remember how he threatened your men and would have abducted your damsel in distress."

"Old enough to be my father, though."

"Then old enough to know better. Thorn, get him out of here and get him a brandy. I'll clean up the mess and keep both your names out of it if I can."

Robin made his way down the back stairs and out into fresh air, where he began to feel better, though he didn't think he'd ever forget the sight of the man dying only yards in front of him. Dying at his hand.

Two soldiers were standing guard by the door. Thorn left Robin with them and went to summon the sedan. When it came, Robin managed to get into it, a hand to his bloody thigh. "Surprised I can tear the stitches by now, but I think that's what I've done."

Thorn swore and ordered the men to make haste.

Robin pulled down the blinds and bobbed by the crowd gathering outside the Arabian, hearing rumors spin.

"Foreign spy . . ."

"Assassin."

"Tried to kill a duke."

"Soldiers took him down. . . ."

He rested his head back and closed his eyes. He sometimes wondered whether there was any solid truth at all in the world.

Robin's mother, rigid with anger and distress, insisted on inspecting the wound herself. Two stitches had given way, leaving dried blood and swollen flesh. "How could you go off to do such a thing? You are an earl. You must behave like one!"

"By staying at home while others do my work?"

"Such work, yes!"

"Thorn went, too," he pointed out.

"Fah! He is no better, and he, he has no brothers so he is worse. It is all to do with that woman, is it not?"

"I believe I was raised to protect the weak."

"Fah! You will stay in bed now until you are completely healed."

He owed her that, so he said, "Yes, *Maman.*"

"And soon you must come home, where I can prevent such follies."

Robin knew he did need to go to Easton Court soon to take full control of his earldom, but not yet. He wasn't ready for that struggle and he needed to find

Petra, to tell her that her enemy was dead. And other things.

"In due course," he said, seeking an excuse. "I must let my leg heal, and then I have a mind to attend Ashart's Venetian masquerade."

Being an invalid did not come naturally, but Robin's friends flowed through the house, ready to gamble, play music, or just share what gossip there was at this time of year. No one brought any news of Petra d'Averio, or of a mysterious Italian beauty by any other name. Robin could be sure that Varzi was no longer a threat to her, but he had to find her. He had to be sure she was well and happy.

He had to try to persuade her to give him another chance. Given his behavior, his untruths, he couldn't blame her for not trusting him. He would never force his attentions on her, but he couldn't endure not knowing where she was.

Even from his bed he could organize searches, starting again from the Gainer farm and from Micklebury, but they achieved nothing. He set a watch on Teresa Cornelys's house, but nothing indicated that Petra was there. Thorn had returned to his estate and had men asking questions all over Kent, but Petra d'Averio had disappeared as if she had never existed. All Robin had as evidence were a few precious remnants—her cross, her rosary, and the one blotched letter.

His mother attempted to choose a new secretary for him, and when he refused to permit it, she left for Easton Court. He was sorry to be at odds with her, but he had to establish his authority, even if only bit by bit. In some way he couldn't quite define, he owed that to Petra. Change had been forced upon her, but she'd faced it with strength, determination, and courage. He could try to do as well.

Once his mother had gone he set about interviewing secretaries, but his mind was on Petra at all times. When Christian dropped by to keep him company, Robin said, "I'll never rest easy until I'm sure Petra is safe and well."

"If it's still eating at you, why not advertise again? It worked last time."

"I won't set hounds after her."

"You don't have to. Make it a message *to* her, asking her to let you know she's safe."

Robin was intrigued, but he said, "What are the chances she'd read it? Do you read those things?"

"Plenty of people commented on the Varzi one. You just have to make it unusual so that people will chatter about it, and put in something that will catch her attention."

"It's an amusement, at least."

With Christian's help and a shared bottle of claret, he came up with: *Who did kill Cock Robin? No, not the sparrow with its bow and arrow, but a bird that has flown, with its sling and stone. News of this bird will be generously received by*—Robin smiled—*Mr. Goodfellow, at the Arabian Coffeehouse, Fernleigh Street, London.*

"That's a little risky," Christian said.

"Why? I want Petra to know I had a hand in Varzi's death, and I need an address where she can send a message. Above all," he said, draining his glass, "I need to receive that message."

"Have you seen this?" Portia asked, entering the tapestry room on Thursday, a newspaper in hand.

Petra was sitting with Rosa, embroidering a smock for Rosa's daughter, Jenny. She only glanced up. Portia had become obsessed with advertisements and notices, seeking hidden meanings in the simplest requests for employment or for assistance finding a lost dog. But when Portia read the strange announcement out loud, she had to struggle not to leap up and grab it.

"Who did kill Cock Robin? No, not the sparrow with its bow and arrow, but a bird that has flown, with its sling and stone. News of this bird will be generously received by Mr. Goodfellow, at the Arabian Coffeehouse, Fernleigh Street, London."

It was a plea, and more, it told her Robin had been connected to Varzi's death.

Of course he was. She'd known that despite her letter, he wouldn't have stopped trying to keep her safe, and guilt at her silence had been eating at her. She had no means to send a letter secretly, however. She went nowhere because her presence was being kept secret until the masquerade, and she was hardly ever alone.

"Isn't it mysterious?" Portia said. "Do you remember, Petra? Your signor Varzi was killed at the Arabian Coffeehouse."

"You think there's a connection?" Petra asked, because she had to say something.

"It's hard to see what," Rosa said. "Your Varzi is dead and gone, and he had nothing to do with birds, did he?"

"No," Petra said. "I'm sure it's a private joke of some sort and the coffeehouse is simply a coincidence."

Varzi's death had been much discussed here, of course, and with great satisfaction. Lord Bryght seemed to suspect that it had been his brother's work, though Rothgar had denied it. Petra believed her father. If anything, he seemed annoyed at being forestalled. Everyone seemed to accept the idea that Varzi had been dabbling in espionage for Austria as well as seeking her, and that that had been his ruin.

Petra had found no connection to Robin in any of the accounts.

He'd been killed by soldiers under the command of a Major Grandiston. A little oblique questioning had revealed that Grandiston was an experienced officer in the Horse Guards who had been on duty at court until recently, so he certainly hadn't been traveling northern France as Robin Bonchurch.

One account had speculated that Varzi had been planning to assassinate a duke, perhaps one of the king's brothers. Robin certainly wasn't one of them.

She'd eventually accepted coincidence, but now it appeared otherwise.

"Why Goodfellow?" Portia muttered, still trying to decipher it.

"He's in Shakespeare, isn't he?" Rosa asked, amiably playing the game. "Another name for Puck?"

"Robin Goodfellow!" Portia declared. "Yes, of course. That fits with the reference to Cock Robin. That poem's all about birds. But I wonder what it *means*."

Robin, Petra thought. *Proof positive.*

"It's not all birds," Rosa pointed out. "The bull tolls the bell, and the fly sees him die. I think I read once that it's some sort of allegory about Walpole."

"Politics?" said Portia. "Ugh."

As the other two teased apart the advertisement and the Cock Robin poem, Petra tried to think of a way to respond to Robin's plea. She must, or she'd never be at peace. Suddenly, she thought of a possibility. That evening, when no one could make any connection, she asked her father how she might send a note of thanks to Mistress Waddle.

"She can't read, but her nephew at the Three Cocks can. She'd be delighted to receive a letter, I think."

"Doubtless," he said with a smile. "Simply write it and put it in the post bag in the hall. It will be paid at this end, so she won't be asked for money."

He seemed unsuspicious, but Petra was more and more aware that Lord Rothgar's reputation for sagacity and omniscience was warranted. He was closely involved in matters of state, and maintained a large administration simply to keep him informed on national and international affairs. Such people could be turned to acquiring other information.

Even Lord Rothgar's brothers found him difficult to comprehend at times. Petra didn't deceive herself that she could do so.

She didn't think he would break a seal, however, so she took the risk. She had a writing desk now, stocked with everything she might need, including a new seal with a PM on it. She wrote her letter, but added a postscript, asking Mistress Waddle to get Mr. Hythe to send on the enclosed letter.

Then she cut a sheet of paper in half and used that for a simple letter to Robin.

I am well, she wrote, *but I could still be a danger to you, even with Varzi dead. I thank you for that, for I'm sure now you played a part. Please fly free, Cock Robin, and avoid all sparrows, arrows, and stones. Petra.*

She folded it and sealed it in the way she'd sealed

the last letter she'd sent him, by pressing down with the handle of her seal and finishing it with her finger. This time she could kiss it, and for some reason that impelled her to address it to Stowting, not London.

She folded it in the other and impressed that seal properly. There. It was a risk, but she hoped her father would only think she'd written her benefactor a long letter.

She held the letter, however, sighing.

Would she ever see Robin again? She'd hoped that her feelings would fade, but if anything they sank deeper roots with every day, fed by hope. She was to enter society, after all, and whatever his true name or title, he was part of that world. Had he not been on his way back from Versailles?

Perhaps, just perhaps, her dream in the Goulart farmyard could come true. Perhaps she might one day meet him at a ball and be properly introduced. Then they could dance and converse, lock eyes and flirt.

If he felt about her as she felt about him, if she meant more to him than a responsibility to be cared for, then perhaps, just perhaps, they might do more, all without shame or scandal.

Perhaps sometimes dreams did come true.

"On the third day," said Robin to Fontaine, "I rise from my bed." He had kept his promise to his mother, and today would be the first day since Varzi's death that he'd attempted normal activities. He walked around his room a little. It didn't hurt much at all.

"I do believe that allowing the new stitches to knit has allowed the rest to heal, too. Damn stiff, though."

"Please take care, sir," Fontaine said, hovering. He had returned yesterday and was still fussing. Coquette hovered and fussed, too, on Robin's other side, as if she could be some help.

"Do you have no idea you're tiny?" Robin asked the dog.

Coquette's look could well say no.

Robin limped to the window, feeling more or less normal. As he stretched, he looked out at a moderately pleasant day for London.

"I shall go down for breakfast," he declared.

That not having distressed him, he ventured farther and took Coquette for a short walk, amused by people's reactions. Nearly everyone he passed stared with a silent *What is that?*

"What will happen when I introduce you to my real dogs at Easton Court?" he asked her when they returned. "I suppose you'll expect to rule the roost." He sat down with a sigh. "This is all very well, little one, but I still have no word of Petra, and until I do I can't seem to grasp the rest of my life."

He snapped out of that and considered the men he'd interviewed for secretary. He decided to trust his instincts and settled on a young, enthusiastic, and extremely bright Oxford man called Nantwich who was in Town and ready to take up a position. Nantwich was also a curate's son who really needed a good position, and Robin knew that swayed him. He sent for the man and informed him of his good fortune.

In the afternoon he ventured to his club in his sedan, where he heard a number of people mention the Cock Robin advertisement, wondering what it might mean, or grumbling about people who wasted ink and paper on nonsense. The company was decidedly dull, so he went on to Angelo's to watch some fencing.

The instructor wanted to know the details of his fight outside Folkestone. Robin told the story and ended up demonstrating some of the moves. He stopped when his leg complained, but began to feel he might be human again soon.

The next day he opened a letter from Thorn, hoping for news of the search. When he saw the enclosure, his heartbeat faltered. It was addressed exactly as the last one, and sent from Micklebury again, but the writing was different. This was fine-quality paper and ink, so he was seeing Petra's true hand, a light, steeply sloping style with its flourishing tails. He turned it to see that again the wax bore no seal. Like last time, it had merely been pressed down when cooling with a finger or thumb. He could clearly see the lines and whorls.

She was still keeping secrets, for with such fine-quality paper and pen, she must have a seal of some sort.

He touched there. Felt an alarming impulse to kiss there.

The pressing finger might not even have been hers, he told himself, but he knew it was and surrendered. Then he snapped the seal, unfolded the heavy paper, and read the words.

I am well, but I could still be a danger to you, even with Varzi dead. I thank you for that, for I'm sure now you played a part. Please fly free, Cock Robin, and avoid all sparrows, arrows, and stones. Petra.

He couldn't imagine why she'd think she was still a danger to him, but clearly she was well and with people who could afford fine paper and ink. Clearly she truly did want him to stop seeking her. He could go to this Micklebury and try to pick up her trail, but she had made her wishes clear.

It hurt like blazes, but he had to respect them, even though he felt that he'd never fly again.

Chapter 30

Lord Rothgar spent some time every day showing Petra different parts of Rothgar Abbey. One day he said, "May I show you my true obsession?"

Of course Petra said yes, but she wondered if she was finally to see the darker side of this world. She followed him into a confusion of ticking sounds to find three men in shirtsleeves completely concentrated on clockwork mechanisms.

One young man at the long center table looked up and nodded with a slight smile; the other didn't twitch away from something he was doing to tiny pieces of shiny brass. A small, older man working on something larger said, "My lord," but then returned to his work.

"Clockwork," Lord Rothgar said, "in all its forms."

Petra could tell from the way he touched a piece of machinery that all this truly was an obsession, but also a love.

"I've never even considered a clock," she confessed, "other than to be annoyed if someone forgot to wind it."

"The mechanism is fascinating and constantly improved. I wish I would be alive in two hundred years to see what is achieved by then." He took her on a tour of the room, but skillfully just long enough. He clearly knew most people didn't share his devotion to wheels, cogs, springs, and pendulums.

Petra's interest grew when he came to the mechanical toys. He demonstrated a monkey that beat a drum, and a lady who danced to the music from a box beneath her feet.

"I have people who find broken and neglected pieces, which I then put to rights."

"You do this yourself?" she asked, sure she must be mistaken.

"When I have the time. Sometimes I need help," he added, with a smile at the older man, who smiled back. "I am only an amateur, but my work then needs a home."

They moved on and came to a bird on the branch of a tree—a bird covered with feathers so that it seemed real. He pressed a switch and it came to life, turning its head and singing, and showing a red breast. It was a robin. A worm popped out of the tree trunk nearby and the bird stopped singing to apparently swallow it.

"It's charming," she said, trying to show no special reaction, though she knew with despair that the omniscient Dark Marquess had somehow learned too much.

She saw his glance at her bodice and realized that she was wearing the cameo, that she'd done that too often. She'd said it was a memento of her mother, but it was not at all an Italian design. Careless, careless, careless, but how could anyone live constantly on guard?

He said nothing else, but picked up the now silent bird. "You may have this if you like."

A shiver went down her spine, but she knew he hadn't meant what she'd heard. When he made no other reference, Petra thanked him and carried the toy up to her room. Once there, she took off the brooch and put it away in a box that already contained a small treasure trove of trinkets, all gifts from her father. She had some more valuable jewelry now, too, kept for safety in Lord Rothgar's safe.

Her father, who was being wonderfully kind, and who planned to acknowledge her before society and provide her with a generous dowry. She gathered that with this support she could be fully accepted in society and could expect to make a good marriage, especially when so many wished to seek a close association with such a powerful man. From the very beginning, she hadn't been able to suppress the thought that perhaps Robin might be a suitable match and might want to marry her.

She wound up the toy again and set it singing, but it couldn't lighten her heart.

"Robin Bonchurch" might be the *only* suitable husband for her. She'd tried to ignore the problem, but her courses were a week overdue.

She sat, a hand over her eyes. How could this happen to her? She'd come so far, struggled so hard, and finally found the haven she sought, but now this, a shame that threatened everything. Soon she was going to have to confess. The marquess would want to know the father, and she didn't see how she could lie. He would find Robin, if he hadn't already, and force him to the altar or to death.

She'd begged him to fly free, but this would cage him.

She inhaled and gathered herself. Robin had never

stopped caring for her, and passion had flared between them at a touch. Perhaps he wouldn't mind too much.

The pressing question was, should she confess before the Cheynings masquerade? That would allow her father to change his mind, and not present his ill-born daughter to his world. No need to decide just yet, she weakly decided. It was always possible she was simply late for once in her life.

Robin dedicated himself grimly to gathering in the strings of his earldom and regaining his physical strength and flexibility. Both were challenging. Again and again he had to deal with people who had his interests at heart, but who couldn't quite accept that he was ready for his responsibilities. He realized that everyone, from servants to estate stewards, but also his family and perhaps himself, had not quite accepted that his father was dead.

Here, Nantwich was a blessing—the proverbial new broom. Robin gave him a free hand, even though the man's enthusiasm could be exhausting. The secretary assumed Robin was interested in national and international affairs and constantly presented him with articles, or even short essays on issues of the moment. Robin dutifully read them.

He was unable to resist asking Nantwich to find out about Milan, and in particular, the d'Averio family. He received, within the day, an authoritative paper. Robin thanked him, skimmed through it, and discovered absolutely nothing of use, so he requested information about the Morcini family, and especially the current conte di Purieri.

That provided more interesting reading, if only because Robin hated Ludovico Morcini's guts. Unfortunately, it came accompanied by a very recent book on the major families of Milan, marked at the page with a picture.

Petra's lover was a darkly handsome fellow, with an elegant stance and smile. The smile didn't hide cold eyes, however. Robin hoped he choked on bile when he heard of Varzi's death and realized Petra had escaped.

Thought of Purieri and visions of vengeance sent him back to Angelo's for some serious work on his swordplay.

"Not bad," he said after a while, but he was running with sweat and his scar was burning.

"Not bad at all, sir," Angelo said, "but to achieve your best you must apply yourself with more seriousness."

Robin laughed wryly. "That seems to be a general opinion. But by all means. By hard work, in due course, I shall become the very epitome of everything."

He also spent time at a Turkish bath, simply for heat and massage of his leg, however, and not for the other exercises available there.

He was being oddly chaste and wouldn't be able to use his leg as an excuse much longer. For some reason, Ashart's masquerade had become a marked day in his mind. The Italian masquerade that was being organized by Teresa Cornelys, and thus felt like a connection to Petra when it was no such thing at all.

After that he would move fully into his new life. He'd go north to tackle Easton Court and then on to his other properties. He'd resume his normal amusements. Perhaps he'd set up a long-term mistress, or even look for a bride.

That business of waiting until he was thirty had been immature nonsense, though he begrudged any penny to Lady Fowler's Fund for the Moral Reform of Society. He didn't approve of a lot that went on in society, but the woman was a sour-faced killjoy who would have everyone on their knees and singing hymns from morn to night. That, after all, was why he, Christian, and Thorn had chosen her as benefactor—as a powerful deterrent.

He'd sort it all out after the masquerade.

Chapter 31

Petra knew herself to be a complete coward, but she set out for Cheynings with the rest of the Mallorens without revealing her secret to anyone, even though by now there could be no doubt.

She clung to Robin's comment about wanting to make a child legitimate. It had been convoluted. Something like *Have you considered that I might . . .* But he'd said it. Even if he did not particularly want to marry her, might that have been true?

She would have to find him and tell him, for the child's sake as much as anything. She would not impose the shame of being a bastard on her child.

The invitations to the Marquess of Ashart's Venetian masquerade had instructed everyone to arrive as darkness fell, wearing their costumes, and the costumes were to be the most traditional and concealing—the enveloping domino cloak and the Venetian half mask. To help conceal identities until midnight, there would be no preliminaries, no official welcomes, no introductions.

There could be some variations in the costume, and Petra had instructed the Mallorens in them. A hat was acceptable instead of the hood, especially if it hid most of the hair, and it was best if hair was powdered to hide its color. Ladies who wanted to be particularly mysterious could wear a dark veil hanging down from the edge of the mask to completely hide the face. As they said, at a Venetian masquerade, a man could find himself in the embarrassing situation of seducing his own wife.

Guests had also been instructed not to bear arms. Petra had questioned that.

"Men so often get carried away," Diana had said, "and a mock duel becomes real. In any case, dress swords are inconvenient. They're always getting in the way. Mistress Cornelys was wise to ban them at her events for that reason alone."

Petra wondered if she might meet her mother's friend tonight. If not tonight, some other time, for she longed to meet someone with whom to share memories.

She traveled to the event with her father and Diana. As they turned up the drive to the house, she fastened the deep blue cloak made of the same fabric as her dress, and put on her mask, which covered her entire face except for a narrow strip from nostrils to chin.

"I do admire that mask," Diana said, fixing her own, which was feathered, with a tiny suggestion of a beak at the nose.

Petra's mask was plainly shaped to her face, but she'd painted it half silver, half midnight blue along a swirling line that itself was marked with spangles.

"I remember that design," said her father dryly.

Petra gasped. "Oh, I'm sorry! I should have realized. . . ." She bit her lip, wondering how she could have been so foolish. "My mother treasured one like this, and I always loved it, but I should have guessed why."

He smiled, perhaps a little sadly. "She will like to see you wearing a copy tonight, I think."

Petra was grateful that the mask hid threatening tears. Her mother would be delighted to see her daughter safe and in the loving care of her father, but if she was witnessing this, she knew Petra's sin and secret. She suppressed a sigh as she put on the traditional three-cornered hat.

Her father's mask was also a bird, the commonest style for a Venetian festival, but in his case the mask had a predatory hooked beak, perhaps of an eagle. His hat was round brimmed and plain. Did it deliberately cast a sinister shadow over his masked eyes? After weeks in his company, she knew he wouldn't disown her for her sin, but she dreaded having to tell him.

Enjoy the night, Petra told herself. *The shadows descend tomorrow.*

They were part of a stream of carriages and riders, all dawdling to take in the magic. The trees lining the drive were hung with colored lanterns, which also illuminated figures that looked like fairies sitting on branches, or dryads peeping out from behind trees. Then, causing laughter and applause, some moved and ran off into shadows. They'd been real people.

"Delightful," Diana said, pulling a garnet cloak closed over her pink gown. "We will have a ball for you soon, Petra, and must think up something equally charming. A shame that Ashart's stolen the Venetian idea. Is there anything distinctive from Milan?"

"Not in the same way," Petra said. "Opera, perhaps."

"You could commission one," Diana said to her husband. "About Petra's adventures, even. *The Fugitive Nun*."

"Alarming," Lord Rothgar said, "but I suppose we could hold it in the old Abbey crypt."

Petra wondered if they were serious, but the event would never happen once she revealed her state. Their coach paused by the open front doors, and it was time to climb down.

The house was also hung with small lanterns, and most of the windows had been covered with color of some sort so that lights inside shone out as through stained glass. All around Petra masked and cloaked people flowed into the house, a river of cheerful anonymity. Some wore the shorter style of cloak, but others the full one that fastened all down the front, making it hard to tell if the wearer was male or female unless a wide skirt spread the cloak, or it parted to reveal legs.

Petra suspected some deliberate deception. Some ladies were wearing skirts without hoops, as she was, so as not to give too much away. Some gentlemen were wearing the older style of stiff-skirted coat to suggest width. Perhaps deception went further. From the back, she was sure one figure was male, but when he turned, she saw that his black cloak hung open over an elaborate ivory-colored gown. A sturdily built woman, or a man dressed in women's clothing?

Her father and Diana were admiring the clever hall decorations designed to suggest Italian ruins, and making plans to outshine them at a grand ball in Petra's honor. That would never happen now. She let the throng carry her up a staircase, through an arch, and into a grand space pretending to be an Italian piazza.

There were even small balconies here and there on a higher level.

"Designed by Madame Cornelys," she heard someone say. "She is Venetian, you know, so it must be quite exact."

It was, in impression, at least. Petra slipped behind some plaster columns and found a dim, concealed walk around the perimeter of the room, ideal for whispered flirtations and even kisses. Walking along it, she eventually found a narrow staircase built against the wall. The simple construction and new wood told her it was part of the fantasy here.

She navigated it carefully to arrive at an equally narrow passageway that circled the room at the higher level. The floor was merely planks and she stepped onto it carefully, but it was solidly made. It was unlit, but light came in now and then through those cunningly constructed balconies. The chatter and music seemed so far away, almost in another world.

Petra walked carefully to the nearest balcony and looked down. She had to smile. The illusion of looking down at a small piazza thronged with a festive crowd was even stronger, and she could imagine herself back in the past, when she'd first attended a masquerade.

She'd been seventeen and thought herself very grown up. It had been the beginning of her flirtation with Ludo, the teasing and kissing she'd been so sure led toward marriage. She could almost imagine this man or that below was he, looking for her while she playfully hid, intending to be found.

"Petra d'Averio," said an Italian voice. Petra turned sharply, but of course it wasn't Ludo. It was a woman, gowned and masked like all the rest, but in her case with scarlet and purple feathers.

"Signora?" Petra asked.

"You don't recognize me. Hardly surprising, but I am Teresa Cornelys, my dear. Teresa Imer once."

"Oh. How did you recognize me, ma'am?"

"The mask. For a moment it was as if Amalia was back with us again. She, too, wore a blue cloak."

Another mistake? No, Mistress Cornelys presented no danger and there was nothing eerie about the coincidence. Blue went with the mask.

"Of course," Mistress Cornelys added, "I was helped by knowing you to be in England."

Petra suddenly wished she weren't in such an isolated spot. "How?"

"I wish you no harm," the woman said with a strange three-pointed smile that made Petra think of a cat.

She pulled herself together. She had only to step onto the false balcony and call for help. "I was simply startled. I'm pleased to meet you, ma'am. My mother spoke warmly of you."

"Dear Amalia. And now dead in a convent, I gather."

"I'm surprised that news has reached England already."

"As I said, questions have been asked about you."

"By whom?" Petra asked, trying to sound only mildly interested, but tingling with excitement. It must have been Robin. This woman must know who he was.

"Signor Varzi. Now so fortunately dead. Dispatched to hell by Lord Grandiston, I understand."

Lord Grandiston? Petra recognized the name of the officer mentioned in the newspapers, but there was a peculiar emphasis in the way it was said. In truth, this woman was a stranger for all she'd been her mother's friend. And her mother had warned that Teresa Imer was not entirely trustworthy. Any impulse to share memories fled, at least for the moment.

"Do you require anything, ma'am? I must rejoin the company."

The woman stepped aside. "Of course. I merely wanted to make myself known. Here, tonight, I will be busy, for this is all my design and I must make sure no problems occur, but perhaps we might have time for more leisurely conversation in London one day."

Petra curtsied and squeezed by to make her escape without commitment.

As she worked her way back down the staircase, she went over the conversation, seeking the traps. Then she paused. Ah. Did Teresa Imer think she had grounds for extortion? If she intended to demand money not to reveal the truth of Petra's birth, she'd soon find that plan exploded.

Robin arrived at Cheynings with Thorn, Christian, and another friend, Lord Duncourt. They'd gathered the previous night at Duncourt's place near Leatherhead and enjoyed a merry party there. Robin just wished he could be as merry as he'd used to be. His friends ascribed his mood to his attempts to take over his earldom. It wasn't entirely true. His failure to find Petra lingered like infection in a wound.

A gathering of friends had been a relief, but he'd forgotten how close Cheynings was to the area where Petra had disappeared. He couldn't stop scanning every street and room, just in case she was there, and as he entered Cheynings he found himself doing the same thing. He wouldn't even recognize her in this noisy mass of cloaks and masks, for heaven's sake, yet still, he couldn't stop. That hand, that back, that laugh, that light step . . .

That perfume?

Petra hadn't worn perfume during their adventures, but he turned, wondering which passing lady he'd detected. The pink, the red, the white, the blue? He grabbed a glass of wine from a tray and let his friends drag him onward in exploration of the transformed house.

Teresa Imer completed a circuit of the house and was satisfied that all was as it should be. She'd had no doubt. She'd become skilled at arranging such events at her own house, and in this case, she hadn't been spending her own money.

Money, money, money. Always such a problem. She had achieved what no one else had—created entertainments so lavish, so exciting, that all the fashionable world begged for tickets. She, a foreigner of no particular birth, who'd arrived in England with nothing, now dictated to the aristocracy. But one must provide the best to attract the best people, and lenders demanded repayment, while tradesmen presented ridiculous bills. And now this Almack was attempting to imitate her assemblies and steal her clientele.

She considered the opportunity she'd discovered, shrugged, and set off in search of a gentleman in purple with only a narrow eye mask. When she found him, she said, "Five hundred guineas, you mentioned?"

The young man turned to her. "She's here?"

"I told you there was a possibility. Dark blue, with a blue-and-silver swirled mask."

Finely carved lips smiled. "How kind of her to be so distinctive," said il conte di Purieri. "You have my gratitude, signora."

"I would rather have payment. That ring would do."

He looked at the gold ring on his right hand, smiled cynically, and slid it off. "True, I will be leaving the country very soon." He gave it to her and moved off into the crowd.

Robin was playing for shillings at the EO table, which provided no excitement but offered escape from other activities. Even with doors and windows open, the place was growing hot, however, and he was thinking of moving outside when a hand touched his arm. He turned to find a woman in a scarlet and purple feathered mask.

He rose. "Ma'am?"

"Would you step aside with me a moment, sir?"

An Italian accent. After one sharp heartbeat, he realized it wasn't Petra. "Madame Cornelys. I congratulate you on your design."

She inclined her head. "Thank you, Lord Huntersdown."

He moved into a quieter corner with her. "You have some means to see through masks, ma'am?"

"No, my lord, but I have long experience of watching masked crowds in search of interlopers and troublemakers."

"Which am I?"

She laughed that away. "When three tall young men enter together and one calls out to Robin, and is later addressed as Christian, I know they must be the Duke of Ithorne, the Earl of Huntersdown, and the dashing Major Lord Grandiston."

"How disappointing to be predictable. But what do you want with me, ma'am?"

"You visited me, did you not?"

Robin came sharply alert. "You have news of Petra d'Averio?"

"I might."

He curbed surging excitement. "What do you want?"

Cunning eyes shone through the slits in her mask. "A promise of gratitude if I am of use to you."

He wanted to say he'd pay anything, but he knew the sort of woman he dealt with. "Too vague, I'm afraid."

She made a moue of distaste. "If you insist on a marketplace, I will give you useful information, my lord, for the promise of five hundred guineas."

"Five hundred guineas if I speak to her," he amended.

"Such a hard bargainer. She is here, my lord, wearing a sapphire blue domino. In fact, her cloak is a very similar color to your own. Her mask is a distinctive blue-and-silver swirl."

Robin moved away, but she said, "Wait." When he turned back, she said, "There is another here seeking her."

"Who?"

"Il conte di Purieri."

Robin inhaled. "Is he, by gad?"

He moved away again, but she caught his cloak. "He is dressed in purple, and armed."

"Ashart will not be pleased," Robin said, and went in search of his host.

He kept alert for both sapphire blue and purple, but

he needed to find Ash. Having obeyed instructions, he now needed a sword.

It was only as he worked against the tide to go downstairs that he thought to wonder if Madame Cornelys had given Lousy Ludovico the same information about Petra, damn her cold, greedy heart.

To Hades with the rules of the masquerade. He grabbed a passing servant and demanded to know what Ash was wearing. The man's eyes went wide, but he said, "Black, with a devil's mask."

Robin soon saw him, observing his guests. "Ash, I need a sword."

"No fighting."

"There's someone here armed and up to no good."

Ash frowned, but led the way out of the hall and unlocked the door to a room that contained a collection of weapons. "Who?" he asked, as Robin took a rapier and tested the balance.

Robin hadn't encountered Ash since his adventures, so hadn't told him the full story. "A certain conte di Purieri from Milan," he said, trying another blade. "It's a long story, but if he's here, he'll try to abduct a lady."

"An Italian lady?"

"In a way." Robin made his choice, buckled on the sword belt, and rearranged his cloak. As he headed for the door, Ash said, "Do try not to kill him, Robin. Blood, you know. So messy."

The Marquess of Ashart found himself talking to an empty doorway. He swiftly loaded a pistol, put it in his pocket, and went to seek his cousin. After all, Rothgar had recently acquired an Italian daughter from Milan.

* * *

Despite everything, Petra was enjoying herself.

She'd forgotten how wonderful it was to flirt, especially in the anonymity of a masquerade. She flitted from one gentleman to another, exchanging only cryptic remarks and teasing smiles, and granting the occasional light kiss.

The company was better behaved than one would find in Venice, probably because everyone knew this company was select and that the masks would come off at midnight. A woman treated too coarsely could turn out to be very well protected. A woman who behaved too rashly could be ruined.

The dancing began, and a gentleman in red swept her into the central chamber to join a line. She laughed as she began the lively steps, and he grinned back at her. He had hopes and would be disappointed, but for now all was joy.

But as she turned, she looked up and saw a man in purple watching from a balcony. He wasn't the only one to have found his way up there, but he seemed to be watching her. When she looked up again at the next turn, however, he'd gone.

Well, it was also a delight to be admired. She concentrated on the dance until the final curtsy to her partner, but then slipped away from him. She worked her way around the edge of the room, seeking other amusements, but an arm came around her waist and she was swept into the shadowy area behind the facade.

"Stop that!" she gasped, thinking it was her dancing partner. But then she realized who it really was.

He didn't say anything, but grasped her face and

kissed her. She knew his taste, she knew his smell, she knew everything about him. After a breathless moment, Petra kissed him back. Somehow, somehow, Robin had found her, and she had no will to resist.

He broke the kiss, breathing hard. "Come." He took her hand and pulled her along the passageway and into a side corridor. He didn't stop there, but led her down some back stairs, through kitchen areas and outside. She found herself on a quiet side of the house lit by a halfhearted scattering of lanterns and completely deserted, though the chatter and music of the masquerade poured out of windows nearby.

Without a word, he tossed aside her hat and tugged at the strings so her mask fell to the ground. His was merely a narrow black strip, and she laughed in delight to see his beloved features again.

He unfastened her cloak to reveal her bare shoulders and low bodice and reverently kissed them. Gasping with pleasure, she fumbled his mask off, then his cloak, and slid arms around him beneath his coat to relish the feel of his long, strong torso as his lips sealed hers.

Oh, sweet heaven, his kiss, his kiss! How had she survived without this?

"Stays," he caught breath to say, laughing with her as his hands ran up her back, then down again, and he kissed her neck and down to the exposed swell of her swollen, tingling breasts. Her whole body tingled. In just moments he could do this to her. She wanted to be insane again, here, in great danger of discovery, but she managed to whisper, "No. Robin, no, please."

This time he didn't protest.

"No," he said, drawing back, taking her hands between his. "But, by heaven, Petra, you've driven me insane. Where did you go? Why? Who are you here with? Tell me it's not another man, beloved."

She laughed shakily. "Not like that. Beloved?"

He stilled, looking into her eyes. "I didn't mean to embarrass you with that. I'm sorry. I vowed not to pester you—"

"Robin, love . . ."

But she stopped her protest. What was he offering?

He'd made it clear that he couldn't marry a penniless bastard, that he could only take her as his mistress. Was that what he had in mind?

She was still a bastard, but she wasn't penniless, and she brought that other dowry he'd spoken of—powerful connections. She could tell him that, but despite her love, despite the child growing inside her, she didn't want him to offer her marriage for dowry or connections or even to make their baby legitimate. She wanted him to offer it when he thought she had none of those, so she would know.

She drew her hands free. "Robin, I still can't enter an unblessed relationship with you or anyone. You don't have to worry about me. As you see, I am in good care."

"Unblessed . . .! Where did you get that idea? 'Struth, on the boat?" He thrust his hand through his already loosened hair, and the ribbon fell off. Petra bit her lip on tender tears.

"I was uncouth," he said. "Unbelievably so. Terrified, to tell the truth. Things did go rather fast, if you remember, and there was no time later to make things right. You gave me no time. You left."

Hands gripped so they wouldn't reach for him, she said, "I read that page in your notebook. The pledge?"

"Good Lord, that? Pure idiocy."

"Idiocy at a thousand guineas' cost?"

"I promised Teresa Cornelys half that just for news of you." He captured her hands again. "Marry me, Petra, please? I'm hollow without you."

Sheer bliss brought tears to Petra's eyes, but then she hesitated again. Tell him first about the baby or simply throw herself into his arms?

She saw the tightening of his face. "I understand if you have a low opinion of me. My foolish levity, my clumsy attempts to find you—"

"Robin . . ."

". . . my failures in the knight errantry business."

"You saved me!" she protested, laughing now at his folly. "You killed Varzi's man."

"That was Dan Fletcher. I did kill Varzi, but—"

"Did you, indeed?" a man said in an Italian accent. "Then I have another score to settle."

Petra went ice-cold as she turned, praying it wasn't so. With such a narrow mask, however, she recognized Ludo immediately. "What are you doing here?" she spat. "Get out! Go away!"

"So imperious. By all means I will go, but with you, and after having killed the man who soiled your lips." He drew a slender but doubtless lethal sword with insolent leisure. Petra remembered with horror that weapons were forbidden here. Robin would be unarmed.

She threw herself between the men. "*Soiled?* Robin wants to marry me. You wish to soil me and always have!"

Ludo shoved her aside. She stumbled but turned, ready to try again to prevent murder. But Robin—oh, thank God—had a sword out, too, and parried Ludo's vicious, killing thrust. But as the swords clashed, she remembered Varzi's man, when Robin hadn't quite been good enough.

She screamed for help.

She scarcely had a sound out when a big hand clapped over her mouth and she was dragged back. Ludo hadn't come alone. Of course he hadn't! Why hadn't she realized that?

People were coming from the house, but it would be too late. Robin was holding his own, but another of Ludo's men was creeping up on him from behind. So like the previous fight, but this time Robin was the one who'd be killed by a cudgel. She fought to free herself, to be able to scream a warning—

But then a pistol cracked, and the man staggered and then collapsed on the ground. Masqueraders were running toward them now, but Robin and Ludo fought on as if none of this was happening. Neither could afford a moment's distraction, for they were too evenly matched. And both were willing to kill. Death danced on every turn and thrust of the long blades.

Petra realized she was crying as she struggled against her captor. She couldn't bite. She couldn't kick. She couldn't escape! But then he grunted and his hold slackened. She wrenched free as he tumbled at her feet. She stared at the knife hilt in his back, but then someone else pulled her into his arms. When she struggled, he said, "It's your father."

She stilled, but stared at the raging fight, tears pouring. "Do something. Please!"

"It's in hand, but I think . . ."

Robin's leg gave way and he staggered to one side. Petra cried, *"No!"*

Ludo cried out, too, in triumph as he drove his sword down to pin Robin in death. It plunged into earth, for Robin rolled, then thrust up and drove his sword into his opponent's heart.

Ludo collapsed on top of Robin, impaled in a bizarre embrace until men ran forward to pull him off and help Robin, bloodstained, to his feet.

Petra ran to him. Her father didn't prevent her, but Robin held her off with his left hand, sucking in breaths. "Don't . . . get his blood . . . on you."

She gripped that hand. "Your leg, your leg! What have you done to it?"

"Only used it, love. A feint . . . I hoped he'd heard of my injury. . . ." He stopped to breathe and Petra wavered, dizzy with emotion. When someone draped her cloak around her shoulders and put an arm around her, she leaned, knowing it was Lord Rothgar again.

He handed her the mask. "Best to become anonymous," he said, and drew her into shadows, concealing her identity from the growing crowd of cloaked and masked men.

She put it on, realizing that Robin's identity was exposed now. That she still didn't know his full name, and he still didn't know about the baby.

But her eyes were drawn to her too-insistent lover. They'd taken out the sword and rolled Ludo onto his back, most of them puzzling over who he was. Ludo—beautiful, arrogant Ludo—the man she'd once adored, was definitely dead, his eyes staring.

"Why pursue me?" she whispered. "Why?"

Robin came over, wiping blood from his hand with a cloth. "None of this was your fault," he said. Blood was all over him, however. Ludo's blood.

"Yes it was. If I'd not—"

"Not now," her father said. "Huntersdown, I gather you are Robert Cockcroft?"

"Who?" Robin asked.

"Quite," Rothgar said dryly. "We will need to discuss various matters very shortly."

Huntersdown? Petra's mind felt scattered into fragments. So that was his real name. Where had she heard it before?

Robin seemed to see Rothgar for the first time. He looked from him to Petra, eyes widening. " 'Struth." But he recovered almost immediately. "I request the honor of Petra's hand in marriage, sir. But my apologies—if you refuse, I'll take it anyway."

"Robin . . ." Petra warned, feeling her father tense.

"Will you?" the Dark Marquess said with a dangerous lack of inflection. "You are owed some tolerance for your assistance to Petra on her way to England, but tolerance can be stretched to breaking point." He turned to a man in a black domino. "Not too many people seem to have come close to events, Ashart. Ah, Fitzroger, too. Excellent. With swift action, this story can be controlled. I leave that up to you. Petra, come with me."

Petra looked at Robin, wondering if love demanded rebellion, but he only gave a rueful smile that seemed to say *Later*.

Yes, later. And she hadn't yet told either man about the baby.

Chapter 32

Her father went with her to a bedchamber, where she cleaned away spots of blood and other dirt. Soon Diana joined them. Neither asked questions, but it was time for explanation. Rothgar poured Petra wine and she drank it gratefully, but longed for Robin with a deep ache.

He loved her. He wanted to marry her. He would defy her powerful father for her. That was rubies and diamonds, but she didn't want to lose the new family she'd found. She didn't want to cause more conflict and discord.

"So, Petra," Rothgar said, "your sober man of Cornwall was the Earl of Huntersdown."

"An earl?" she gasped. "He said he wasn't a lord!"

"He lied to you?" her father said icily.

Petra hastily thought back. "No, no! He only said he wasn't the younger son of a duke. And after all, I was pretending to be a full nun. Half-truth for half-truth is fair, I suppose."

Her babble didn't create a thaw.

Robin was an earl, but that clearly didn't make him acceptable, and she was going to have to make it worse.

Hands tight on her wineglass, Petra faced her father, dry throated. "I love him, my lord, and I'm carrying his child." She saw the Dark Marquess then and hurried on. "I'm sorry, but . . . I wasn't a virgin! Ludo. Il conte . . ."

Diana took her in her arms and settled her on the sofa. "It's all right, Petra. Don't be afraid."

Petra cast a dubious look at her father's face.

"Yes, she's your daughter," Diana said to him without a trace of nervousness, "and as you suspected, her protector in France was Huntersdown. I know you disapprove of him, but love will do what love will do."

"Not always," he said, "and not without retribution. Petra, you do not have to marry Huntersdown simply because you're carrying his child. Other arrangements can be made."

Petra found the courage to say, "I don't want that. And I *am* carrying his child."

"Unfortunately. He's not a young man known for sober living and responsibility. Or for anything close to chastity. You do not know him. Unless I am much mistaken, you've spent very little time with him."

Petra knew he was correct, but she could only say, "I know I love him. I know I *need* him." What argument could she make? "I thought perhaps my feelings would fade. After all, I thought once that I would die for love of Ludo. But they didn't. Not even for a day. Not even when I believed I'd never see him again. Not even," she added, "when I found myself surrounded by other people willing to love and care for me. I value that deeply, but I am not complete without Robin."

His face was set and he went to stand by the empty fireplace. Petra took Diana's hand and prayed.

"In other circumstances," he said at last, "I would insist on time. Time in normal society and normal interactions during which you could become sure of your heart. Yes, I know you believe yourself sure, Petra, but it might not be so. As it is, however, if you truly feel that way, it would be best if you married quickly."

"Thank you!"

His expression turned wry. "I hope you always feel that way. We cannot keep you out of tonight's events, as we don't intend to hide the essentials of your story, and the Italian's death cannot be concealed. We will stick close to the truth. He pursued you out of misplaced love, and when you rejected him again, he tried to kill you. A number of men rushed to your aid, but it was Huntersdown who struck the fatal blow. This gallant act naturally drew him to your attention, and over the next few days a love will develop of such intensity that there will be nothing for it but to permit the marriage. I will, of course, make very clear to him that he is required to be the perfect husband."

Petra saw Diana fighting a smile, and perhaps to her the Dark Marquess as protective father was amusing. It terrified Petra. Even so, she met his eyes. "He will always be under *my* protection, sir. Harm him at your peril."

Those dark eyes widened, but then he laughed. "My dear," he said to Diana, "imagine more in her mold."

"A delightful thought," Diana said.

He turned to Petra again. "When you arrived at Rothgar Abbey, I told you that you brought a gift. It was yourself. As you know by now, my mother went mad and murdered her second-born baby. It made me reluctant to pass on her blood. I have come to see that at least part of her problem was the strain of indulgence and marrying too young. In addition, it seems some women are badly affected by giving birth. These things have lessened my concerns. But you, you are a daughter any man could be proud of, as much to be valued as any taint is to be feared. I can only pray that any children Diana bears me are as splendid." He smiled at his wife. "Given her nature, how can it be otherwise?"

"I'm glad I have a gift to give," Petra said, tears threatening at this tenderness, "for you have given me so much."

"It truly has been my pleasure, my dear. I hope Amalia can now forgive me any carelessness of the past."

Petra went to him. "She never blamed you for anything. And she did have complete trust that you would accept me and treat me well." She cocked her head. "I know you intend to speak to Robin, but may I first? You can threaten him later."

He laughed, and for a moment she glimpsed the lighthearted youth her mother had loved. "Very well."

Petra hurried to the door, but at the last moment she remembered the automaton he'd given her. "Did you *know*? Who Robert Cockcroft was, I mean."

His lips twitched. "Your adventures did seem unlikely for a sober man of Cornwall, and Huntersdown has often made play of the Cock Robin rhyme. You showed a reaction to the robin automaton, and wore a cameo depicting a bird."

"A robin," Petra said. "That was so careless."

"If you study that brooch, you'll see it's not a robin but a sparrow. The twigs at its feet are in fact a bow and arrow."

Petra shook her head. "Why would he have an image of Cock Robin's murderer?"

"Whimsy, which is a flaw of his. But also, during the war, he and Ithorne, and sometimes Grandiston, undertook some work for the king on Ithorne's ship, the *Black Swan*."

"The *Black Swan*!" she gasped, and told him about the address she'd used.

"Three wild young men," he said, "though Grandiston's a good officer. Then, of course, Grandiston was reported to have killed Varzi, which added another thread."

"Good heavens," Petra said, and glanced at Diana.

Diana shrugged, smiling. "It is his way. Omniscience plus a devilish skill at puzzles."

"I really needed nothing more, but I did know that Huntersdown had recently been at Versailles, and quite likely had been traveling home at about that time."

"How did you know that?" Diana asked.

"Because he was engaged in a minor matter for the king. A lady there had information that could be of use, but she was frightened to meet with anyone the least bit suspicious. No one would suspect Huntersdown of ulterior motives in seduction."

"I suppose she adores papillon dogs," Petra said.

"Ah yes, I heard that he'd acquired one, much to the world's astonishment. And a wound during a mysterious bout near Folkestone. Lastly—"

"There's more?" Diana asked.

"I do like to be thorough. Discreet inquiries of Lady Sodworth uncovered complaints about a young woman foisted on her in Milan as a nun who turned out to be completely unreliable and a harlot to boot, running off at first chance with a young man who quite clearly had the worst of intentions and whose description fit exactly the Earl of Huntersdown."

"What would you have done if not for the child?" Petra asked.

"I intended to observe the two of you and consider matters. I have no wish to lose you so soon, Petra."

She sighed. "I, too, wish . . . but I cannot wish to be apart from him. Huntingdonshire is not so very far, is it?"

"And the roads become more tolerable all the time. Go. Huntersdown will have needed to restore his appearance, but wherever he is, I'm sure you'll find him. Love has its ways. But at midnight, you must be with us for the unmasking and the announcement. After that, you can dance with him all night if you wish. Only dance," he added, and she saw he meant it.

Petra emerged into a quiet corridor, restoring her mask. Her father had set her a challenge—to find Robin by the compass of love. Because he would have needed to wash and change, she walked some of the quiet corridors, but if he was in this part of the house she couldn't sense him.

She returned to the melee of the masquerade, wishing she could remember the color of his cloak. Outside in the dark, she hadn't noticed. The noise and wild atmosphere were building, perhaps increased by stories of danger and violence. She heard exclamations about evil Italians and death.

No gloom, however. No mourning.

She paused in a quiet corner to feel sorrow for Ludo's family and friends. She didn't think his wife would suffer deep regrets. She'd been married for her money, and from what Petra had heard, had received no warmth from a man obsessed by another.

Such a strange obsession, too. Perhaps he had thought it love, but love would have led him to offer marriage, not insult. Love didn't seek to compel, hurt, and imprison. His emotions had been something dark and vile, for love, in the end, could only set the beloved free—as Robin had done for her, as she had tried to do for him.

So where was he? She felt her father's words should be true. She should know him by some secret sense.

She went to the central chamber and up to a balcony to scan the dancers below. No, she felt strangely certain that none of the gentlemen below was he. She looked up—and then she saw him, on a balcony across from her, searching as she had done.

As if alerted, he looked up, then smiled across at her. She smiled back, love rising in her, warm and bright. She would have flown across to him if she'd had wings, but for now this was enough, to see him, to know he was hers, that they had their precious future, all secrets and mysteries burned away.

Then he stepped back into shadows and she waited, waited calmly, until he came behind her, and then she turned.

They joined hands. "My lord the Earl of Huntersdown, I gather," Petra said, smiling, then smiling wider for sheer joy.

"My sweet Sister Immaculata. Who are you now?"

"Petra Malloren."

"He accepts you fully, then?"

"There are images of him as a youth that make it impossible not to."

He laughed. "A warning to all loose-loving lads. I have not been immaculate. Will you mind if some chickens come home to roost?"

"No." She tightened her hands on his and stepped closer, looking into his eyes. "But there is something of Sister Immaculata in me, Robin. Will you be true to me?"

He pulled her into his arms. "Till death do us part. I promise you that." He raised her face to his. "You will marry me?"

"With all my heart. But I warn you, Lord Rothgar will not be a tolerant father-in-law."

"Good God. Son-in-law to the Dark Marquess."

She touched his cheek. "But I will bring a handsome dowry and powerful connections."

He turned his face into her hand, to kiss her palm. "So you will, so you will."

"And I've already told him you're under my protection." She turned his face back to her. "But if you're ever inclined to stray, my lord, remember that I am the Dark Marquess's daughter."

"I am suitably terrified." He kissed her then, a long, cherishing kiss such as they'd never shared before, but she had to break free.

She looked into his eyes. "Robin, I'm carrying your child."

He stared, and she thought perhaps she'd misjudged everything, that somehow it could still go awry. But then he cradled her face. "You must have been worried. I'm sorry. I'm sorry I wasn't there."

She shook her head, her vision blurring. "That was entirely my fault, my dear beloved. Kiss me again."

They explored one another then with mouths and hands and with so much more, stirring familiar fires that crackled with searing heat, that demanded surrender.

Petra broke free again, held him off with one hand. "We can't. We mustn't. I must be with Lord Rothgar at midnight for the unmasking. He is to introduce me. I'm apparently going to fall in love with you because you saved me from Ludovico. We can marry soon, though."

"Some hope of sanity, then," he said, capturing her hand and kissing each finger.

"We have his permission to dance."

"He treats everyone as puppets."

Her mind was melting again, from only lips on fingers, but she said, "He is my father, Robin. I'm fond of him, of all the Mallorens. . . ."

He drew her index finger into his mouth.

Her knees went weak, but she found the words. "Please don't make me choose."

He slowly released her finger, but the heat in his eyes could complete her destruction. "I won't," he said at last. "He cares for you. But there's an hour before midnight. Shall we dance?" He drew her to him, sliding one hand under her cloak to her bare shoulders, to her neck. . . .

Petra shifted against him with yearning, but she found the strength to say "No."

"Truly no?" he asked, fingers playing there, promising fiery delights.

She swallowed. "Truly no," she said, and moved back out of his arms. "I promised. But also, despite my sins, I am a shockingly moral woman, Robin. You'd best know that now. We can marry. We soon will marry. We must wait."

He smiled. "With all the riches of the universe in

sight, what need of haste? Come, love," he said, taking her hand to lead her away. "Of all the many pleasures we haven't tasted yet, one is an ordinary dance. It seems an excellent place to start."

Chapter 33

The grounds of Rothgar Abbey were thronged again for the grand celebration of the wedding of the marquess's rather scandalous daughter to the handsome Earl of Huntersdown. Petra watched from her bedroom window, for she wouldn't go down to mingle until after the ceremony. That would take place shortly in the private chapel, which was a remnant of the abbey that had once stood on this site.

She was ready, dressed in a gown of green silk sprigged with spring flowers, a costly replication of the one Robin had bought for her in Montreuil, the one he'd loved her in when passion had first hit them in full force. The one she'd opened for him on the *Courlis,* the one she'd worn to arrive here, to find a loving home.

She turned his ring on her finger, a star sapphire, exactly what she'd asked for. She touched the pearls around her neck, a gift from her father. A three-strand bracelet of pearls was a gift from Diana. Though it didn't quite fit the outfit, she wore Robin's cameo brooch among the fine lace that trimmed her bodice.

She'd asked him about that.

"The sparrow?" he'd said, as they strolled through the gardens. "I commissioned it after my father's death, though I'm not sure why. I've always been puzzled by that story. Why did the sparrow kill the friendly robin? Was he punished for it? There's no mention. I suppose I was simply thinking on death."

"And realizing that your days as Cock Robin were numbered." She quoted the end of the poem. *"All the birds of the air fell a-crying and a-sobbing when they heard the bell toll for poor Cock Robin."* She squeezed his hand. "He'll never die for me."

"That's as well," he'd said, eyes twinkling, and it was then he told her the cruder meaning of "cock." She laughed again now at the memory.

Portia came in to ask if Petra was ready, and she went out to take her father's arm to be led down to the chapel. There she found Robin, in a grand suit of blue velvet that had sapphire-and-diamond buttons that she remembered. That almost made her laugh again. She was fighting laughter, anyway, simply because she was so happy.

Robin's mother was here, along with his sisters and brothers. There hadn't been enough time to truly get to know them, but she sensed harmony was possible. His mother, to her amusement, had been disapproving rather than approving of Petra's devotion to the faith they shared, but once Petra had assured her she would accept her children being raised in the Protestant faith, that barrier had fallen away.

She was a strong-minded, proud woman, the Dowager Countess of Huntersdown, and used to having her own way. She was also used to having Robin to herself and not entirely happy about Petra's unorthodox origins, but a handsome dowry and grand connections had sweetened matters, and she and Petra had love for Robin in common.

Even Coquette had her place here, sitting by Robin's feet in perfect, courtly dignity.

Petra said her vows, content that they made the same promises to Robin as the Catholic ones, and in the sight of the same God. She knew from the way he made his vows to her that he meant them in the truest, deepest sense. She sent prayers of thanks to her mother, and to God, who had brought her here.

Then she and Robin went out among a merry crowd to share their happiness with her father's servants, tenants, neighbors, and friends. The day was made better by it being the anniversary of the marquess's wedding, and by the recent announcement that the marchioness expected a child at Christmas. Most people here thought it a simple matter for rejoicing, but some, especially in the family, knew what it signified.

Her father and Diana had known about their baby before Petra had arrived. They'd been happy, but the old concerns had lingered. That was why he'd seen her as a special blessing, as a special promise. Strange, however, to think that her baby and Diana's would be so close in age.

Petra took Robin in search of a special guest. She'd sent a coach for Mistress Waddle, and the old lady had traveled here with her daughter and son-in-law and one of her granddaughters, a bright-eyed eight-year-old called Tess. Petra had arranged for handsome clothes for them all, so they wouldn't feel out of place, and she would soon do more for the woman who'd been so kind.

Seeing her now, she hugged the old lady tight. "You were an angel to me."

"Go on with you," Mistress Waddle said, pink under a wide, flowered hat. "If a person can't offer a bed and a bit of soup, what's the world coming to? So pretty, you look, and I gather as this fine gentleman isn't the pestifying husband."

Robin laughed and kissed her, making her swat at him. "I can see you'll be trouble. You keep him in line, dearie. It's the only way."

Petra could tell they were still feeling a bit out of place, so she took them to meet the Harsteads, and left them all happily comparing their part in the adventure. She saw Mistress Digby, but that lady was avoiding her.

As darkness fell a bonfire was lit, but Petra and Robin had already slipped away, up to her pink-and-white room and to their nuptial bed. "Clean," she said, smiling, "but not to myself, thank heavens."

They had no need of servants, for they undressed each other, taking their time now that there was all the time in the world, but having to fight the wild pull of passion.

"No need of haste," he murmured, "but no need to wait, either."

Half undressed, they tumbled onto the bed, pushing at shirt and shift, mouths still joined, tangling together in turned-back sheets, exploring by candlelight this time, the leg, the hip, the breast, the back, and the magnificently upstanding cock.

As they joined together, soaring higher and higher, a great boom and crackle announced the beginning of the fireworks. They exploded together in passion and laughter.

When he had breath to speak, Robin gasped, "Trust Rothgar."

He gathered Petra in close, and closer yet, to kiss again, hot skin to skin as crackles and explosions sounded outside and colored lights blazed against the night sky.

But then, in time, as peace reigned again, he rested his head against hers.

"There can be only one word to describe this and you, my love."

"And what is that?" she asked, smiling.

"Heaven," he said.

Author's Note

What fun to return to the Malloren world. I hope you enjoyed this foray as much as I did. This book had a weird start, however, and I thought you might enjoy reading about it.

Sometimes ideas come to me in a video flash, a vignette, and this time it was a gentleman at a coaching inn who hears a plainly dressed woman swearing. Any lady using strong language would be surprising, but she seems such a sober sort. He asks if he can assist her and ends up offering to take her to her destination. Somewhat warily, she agrees.

This might seem like the beginning to *A Lady's Secret,* but in my first vision the inn was in England, he was a respectable Regency gentleman, and she was wearing ordinary dress and was a normal sort of governess. Still, it was intriguing, and I pondered possible motivations and outcomes. Clearly she was escaping something or striving to get somewhere, or both. One idea that popped into my mind was that she was a young woman trying to get to her trustees in London to complain about her thieving guardian.

So how did I get from there to northern France, a

Georgian rake with a papillon dog, and a nun on the run? As with everything to do with writing a book, it's a mystery.

I can remember some factors, however. The original spark felt like the setup for a road book, where most of the action takes place during a desperate journey. Regency England isn't the best setting for a road book, however. It was too civilized. The main routes were heavily traveled toll roads, and law and order was fairly well established. When I found myself trying to come up with plot reasons to send them over minor roads across the Pennines or the North York Moors, I knew I was getting desperate.

So I decided to move the book back fifty years to my Malloren world, when roads were much rougher and many parts of England could still be lawless. Even so, I was still looking for desolate spots so they would be far from help, and it wasn't feeling right. I mentioned this to my husband and for some reason—even he doesn't remember what—he said, "They're in France."

And so they were. As I said, it's all a mystery, but once I made that switch and opened my mind to my heroine not being English, things started to gel.

A while ago on my e-mail chat list some readers had been speculating about possible spin-off books. Somewhere in that discussion the idea arose of Rothgar having fathered a child during his Grand Tour of Europe. As you know, in the earlier Malloren books, his concerns about having children, his fear of them turning out to be mad like his mother, had been a strong thread, so an unknown adult child was a powerful idea. Now I realized I'd found her.

Figuring out a book is often a matter of fighting through my preconceptions and controlling thoughts to discover what the story already is.

The Grand Tour, by the way, was an essential part of an upper-class gentleman's education in the eighteenth century. In his mid-to-late teens, he would set off to visit the cultural highlights of Europe under the tutelage of a tutor-guide—sometimes called a bear leader—and with a small or large entourage of servants. He would visit various courts in order to learn international savoir faire, and visit various locations in Italy and Greece to round out his classical education. In those days a gentleman's education was largely in the classics. Boys being boys, these young gentlemen would also have fun far from ordinary restraints and scrutiny. Sort of like a very long Spring Break in Florida.

So I realized that my cursing woman was Rothgar's daughter and off to find her father. Then I had to figure out why, and why she was wearing a nun's habit. It could be a straight disguise, but that seemed like a cheap shot. On the other hand, it would cramp the story to have her a true nun. My research turned up the common practice of highborn Italian ladies living in convents and the complexities of the rules about nuns in cloisters. I had my situation. I just needed to know why she was on this desperate flight.

"Why?" is the most important question an author asks. Slowly, as I wrote, her story revealed itself. That's the way I have to do it. Simply thinking about a story or plotting it on paper doesn't work for me.

Once I had enough understanding to begin, I needed to research eighteenth-century northern

France, in particular travel in northern France, which was new territory for me. What fun!

It was especially fun because of Google Book Search. Google Book Search is the new service by Google in which they are scanning and making available many books from university libraries. This is an incredibly important service. Some of these books may only exist in one or two copies, and thus can only be consulted if a person travels to the library in question. What's more, a natural disaster or a fire could destroy an only copy.

Now these books are in electronic form and thus held in many locations. Even better, Google puts them on the Web for all to read and even download. I've acquired an electronic library of books I could only dream about a few years ago.

My best find in this instance was *The Gentleman's Guide in his Tour through France wrote* [sic] *by An Officer, who lately travelled on a Principle which he most sincerely recommends to his Countrymen, viz. Not to spend more Money in the Country of our natural Enemy, than is requisite to support, with Decency, the Character of an Englishman.* It was published in 1770, only a few years after the events in *A Lady's Secret*. There may be only one print copy in existence.

The Officer records his journey from England to France, sharing many details. He tells his contemporaries, and now me, that a person may travel post to Dover or by the "Dover machine," which means stagecoach. Modern readers can think of these as the difference between hiring a car and taking a bus.

The Dover machine, he says, will cost twenty shillings and complete its journey of seventy-two miles in one day. Note the time that journey took. It was probably at least a ten-hour day, so about seven miles an hour. A post chaise cost a shilling a mile, or seventy-two shillings for the same journey, but would be a bit faster.

The packet from Dover to Calais was a half guinea per person. (A half guinea is about ten shillings.) The hire of a vessel for oneself or a party was five guineas. The book was so full of lovely detail that it was hard to resist cramming it all into the novel.

Another interesting source was Tobias Smollett, who wrote at length about his travels at this time. Most of what I learned from various sources didn't end up in the book, of course, but it enabled me to feel in place with my characters.

Now on to Teresa Cornelys. She was an important person in the London of the 1760s, but I missed her during the earlier research for my Malloren books. She was a natural fit for this one, however, being Italian. I would have liked to have given her a bigger part, but the story flow takes precedence.

She was a bold, adventurous, and unscrupulous woman who started out as an opera singer on the Continent and then became an entrepreneur in London, despite being broke and speaking little English. You have to admire that kind of spirit.

She talked her way into possession of a grand house on Soho Square and tricked and/or seduced men into paying for her schemes, becoming outraged if they wanted their loans repaid. She had patrons among the aristocracy, and for a while her Venetian entertainments at Carlisle House were some of the must-attend events of the London season. She limited the tickets, had a group of English ladies to decide who should be allowed to purchase them, and even dictated what people could and couldn't wear at the events.

Unfortunately, she was a terrible businesswoman, constantly on the edge of financial disaster, and narrowly escaped being imprisoned for debt. Eventually her business failed and she died in debtors' prison.

Her assemblies were so successful, however, that others tried to imitate her, and one succeeded very well indeed. That was a Scot called Mr. Almack, and his events became the Almack's Assemblies so famous in the Regency period.

For more about Teresa Cornelys, read *The Empress of Pleasure* by Judith Summers (Viking, 2003).

Amazingly, Teresa Cornelys was a lover of Giacomo Casanova. He was a longtime friend and the father of her daughter. Teresa confronted him with little Sophie at a London event and the resemblance was so marked that he had no choice but to believe her to be his. Truth sometimes is stranger than fiction, but it can also inspire fiction very nicely.

Incidentally, Teresa also missed hosting Mozart's first performance in London simply because her rooms were fully booked. Such is history.

It's such a journey of discovery, writing a novel, and now I'm beginning to discover more about Lord Grandiston. It's all very intriguing and mysterious. . . .

Right now, there's more! NAL is republishing two of my early novels. These have been very hard to find for years, but now *The Fortune Hunter* and *Deirdre and Don Juan* are in your bookstore in a lovely trade paperback edition called *Lovers and Ladies*.

This is love in the world of Jane Austen, with spirited ladies and dashing lovers constrained by the pressures of an orderly, elegant society. *Deirdre and Don Juan* won a RITA Award for Best Regency Romance and has been described as "pure storytelling genius" by *Romantic Times*. *Romantic Times* described *The Fortune Hunter* as "the kind of wonderful reading experience that every fan desires but all too infrequently gets."

I hope you'll enjoy these oldies-but-goodies. I'm sure there'll be more to come.

I love to hear from my readers, and you can e-mail me at jo@jobev.com. You can also subscribe to an e-mail newsletter. The links are on my Web page, www.jobev.com, where you'll also find background to my novels and even some free fiction.

You'll see there that I have spots on MySpace and Facebook, and occasionally post to a couple of personal blogs. I'm also part of a group of historical authors who blog as The Word Wenches. Visit us at www.wordwenches.com. We love reader participation, and there are often prizes.

If you're not into cyberspace yet, you can write to me care of my agent, Margaret Ruley, 318 East 51st Street, New York, NY 10022. I appreciate a SASE.

All best wishes,

Jo

Something Wicked

Disguised as the mysterious beauty Lisette, Lady Elfred Malloren anticipates only fun and flirtation at the Vauxhall Gardens Masquerade. Instead, the dark walkways lead to an encounter with treason, a brush with death, and a night of riotous passion with her family's most dangerous enemy—the elusive Fortitude Ware, Earl of Walgrave. His control is indisputable, his power unquestionable, his attraction undeniable. And after just one night, Elf knows she will never forget the man she should not love. . . .

"A fast-paced adventure with strong, vividly portrayed characters . . . wickedly, wonderfully sensual and gloriously romantic."   —Mary Balogh

"*Something Wicked* will delight."
                                        —*Lake Worth Herald*

Secrets of the Night

Rosamunde Overton is forced into a daring deceit when her elderly husband's inability to sire an heir threatens everyone she cares for. Fleeing a scandalous masquerade, she rescues a handsome, injured gentleman, seeing the answer to her prayers—but instead of a nobody, she has snared a member of the powerful Malloren family. Intrigued, Lord Brand Malloren follows the lead of the lovely masked lady, but neither he nor Rosa is prepared for impossible, disastrous love.

"Jo Beverley is up to her usual magic. . . . She sprinkles a bit of intrigue, a dash of passion and a dollop of lust, a pinch of poison, and a woman's need to protect all those she loves." —*Affaire de Coeur*

"Incredibly sensual . . . sexy and funny. . . . These characters [are] wonderfully real."
—All About Romance

Devilish

Two of the strongest wills in England clash when Lord Rothgar is commanded by the king to escort fiercely independent Diana Westmount, the Countess of Arradale, to London. Though Rothgar, tortured by a tragic secret, has become a master of resisting temptation, Diana proves a challenge to his steely resolve. Then his icy self-control melts in a moment of peril—and a night of passion—and he must find the strength to surrender his heart to another. . . .

"Beverley beautifully captures the flavor of Georgian England. . . . Her fast-paced, violent, and exquisitely sensual story is one that readers won't soon forget."
—*Library Journal*

"Jo [Beverley] has truly brought to life a fascinating, glittering, and sometimes dangerous world."
—Mary Jo Putney

RITA Award Winner

Winter Fire

Genova Smith is a resourceful woman, but the arrogant Marquess of Ashart is a challenge even for her—especially when they're caught in a kiss and have to arrive at the house of his cousin, the Marquess of Rothgar, pretending to be betrothed. There, beneath Christmas glitter and joy, she realizes that Ashart is determined to destroy his cousin, and could easily destroy her at the same time—for he has already captured her heart.

"Holiday fun, lively family interactions, and romance abound in this heartwarming tale. . . ."
                                            —Library Journal

"An intelligent, ever sensible heroine and an elegant, sinfully seductive rake spar with splendidly sexy results."   *—Booklist*

A Most Unsuitable Man

Damaris Myddleton never expected to inherit a vast fortune, but she's ready to use it to buy the most eligible title in England. When disappointed by a marquess, she simply sets her sights higher—on a duke. But then there's plain Mr. Fitzroger, the dashing but penniless adventurer who first saves her from social disaster and then saves her life. Entangled in mystery, danger, and forbidden intimacy, Damaris fights not to surrender her freedom and her heart to a most unsuitable man. . . .

"Her strong characters and finely honed dialogue, combined with a captivating love story, are a pleasure to read."   —*Romantic Times BOOKclub* (Top Pick)

"Once again readers are treated to a delightful, intricately plotted, and sexy romp set in the slightly bawdy Georgian world of Beverley's beloved Malloren Chronicles."   —*Library Journal*

"Wickedly, wonderfully sensual and gloriously romantic."
—Mary Balogh

"A delicious...sensual delight."
—Teresa Medeiros

New York Times Bestselling Author
Jo Beverley

**Available wherever books are sold or at
penguin.com**